W9-BSY-569
TIERRA DEL FUEGO
AND
CAPE HORN
Nautical Miles at 54° South
0
10
20
30
40
50
68°
66°
53°
54°
55°
56°
64°
Estrecho de Magallanes
(Strait of Magellan)
ARGENTINA
RA
FUEGO
SOUTH
ATLANTIC
OCEAN
Beagle Channel
Puerto Williams
ISLA
NAVARINO
Strait
of
Le Maire
STATEN ISLAND
Isla Desolacíon
False Cape
Horn
Isla
Barnevelt
Cape Horn
Cape Horn Islands
ASSAGE
Diego
Ramirez
Island
N
W
E
S

THE ICE LIMIT

By Douglas Preston and Lincoln Child

Relic
Mount Dragon
Reliquary
Riptide
Thunderhead

By Douglas Preston

Dinosaurs in the Attic
Cities of Gold
Jennie
Talking to the Ground
The Royal Road

Edited by Lincoln Child

Dark Company
Dark Banquet
Tales of the Dark 1–3

DOUGLAS PRESTON
AND LINCOLN CHILD

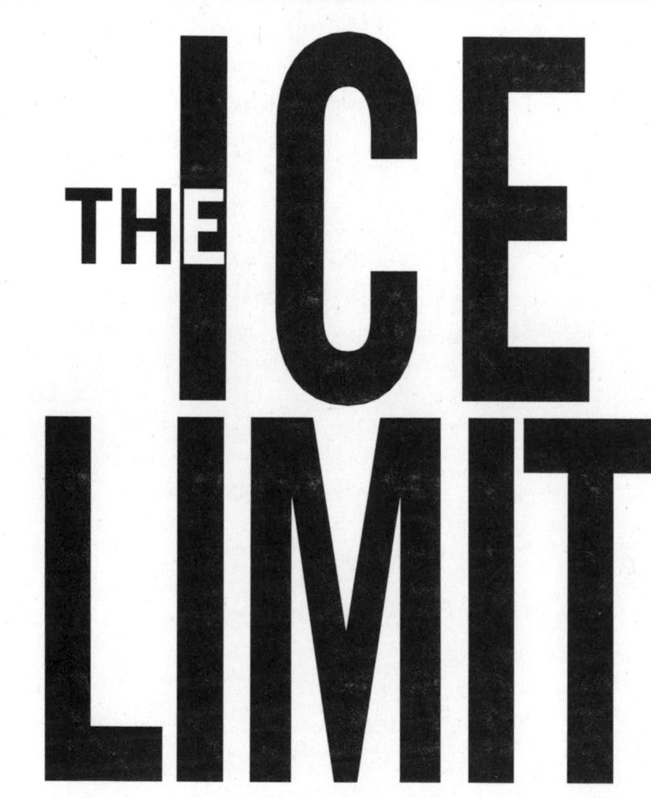

A Time Warner Company

This book is a work of fiction. Names, characters, places, and incidents are the product of the authors' imagination or are used fictitiously. Any resemblance to actual events, locales, or persons, living or dead, is coincidental. The authors wish to state most emphatically that the Chilean characters in *The Ice Limit* are entirely fictitious and are in no way meant to be representative of the fine people of Chile or that country's navy.

Grateful acknowledgment is given for permission to reprint excerpts from the following:
"Musee des Beaux Arts" from *W. H. Auden Collected Poems* by W. H. Auden. Copyright © 1940 and renewed 1968 by W. H. Auden. Reprinted by permission of Random House, Inc., and Curtis Brown, Ltd.
"Atlantis" from *W. H. Auden Collected Poems* by W. H. Auden. Copyright © 1945 by W. H. Auden. Reprinted by permission of Random House, Inc., and Curtis Brown, Ltd.

Warner Books, Inc., 1271 Avenue of the Americas, New York, NY 10020
Visit our Web site at www.twbookmark.com

A Time Warner Company

Printed in the United States of America
First Printing: July 2000
10 9 8 7 6 5 4 3 2 1

Library of Congress Cataloging-in-Publication Data
Preston, Douglas J.
The ice limit / Douglas Preston and Lincoln Child.
p. cm.
ISBN 0-446-52587-1
1. Antarctic regions—Fiction. 2. Meteorites—Fiction.
I. Child, Lincoln. II. Title.
PS3566.R3982 I27 2000
813'.54—dc21 99-087229

Lincoln Child dedicates this book to his daughter, Veronica

Douglas Preston dedicates this book to Walter Winings Nelson,
artist, photographer, and partner in adventure

Acknowledgments

The authors would like to acknowledge Commander Stephen Littfin, United States Naval Reserve, for his invaluable help with the naval aspects of *The Ice Limit*. Our deep gratitude also goes out to Michael Tusiani, who corrected various tanker-related elements of the manuscript. We would also like to thank Tim Tiernan for his advice on metallurgy and physics, the meteorite hunter Charlie Snell of Santa Fe for information on how meteorite hunters actually operate, and Frank Ryle, senior structural engineer at Ove Arup & Partners. We also want to express our appreciation to various other anonymous engineers who shared with us confidential engineering details related to moving extremely heavy objects.

Lincoln Child would like to thank his wife, Luchie, for just about everything; Sonny Baula for the Tagalog translations; Greg Tear for being such an eager and competent critic; and his daughter, Veronica, for making every day precious. Also, thanks to Denis Kelly, Malou Baula, and Juanito "Boyet" Nepomuceno for their various and sundry ministrations. And my heartfelt gratitude to Liz Ciner, Roger Lasley, and especially George Soule, my adviser (had I but known it!) all this last quarter century. May the warm enlightening sun shine always upon Carleton College and its progeny.

Douglas Preston would like to thank his wife, Christine, and his three children, Selene, Aletheia, and Isaac, for their love and support.

We also wish to thank Betsy Mitchell and Jaime Levine of Warner Books, Eric Simonoff of Janklow & Nesbit Associates, and Matthew Snyder of CAA.

THE ICE LIMIT

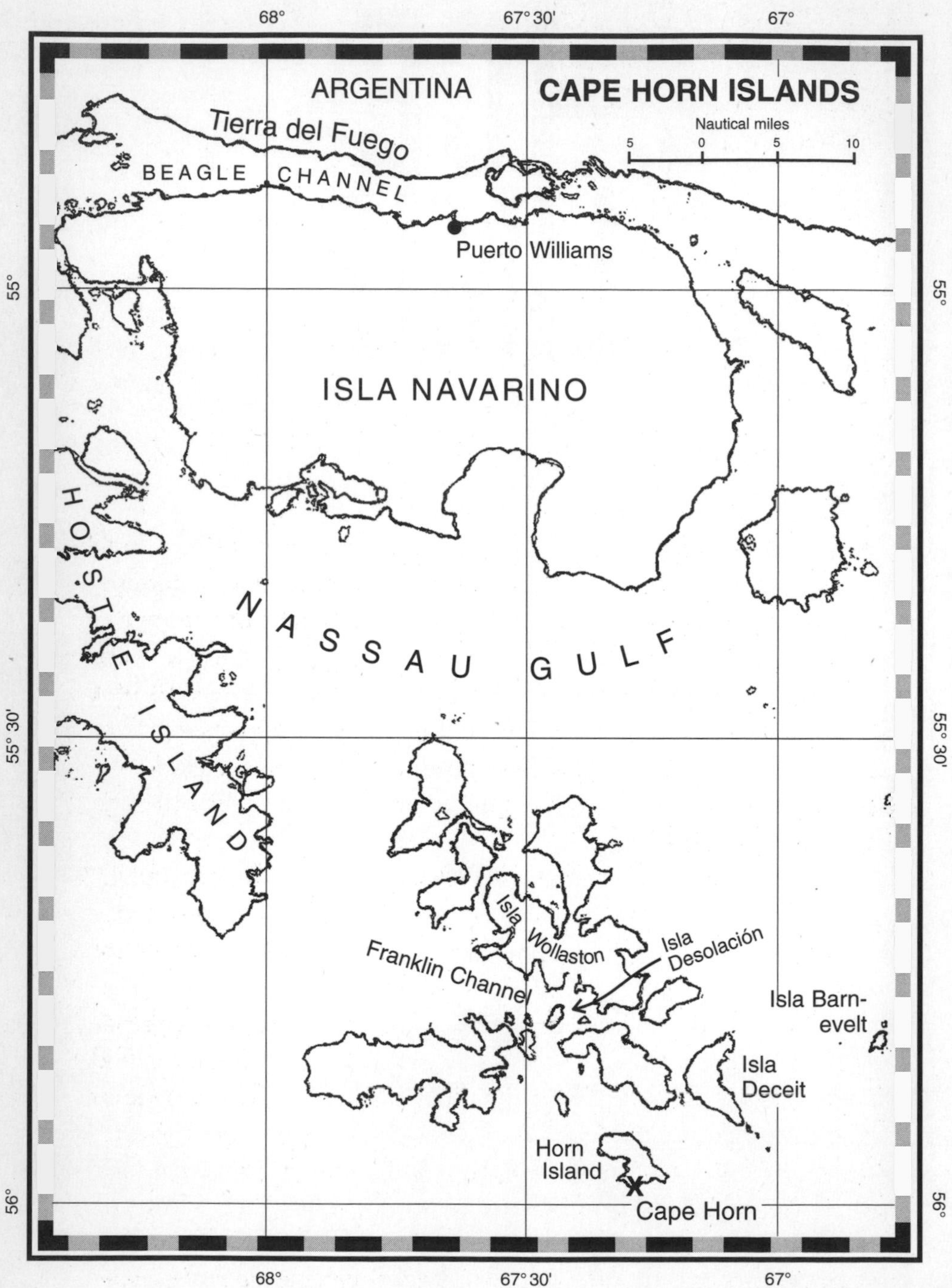

CAPE HORN ISLANDS
ARGENTINA
Tierra del Fuego
BEAGLE CHANNEL
Puerto Williams
Nautical miles
5 0 5 10
68°
67° 30'
67°
55°
55° 30'
56°
ISLA NAVARINO
HOSTE ISLAND
NASSAU GULF
Isla Wollaston
Isla Desolación
Franklin Channel
Isla Barnevelt
Isla Deceit
Horn Island
Cape Horn

Isla Desolación, January 16, 1:15 P.M.

The valley that had no name ran between barren hills, a long mottled floor of gray and green covered with soldier moss, lichens, and carpha grasses. It was mid-January—the height of summer—and the crevasses between the patches of broken rock were mortared with tiny pinguicula flowers. To the east, the wall of a snowfield gleamed a bottomless blue. Blackflies and mosquitoes droned in the air, and the summer fogs that shrouded Isla Desolación had temporarily broken apart, allowing a watery sunlight to speckle the valley floor.

A man walked slowly across the island's graveled flats, stopping, moving, then stopping again. He was not following a trail—in the Cape Horn islands, at the nethermost tip of South America, there were none.

Nestor Masangkay was dressed in worn oilskins and a greasy leather hat. His wispy beard was so thick with sea salt that it had divided itself into forked tips. It waggled like a snake's tongue as he led two heavily burdened mules across the flats. There was no one to hear his voice commenting unfavorably on the mules' parentage, character, and right to existence. Once in a while the complaints were punctuated with the thwack of a sucker rod that he carried in one brown hand. He had never met a mule, especially a rented mule, that he liked.

But Masangkay's voice held no anger, and the thwacks of his sucker rod held little force. Excitement was rising within him. His eyes roamed over the landscape, taking in every detail: the columnar basaltic escarpment a mile away, the double-throated volcanic plug, the unusual outcropping of sedimentary rock. The geology was promising. Very promising.

He walked across the valley floor, eyes on the ground. Once in a while a hobnailed boot would lash out and kick a rock loose. The beard waggled; Masangkay grunted; and the curious pack train would move on once again.

In the center of the valley, Masangkay's boot dislodged a rock from the flat. But this time he stopped to pick it up. The man examined the soft rock, rubbing it with his thumb, abrading small granules that clung to his skin. He brought it to his face and peered at the grit with a jeweler's loupe.

He recognized this specimen—a friable, greenish material with white inclusions—as a mineral known as coesite. It was this ugly, worthless rock that he had traveled twelve thousand miles to find.

His face broke into a broad grin, and he opened his arms to heaven and let out a terrific whoop of joy, the hills trading echoes of his voice, back and forth, back and forth, until at last it died away.

He fell silent and looked around at the hills, gauging the alluvial pattern of erosion. His gaze lingered again on the sedimentary outcrop, its layers clearly delineated. Then his eyes returned to the ground. He led the mules another ten yards and pried a second stone loose from the valley floor with his foot, turning it over. Then he kicked loose a third stone, and a fourth. It was all coesite—the valley floor was practically paved with it.

Near the edge of the snowfield, a boulder—a glacial erratic—lay atop the tundra. Masangkay led his mules over to the boulder and tied them to it. Then, keeping his movements as slow and deliberate as possible, he walked back across the flats, picking up rocks, scuffing the ground with his boot, drawing a mental map of the coesite distribution. It was incredible, exceeding even his most optimistic assumptions.

He had come to this island with realistic hopes. He knew from personal experience that local legends rarely panned out. He recalled the dusty museum library where he had first come across the legend of Hanuxa: the smell of the crumbling anthropological monograph, the faded pictures of artifacts and long-dead Indians. He almost hadn't bothered; Cape Horn was a hell of a long way from New York City. And his instincts had often been wrong in the past. But here he was.

And he had found the prize of a lifetime.

Masangkay took a deep breath. He was getting ahead of himself. Walking back to the boulder, he reached beneath the belly of the lead packmule. Working swiftly, he unraveled the diamond hitch, pulled the hemp rope from the pack, and unbuckled the wooden box panniers. Unlatching the lid of one pannier, he pulled out a long drysack and laid it on the ground. From it he extracted six aluminum cylinders, a small computer keyboard and screen, a leather strap, two metal spheres, and a nicad battery. Sitting cross-legged on the ground, he assembled the equipment into an aluminum rod fifteen feet long, with spherical projections at either end. He fitted the computer to its center, clipped on the leather strap, and slapped the battery into a slot on one side. He stood up, examining the high-tech object with satisfaction: a shiny anachronism among the grubby pack gear. It was an electromagnetic tomographic sounder, and it was worth over fifty thousand dollars—a ten-thousand down payment and financing for the rest, which was proving to be a struggle to pay off atop all his other debts. Of course, when this project paid off, he could settle with everyone—even his old partner.

Masangkay flicked the power switch and waited for the machine to warm up. He raised the screen into position, grasped a handle at the center of the rod, and let the weight settle around his neck, balancing the sounder the way a high-wire artist balances his pole. With his free hand he checked the settings, calibrated and zeroed the instrument, and then began walking steadily across the long flat, staring fixedly at the screen. As he walked, fog drifted in and the sky grew dark. Near the center of the flat, he suddenly stopped.

Masangkay stared at the screen in surprise. Then he adjusted some settings and took another step. Once again he paused, brow furrowed. With a curse he switched the machine off, returned to the edge of the flat, rezeroed the machine, and walked at right angles to his previous path. Again he paused, surprise giving way to disbelief. He marked the spot with two rocks, one atop the other. Then he walked to the far side of the flat, turned, and came back, more quickly now. A soft rain was beading on his face and shoulders, but he ignored it. He pressed a button, and a narrow line of paper began spooling out of the computer. He examined it closely, ink bleeding down the paper in the mist. His breath came faster. At first he thought the data was wrong: but there it was, three passes, all perfectly consistent. He made yet another pass, more reckless than the last, tearing off another spool of paper, examining it quickly, then balling it into his jacket pocket.

After the fourth pass, he began talking to himself in a low, rapid monotone. Veering back toward the mules, he dropped the tomographic sounder on the drysack and untied the second mule's pack with trembling hands. In his haste, one of the panniers fell to the ground and split open, spilling picks, shovels, rock hammers, an auger, and a bundle of dynamite. Masangkay scooped up a pick and shovel and jogged back to the center of the flat. Flinging the shovel to the ground, he began feverishly swinging the pick, breaking up the rough surface. Then he scooped out the loosened gravel with the shovel, throwing it well to the side. He continued in this fashion, alternating pick and shovel. The mules watched him with complete impassivity, heads drooping, eyes half-lidded.

Masangkay worked as the rain began to stiffen. Shallow pools collected at the lowest points of the graveled flat. A cold smell of ice drifted inland from Franklin Channel, to the north. There was a distant roll of thunder. Gulls came winging over his head, circling in curiosity, uttering forlorn cries.

The hole deepened to a foot, then two. Below the hard layer of gravel, the alluvial sand was soft and easily dug. The hills disappeared behind shifting curtains of rain and mist. Masangkay worked on, heedless, stripping off his coat, then his shirt, and eventually his undershirt, flinging them out of the hole. Mud and water mingled with the sweat that ran across his back and chest, defining the ripples and hollows of his musculature, while the points of his beard hung with water.

Then, with a cry, he stopped. He crouched in the hole, scooping the sand and mud away from a hard surface beneath his feet. He let the rain wash the last bit of mud from the surface.

Suddenly, he started in shock and bewilderment. Then he knelt as if praying, spreading his sweaty hands reverently on the surface. His breath came in gasps, eyes wild with astonishment, sweat and rain streaming together off his forehead, his heart pounding from exertion, excitement, and inexpressible joy.

At that moment, a shock wave of brilliant light burst out of the hole, followed by a prodigious boom that rolled off across the valley, echoing and dying among the far hills. The two mules raised their heads in the direction of the noise. They saw a small body of mist, which became crablike, broke apart, and drifted off into the rain.

The tethered mules looked away from the scene with indifference as night settled upon Isla Desolación.

Isla Desolación, February 22, 11:00 A.M.

The long bark canoe cut through the water of the channel, moving swiftly with the tidal current. A single figure, small and bent, knelt inside, expertly feathering a paddle, guiding the canoe through the chop. A thin trail of smoke rose from the smoldering fire built on a pad of wet clay in the center of the canoe.

The canoe rounded the black cliffs of Isla Desolación, turned into the smoother water of a little cove, and crunched onto the cobbled beach. The figure leapt out and pulled the canoe above the high tide mark.

He had heard the news, in passing, from one of the nomadic fishermen who lived alone in these cold seas. That a foreign-looking man would visit such a remote and inhospitable island was unusual indeed. But even more unusual was the fact that a month had passed, and the man had apparently not left.

He paused, catching sight of something. Moving forward, he picked up a piece of shattered fiberglass, and then another, looking at them, peeling some strands from the broken edges and tossing them aside. The remains of a freshly wrecked boat. Perhaps there was a simple explanation after all.

He was a peculiar-looking man—old, dark, with long gray hair and a thin little mustache that drooped down from his chin like the film of a spiderweb. Despite the freezing weather, he was dressed only in a soiled T-shirt and a baggy pair of shorts. Touching a finger to his nose, he blew snot out of his nostrils, first one, then the other, with a delicate motion. Then he scrambled up the cliff at the head of the little cove.

He paused at its brink, his bright black eyes scanning the ground for signs. The gravelly floor, dotted with mounds of moss, was spongy from the freeze-thaw cycle, and it had preserved the footprints—and hoofprints—excellently.

He followed the trail as it made its irregular way up a rise to the snowfield. There it followed the edge of the field, eventually cutting down into the valley beyond. At a brow overlooking the valley the prints stopped, milling around in a crazy pattern. The man paused, gazing down into the barren draw. There was something down there: bits of color against the landscape, and the glint of sunlight off polished metal.

He hurried down.

He reached the mules first, still tied to the rock. They were long dead. His eyes traveled hungrily across the ground, glittering with avarice as they registered the supplies and equipment. Then he saw the body.

He approached it, moving much more cautiously. It lay on its back, about a hundred yards from the mouth of a recently dug hole. It was naked, with just a shred of charred clothing clinging to the carbonized flesh. Its black, burnt hands were raised to the sky, like the claws of a dead crow, and its splayed legs were drawn up to its crushed chest. The rain had collected in the hollow eye sockets, making two little pools of water that reflected the sky and clouds.

The old man backed away, one foot at a time, like a cat. Then he stopped. He remained rooted to the spot, staring and wondering, for a long time. And then—slowly, and without turning his back on the blackened corpse—he turned his attention to the trove of valuable equipment that lay scattered about.

New York City, May 20, 2:00 P.M.

The sale room at Christie's was a simple space, framed in blond wood and lit by a rectangle of lights suspended from the ceiling. Although the hardwood floor had been laid in a beautiful herringbone pattern, almost none of it was visible beneath the countless rows of chairs—all filled—and the feet of the reporters, latecomers, and spectators who crowded the rear of the room.

As the chairman of Christie's mounted the center podium, the room fell silent. The long, cream-colored screen behind him, which in a normal auction might be hung with paintings or prints, was vacant.

The chairman rapped on the podium with his gavel, looked around, then drew a card from his suit and consulted it. He placed the card carefully at one side of the podium and looked up again.

"I imagine," he said, the plummy English vowels resonating under the slight amplification, "that a few of you may already be aware of what we're offering today."

Decorous amusement rippled through the assembly.

"I regret that we could not bring it to the stage for you to see. It was a trifle large."

Another laugh floated through the audience. The chairman was clearly relishing the importance of what was about to happen.

"But I have brought a small piece of it—a token, so to speak—

as assurance you will be bidding on the genuine article." With that he nodded, and a slender young man with the bearing of a gazelle walked out onstage, holding a small velvet box in both arms. The man unlatched it, opened the lid, and turned in a semicircle for the audience to see. A low murmur rose among the crowd, then fell away again.

Inside, a curved brown tooth lay nestled on white satin. It was about seven inches long, with a wickedly serrated inner edge.

The chairman cleared his throat. "The consigner of lot number one, our only lot today, is the Navajo Nation, in a trust arrangement with the government of the United States of America."

He surveyed the audience. "The lot is a fossil. A *remarkable* fossil." He consulted the card on the podium. "In 1996, a Navajo shepherd named Wilson Atcitty lost some sheep in the Lukachukai mountains along the Arizona–New Mexico border. In attempting to find his sheep, he came across a large bone protruding from a sandstone wall in a remote canyon. Geologists call this layer of sandstone the Hell Creek Formation, and it dates back to the Cretaceous era. Word got back to the Albuquerque Museum of Natural History. Under an agreement with the Navajo Nation, they began excavating the skeleton. As work proceeded they realized they had not one but two entwined skeletons: a *Tyrannosaurus rex* and a *Triceratops*. The Tyrannosaurus had its jaws fastened about the Triceratops' neck, just beneath its crest, virtually decapitating the creature with a savage bite. The Triceratops, for his part, had thrust his central horn deep into the chest of the Tyrannosaurus. Both animals died together, locked in a terrible embrace."

He cleared his throat. "I can't wait for the movie."

There was another round of laughter.

"The battle was so violent that beneath the Triceratops, paleontologists found five teeth from the Tyrannosaurus that had apparently broken off during the heat of the fight. This is one of them." He nodded to the assistant, who closed the box.

"A block of stone containing the two dinosaurs, weighing some three hundred tons, was removed from the mountainside and stabilized at the Albuquerque Museum. It was then taken to the New York Museum of Natural History for further preparation. The two skeletons are still partly embedded in the sandstone matrix."

He glanced at his card again.

"According to scientists consulted by Christie's, these are the two most perfect dinosaur skeletons ever found. They are of incalculable value to science. The chief paleontologist at the New York Museum has called it the greatest fossil discovery in history."

He carefully replaced the card and picked up the gavel. As if on signal, three bid spotters moved wraithlike onto the stage, waiting at quiet attention. Employees at the telephone stations stood motionless, phones in hand, lines open.

"We have an estimate on this lot of twelve million dollars, and an opening price of five million." The chairman tapped his gavel.

There was a faint smattering of calls, nods, and genteelly raised paddles.

"I have five million. Six million. Thank you, I have seven million." The spotters craned their necks, catching the bids, relaying them to the chairman. The *sotto voce* hubbub in the hall gradually increased.

"I have eight million."

A scattering of applause erupted as the record price for a dinosaur fossil was broken.

"Ten million. Eleven million. Twelve. Thank you, I have thirteen. I have fourteen. Fifteen."

The show of paddles had dwindled considerably, but several telephone bidders were still active, along with half a dozen in the audience. The dollar display to the chairman's right rose rapidly, with the English and Euro equivalents beneath following in lockstep.

"Eighteen million. I have eighteen million. Nineteen."

The murmuring became a groundswell and the chairman gave a cautionary rap with his gavel. The bidding continued, quietly but furiously. "Twenty-five million. I have twenty-six. Twenty-seven to the gentleman on the right."

The murmuring rose once again, and this time the chairman did not quell it.

"I have thirty-two million. Thirty-two and a half on the phone. Thirty-three. Thank you, I have thirty-three and a half. Thirty-four to the lady in the front."

An electricity was building in the sale room: the price was mounting far higher than even the wildest predictions.

"Thirty-five on the phone. Thirty-five and a half to the lady. Thirty-six."

Then there was a small stir in the crowd; a rustle, a shifting of attention. A number of eyes turned toward the door leading out into the main gallery. Standing on the crescent-moon steps was a remarkable-looking man of about sixty, a massive, even overwhelming presence. He had a shaved head and a dark Vandyke beard. A Valentino suit of dark blue silk was draped over his imposing frame, shimmering slightly in the light when he moved. A Turnbull & Asser shirt, uncompromisingly white, lay open at the neck. Over it was a string tie, held in place by a fist-size piece of amber, containing the only *Archaeopteryx* feather ever found.

"Thirty-six million," the chairman repeated. But his eyes, like everyone else's, had strayed toward the new arrival.

The man stood on the steps, his blue eyes sparkling with vitality and some private amusement. He slowly raised his paddle. A hush fell. On the remote chance anybody in the crowd had not recognized the man, the paddle was a giveaway: it was numbered 001, the only number Christie's had ever allowed to be given permanently to a client.

The chairman looked at him, expectantly.

"One hundred," the man said at last, softly but precisely.

The hush deepened. "I beg your pardon?" The chairman's voice was dry.

"One hundred million dollars," the man said. His teeth were very large, very straight, and very white.

Again the silence was absolute.

"I have a bid of one hundred million," said the chairman, a little shakily.

Time seemed to have been suspended. A telephone rang somewhere in the building, at the edge of audibility, and the sound of a car horn filtered up from the avenue.

Then the spell was broken with a smart rap of the gavel. "Lot number one, for one hundred million dollars, sold to Palmer Lloyd!"

The room erupted. In a flash everyone was on their feet. There was exuberant clapping, cheers, a call of "bravo" as if a great tenor had just concluded the performance of his career. Others were not as pleased, and the cheering and clapping was interlaced with hisses of disapproval, catcalls, low boos. Christie's had never witnessed a crowd so close to hysteria: all the participants, pro and con, were well aware that history had just been made. But the man who had caused it all was gone, out through the main gallery, down the green carpet past the cashier—and the multitude found themselves addressing an empty doorway.

Kalahari Desert, June 1, 6:45 P.M.

Sam McFarlane sat cross-legged in the dust. The evening fire, built of twigs on bare ground, cast a trembling net of shadows over the thorn scrub surrounding the camp. The nearest settlement lay one hundred miles behind his back.

He looked around at the wizened figures squatting on their heels around the fire, naked except for dusty breechclouts, their alert eyes gleaming. San Bushmen. It took a long time to gain their trust, but once gained, it was unshakable. Very different, McFarlane thought, from back home.

In front of each San lay a battered secondhand metal detector. The San remained immobile as McFarlane rose to his feet. He spoke slowly, awkwardly, in their strange click language. At first there were some snickers as he struggled with the words, but McFarlane had a natural affinity for languages, and as he continued the men fell back into respectful silence.

At the conclusion of his speech, McFarlane smoothed out a patch of sand. Using a stick, he began to draw a map. The San squatted on their heels, craning their necks to look at the drawing. Slowly the map took shape, and the San nodded their understanding as McFarlane pointed out the various landmarks. It was the Makgadikgadi Pans that lay north of the camp: a thousand square miles of dry lakebeds, sand hills, and alkali flats, desolate and uninhabited. In the deep interior of the Pans, he drew a small circle with his stick. Then he stabbed the stick in the center of the circle and looked up with a broad smile.

There was a moment of silence, punctuated by the lonely sound of a ruoru bird calling across the distant flats. The San began talking among themselves in low voices, the clicks and clucks of their language like the rattling of pebbles in a stream. A gnarled old figure, the headman of the band, pointed at the map. McFarlane leaned forward, straining to understand the rapid speech. Yes, they knew the area, the old man said. He began to describe trails, known only to the San, that crossed the remote area. With a twig and some pebbles, the headman began marking where the seeps were, where the game was, where edible roots and plants could be found. McFarlane waited patiently.

At last, quiet again settled on the group. The headman spoke to McFarlane, more slowly this time. Yes, they were willing to do what the white man wanted. But they were afraid of the white man's machines, and they also did not understand this thing the white man was looking for.

McFarlane rose again, pulled the stick out of the map. Then he took a small, dark lump of iron from his pocket, no bigger than a marble, and placed it in the hole left by the stick. He pushed it down and concealed it with sand. Then he stood, picked up his metal detector, and snapped it on. There was a brief, high-pitched whine. Everyone watched in nervous silence. He took two steps away from the map, turned, and began walking forward, making low sweeps over the ground with the detector. As it swept over the buried lump of iron, there was a squawk. The San jumped backward in alarm and there was a burst of rapid talk.

McFarlane smiled, spoke a few words, and the San crept back into their seating places. He turned off the metal detector and held it toward the headman, who took it reluctantly. McFarlane showed him how to turn it on, and then guided him, in sweeping motions, over the circle. A second squawk sounded. The headman flinched but then smiled. He tried it again, and again, his smile growing broader, his face breaking into a mass of wrinkles. "Sun'a ai, Ma!gad'i!gadi !iaad'mi," he said, gesturing to his band.

With McFarlane's patient help, each San Bushman in turn picked up a machine and tested it on the hidden iron nugget. Slowly, the apprehension was replaced by laughter and speculative discussion. Eventually McFarlane raised his hands, and all sat down again, each with his machine in his lap. They were ready to begin the search.

McFarlane took a leather bag from his pocket, opened it, inverted it. A dozen gold Krugerrands fell into his outstretched palm. The ruoru bird began its mournful call again as the last light died from the sky. Slowly and with ceremony, he gave a gold coin to each man in turn. They took them reverently, with paired hands, bowing their heads.

The headman spoke again to McFarlane. Tomorrow, they would move camp and begin the journey into the heart of the Makgadikgadi Pans with the white man's machines. They would look for this big thing the white man wanted. When they found it, they would return. They would tell the white man where it was . . .

The old man suddenly darted his eyes to the sky in alarm. The others did the same as McFarlane watched, his brow creasing in puzzlement. Then he heard it himself: a faint, rhythmic throbbing. He followed their gaze to the dark horizon. Already the Bushmen were on their feet, birdlike, apprehensive. There was rapid, urgent talk. A cluster of lights, faint but growing brighter, rose in the distant sky. The throbbing sound grew stronger. The pencil-like beam of a spotlight stabbed downward into the scrub.

With a soft cry of alarm, the old man dropped his Krugerrand and disappeared into the darkness. The rest followed suit. Instantly, it seemed, McFarlane was left alone, staring into the still darkness of the brush. He turned wildly as the light grew in intensity. It was coming straight for the camp. And now he could see it was a big Blackhawk helicopter, its rotors tearing up the night air, running lights winking, the oversize spotlight racing across the ground until at last it fixed him in its glare.

McFarlane threw himself into the dust behind a thornbush and lay there, feeling exposed in the brilliant light. Digging a hand into his boot, he pulled out a small pistol. Dust whipped up around him, stinging his eyes as the desert bushes gyrated maniacally. The helicopter slowed, hovered, and descended to an open area at one side of the camp, the backwash blowing a cascade of sparks from the fire. As the chopper settled, a lightbar on its roof lit up, bathing the area in an even harsher glare. The rotors powered down. McFarlane waited, wiping dirt from his face, keeping his eyes on the helicopter's hatch, gun at the ready. Soon it swung open, and a large, solid man stepped out, alone.

McFarlane peered through the thorny scrub. The man was dressed in khaki shorts and a cotton bush shirt, and a Tilley hat sat on his massive shaven head. There was something heavy swinging in one of the shorts' oversize pockets. The man began walking toward McFarlane.

McFarlane slowly rose, keeping the bush between himself and the chopper, training his gun on the man's chest. But the stranger seemed unconcerned. Although he was in shadow, silhouetted by the chopper's takedown lights, McFarlane thought he saw teeth gleaming in a smile. He stopped five paces away. He had to be six foot eight, at least—McFarlane was not sure he had ever seen anybody quite as tall before.

"You're a difficult man to find," the man said.

In the deep, resonant voice McFarlane heard nasal traces of an East Coast accent. "Who the hell are you?" he replied, keeping the gun leveled.

"Introductions are so much more pleasant after the firearms have been put away."

"Take the gun out of your pocket and toss it in the dirt," said McFarlane.

The man chuckled and withdrew the lump: it was not a gun, but a small thermos. "Something to keep out the chill," he said, holding it up. "Care to share it with me?"

McFarlane glanced back at the helicopter, but the only other occupant was the pilot. "It took me a month to gain their trust," he said in a low voice, "and you've just scattered them all to hell and gone. I want to know who you are, and why you're here. And it had better be good."

"It's not good, I'm afraid. Your partner, Nestor Masangkay, is dead."

McFarlane felt a sudden numbness. His gun hand slowly dropped. "Dead?"

The man nodded.

"How?"

"Doing just what you're doing. We don't really know how." He gestured. "Shall we move by the fire? I didn't expect these Kalahari nights to be so nippy."

McFarlane edged toward the remains of the fire, keeping the gun loosely by his side, his mind full of conflicting emotions. He noticed, distantly, that the backwash of the chopper had erased his sand map, exposing the little nugget of iron.

"So what's your connection to Nestor?" he asked.

The man did not answer right away. Instead, he surveyed the scene—the dozen metal detectors scattered willy-nilly by the fleeing San, the gold coins lying in the sand. He bent down and picked up the brown fingernail of iron, hefted it, and then held it up to his eye. Then he glanced up at McFarlane. "Looking for the Okavango meteorite again?"

McFarlane said nothing, but his hand tightened on the gun.

"You knew Masangkay better than anybody. I need you to help me finish his project."

"And just what project was that?" McFarlane asked.

"I'm afraid I've said all I can say about it."

"And I'm afraid I've heard all I want to hear. The only person I help anymore is myself."

"So I've heard."

McFarlane stepped forward quickly, the anger returning. The man raised a pacifying hand. "The least you can do is hear me out."

"I haven't even heard your name, and, frankly, I don't want to.

Thanks for bringing me the bad news. Now why don't you get back in your chopper and get the hell out of here."

"Forgive me for not introducing myself. I'm Palmer Lloyd."

McFarlane began to laugh. "Yeah, and I'm Bill Gates."

But the big man wasn't laughing—just smiling. McFarlane looked closer at his face, really studying it for the first time. "Jesus," he breathed.

"You may have heard that I'm building a new museum."

McFarlane shook his head. "Was Nestor working for you?"

"No. But his activities recently came to my attention, and I want to finish what he started."

"Look," said McFarlane, shoving the gun into his waistband. "I'm not interested. Nestor Masangkay and I parted ways a long time ago. But I'm sure you know all about that."

Lloyd smiled and held up the thermos. "Shall we talk about it over a toddy?" Without waiting for an answer, he settled himself by the fire—white man style, with his butt in the dust—unscrewed the cap, and poured out a steaming cup. He offered it to McFarlane, who shook his head impatiently.

"You like hunting meteorites?" Lloyd asked.

"It has its days."

"And you really think you'll find the Okavango?"

"Yes. Until you dropped out of the sky." McFarlane crouched beside him. "I'd love to chitchat with you. But every minute you sit here with that idling chopper, the Bushmen are getting farther away. So I'll say it again. I'm not interested in a job. Not at your museum, not at *any* museum." He hesitated. "Besides, you can't pay me what I'm going to make on the Okavango."

"And just what might that be?" Lloyd asked, sipping the cup himself.

"A quarter million. At least."

Lloyd nodded. "Assuming you find it. Subtract what you owe everyone over the Tornarssuk fiasco, and I imagine you'll probably break even."

McFarlane laughed harshly. "Everyone's entitled to one mistake. I'll have enough left over to get me started on the next rock.

There's a lot of meteorites out there. It sure beats a curator's salary."

"I'm not talking about a curatorship."

"Then what are you talking about?"

"I'm sure you could make a pretty good guess. I can't talk about particulars until I know you're on board." He sipped at the toddy. "Do this one for your old partner."

"Old ex-partner."

Lloyd sighed. "You're right. I know all about you and Masangkay. It wasn't entirely your fault, losing the Tornarssuk rock like that. If anyone's to blame, it's the bureaucrats at the New York Museum of Natural History."

"Why don't you give up? I'm not interested."

"Let me tell you about the compensation. As a signing bonus, I'll pay off the quarter million you owe, get the creditors off your back. If the project is successful, you'll get another quarter million. If it isn't, you'll have to settle for being debt free. Either way, you can continue at my museum as director of the Planetary Sciences Department—if you wish. I'll build you a state-of-the-art laboratory. You'll have a secretary, lab assistants, a six-figure salary—the works."

McFarlane began to laugh again. "Beautiful. So how long is this project?"

"Six months. On the outside."

McFarlane stopped laughing. "Half a million for six months' work?"

"*If* we're successful."

"What's the catch?"

"No catch."

"Why me?"

"You knew Masangkay: his quirks, his work patterns, his thoughts. There's a big mystery lingering over what he was doing, and you're the man who can solve it. And besides, you're one of the top meteorite hunters in the world. You've got an intuitive sense about them. People say you can *smell* them."

"I'm not the only one out there." The praise irritated McFarlane: it smacked of manipulation.

In response, Lloyd extended one hand, the knuckle of the ring finger raised. There was a wink of precious metal as he turned it in McFarlane's direction.

"Sorry," McFarlane answered. "I only kiss the ring of the pope."

Lloyd chuckled. "Look at the stone," he said.

Peering more closely, McFarlane saw that the ring on Lloyd's finger consisted of a milky gemstone, deep violet, in a heavy platinum setting. He recognized it immediately. "Nice stone. But you could have bought it from me wholesale."

"No doubt. After all, you and Masangkay are the ones that *got* the Atacama tektites out of Chile."

"Right. And I'm still a wanted man in those parts as a result."

"We will offer you suitable protections."

"So it's Chile, huh? Well, I know what the insides of their jails look like. Sorry."

Lloyd didn't respond immediately. Picking up a stick, he banked the scattered embers, then tossed the stick onto them. The fire crackled up, beating back the darkness. On anybody else, the Tilley hat would look a little silly; somehow, Lloyd managed to pull it off. "If you knew what we were planning, Dr. McFarlane, you'd do it for free. I'm offering you the scientific prize of the century."

McFarlane chuckled, shaking his head. "I'm done with *science*," he said. "I've had enough dusty labs and museum bureaucracies to last me a lifetime."

Lloyd sighed and stood up. "Well, it looks like I've wasted my time. I guess we'll have to go with our number two choice."

McFarlane paused. "And who would that be?"

"Hugo Breitling would love to be in on this."

"Breitling? He couldn't find a meteorite if it hit him in the ass."

"He found the Thule meteorite," Lloyd replied, slapping the dust from his pants. He gave McFarlane a sidelong glance. "Which is bigger than anything you've found."

"But that's *all* he found. And that was sheer luck."

"Fact is, I'm going to *need* luck for this project." Lloyd screwed the top back on the thermos and tossed it into the dust at McFarlane's feet. "Here, have yourself a party. I've got to get going."

He began striding toward the helicopter. As McFarlane watched, the engine revved and the heavy rotors picked up speed, beating the air, sending skeins of dust swirling erratically across the ground. It suddenly occurred to him that, if the chopper left, he might never learn how Masangkay died, or what he had been doing. Despite himself, he was intrigued. McFarlane looked around quickly: at the metal detectors, dented and scattered; at the bleak little camp; at the landscape beyond, parched and unpromising.

At the helicopter's hatch, Lloyd paused.

"Make it an even million!" called McFarlane to the man's broad back.

Carefully, so as not to upset the hat, Lloyd ducked his head and began stepping into the chopper.

"Seven fifty, then!"

There was another pause. And then Palmer Lloyd slowly turned, his face breaking into a broad smile.

The Hudson River Valley, June 3, 10:45 A.M.

Palmer Lloyd loved many rare and valuable things, but one of the things he loved most was Thomas Cole's painting *Sunny Morning on the Hudson River.* As a scholarship student in Boston, he had often gone to the Museum of Fine Arts, walking through the galleries with his eyes downcast so as not to sully his vision before he could stand before that glorious painting.

Lloyd preferred to own the things he loved, but the Thomas Cole painting was not to be had at any price. Instead, he had purchased the next best thing. On this sunny morning he sat in his upper Hudson Valley office, gazing out a window that framed precisely the view in Cole's painting. There was a very beautiful line of light penciling the extreme horizon; the fields, seen through the breaking mists, were exquisitely fresh and green. The mountainside in the foreground, limned by the rising sun, sparkled. Not much had changed in the Clove Valley since Cole had painted this scene in 1827, and Lloyd had made sure, with vast land purchases along his line of sight, that nothing would.

He swiveled in his chair, gazing across a desk of spaulded maple into a window that looked in the opposite direction. From here, the hillside fell away beneath him, a brilliant mosaic of glass and steel. Hands behind his head, Lloyd surveyed the scene of frantic activity with satisfaction. Work crews swarmed over the landscape, fulfilling a vision—*his* vision—unparalleled in the world. "A miracle of rare device," he murmured beneath his breath.

At the center of the activity, green in the Catskill morning light, was a massive dome: an oversize replica of London's Crystal Palace, which had been the first structure made entirely of glass. Upon its completion in 1851 it was considered one of the most beautiful buildings ever constructed, but it had been demolished during World War II because its glittering presence acted as a guide to Nazi bombers.

Beyond the overarching dome, Lloyd could see the first blocks being laid of the pyramid of Khefret II, a small Old Kingdom pyramid. He smiled a little ruefully at the memory of his trip to Egypt: his byzantine dealings with government officials, the Keystone Kops uproar about the suitcase full of gold that no one could lift, all the other tedious melodrama. That pyramid had cost him more than he liked, and it wasn't exactly Cheops, but it was impressive nonetheless.

Thinking of the pyramid reminded him of the outrage its purchase had caused in the archaeological world, and he glanced up at the newspaper articles and magazine covers framed on a nearby wall. "Where Have All the Artifacts Gone?" read one, accompanied by a grotesque caricature of Lloyd, complete with shifty eyes and slouch hat, slipping a miniature pyramid under his dark cloak. He scanned the other framed headlines. "The Hitler of Collectors?" read one; and then there were all the ones decrying his recent purchase: "Bones of Contention: Paleontologists Outraged by Sale." And a *Newsweek* cover: "What Do You Do with Thirty Billion? Answer: Buy the Earth." The wall was covered with them, the shrill utterances of the naysayers, the self-appointed guardians of cultural morality. Lloyd found it all an endless source of amusement.

A small chime rang on a flat panel laid into his desk, and the voice of his secretary fluted: "There's a Mr. Glinn to see you, sir."

"Send him in." Lloyd didn't bother to suppress the excitement in his voice. He had not met Eli Glinn before, and it had been surprisingly difficult to get him to come in person.

He closely observed the man as he entered the office, without even a briefcase in his hand, sunburnt face expressionless. Lloyd had found, in his long and fruitful business career, that first impressions, if carefully made, were exceedingly revealing. He took in the close-cropped brown hair, the square jaw, the thin lips. The man looked, at first glance, as inscrutable as the Sphinx. There was nothing distinctive about him, nothing that gave anything away. Even his gray eyes were veiled, cautious, and still. Everything about him looked ordinary: ordinary height, ordinary build, good-looking but not handsome, well-dressed but not dapper. His only unusual feature, Lloyd thought, was the way he moved. His shoes made no sound on the floor, his clothes did not rustle on his person, his limbs moved lightly and easily through the air. He glided through the room like a deer through a forest.

And, of course, there was nothing ordinary in the man's résumé.

"Mr. Glinn," Lloyd said, walking toward him and taking his hand. "Thank you for coming."

Glinn nodded silently, shook the proffered hand with a shake that was neither too long nor too short, neither limp nor bone-crushingly macho. Lloyd felt moderately disconcerted: he was having trouble forming that invaluable first impression. He swept his hand toward the window and the sprawling, half-finished structures beyond. "So. What do you think of my museum?"

"Large," Glinn said without smiling.

Lloyd laughed. "The Getty of natural history museums. Or it will be, soon—with three times the endowment."

"Interesting that you decided to locate it here, a hundred miles from the city."

"A nice touch of hubris, don't you think? Actually, I'm doing the New York Museum of Natural History a favor. If we'd built there instead of up here, we'd have put them out of business within a month. But since we'll have the biggest and the best of everything, they'll be reduced to serving school field trips." Lloyd chuckled. "Come on, Sam McFarlane is waiting for us. I'll give you a tour on the way."

"Sam McFarlane?"

"He's my meteorite expert. Well, he's still only about half mine, I'd say, but I'm working on him. The day is young."

Lloyd placed a hand on the elbow of Glinn's well-tailored but anonymous dark suit—the material was better than he expected—and guided him back through the outer office, down a sweeping circular ramp of granite and polished marble, and along a large corridor toward the Crystal Palace. The noise was much louder here, and their footsteps were punctuated by shouts, the steady cadence of nailguns, and the stutter of jackhammers.

With barely contained enthusiasm, Lloyd pointed out the sights as they walked. "That's the diamond hall, there," he said, waving his hand toward a large subterranean space, haloed in violet light. "We discovered there were some old diggings in this hillside, so we tunneled our way in and set up the exhibit within an entirely natural context. It's the only hall in any major museum devoted exclusively to diamonds. But since we've acquired the three largest specimens in the world, it seemed appropriate. You must have heard about how we snapped up the Blue Mandarin from De Beers, just ahead of the Japanese?" He gave a wicked chuckle at the memory.

"I read the papers," Glinn said dryly.

"And that," said Lloyd, becoming more animated, "will house the Gallery of Extinct Life. Passenger pigeons, a dodo bird from the Galápagos, even a mammoth removed from the Siberian ice, still perfectly frozen. They found crushed buttercups in its mouth—remnants of its last meal."

"I read about the mammoth, too," Glinn said. "Weren't there several shootings in Siberia in the aftermath of its acquisition?"

Despite the pointedness of the question, Glinn's tone was mild, without any trace of censure, and Lloyd didn't pause in his answer. "You'd be surprised, Mr. Glinn, how quickly countries waive their so-called cultural patrimony when large sums of money become involved. Here, I'll show you what I mean." He beckoned his guest forward, through a half-completed archway flanked by two men in hard hats, into a darkened hall that stretched for a hundred yards. He paused to flick on the lights, then turned with a grin.

Before them stretched a hardened, mudlike surface. Wandering across this surface were two sets of small footprints. It looked as if people had wandered into the hall while the cement on the floor was setting.

"The Laetoli footprints," Lloyd said reverently.

Glinn said nothing.

"The oldest hominid footprints ever discovered. Think about it: three and a half million years ago our first bipedal ancestors made those footprints, walking across a layer of wet volcanic ash. They're unique. Nobody knew that *Australopithecus afarensis* walked upright until these were found. They're the earliest proof of our humanity, Mr. Glinn."

"The Getty Conservation Institute must have been interested to hear of this acquisition," Glinn said.

Lloyd looked at his companion more carefully. Glinn was an exceptionally difficult man to read. "I see you've done your homework. The Getty wanted to leave them buried in situ. How long do you think *that* would have lasted, with Tanzania in the state it's in?" He shook his head. "The Getty paid one million dollars to cover them back up. I paid *twenty* million to bring them here, where scholars and countless visitors can benefit."

Glinn glanced around at the construction. "Speaking of scholars, where are the scientists? I see a lot of blue collars, but very few white coats."

Lloyd waved his hand. "I bring them on as I need them. For the most part, I know what I want to buy. When the time comes, though, I'll get the best. I'll stage a raiding party through the country's curatorial offices that will leave them spinning. It'll be just like Sherman marching to the sea. The New York Museum won't know what hit them."

More quickly now, Lloyd directed his visitor away from the long hallway and into a warren of corridors that angled deeper into the Palace. At the end of one corridor, they stopped before a door marked CONFERENCE ROOM A. Lounging beside the door was Sam

McFarlane, looking every inch the adventurer: lean and rugged, blue eyes faded by the sun. His straw-colored hair had a faint horizontal ridge to it, as if years of wearing heavy-brimmed hats had permanently creased it. Just looking at him, Lloyd could see why the man had never taken to academia. He seemed as out of place among the fluorescent lights and drab-colored labs as would the San Bushmen he had been with just the other day. Lloyd noted, with satisfaction, that McFarlane looked tired. No doubt he had gotten very little sleep over the last two days.

Reaching into his pocket, Lloyd withdrew a key and opened the door. The space beyond was always a shock to first-time visitors. One-way glass covered three of the room's walls, looking down on the grand entrance to the museum: a vast octagonal space, currently empty, in the very center of the Palace. Lloyd glanced to see how Glinn would take it. But the man was as inscrutable as ever.

For months Lloyd had agonized over what object would occupy the soaring octagonal space below—until the auction at Christie's. The battling dinosaurs, he had thought, would make a perfect centerpiece. You could still read the desperate agony of their final struggle in the contorted bones.

And then his eyes fell on the table littered with charts, printouts, and aerial photographs. When *this* happened, Lloyd had forgotten all about the dinosaurs. This would be the pièce de résistance, the crowning glory of the Lloyd Museum. Mounting *this* in the center of the Crystal Palace would be the proudest moment of his life.

"May I introduce Dr. Sam McFarlane," Lloyd said, turning away from the table and looking at Glinn. "The museum's retaining his services for the duration of this assignment."

McFarlane shook Glinn's hand.

"Until last week, Sam was wandering around the Kalahari Desert looking for the Okavango meteorite. A poor use of his talents. I think you'll agree we've found something much more interesting for him to do."

He gestured at Glinn. "Sam, this is Mr. Eli Glinn, president of Effective Engineering Solutions, Inc. Don't let the dull name fool you—it's a remarkable company. Mr. Glinn specializes in such things as raising Nazi subs full of gold, figuring out why space shuttles blow up—that sort of thing. Solving unique engineering problems and analyzing major failures."

"Interesting job," said McFarlane.

Lloyd nodded. "Usually, though, EES steps in after the fact. Once things have gotten *fucked up*." The vulgarity, enunciated slowly and distinctly, hung in the air. "But I'm bringing them in now to help make sure a certain task *doesn't* get fucked up. And that task, gentlemen, is why we're all here today."

He gestured toward the conference table. "Sam, I want you to tell Mr. Glinn what you've found, looking at this data over the last few days."

"Right now?" McFarlane asked. He seemed uncharacteristically nervous.

"When else?"

McFarlane glanced over the table, hesitated, and then spoke. "What we have here," he said, "is geophysical data about an unusual site in the Cape Horn islands of Chile."

Glinn nodded encouragingly.

"Mr. Lloyd asked me to analyze it. At first, the data seemed . . . impossible. Like this tomographic readout." He picked it up, glanced at it, let it drop. His eyes swept over the rest of the papers, and his voice faltered.

Lloyd cleared his throat. Sam was still a little shaken by it all; he was going to need some help. He turned to Glinn. "Perhaps I'd better bring you up to speed on the history. One of our scouts came across a dealer in electronic equipment in Punta Arenas, Chile. He was trying to sell a rusted-out electromagnetic tomographic sounder. It's a piece of mining survey equipment, made here in the States by DeWitter Industries. It had been found, along with a bag of rocks and some papers, near the remains of a prospector on a remote island down near Cape Horn. On a whim, my scout bought it all. When he took a closer look at the papers—those that he could decipher—the scout noticed they belonged to a man named Nestor Masangkay."

Lloyd's eyes drifted toward the conference table. "Before his death on the island, Masangkay had been a planetary geologist. More specifically, a meteorite hunter. And, up until about two years ago, he'd been the partner of Sam McFarlane here."

He saw McFarlane's shoulders stiffen.

"When our scout learned this, he sent everything back here for analysis. The tomographic sounder had a floppy disk rusted into its drive bay. One of our technicians managed to extract the data. Some of my people analyzed the data, but it was simply too far outside the bell curve for them to make much sense of it. That's why we hired Sam."

McFarlane had turned from the first page to the second, and then back again. "At first I thought that Nestor had forgotten to calibrate his machine. But then I looked at the rest of the data." He dropped the readout, then pushed the two weathered sheets aside with a slow, almost reverent motion. He began leafing through the scatter and removed another sheet.

"We didn't send a ground expedition," Lloyd continued, speaking again to Glinn, "because the last thing we want to do is attract attention. But we did order a flyover of the island. And that sheet Sam's holding now is a dump from the LOG II satellite—the Low Orbit Geosurvey."

McFarlane carefully put down the data dump. "I had a lot of trouble believing this," he finally said. "I must have gone over it a dozen times. But there's no getting away from it. It can mean only one thing."

"Yes?" Glinn's voice was low, encouraging, holding no trace of curiosity.

"I think I know what Nestor was after."

Lloyd waited. He knew what McFarlane was going to say. But he wanted to hear it again.

"What we've got here is the largest meteorite in the world."

Lloyd broke into a grin. "Tell Mr. Glinn just how large, Sam."

McFarlane cleared his throat. "The largest meteorite recovered in the world so far is the Ahnighito, in the New York Museum. It weighs sixty-one tons. This one weighs four thousand tons. At an absolute minimum."

"Thank you," Lloyd said, his frame swelling with joy, his face breaking into a radiant smile. Then he turned and looked again at Glinn. The man's face still betrayed nothing.

There was a long moment of silence. And then Lloyd spoke again, his voice low and hoarse with emotion.

"I want that meteorite. Your job, Mr. Glinn, is to make sure I get it."

New York City, June 4, 11:45 A.M.

The Land Rover jounced its way down West Street, the sagging piers along the Hudson flashing by the passenger window, the sky over Jersey City a dull sepia in the noon light. McFarlane braked hard, then swerved to avoid a taxi angling across three lanes to catch a fare. It was a smooth, automatic motion. McFarlane's mind was far away.

He was remembering the afternoon when the Zaragosa meteorite fell. He'd finished high school, had no job or plans of one, and was hiking across the Mexican desert, Carlos Castaneda in his back pocket. The sun had been low, and he'd been thinking about finding a place to pitch his bedroll. Suddenly, the landscape grew bright around him, as if the sun had emerged from heavy clouds. But the sky was already perfectly clear. And then he'd stopped dead in his tracks. On the sandy ground ahead of him, a *second* shadow of himself had appeared; long and ragged at first, but quickly compacting. There was a sound of singing. And then, a massive explosion. He'd fallen to the ground, thinking earthquake, or nuclear blast, or Armageddon. There was a patter of rain. Except it was not rain: it was thousands of tiny rocks dropping around him. He picked one up; a little piece of gray stone, covered in black crust. It still held the deep cold of outer space inside, despite its fiery passage through the atmosphere, and it was covered with frost.

As he stared at the fragment from outer space, he suddenly knew what he wanted to do with the rest of his life.

But that had been years ago. Now, he tried to think as little about those idealistic days as possible. His eye strayed to a locked briefcase on the passenger seat, which contained Nestor Masangkay's battered journal. He tried to think as little as possible about that, too.

A light ahead turned green, and he made a turn into a narrow one-way street. This was the meat-packing district, perched at the uttermost edge of the West Village. Old loading docks yawned wide, filled with burly men manhandling carcasses in and out of trucks. Along the far side of the street, as if to take advantage of the proximity, was a crowd of restaurants with names like The Hog Pit and Uncle Billy's Backyard. It was the antithesis of the chrome-and-glass Park Avenue headquarters of Lloyd Holdings, from which he had just come. *Nice place for a corporate presence*, McFarlane thought, *if you deal in pork-belly futures*. He double-checked the scribbled address lying on his dashboard.

He slowed, then guided the Land Rover to a stop on the far side of an especially decrepit loading dock. Killing the engine, he stepped into the meat-fragrant humidity and looked around. Halfway down the block a garbage truck idled, grinding busily away at its load. Even from this distance, he caught a whiff of the green juice that dribbled off its rear bumper. It was a stench unique to New York City garbage trucks; once smelled, never forgotten.

He took a deep breath. The meeting hadn't begun yet, and already he felt himself tense, the defensiveness rising. He wondered how much Lloyd had told Glinn about himself and Masangkay. It didn't really matter; what they didn't know they'd learn soon enough. Gossip moved even faster than the impactors he hunted.

He pulled a heavy portfolio from the back of the Land Rover, then closed and locked the door. Before him rose the grimy brick facade of a fin de siècle building, a massive structure taking up most of the block. His eye traveled up a dozen stories, coming to rest at the words PRICE & PRICE PORK PACKING INC. The paint was almost effaced by time. Although the windows on the lower floors had been bricked over, he could see fresh glass and chrome winking on the upper stories.

The only entrance seemed to be a brace of metal loading doors. He pressed a buzzer at their side and waited. After a few seconds there came a faint click and the doors parted, moving noiselessly on oiled bearings.

He stepped into a poorly lit corridor that ended in another set of steel doors, much newer, flanked with security keypads and a retinal scanning unit. As he approached, one of the doors opened and a small, dark, heavily muscled man in an MIT warm-up suit came forward, an athletic spring to his step. Tightly curled black hair, fringed with white at the temples, covered his head. He had dark, intelligent eyes and an easygoing air that was very uncorporate.

"Dr. McFarlane?" the man asked in a friendly growl, extending a hairy hand. "I'm Manuel Garza, construction engineer for EES." His grip was surprisingly gentle.

"Is this your corporate headquarters?" McFarlane asked with a wry smile.

"We prefer our anonymity."

"Well, at least you don't have to go far for a steak."

Garza laughed gruffly. "Not if you like it rare."

McFarlane followed him through the open door. He found himself in a cavernous room, brilliantly lit with halogen lights. Acres of steel tables stood in long, neat rows. On them rested numerous tagged objects—piles of sand, rocks, melted jet engines, ragged pieces of metal. Technicians in lab coats moved around. One passed him, cradling a piece of asphalt in white-gloved hands as if it were a Ming vase.

Garza followed McFarlane's gaze around the room, and then glanced at his watch. "We've got a few minutes. Care for a tour?"

"Why not? I always love a good junkyard."

Garza threaded his way among the tables, nodding to various technicians. He paused at an unusually long table, covered with twisted black lumps of rock. "Recognize these?"

"That's pahoehoe. There's a nice example of aa. Some volcanic bombs. You guys building a volcano?"

"No," said Garza. "Just blew one apart." He nodded to a scale model of a volcanic island at the far end of the table, complete with a city, canyons, forests, and mountains. He reached beneath the lip of the table and pressed a button. There was a brief whirr, a groaning noise, and the volcano began to belch lava, spilling in sinuous flows down its flanks and creeping toward the scale city. "The lava is specially formulated methyl cellulose."

"Beats my old N-scale railroad."

"A Third World government needed our assistance. A dormant volcano had erupted on one of their islands. A lake of lava was building up in the caldera and was about to bust out and head straight for this city of sixty thousand. Our job was to save the city."

"Funny, I didn't read anything in the news about this."

"It wasn't funny at all. The government wasn't going to evacuate the city. It's a minor offshore banking haven. Mostly drug money."

"Maybe you should have let it burn, like Sodom and Gomorrah."

"We're an engineering firm, not God. We don't concern ourselves with the moral status of paying clients."

McFarlane laughed, feeling himself relax a little. "So how'd you stop it?"

"We blocked those two valleys, there, with landslides. Then we punched a hole in the volcano with high explosives and blasted an overflow channel on the far side. We used a significant portion of the world's nonmilitary supply of Semtex in the process. All the lava went into the sea, creating almost a thousand acres of new real estate for our client in the process. That didn't quite pay our fee, of course. But it helped."

Garza moved on. They passed a series of tables covered with

bits of fuselage and burnt electronics. "Jet crash," said Garza, "terrorist bomb." He dismissed it with a quick wave of his hand.

Reaching the far side of the room, Garza opened a small white door and led McFarlane down a series of sterile corridors. McFarlane could hear the hush of air scrubbers; the clatter of keys; a strange, regular thudding sound from far below his feet.

Then Garza opened another door and McFarlane stopped short in surprise. The space ahead of him was vast—at least six stories tall and two hundred feet deep. Around the edges of the room was a forest of high-tech equipment: banks of digital cameras, category-5 cabling, huge "green screens" for visual effects backdrops. Along one wall sat half a dozen Lincoln convertibles of early sixties vintage, long and slab-sided. Inside each car sat four carefully dressed dummies, two in the front and two in the rear.

The center of the enormous space was taken up by a model of a city intersection, complete down to working stoplights. Building facades of various heights rose on either side. A groove ran down the asphalted road, and a pulley system within it was fixed to the front bumper of yet another Lincoln, its four dummies in careful place. An undulating greensward of sculpted AstroTurf lined the roadway. The roadway ended in an overpass, and there stood Eli Glinn himself, bullhorn in one hand.

McFarlane stepped forward in Garza's wake, halting at last on the pavement in the artificial shade of some plastic bushes. Something about the scene looked strangely familiar.

On the overpass, Glinn raised the bullhorn. "Thirty seconds," he called out.

"Syncing to digital feed," came a disembodied voice. "Sound off."

There was a flurry of responses. "Green across the board," the voice said.

"Everyone clear," said Glinn. "Power up and let's go."

Activity seemed to come from everywhere. There was a hum and the pulley system moved forward, pulling the limo along the direction of the groove. Technicians stood behind the digital cameras, recording the progress.

There was the crack of an explosion nearby, then two more in quick succession. McFarlane ducked instinctively, recognizing the sound as gunfire. Nobody else seemed alarmed, and he looked in the direction of the noise. It seemed to have come from some bushes to his right. Peering closely into the foliage, he could make out two large rifles, mounted on steel pedestals. Their stocks had been sawn off, and leads ran from the triggers.

Suddenly, he knew where he was. "Dealey Plaza," he murmured.

Garza smiled.

McFarlane stepped onto the AstroTurf and peered closer at the two rifles. Following the direction of their barrels, he noticed that the rear right dummy was leaning to one side, its head shattered.

Glinn approached the side of the car, inspected the dummies, then murmured to someone beside him, pointing out bullet trajectories. As he stepped away and came toward McFarlane, the technicians crowded forward, taking pictures and jotting down data.

"Welcome to *my* museum, Dr. McFarlane," he said, shaking his hand. "I'll thank you to step off our grassy knoll, however. That rifle still holds several live rounds." He turned toward Garza. "It's a perfect match. We've cracked this one. No need for additional run-throughs."

"So *this* is the project you're just wrapping up?" McFarlane asked.

Glinn nodded. "Some new evidence turned up recently that needed further analysis."

"And what have you found?"

Glinn gave him a cool glance. "Perhaps you'll read about it in the *New York Times* someday, Dr. McFarlane. But I doubt it. For now, let me just say that I have a greater respect for conspiracy theorists than I did a month ago."

"Very interesting. This must've cost a fortune. Who paid for it?"

There was a conspicuous silence.

"What does this have to do with engineering?" McFarlane finally asked.

"Everything. EES was a pioneer in the science of failure analysis, and half our work is still in that area. Understanding how things fail is the most important component in solving engineering problems."

"But *this* . . . ?" McFarlane jerked his hand in the direction of the re-created plaza.

Glinn smiled elusively. "Assassination of a president is a rather major failure, don't you think? Not to mention the botched investigation that followed. Besides, our work in analyzing failures such as this helps us maintain our perfect engineering record."

"Perfect?"

"That's right. EES has never failed. *Never.* It is our trademark." He gestured to Garza, and they moved back toward the doorway. "It's not enough to figure out *how* to do something. You must also analyze every possible path to failure. Only then can you be certain of success. That is why we have never failed. We do not sign a contract until we know we can succeed. And then we guarantee success. There are no disclaimers in our contracts."

"Is that why you haven't signed the Lloyd Museum contract yet?"

"Yes. And it's why you're here today." Glinn removed a heavy, beautifully engraved gold watch from his pocket, checked the time, and slid it back. Then he turned the door handle briskly and stepped through. "Come on. The others are waiting."

EES Headquarters, 1:00 P.M.

A short ascent in an industrial elevator, a mazelike journey through white hallways, and McFarlane found himself ushered into a conference room. Low-ceilinged and austerely furnished, it was as understated as Palmer Lloyd's had been lavish. There were no windows, no prints on the walls—only a circular table made out of an exotic wood, and a darkened screen at the far end of the room.

Two people were seated at the table, staring at him, evaluating him with their eyes. The closest was a black-haired young woman, dressed in Farmer Brown–style bib overalls. She was not exactly pretty, but her brown eyes were quick and had glimmers of gold in their depths. They lingered over him in a sardonic way that McFarlane found unsettling. She was of average size, slender, unremarkable, with a healthy tan browning her cheekbones and nose. She had very long hands with longer fingers, currently busy cracking a peanut into a large ashtray on the table in front of her. She looked like an overgrown tomboy.

The man beyond her was dressed in a white lab coat. He was blade thin, with a badly razor-burned face. One eyelid seemed to droop slightly, giving the eye a jocular look, as if it was about to wink. But there was nothing jocular about the rest of the man: he looked humorless, pinched, as tense as catgut. He fidgeted restlessly with a mechanical pencil, turning it over and over.

Glinn nodded. "This is Eugene Rochefort, manager of engineering. He specializes in one-of-a-kind engineering designs."

Rochefort accepted the compliment with a purse of his lips, the pressure briefly turning them white.

"And this is Dr. Rachel Amira. She started out as a physicist with us, but we soon began to exploit her rare gifts as a mathematician. If you have a problem, she will give you an equation. Rachel, Gene, please welcome Dr. Sam McFarlane. Meteorite hunter."

They nodded in reply. McFarlane felt their eyes on him as he busied himself with opening the portfolio case and distributing folders. He felt the tension return.

Glinn accepted his folder. "I'd like to go over the general outline of the problem, and then open the floor for discussion."

"Sure thing," said McFarlane, settling into a chair.

Glinn glanced around, his gray eyes unreadable. Then he withdrew a sheaf of notes from inside his jacket. "First, some general information. The target area is a small island, known as Isla Desolación, off the southern tip of South America in the Cape Horn islands. It lies in Chilean national territory. It is about eight miles long and three miles wide."

He paused and looked around. "Our client, Palmer Lloyd, insists upon moving ahead with the utmost possible speed. He is concerned about possible competition from other museums. That means working in the depths of the South American winter. In the Cape Horn islands, temperatures in July range from above freezing to as much as thirty below zero, Fahrenheit. Cape Horn is the southernmost major landmass outside of Antarctica itself, more than a thousand miles closer to the South Pole than Africa's Cape of Good Hope. During the target month, we can expect five hours of daylight.

"Isla Desolación is not a hospitable place. It is barren, windswept, mostly volcanic with some Tertiary sedimentary basins. The island is bisected by a large snowfield, and there is an old volcanic plug toward the north end. The tides range from thirty to thirty-five vertical feet, and a reversing six-knot current sweeps the island group."

"Lovely conditions for a picnic," Garza muttered.

"The closest human settlement is on Navarino Island, in the Beagle Channel, about forty miles north of the Cape Horn islands. It is a Chilean naval base called Puerto Williams, with a small mestizo Indian shantytown attached to it."

"Puerto *Williams?*" Garza said. "I thought this was Chile we were talking about."

"The entire area was originally mapped by Englishmen." Glinn placed the notes on the table. "Dr. McFarlane, I understand you've been in Chile."

McFarlane nodded.

"What can you tell us about their navy?"

"Charming fellows."

There was a silence. Rochefort, the engineer, began tapping his pencil on the table in an irritated tattoo. The door opened, and a waiter began serving sandwiches and coffee.

"They belligerently patrol the coastal waters," McFarlane went on, "especially in the south, along the border with Argentina. The two countries have a long-running border dispute, as you probably know."

"Can you add anything to what I've said about the climate?"

"I once spent time in Punta Arenas in late fall. Blizzards, sleet storms, and fog are common. Not to mention williwaws."

"Williwaws?" Rochefort asked in a tremulous, reed-thin voice.

"Basically a microburst of wind. It lasts only a minute or two, but it can peak at about a hundred and fifty knots."

"What about decent anchorages?" Garza asked.

"I've been told there *are* no decent anchorages. In fact, from what I've heard, there's no good holding ground for a ship anywhere in the Cape Horn islands."

"We like a challenge," said Garza.

Glinn collected the papers, folded them carefully, and returned them to his jacket pocket. Somehow, McFarlane felt the man had already known the answers to his own questions.

"Clearly," Glinn said, "we have a complex problem, even without considering the meteorite. But let's consider it now. Rachel, I believe you have some questions about the data?"

"I have a *comment* about the data." Amira's eyes glanced at a folder before her, then hovered on McFarlane with faint amusement. She had a superior attitude that McFarlane found annoying.

"Yes?" said McFarlane.

"I don't believe a word of it."

"What exactly don't you believe?"

She waved her hand over his portfolio. "You're the meteorite expert, right? Then you know why no one has ever found a meteorite larger than sixty tons. Any larger, and the force of impact causes the meteorite to shatter. Above two hundred tons, meteorites vaporize from the impact. So how could a monster like this still be intact?"

"I can't—" McFarlane began.

But Amira interrupted. "The second thing is that iron meteorites *rust*. It only takes about five thousand years to rust even the biggest one into a pile of scale. So if it somehow did survive the impact, why is it still there? How do you explain this geological report that says it fell thirty million years ago, was buried in sediment, and is only now being exposed through erosion?"

McFarlane settled back in his chair. She waited, raising her eyebrows quizzically.

"Have you ever read Sherlock Holmes?" McFarlane asked with a smile of his own.

Amira rolled her eyes. "You're not going to quote that old saw about how once you've eliminated the impossible, whatever remains, no matter how improbable, must be the truth—are you?"

McFarlane shot a surprised glance at her. "Well, isn't it true?"

Amira smirked her triumph, while Rochefort shook his head.

"So, Dr. McFarlane," Amira said brightly, "is that your source of scientific authority? Sir Arthur Conan Doyle?"

McFarlane exhaled slowly. "Someone else collected the base data. I can't vouch for it. All I can say is, if that data's accurate, there's no other explanation: it's a meteorite."

There was a silence. "Someone else's data," Amira said, cracking another shell and popping the nuts into her mouth. "Would that be a Dr. Masangkay, by chance?"

"Yes."

"You knew each other, I believe?"

"We were partners."

"Ah." Amira nodded, as if hearing this for the first time. "And so, if Dr. Masangkay collected this data, you have a high degree of confidence in it? You trust *him?*"

"Absolutely."

"I wonder if he'd say the same about you," Rochefort said in his quiet, high, clipped voice.

McFarlane turned his head and looked steadily at the engineer.

"Let's proceed," Glinn said.

McFarlane looked away from Rochefort and tapped his portfolio with the back of one hand. "There's an enormous circular deposit of shocked and fused coesite on that island. Right in the center is a dense mass of ferromagnetic material."

"A natural deposit of iron ore," said Rochefort.

"The flyover indicates a reversal of the sedimentary strata around the site."

Amira looked puzzled. "A what?"

"Flipped sedimentary layers."

Rochefort sighed heavily. "Signifying . . . ?"

"When a large meteorite strikes sedimentary layers, the layers get reversed."

Rochefort continued tapping his pencil. "How? By magic?"

McFarlane looked at him again, longer this time. "Perhaps Mr. Rochefort would like a demonstration?"

"I would," said Rochefort.

McFarlane picked up his sandwich. He examined it, smelled it. "Peanut butter and jelly?" He made a face.

"May we just have the demonstration, please?" Rochefort asked in a tight, exasperated voice.

"Of course." McFarlane placed the sandwich on the table between himself and Rochefort. Then he tilted his coffee cup and carefully poured liquid over it.

"What is he doing?" said Rochefort, turning to Glinn, his voice high. "I knew this was a mistake. We should have required one of the principals to come in."

McFarlane held up his hand. "Bear with me. We're just preparing our sedimentary deposit here." He reached for another sandwich and placed it on top, then tipped on more coffee until it was saturated. "There. This sandwich is the sedimentary deposit: bread, peanut butter, jelly, more bread, in layers. And my fist"—he raised his hand above his head—"is the meteorite."

He brought his fist down on the sandwich with a jarring crash.

"For Christ's sake!" Rochefort cried, jumping back, his shirt splattered with peanut butter. He stood up, flicking bits of sodden bread from his arms.

At the far end of the table, Garza sat with an astonished look on his face. Glinn was expressionless.

"Now, let us examine the remains of the sandwich on the table," McFarlane continued as calmly as if he were giving a college lecture. "Please note that all the pieces have been flipped over. The bottom layer of bread is now on the top, the peanut butter and jelly have reversed places, and the top layer of bread is now on the bottom. It's what a meteorite does when it hits sedimentary rock: it pulverizes the layers, flips them over, and lays them back down in reversed sequence." He glanced at Rochefort. "Any further questions or comments?"

"This is outrageous," said Rochefort, wiping his glasses with a handkerchief.

"Sit down, please, Mr. Rochefort," said Glinn quietly.

To McFarlane's surprise, Amira began to laugh: a deep, smooth laugh. "That was very good, Dr. McFarlane. Very entertaining. We need a little excitement in our meetings." She turned to Rochefort.

"If you had ordered club sandwiches like I suggested, this wouldn't have happened."

Rochefort scowled as he returned to his seat.

"Anyway," said McFarlane, sitting back and wiping his hand with a napkin, "strata reversal means only one thing: a massive impact crater. Taken together, everything points to a meteorite strike. Now if you have a better explanation for what is down there, I'd like to hear it."

He waited.

"Perhaps it's an alien spaceship?" Garza asked hopefully.

"We considered that, Manuel," Amira replied dryly.

"And?"

"Occam's razor. It seemed unlikely."

Rochefort was still cleaning the peanut butter from his glasses. "Speculation is useless. Why not send a ground party to check it out, and get some better data?"

McFarlane glanced at Glinn, who was listening with half-lidded eyes. "Mr. Lloyd and I trust the data we have in hand. And he doesn't want to draw any more attention to the site than he has already. With good reason."

Garza suddenly spoke up. "Yeah, and that brings up the second problem we need to discuss: how we're going to get whatever it is out of Chile. I believe you're familiar with that sort of—shall we say—operation?"

More polite than calling it smuggling, McFarlane thought. Aloud, he said, "More or less."

"And your thoughts?"

"It's metal. It's basically an ore body. It doesn't fall under the laws of cultural patrimony. At my recommendation, Lloyd created a company that is in the process of acquiring mineral leases to the island. I suggested that we go down there as a mining operation, dig it up, and ship it home. There's nothing illegal in it—according to the lawyers."

Amira smiled again. "But if the government of Chile realized this was the world's largest meteorite and not just some ordinary iron deposit, it might take a dim view of your operation."

"A 'dim view' is an understatement. We might all get shot."

"A fate you barely escaped smuggling the Atacama tektites out of the country, right?" Garza asked.

Throughout the meeting, Garza had remained friendly, showing none of Rochefort's hostility or Amira's sardonic attitude. Still, McFarlane found himself coloring. "We took a few chances. It's part of the job."

"So it seems." Garza laughed, turning over the sheets in his folder. "I'm amazed you'd consider going back there. This project could create an international incident."

"Once Lloyd unveils the meteorite in his new museum," McFarlane replied, "I can guarantee you there *will* be an international incident."

"The point," Glinn interjected smoothly, "is that this must be carried out in secrecy. What happens after we conclude our part of the business is up to Mr. Lloyd."

Nobody spoke for a moment.

"There is one other question," Glinn continued at last. "About your ex-partner, Dr. Masangkay."

Here it comes, McFarlane thought. He steeled himself.

"Any idea what killed him?"

McFarlane hesitated. This was not the question he'd expected. "No idea," he said after a moment. "The body hasn't been recovered. It could well have been exposure or starvation. That climate isn't exactly hospitable."

"But there were no medical problems? No history that might have contributed?"

"Malnutrition as a kid. Nothing else. Or if there was, I didn't know about it. There was no mention of illness or starvation in the diary."

McFarlane watched Glinn page through his folder. The meeting seemed to be over. "Lloyd told me to bring back an answer," he said.

Glinn put the folder aside. "It's going to cost a million dollars."

McFarlane was momentarily taken aback. The amount was less than he had expected. But what surprised him most was how quickly Glinn had arrived at it. "Naturally, Mr. Lloyd will have to sign off, but that seems very reasonable—"

Glinn raised his hand. "I'm afraid you've misunderstood. It's going to cost a million dollars to determine whether we can undertake this project."

McFarlane stared at him. "You mean it's going to cost a million dollars just for the *estimate?*"

"Actually, it's worse than that," Glinn said. "We might come back and tell you EES can't sign on at all."

McFarlane shook his head. "Lloyd's going to love this."

"There are many unknowns about this project, not the least of which is what we're going to find when we get there. There are political problems, engineering problems, scientific problems. To analyze them, we'll need to build scale models. We'll need hours of time on a supercomputer. We'll need the confidential advice of physicists, structural engineers, international lawyers, even historians and political scientists. Mr. Lloyd's desire for speed will make things even more expensive."

"Okay, okay. So when will we get our answer?"

"Within seventy-two hours of our receipt of Mr. Lloyd's certified check."

McFarlane licked his lips. It was beginning to occur to him that he himself was being underpaid. "And what if the answer's no?" he asked.

"Then Lloyd will at least have the consolation of knowing the project is impossible. If there's a way to retrieve that meteorite, we'll find it."

"Have you ever said no to anyone?"

"Often."

"Oh, really? Like when?"

Glinn coughed slightly. "Just last month a certain eastern European country wanted us to entomb a defunct nuclear reactor in concrete and move it across an international border, undetected, for a neighboring country to deal with."

"You're joking," said McFarlane.

"Not at all," said Glinn. "We had to turn them down, of course."

"Their budget was insufficient," said Garza.

McFarlane shook his head and snapped his portfolio shut. "If you show me to a phone, I'll relay your offer to Lloyd."

Glinn nodded to Garza, who stood up. "Come this way, please, Dr. McFarlane," said Garza, holding open the door.

As the door hissed shut, Rochefort let out another sigh of irritation. "We don't really have to work with him, do we?" He flicked a clot of purple jelly from his lab coat. "He's not a scientist, he's a scavenger."

"He has a doctorate in planetary geology," said Glinn.

"That degree died long ago from neglect. But I'm not just talking about the man's ethics, what he did to his partner. Look at this." He gestured at his shirt. "The man's a loose cannon. He's unpredictable."

"There is no such thing as an unpredictable person," Glinn replied. "Only a person we don't understand." He gazed at the mess on his fifty-thousand-dollar Accawood table. "Naturally, we'll make it our business to understand everything about Dr. McFarlane. Rachel?"

She turned to him.

"I'm going to give you a very special assignment."

Amira flashed another sardonic smile at Rochefort. "Of course," she said.

"You're going to be Dr. McFarlane's assistant."

There was a sudden silence as the smile disappeared from Amira's face.

Glinn went on smoothly, without giving her time to react. "You will keep an eye on him. You will prepare regular reports on him and give them to me."

"I'm no damn shrink!" Amira exploded. "And I'm sure as hell no rat!"

Now it was Rochefort whose face was mottled with an expression that might have passed for amusement, if it had not been so laced with ill will.

"Your reports will be strictly observational," Glinn said. "They will be thoroughly evaluated by a psychiatrist. Rachel, you're a shrewd analyst, of human beings as well as mathematics. You will, of course, be an assistant in name only. As for your being a rat, that's entirely incorrect. You know Dr. McFarlane has a checkered past. He will be the only one on this expedition not of our choosing. We must keep a close watch on him."

"Does that give me license to spy on him?"

"Say I hadn't asked you to do this. If you were to catch him doing anything that might compromise the expedition, you'd have told me without a second thought. All I'm asking you to do is formalize the process a little."

Amira flushed and was silent.

Glinn gathered up his papers, and they swiftly disappeared into the folds of his suit. "All this may be moot if the project turns out to be impossible. There's one little thing I have to look into first."

Lloyd Museum,
June 7, 3:15 P.M.

McFarlane paced his office in the museum's brand-new administration building, moving restlessly from wall to wall like a caged animal. The large space was half filled with unopened boxes, and the top of his desk was littered with blueprints, memos, charts, and printouts. He had only bothered to tear the plastic wrap off a single chair. The rest of the furniture remained shrink-wrapped, and the office smelled raw with new carpeting and fresh paint. Outside the windows, construction continued at a frantic pace. It was unsettling to see so much money being spent so quickly. But if anyone could afford it, he supposed Lloyd could. The diversified companies that made up Lloyd Holdings—aerospace engineering, defense contracting, supercomputer development, electronic data systems—brought in enough revenue to make the man one of the two or three richest in the world.

Forcing himself to sit down, McFarlane shoved the papers aside to clear a space, opened the bottom desk drawer, and pulled out Masangkay's moldy diary. Just seeing the Tagalog words on paper had brought back a host of memories, almost all of them bittersweet, faded, like old sepia-toned photographs.

He opened the cover, turned the pages, and gazed again at the strange, crabbed script of the final entry. Masangkay had been a poor diary keeper. Exactly how many hours or days passed between this entry and his death was impossible to know.

Nakaupo ako at nagpapausok para umalis ang mga lintik na lamok. Akala ko masama na ang South Greenland, mas grabe pala dito sa Isla Desolación . . .

McFarlane glanced down at the translation he had written out for Lloyd:

I am sitting by my fire, in the smoke, trying to keep the damned mosquitoes at bay. And I thought South Greenland was bad. Isla Desolación: good name. I always wondered what the end of the world looked like. Now I know.

It looks promising: the reversed strata, the bizarre vulcanism, the satellite anomalies. It all meshes with the Yaghan legends. But it doesn't make sense. It must have come in damn fast, maybe even too fast for an elliptical orbit. I keep thinking about McFarlane's crazy theory. Christ, I find myself almost wishing the old bastard were here to see this. But if he was *here, no doubt he'd find some way to screw things up.*

Tomorrow, I'll start the quantitative survey of the valley. If it's there, even deep, I'll find it. It all depends on tomorrow.

And that was it. He had died, all alone, in one of the remotest places on earth.

McFarlane leaned back in his chair. *McFarlane's crazy theory . . .* The truth was, *walang kabalbalan* didn't precisely translate as "crazy"—it meant something a lot more unflattering—but Lloyd didn't need to know everything.

But that was beside the point. The point was, his own theory *had* been crazy. Now, with the wisdom of hindsight, he wondered why he had held on to it so tenaciously, for so long, and at such a terrible price.

All known meteorites came from inside the solar system. His theory of interstellar meteorites—meteorites that originated outside, from other star systems—appeared ridiculous in hindsight. To think that a rock could wander across the vastness of the space between the stars and just happen to land on Earth. Mathematicians always said the probabilities were on the order of a quintillion to one. So why hadn't he left it at that? His idea that someday someone—preferably himself—would find an interstellar meteorite had been fanciful, ridiculous, even arrogant. And what was more to the point, it had twisted his judgment and, ultimately, messed up his life almost beyond redemption.

How strange it was to see Masangkay bringing up the theory now in his journal. The reversed strata were to be expected. What was it that didn't make sense to him? What had been so puzzling?

He closed the diary and stood up, returning to the window. He remembered Masangkay's round face, the thick, scruffy black hair, the sarcastic grin, the eyes dancing with humor, vivacity, and intelligence. He remembered that last day outside the New York Museum—bright sunlight gilding everything to a painful brilliance—where Masangkay had come rushing down the steps, glasses askew, shouting, "Sam! They've given us the green light! We're on our way to Greenland!" And—more painfully—he remembered that night after they actually found the Tornarssuk meteorite, Masangkay tilting the precious bottle of whiskey up, the firelight flickering in its amber depths as he took a long drink, his back against the dark metal. God, the hangover the next day . . . But they had *found* it—sitting right there, as if someone had carefully placed it on the gravel for all to see. Over the years, they had found many meteorites together, but nothing like this. It had come in at an acute angle and had actually bounced off the ice sheet, tumbling for miles. It was a beautiful siderite, shaped like a sea horse . . .

And now it sat in some Tokyo businessman's backyard garden. It had cost him his relationship with Masangkay. And his reputation.

He stared out the window, returning to the present. Above the leafy maples and white oaks a structure was rising, incomprehensibly out of place in the upper Hudson Valley: an ancient, sun-weathered Egyptian pyramid. As he watched, a crane swung another block of limestone above the treetops and began lowering it gently onto the half-built structure. A finger of sand trailed off the block and feathered away into the wind. In the clearing at the base of the pyramid he could see Lloyd himself, oversized safari hat dappled by the leafy shade. The man had a weakness for melodramatic headgear.

There was a knock on the door and Glinn entered, a folder beneath one arm. He glided his way among the boxes to McFarlane's side and gazed at the scene below.

"Did Lloyd acquire a mummy to accessorize it?" he asked.

McFarlane grunted a laugh. "As a matter of fact, he did. Not the original—that was looted long ago—but another one. Some poor soul who had no idea he'd be spending eternity in the Hudson River Valley. Lloyd is having some of King Tut's golden treasures replicated for the burial chamber. Couldn't buy the originals, apparently."

"Even thirty billion has its limits," said Glinn. He nodded out the window. "Shall we?"

They left the building, descending a graveled path into the woods. Cicadas droned in the canopy over their heads. They soon struck the sandy clearing. Here the pyramid rose directly above them, stark yellow against the cerulean sky. The half-built structure gave off a smell of ancient dust and limitless desert wastes.

Lloyd caught sight of them and came forward immediately, both hands extended. "Eli!" he boomed good-naturedly. "You're late. One would think you were planning to move Mount Everest instead of a lump of iron." He took Glinn's elbow and steered him toward a set of stone benches on the far side of the pyramid.

McFarlane settled on a bench opposite Lloyd and Glinn. Here, in the shadow of the pyramid, it was cool.

Lloyd pointed at the slim folder under Glinn's arm. "Is that all my million dollars bought me?"

Glinn did not reply directly; he was gazing at the pyramid. "How high will it be when completed?" he asked.

"Seventy-seven feet," Lloyd replied proudly. "It's the tomb of an

Old Kingdom pharaoh, Khefret II. A minor ruler in every way—poor kid died at thirteen. I wanted a bigger one, of course. But it *is* the only pyramid outside of the Nile Valley."

"And the base, what does it measure?"

"One hundred and forty feet on a side."

Glinn was silent for a moment, his eyes veiled. "Interesting coincidence," he said.

"Coincidence?"

Glinn's eyes slid back to Lloyd. "We reanalyzed the data on your meteorite. We think it weighs closer to ten thousand tons. Same as your pyramid over there. Using standard nickel-iron meteorites as a basis, that would make your rock about forty feet in diameter."

"That's wonderful! The bigger the better."

"Moving the meteorite will be like moving this pyramid of yours. Not block by block, but all together."

"So?"

"Take the Eiffel Tower, for instance," Glinn said.

"I wouldn't want to. Ugly as hell."

"The Eiffel Tower weighs about five thousand tons."

Lloyd looked at him.

"The Saturn V rocket—the heaviest land-based object ever moved by human beings—weighs three thousand tons. Moving your meteorite, Mr. Lloyd, will be like moving two Eiffel towers. Or three Saturn V rockets."

"What's the point?" Lloyd asked.

"The point is that ten thousand tons, when you actually consider it, is a staggering weight. Twenty *million* pounds. And we're talking about lugging it halfway around the world."

Lloyd grinned. "The heaviest object ever moved by mankind—I like that. You couldn't ask for a better publicity hook. But I don't see the problem. Once it's on board the ship, you can bring it right up the Hudson practically to our doorstep."

"Getting it on board the ship *is* the problem—especially those last fifty feet from shore into the hold. The biggest crane in the world picks up less than a thousand tons."

"So build a pier and slide it out to the boat."

"Off the coast of Isla Desolación, the depth drops to two hundred feet a mere twenty feet from shore. So you can't build a fixed pier. And the meteorite would sink an ordinary floating pier."

"Find a shallower place."

"We've checked. There *is* no other place. In fact, the only possible loading point is on the eastern coast of the island. A snowfield lies between that point and the meteorite. The snow is two hundred feet deep in the center. Which means we have to move your rock around the snowfield to get it to the ship."

Lloyd grunted. "I'm beginning to see the problem. Why don't we just bring a big ship in there, back it up to shore, and roll the damn thing into the hold? The biggest supertankers hold half a million tons of crude. That's more than enough to spare."

"If you roll this meteorite into the hold of a ship, it would simply drop right through the bottom. This is not crude oil, which conveniently displaces its weight as it fills a hold."

"What's all this dancing around, then?" Lloyd asked sharply. "Is this leading up to a refusal?"

Glinn shook his head. "On the contrary. We're willing to take on the job."

Lloyd beamed. "That's terrific! Why all the gloomy talk?"

"I simply wanted to prepare you for the enormity of the task you want to accomplish. And for the commensurate enormity of our bill."

Lloyd's broad features narrowed. "And that is . . . ?"

"One hundred and fifty million dollars. Including chartering the transport vessel. FOB the Lloyd Museum."

Lloyd's face went pale. "My God. One hundred and fifty million . . ." His chin sank onto his hands. "For a ten-thousand-ton rock. That's . . ."

"Seven dollars and fifty cents a pound," said Glinn.

"Not bad," McFarlane said, "when you consider that the going rate for a decent meteorite is about a hundred bucks a pound."

Lloyd looked at him. "Is that so?"

McFarlane nodded.

"In any case," Glinn continued, "because of the unusual nature of the job, our acceptance comes with two conditions."

"Yes?"

"The first condition is double overage. As you'll see in the report, our cost estimates haven't been especially conservative. But we feel that, to be absolutely safe, *twice* that amount must be budgeted for."

"Meaning it's really going to cost three hundred million dollars."

"No. We believe it's going to cost one hundred and fifty, or we wouldn't have presented you with that figure. But given all the unknown variables, the incomplete data, and the immense weight of the meteorite, we need some maneuvering room."

"Maneuvering room." Lloyd shook his head. "And the second condition?"

Glinn took the folder from under his arm and placed it on one knee. "A dead man's switch."

"What's that?"

"A special trapdoor, built into the bottom of the transport vessel, so that in the direst emergency the meteorite can be jettisoned."

Lloyd seemed not to understand. "Jettison the meteorite?"

"If it ever shook loose from its berth, it could sink the ship. If that happened, we'd need a way to get rid of it, fast."

As Lloyd listened to this, the pallor that had come across his face gave way to a flush of anger. "You mean to say the first time we hit a rough sea, you dump the meteorite overboard? Forget it."

"According to Dr. Amira, our mathematician, there's only a one-in-five-thousand chance of it being necessary."

McFarlane spoke. "I thought he was paying the big bucks because you guaranteed success. Dumping the meteorite in a storm sounds like a failure to me."

Glinn glanced at him. "Our guarantee is that EES will *never* fail in *our* work. And that guarantee is unequivocal. But we can't guarantee against an act of God. Natural systems are inherently unpredictable. If a freak storm came out of nowhere and foundered the vessel, we wouldn't necessarily consider that a failure."

Lloyd bounded to his feet. "Well, there's no way in hell I'm going to drop the meteorite to the bottom of the ocean. So there's no point in letting you build a dead man's switch." He took several steps away from them, then stopped, facing the pyramid, arms folded.

"It's the price of the dance," Glinn said. He spoke quietly, but his voice carried total conviction.

For a time, Lloyd made no reply. The big man shook his head, clearly in the grip of an inner struggle. At last he turned.

"All right," he said. "When do we start?"

"Today, if you like." Glinn stood up, carefully placing his folder on the stone bench. "This contains an overview of the preparations we'll need to make, along with a breakdown of the associated costs. All we need is your go-ahead and a fifty-million retainer. As you will see, EES will handle all the details."

Lloyd took the folder. "I'll read it before lunch."

"I think you'll find it interesting. And now, I'd better get back to New York." Glinn nodded at the two men in turn. "Gentlemen, enjoy your pyramid."

Then he turned, made his way across the sandy clearing, and disappeared into the tightly woven shade of the maple trees.

Millburn, New Jersey, June 9, 2:45 P.M.

Eli Glinn sat, motionless, behind the wheel of a nondescript four-door sedan. By instinct, he had parked at an angle that maximized sun glare off the windshield, making it difficult for passersby to observe him. He dispassionately took in the sights and sounds of the typical East Coast suburb: tended lawns, ancient trees, the distant hum of freeway traffic.

Two buildings down, the front door of a small Georgian opened and a woman appeared. Glinn straightened up with an almost imperceptible motion. He watched attentively as she descended the front steps, hesitated, then looked back over her shoulder. But the door had already shut. She turned away and began walking toward him briskly, head held high, shoulders straight, light yellow hair burnished by the afternoon sun.

Glinn opened a manila folder lying on the passenger seat and studied a photograph clipped to the papers inside. This was her. He slipped the folder into the rear of the car and looked back through the window. Even out of uniform the woman radiated authority, competence, and self-discipline. And nothing about her betrayed how difficult the last eighteen months must have been. That was good, very good. As she approached, he lowered the passenger window: according to his character profile, surprise offered the highest hope of success.

"Captain Britton?" he called out. "My name is Eli Glinn. Could I have a word with you?"

She paused. He noted that, already, the surprise on her face was giving way to curiosity. There was no alarm or fear; merely quiet confidence.

The woman stepped toward the car. "Yes?"

Automatically, Glinn made a number of mental notes. The woman wore no perfume, and she kept her small but functional handbag clasped tightly against her side. She was tall, but fine-boned. Although her face was pale, tiny crinkles around the green eyes and a splash of freckles gave evidence of years spent in the sun and wind. Her voice was low.

"Actually, what I have to say might take a while. Can I drop you somewhere?"

"Unnecessary, thank you. The train station's just a few blocks away."

Glinn nodded. "Heading home to New Rochelle? The connections are very inconvenient. I'd be happy to drive you."

This time the surprise lingered a little longer, and when it died away it left a look of speculation in the sea green eyes. "My mother always told me never to get into a stranger's car."

"Your mother taught you well. But I think what I have to say will be of interest to you."

The woman considered this a moment. Then she nodded. "Very well," she said, opening the passenger door and taking a seat. Glinn noticed that she kept her purse in her lap, and her right hand, significantly, stayed on the door handle. He was not surprised she had accepted. But he was impressed by her ability to size up a situation, examine the options, and quickly arrive at a solution. She was willing to take a risk, but not a foolish one. This is what the dossier had led him to expect.

"You'll have to give me directions," he said, pulling away from the curb. "I'm not familiar with this part of New Jersey." This was not precisely true. He knew half a dozen ways to get to Westchester County, but he wanted to see how she handled command, even one as small as this. As they drove, Britton remained collected, giving terse directions in the manner of someone accustomed to having her orders obeyed. A very impressive woman indeed, perhaps all the more impressive for her single catastrophic failure.

"Let me get something out of the way from the beginning," he said. "I know your past history, and it has no bearing on what I'm about to say."

From the corner of his eye, he saw her stiffen. But when she spoke, her voice was calm. "I believe that at this point, a lady is supposed to say, 'You have me at a disadvantage, sir.' "

"I can't go into details at the moment. But I'm here to offer you the captaincy of an oil tanker."

They rode for several minutes in silence.

At last she glanced over at him. "If you knew my history as well as you say, I doubt you'd be making such an offer."

Her voice remained calm, but Glinn could read many things in her face: curiosity, pride, suspicion, perhaps hope. "You're wrong, Captain Britton. I know the whole story. I know how you were one of the few female masters in the tanker fleet. I know how you were ostracized, how you tended to catch the least popular routes. The pressures you faced were immense." He paused. "I know that you were found on the bridge of your last command in a state of intoxication. You were diagnosed an alcoholic and entered a rehabilitation center. As a result of rehab, you successfully retained your master's license. But since leaving the center over a year ago, you've had no new offers of command. Did I miss anything?" He carefully waited for the reaction.

"No," she replied, steadily. "That about covers it."

"I'll be frank, Captain. This assignment is very unusual. I have a short list of other masters I could approach, but I think they might well turn down the command."

"While I, on the other hand, am desperate." Britton continued staring out the windshield, speaking in a low voice.

"If you had been desperate, you would have taken that tramp Panama steamer offered you last November, or that Liberian freighter, with its armed guards and suspicious cargo." He watched her eyes narrow slightly. "You see, Captain Britton, in my line of work, I analyze the nature of failure."

"And just what *is* your line of work, Mr. Glinn?"

"Engineering. Our analysis has shown that people who failed once are ninety percent less likely to fail again." *I myself am a living example of the truth of this theory.*

Glinn did not actually utter this last sentence, but he had been about to. He allowed his eyes to sweep over Captain Britton for a moment. What had prompted him to almost drop a reserve as habitual as breathing? This merited later consideration.

He returned his eyes to the road. "We have evaluated your overall record thoroughly. Once you were a superb captain with a drinking problem. Now you are merely a superb captain. One on whose discretion I know I can rely."

Britton acknowledged this with a slight nod of her head. "Discretion," she repeated, with a faint sardonic note.

"If you accept the assignment, I will be able to say much more. But what I can tell you now is this. The voyage will not be a long one, perhaps three months at most. It will have to be conducted under great secrecy. The destination is the far southern latitudes, an area you know well. The financial backing is more than adequate, and you may handpick your crew, as long as they pass our background checks. All officers and crew will draw triple the normal pay."

Britton frowned. "If you know I turned down the Liberians, then you know I don't smuggle drugs, run guns, or deal in contraband. I will not break the law, Mr. Glinn."

"The mission is legal, but it is unique enough to require a motivated crew. And there is something else. If the mission is successful—I should say, *when* the mission is successful, because my job is to make sure it is—there will be publicity, largely favorable. Not for me—I avoid that sort of thing—but for you. It could be useful in a number of ways. It could get you reinstated onto the list of active masters, for example. And it would carry some weight with your child custody hearings, perhaps making these long weekend visitations unnecessary."

This last observation had the effect Glinn hoped for. Britton looked at him quickly, then glanced over her shoulder, as if at the swiftly retreating Georgian house, now many miles behind them. Then she looked back at Glinn.

"I've been reading W. H. Auden," she said. "On the train coming out this morning, I came across a poem called 'Atlantis.' The last stanza started out something like this:

All the little household gods
Have started crying, but say
Good-bye now, and put to sea."

She smiled. And, if Glinn paid attention to such things, he would have insisted that the smile was distinctly beautiful.

Port of Elizabeth, June 17, 10:00 A.M.

Palmer Lloyd paused before the windowless door, a grimy rectangle in the vast expanse of metal building that reared up before him. From behind, where his driver leaned against a limousine reading a tabloid, he could hear the roar of the New Jersey Turnpike echoing across the dead swamplands and old warehouses. Ahead, beyond the Marsh Street dry docks, the Port of Elizabeth glittered in the summer heat. The immense oil tankers and LNG carriers docked along the quays were like so many dories snugged against a fishing pier. Nearby, a crane nodded maternally above a container ship. Beyond the port, a brace of tugboats was pushing a barge burdened with cubed cars. And even farther beyond, poking above the blackened backside of Bayonne, the Manhattan skyline beckoned, gleaming in the sun like a row of jewels.

Lloyd was momentarily swept by a feeling of nostalgia. It had been years since he was last here. He remembered growing up in ironbound Rahway, near the port. In his poverty-stricken boyhood, Lloyd had spent many days prowling the docks, yards, and factories.

He inhaled the industrial air, the familiar acrid odor of artificial roses mingling with the smell of the salt marshes, tar, and sulfur. He still loved the feel of the place, the stacks trailing steam and smoke, the gleaming refineries, the thickets of power lines. The naked industrial muscle had a Sheeler-like beauty to it. It was places like Elizabeth, he mused, with their synergy of commerce and industry, that gave the residents of the suburbs and the phony boutique artiste towns the very wherewithal that allowed them to sneer at its ugliness from their own perches of comfort. Strange how much he missed those lost boyhood days, even though all his dreams had come true.

And even stranger that his greatest achievement should be launched from here, where his own roots lay. Even as a boy he had loved collecting. Having no money, he had to build up his natural history collection by finding his own specimens. He picked up arrowheads out of eroded embankments, shells from the grimy shoreline, rocks and minerals from abandoned mines; he dug fossils from the Jurassic deposits of nearby Hackensack and caught butterflies by the dozen from these very marshes. He collected frogs, lizards, snakes, and all manner of animal life, preserving them in gin swiped from his father. He had amassed a fine collection—until his house burned down on his fifteenth birthday, taking all his treasures with it. It was the most painful loss of his life. After that, he never collected another specimen. He'd gone to college, then into business, piling success upon success. And then one day, it dawned on him that he could now afford to buy the very best the world could offer. He could, in an odd way, erase that early loss. What started as a hobby became a passion—and his vision for the Lloyd Museum was born. And now here he was, back at the Jersey docks, about to set off to claim the greatest treasure of all.

He took a deep breath and gripped the handle of the door, a tingle of anticipation coursing through him. Glinn's thin folder had been a masterpiece—well worth the million he had paid for it. The plan it outlined was brilliant. Every contingency had been accounted for, every difficulty anticipated. Before he'd finished reading, his shock and anger at the price tag had been replaced by eagerness. And now, after ten days of impatient waiting, he would see the first stage of the plan nearing completion. *The heaviest object ever moved by mankind.* He turned the handle and stepped inside.

The building's facade, large as it was, only hinted at the vastness of its interior. Seeing such a large space without internal floors or walls, completely open to its high ceiling, temporarily defeated the eye's ability to judge distances, but it seemed at least a quarter mile in length. A network of catwalks stretched through the dusty air like metal spiderwebbing. A cacophony of noise rolled through the cavernous space toward him: the chatter of riveting, the clang of steel, the crackle of welding.

And there, at the center of furious activity, *it* lay: a stupendous vessel, propped up in dry dock by great steel buttresses, its bulbous bows towering above him. As oil tankers go, it was not the biggest, but out of the water it was just about the most gigantic thing Lloyd had ever seen. The name *Rolvaag* was stenciled in white paint along the port side. Men and machines were crawling around it like a colony of ants. A smile broke out on Lloyd's face as he inhaled the heady aroma of burnt metal, solvents, and diesel fumes. A part of him enjoyed watching the flagrant expenditure of money—even his own.

Glinn appeared, rolled-up blueprints in one hand, an EES hard hat on his head. Lloyd looked at him, still smiling, and shook his head wordlessly in admiration.

Glinn handed him a spare hard hat. "The view from the catwalks is even better," he said. "We'll meet Captain Britton up there."

Lloyd fitted the hard hat to his head and followed Glinn onto a small lift. They ascended about a hundred feet, then stepped out onto a catwalk that ran around all four walls of the dry dock. As he moved, Lloyd found himself unable to take his gaze off the immense ship that stretched away below him. It was incredible. And it was *his*.

"It was built in Stavanger, Norway, six months ago." Glinn's dry voice was almost lost in the din of construction that rose up to meet them. "Given everything we're doing to it, we couldn't opt for a spot charter. So we had to buy it outright."

"Double overage," Lloyd murmured.

"We'll be able to sell it later and recoup almost all the expense, of course. And I think you'll find the *Rolvaag* worth it. It's state of the art, triple-hulled and deep drafted for rough seas. It displaces a hundred and fifty thousand tons—smallish when you consider that VLCCs displace up to half a million."

"It's remarkable. If there was only some way of running my affairs remotely, I'd give anything to be able to go along."

"We'll document everything, of course. There will be daily conferences via satellite uplink. I think you'll share everything but the seasickness."

As they continued along the catwalk, the entire port side of the vessel became visible. Lloyd stopped.

"What is it?" Glinn asked.

"I . . ." Lloyd paused, temporarily at a loss for words. "I just never thought it would look so *credible*."

Amusement gleamed briefly in Glinn's eyes. "Industrial Light and Magic is doing a fine job, don't you think?"

"The Hollywood firm?"

Glinn nodded. "Why reinvent the wheel? They've got the best visual effects designers in the world. And they're discreet."

Lloyd did not reply. He simply stood at the railing, gazing down. Before his very eyes, the sleek, state-of-the-art oil tanker was being transformed into a shabby ore carrier bound for its graveyard voyage. The forward half of the great ship presented beautiful, clean expanses of painted metal, lines of rivets and plates in crisp geometrical perfection: all the sparkling newness of a six-month-old vessel. From amidships to the stern, however, the contrast could not have been more outrageous. The rear section of the ship looked like a wreck. The aft superstructure seemed to have been coated in twenty layers of paint, each flaking off at a different rate. One of the bridge wings, a queer-looking structure to begin with, had been apparently crushed, then welded back together. Great rivers of rust cascaded down the dented hull. The railings were warped, and missing sections had been crudely patched with welded pipe, rebar, and angle iron.

"It's a perfect disguise," said Lloyd. "Just like the mining operation."

"I'm especially pleased with the radar mast," said Glinn, pointing aft.

Even from this distance, Lloyd could see the paint was largely stripped off, and bits of metal dangled from old wires. A few antennae had been broken, crudely spliced, then broken again. Everything was streaked with stack soot.

"Inside that wreck of a mast," Glinn went on, "you'll find the very latest equipment: P-Code and differential GPS, Spizz-64, FLIR, LN-66, Slick 32, passive ESM, and other specialized radar equipment, Tigershark Loran C, INMARSAT, and Sperry GMDSS communications stations. If we run into any, ah, special situations, there are some mast electronics that can be raised at the push of a button."

As Lloyd watched, a crane holding a huge wrecking ball swiveled toward the hull; with exquisite care the ball was brought in contact with the port side of the ship once, twice, then three times, adding fresh indignities. Painters with thick hoses swarmed over the ship's midsection, turning the spotless deck into a storm of simulated tar, oil, and grit.

"The real job will be cleaning all this up," Glinn said. "Once we unload the meteorite and are ready to resell the ship."

Lloyd tore his gaze away. *Once we unload the meteorite* . . . In less than two weeks, the ship would be heading to sea. And when it returned—when, at last, his prize could be unveiled—the whole world would be talking about what had been accomplished.

"Of course, we're not doing much to the interior," Glinn said as they started along the catwalk again. "The quarters are quite luxurious—large staterooms, wood paneling, computer-controlled lighting, lounges, exercise rooms, and so forth."

Lloyd stopped once again as he noticed activity around a hole cut into the forward hull. A line of bulldozers, D-cats, front-end loaders, skidders with house-size tires, and other heavy mining equipment snaked away from the hole, a heavyweight traffic jam, waiting to be loaded onto the ship. There was a roar of diesel engines and the grinding of gears as, one by one, the equipment drove in and disappeared from view.

"An industrial-age Noah's ark," said Lloyd.

"It was cheaper and faster to make our own door than to position all the heavy equipment with a crane," Glinn said. "The *Rolvaag* is designed like a typical tanker. The cargo-oil spaces occupy little more than half of the hull. The rest is taken up with general holds, compartments, machinery spaces, and the like. We've built special bays to hold the equipment and raw material we'll need for the job. We've already loaded a thousand tons of the best Mannsheim high-tensile steel, a quarter million board feet of laminated timbers, and everything from aircraft tires to generators."

Lloyd pointed. "And those boxcars on the deck?"

"They're designed to look like the *Rolvaag* is making some extra bucks on the side piggybacking containers. Inside are some very sophisticated labs."

"Tell me about them."

"The gray one closest to the bow is a hydro lab. Next to it is a clean room. And then we have a high-speed CAD workstation, a darkroom, tech stores, a scientific freezer, electron microscope and X-ray crystallography labs, a diver's locker, and an isotope and radiation chamber. Belowdecks are medical and surgical spaces, a biohazard lab, and two machine shops. No windows for any of them, I'm afraid; that would give the game away."

Lloyd shook his head. "I'm beginning to see where all my money is going. Don't forget, Eli, what I'm buying is basically a *recovery* operation. The science can wait."

"I haven't forgotten. But given the high degree of unknowns, and the fact that we'll only get one chance at this recovery, we must be prepared for anything."

"Of course. That's why I'm sending Sam McFarlane. But as long as things go according to plan, his expertise is for use with the *engineering* problem. I don't want a lot of time-wasting scientific tests. Just get the thing the hell out of Chile. We'll have all the time in the world to fuss with it later."

"Sam McFarlane," Glinn repeated. "An interesting choice. Curious fellow."

Lloyd looked at him. "Now don't *you* start telling me I made a mistake."

"I didn't say that. I merely express surprise at your choice of planetary geologists."

"He's the best guy for the job. I don't want a crowd of wimpy scientists down there. Sam's worked both the lab *and* the field. He can do it all. He's tough. He knows Chile. The guy who found the thing was his ex-partner, for chrissakes, and his analysis of the data was brilliant." He leaned confidentially toward Glinn. "So he made an error of judgment a couple of years back. And, yes, it wasn't a small one. Does that mean nobody should trust him for the rest of his life? Besides"—and here he placed a hand on Glinn's shoulder—"you'll be there to keep an eye on him. Just in case temptation comes his way." He released his hold and turned back to the ship. "And speaking of temptation, where exactly will the meteorite go?"

"Follow me," Glinn said. "I'll show you."

They climbed another set of stairs and continued along a high catwalk that bridged the ship's beam. Here, a lone figure stood at the rail: silent, erect, dressed in a captain's outfit, looking every inch the ship's officer. As they approached, the figure detached itself from the railing and waited.

"Captain Britton," said Glinn, "Mr. Lloyd."

Lloyd extended his hand, then froze. "A woman?" he blurted involuntarily.

Without a pause, she grasped his hand. "Very observant, Mr. Lloyd." She gave his hand a firm, short shake. "Sally Britton."

"Of course," said Lloyd. "I just didn't expect—" Why hadn't Glinn warned him? His eyes lingered on the trim form, the wisp of blond hair escaping from beneath her cap.

"Glad you could meet us," said Glinn. "I wanted you to see the ship before it was completely disguised."

"Thank you, Mr. Glinn," she said, the faint smile holding. "I don't think I've ever seen anything quite so repulsive in my life."

"It's purely cosmetic."

"I intend to spend the next several days making sure of that." She pointed toward some large projections from the side of the superstructure. "What's behind those forward bulkheads?"

"Additional security equipment," Glinn said. "We've taken every possible safety precaution, and then some."

"Interesting."

Lloyd gazed at her profile curiously. "Eli here has said nothing about you," he said. "Can you fill me in on your background?"

"I was a ship's officer for five years, and a captain for three."

Lloyd caught the past tense. "What kind of ships?"

"Tankers and VLCCs."

"I'm sorry?"

"Very Large Crude Carriers. Over two hundred and fifty thousand tons displacement. Tankers on steroids, basically."

"She's gone around the Horn on several occasions," said Glinn.

"Around the Horn? I didn't know that route was still used."

"The big VLCCs can't go through the Panama Canal," said Britton. "The preferred route is around the Cape of Good Hope, but occasionally schedules require a Horn passage."

"That's one reason we hired her," said Glinn. "The seas down there can be tricky."

Lloyd nodded, still gazing at Britton. She returned the look calmly, unruffled by the pandemonium taking place below her. "You know about our unusual cargo?" he asked.

She nodded.

"And you have no problem with it?"

She looked at him. "I have no problem with it."

Something in those clear green eyes told Lloyd a different story. He opened his mouth to speak, but Glinn interrupted smoothly. "Come on," he said. "I'll show you the cradle."

He motioned them farther down the catwalk. Here the ship's deck lay directly below, wreathed in clouds of welding smoke and diesel. Deckplates had been removed, exposing a vast hole in the ship. Manuel Garza, chief engineer for EES, stood at its edge, holding a radio to his ear with one hand and gesturing with the other. Catching sight of them overhead, he waved.

Peering down into the exposed space, Lloyd could make out an amazingly complex structure, with the elegance of a crystal lattice. Strings of yellow sodium lights along its edges made the dark hold sparkle and glow like a deep, enchanted grotto.

"That's the hold?" Lloyd asked.

"Tank, not hold. Number three center tank, to be precise. We'll be placing the meteorite at the very center of the ship's keel, to maximize stability. And we've added a passageway beneath the maindeck, running from the superstructure forward, to aid access. Note the mechanical doors we've installed on each side of the tank opening."

The cradle was a long way down. Lloyd squinted against the glow of the countless lights.

"I'll be damned," he said suddenly. "Half of it's made of wood!" He turned to Glinn. "Cutting corners already?"

The corners of Glinn's mouth jerked upward in a brief smile. "Wood, Mr. Lloyd, is the ultimate engineering material."

Lloyd shook his head. "Wood? For a ten-thousand-ton weight? I can't believe it."

"Wood is ideal. It gives ever so slightly, but never deforms. It tends to bite into heavy objects, locking them in place. The type of oak we're using, greenheart laminated with epoxy, has a higher shear strength than steel. And wood can be carved and shaped to fit the curves of the hull. It won't wear through the steel hull in a heavy sea, and it doesn't suffer metal fatigue."

"But why so complicated an arrangement?"

"We had to solve a little problem," said Glinn. "At ten thousand tons, the meteorite must be absolutely locked into place, immobilized in the hold. If the *Rolvaag* encounters heavy weather on the way back to New York, even a tiny shift of the meteorite's position could fatally destabilize the ship. That network of timbers not only locks the thing into place, but distributes its weight evenly throughout the hull, simulating the loading of crude oil."

"Impressive," said Britton. "You took the internal frames and partitioning into account?"

"Yes. Dr. Amira is a computational genius. She worked up a calculation that took all of ten hours on a Cray T3D supercomputer, but it gave us the configuration. We can't finish it, of course, until we get the exact dimensions of the rock. We've built this based on Mr. Lloyd's flyover data. But when we actually unearth the meteorite, we'll build a second cradle around it that we can plug into this one."

Lloyd nodded. "And what are those men doing?" He pointed to the deepest depths of the hold, where a gaggle of workmen, barely visible, were cutting through the hull plates with acetylene torches.

"The dead man's switch," said Glinn evenly.

Lloyd felt a surge of irritation. "You're not really going through with that."

"We've already discussed it."

Lloyd struggled to sound reasonable. "Look. If you open up the bottom of the ship to dump the meteorite in the middle of some storm, the damn ship's going to sink anyway. Any idiot can see that."

Glinn held Lloyd with his gray, impenetrable eyes. "If the switch is thrown, it will take less than sixty seconds to open the tank, release the rock, and reseal it. The tanker won't sink in sixty seconds, no matter how heavy the seas are. On the contrary, the inrush of water will actually *compensate* for the sudden loss of ballast when the meteorite goes. Dr. Amira worked that all out, too. And a pretty little equation it was."

Lloyd stared back at him. This man actually derived pleasure from having solved the problem of how to send a priceless meteorite to the bottom of the Atlantic. "All I can say is, if anyone throws that dead man's switch on my meteorite, he's a dead man himself."

Captain Britton laughed—a high, ringing sound that carried above the clangor below. Both men turned toward her.

"Don't forget, Mr. Lloyd," she said crisply, "it's nobody's meteorite yet. And there's a long stretch of water ahead of us before it is."

Aboard the *Rolvaag,* June 26, 12:35 A.M.

McFarlane stepped through the hatchway, carefully closed the steel door behind him, and walked out onto the fly deck. It was the very highest point of the ship's superstructure, and it felt like the roof of the world. The smooth surface of the Atlantic lay more than a hundred feet below him, dappled in faint starlight. The gentle breeze carried the distant cry of gulls, and smelled wonderfully of the sea.

He walked over to the forward railing and wrapped his hands around it. He thought about the huge ship that would be his home for the next few months. Directly below his feet lay the bridge. Below that lay a deck left mysteriously empty by Glinn. Farther below lay the rambling quarters of the senior officers. And a full six stories down, the maindeck, stretching ahead a sixth of a mile to the bow. An occasional dash of starlit spray washed over the forecastle head. The network of piping and tank valves remained, and placed around it were a maze of old containers—the laboratories and workspaces—like a child's woodblock city.

In a few minutes his presence would be required at the "night lunch," which would be their first formal meal on board ship. But he had come up here first to convince himself that the voyage had really begun.

He breathed in, trying to clear his head of the last frantic days, setting up labs and beta-testing equipment. He gripped the railing tighter, feeling a swell of exhilaration. *This is more like it,* he thought. Even a jail cell in Chile seemed preferable to having Lloyd constantly looking over his shoulder, second-guessing, worrying over trivial details. Whatever lay at the end of their journey—whatever it was that Nestor Masangkay had found—at least they were on their way.

McFarlane turned and made the long walk across the deck to the rearward rail. Although the thrum of engines came faintly from the depths of the ship, up here he could feel no hint of vibration. In the distance he could see the Cape May lighthouse winking, one short, one long. After Glinn secured their embarkation papers through some private means of his own, they had left Elizabeth under cover of darkness, maintaining secrecy to the last. They would soon be in the main shipping lanes, beyond the continental shelf, and would then turn due south. Five weeks from now, if all went as planned, they would see the same light again. McFarlane tried to imagine what it would be like if they *did* recover it successfully: the furious outcry, the scientific coup—and, perhaps, his own personal exoneration.

Then he smiled cynically to himself. Life didn't work like that. It was so much easier to see himself back again in the Kalahari, a little more money in his pocket, a little chubby from ship's food, tracking down the elusive Bushmen and renewing his search for the Okavango. And nothing would erase what he had done to Nestor—particularly now that his old friend and partner was dead.

As he gazed out over the ship's stern, McFarlane became aware of another odor on the sea air: tobacco. Looking around, he realized he wasn't alone. From the far side of the fly deck, a small pinpoint of red winked against the dark, then disappeared again. Someone had been quietly standing there; a fellow passenger enjoying the night.

Then the red ember jerked and bobbed as the person rose to approach him. With surprise, he realized it was Rachel Amira, Glinn's physicist, and his own alleged assistant. Between the fingers of her right hand were the final inches of a thick cigar. McFarlane sighed inwardly at having his solitary reverie intruded upon, especially by this sardonic woman.

"Ciao, boss. Any orders for me?"

McFarlane remained silent, feeling a swell of annoyance at the word "boss." He hadn't signed on to be a manager. Amira didn't need a nursemaid. And she didn't seem too pleased with the arrangement either. What could Glinn have been thinking?

"Three hours at sea, and I'm bored already." She waved the cigar. "Want one?"

"No thanks. I want to taste my dinner."

"Ship's cooking? You must be a masochist." She leaned against the rail beside him with a bored sigh. "This ship gives me the willies."

"How so?"

"It's just so cold, so robotic. When I think of going to sea, I think of iron men running all over the decks, jumping at barked orders. But look at this." She jerked a finger over her shoulder. "Eight hundred feet worth of deck, and nothing stirring. *Nothing*. It's a haunted ship. Deserted. Everything's done by computer."

She has a point, McFarlane thought. Even though by modern supertanker standards the *Rolvaag* was only moderate sized, it was still huge. Yet only a skeleton crew was necessary to man it. With all the ship's complement, the EES specialists and engineers, and the construction crew, there were still fewer than one hundred people aboard. A cruise ship half the *Rolvaag*'s size might carry two thousand.

"And it's so damned *big*," he heard her say, as if answering his own thoughts.

"Talk to Glinn about that. Lloyd would have been happier spending less money for less boat."

"Did you know," said Amira, "that these tankers are the first man-made vessels big enough to be affected by the earth's rotation?"

"No, I didn't." Here was a woman who liked the sound of her own voice.

"Yeah. The engine thrust has to be adjusted slightly to take into account the Coriolis effect. And it takes three sea miles to stop this baby."

"You're a regular fund of tanker trivia."

"Oh, I'm good at cocktail conversation." Amira blew a smoke ring into the darkness.

"What else are you good at?"

Amira laughed. "I'm not too bad at math."

"So I've heard." McFarlane turned away, leaning over the rail, hoping she would take the hint.

"Well, we can't all be airline stewardesses when we grow up, you know." There was a moment of blessed silence as Amira puffed at the cigar. "Hey, you know what, boss?"

"I'd appreciate it if you didn't call me that."

"It's what you are, right?"

McFarlane turned to her. "I didn't ask for an assistant. I don't need an assistant. I don't like this arrangement any more than you do."

Amira puffed, a sardonic smile hovering, her eyes full of amusement.

"So I've got an idea," McFarlane said.

"What's that?"

"Let's just pretend you're not my assistant."

"What, you firing me already?"

McFarlane sighed, suppressing his first, impulsive reaction. "We're going to be spending a lot of time together. So let's work together as equals, okay? Glinn doesn't need to know. And I think we'd both be happier."

Amira examined the lengthening ash, then tossed the cigar over the rail into the sea. When she spoke, her voice sounded a little more friendly. "That thing you did with the sandwich cracked me up. Rochefort's a control freak. It really pissed him off, getting covered with jelly. I liked that."

"I made my point."

Amira giggled and McFarlane glanced in her direction, at the eyes glinting in the half-light, at the dark hair disappearing into the velvet behind her. There was a complex person in there, hiding behind the tomboy, one-of-the-guys facade. He looked back out to sea. "Well, I'm sure I'm not going to be Rochefort's good buddy."

"Nobody is. He's only half human."

"Like Glinn. I don't think Glinn would even take a leak without first analyzing all possible trajectories."

There was a pause. He could tell his joke had displeased her.

"Let me tell you a little about Glinn," Amira said. "He's only had two jobs in his life. Effective Engineering Solutions. And the military."

There was something in her voice that made McFarlane glance back at her.

"Before starting EES, Glinn was an intelligence specialist in the Special Forces. Prisoner interrogation, photo recon, underwater demolition, that kind of stuff. Head of his A-Team. Came up through Airborne, then the Rangers. Earned his bones in the Phoenix program during Vietnam."

"Interesting."

"Damn right." Amira spoke almost fiercely. "They excelled in hot-war situations. From what Garza tells me, the team's kill-loss ratio was excellent."

"Garza?"

"He was engineer specialist on Glinn's team. Second in command. Back then, instead of building things, he blew stuff up."

"Garza told you all this?"

Amira hesitated. "Eli told me some of it himself."

"So what happened?"

"His team got their asses kicked trying to secure a bridge on the Cambodian border. Bad intel on enemy placements. Eli lost his whole team, everyone except Garza." Amira dug into her pocket, pulled out a peanut, shelled it. "And now Glinn runs EES. And does all the intel himself. So you see, Sam, I think you've misread him."

"You seem to know a lot about him."

Amira's eyes suddenly grew veiled. She shrugged, then smiled. The ardent look faded as quickly as it had appeared. "It's a beautiful sight," she said, nodding out across the water toward the Cape May light. It wavered in the velvety night: their last contact with North America.

"That it is," McFarlane replied.

"Care to bet how many miles away it is?"

McFarlane frowned. "Excuse me?"

"A small wager. On the distance to that lighthouse."

"I'm not a betting man. Besides, you probably have some arcane mathematical formula at your fingertips."

"You'd be right about that." Amira shelled some more peanuts, tossed the nuts into her mouth, then flung the shells into the sea. "So?"

"So what?"

"Here we are, bound for the ends of the earth, out to snag the biggest rock anybody's ever seen. So, Mr. Meteorite Hunter, what do you *really* think?"

"I think—" McFarlane began. Then he stopped. He realized he wasn't allowing himself to hope that this second chance—which after all had come out of nowhere—might actually work out.

"I think," he said aloud, "that we'd better get down to dinner. If we're late, that captain of ours will probably keelhaul us. And that's no joke on a tanker."

Rolvaag,
June 26, 12:55 A.M.

They stepped out of the elevator onto the forecastle deck. Here, five decks closer to the engines, McFarlane could feel a deep, regular vibration: still faint, yet always present in his ears and his bones.

"This way," Amira said, motioning him down the blue-and-white corridor.

McFarlane followed, glancing around as they went. In dry dock, he'd spent his days and even most nights in the container labs on deck, and today marked his first time inside the superstructure. In his experience, ships were cramped, claustrophobic spaces. But everything about the *Rolvaag* seemed built to a different scale: the passages were wide, the cabins and public areas spacious and carpeted. Glancing into doorways, he noticed a large-screen theater with seats for at least fifty people, and a wood-paneled library. Then they rounded a corner, Amira pushed open a door, and they stepped into the dining saloon.

McFarlane stopped. He had been expecting the indifferent dining area of a working ship. But once again the *Rolvaag* surprised him. The officers' mess was a vast room, extending across the entire stern of the forecastle deck. Huge windows looked out onto the ship's wake, boiling back into the darkness. A dozen round tables, each set for eight and covered with crisp linen and fresh flowers, were arranged around the center of the room. Dining stewards in starched uniforms stood at their stations. McFarlane felt underdressed.

Already, people were beginning to gravitate toward the tables. McFarlane had been warned that seating arrangements on board ship were regimented, at least at first, and that he was expected to sit at the captain's table. Glancing around, he spotted Glinn standing at the table closest to the windows. He made his way across the polished oak deck.

Glinn had his nose in a small volume, which he quickly slipped into his pocket as they approached. Just before it vanished, McFarlane caught the title: *Selected Poetry of W. H. Auden*. Glinn had never struck him as a reader of poetry. Perhaps he had misjudged the man after all.

"Luxurious," McFarlane said as he looked around. "Especially for an oil tanker."

"Actually, this is fairly standard," Glinn replied. "On such a large vessel, space is no longer at a premium. These ships are so expensive to operate, they spend practically no time in port. That means the crews are stuck on board for many, many months. It pays to keep them happy."

More people were taking their places beside the tables, and the noise level in the room had increased. McFarlane looked around at the cluster of technicians, ship's officers, and EES specialists. Things had happened so quickly that he only recognized perhaps a dozen of the seventy-odd people now in the room.

Then quiet fell across the mess. As McFarlane glanced toward the door, Britton, the captain of the *Rolvaag*, stepped in. He had known she was a woman, but he wasn't expecting either her youth—she couldn't be more than thirty-five—or her stately bearing. She carried herself with a natural dignity. She was dressed in an impeccable uniform: naval blazer, gold buttons, crisp officer's skirt. Small gold bars were affixed to her graceful shoulders. She came toward them with a measured step that radiated competence and something else—perhaps, he thought, an iron will.

The captain took her seat, and there was a rustle as the rest of the room followed her lead. Britton removed her hat, revealing a tight coil of blond hair, and placed it on a small side table that seemed specially set up for that purpose. As McFarlane looked closer, he noticed her eyes betrayed a look older than her years.

A graying man in an officer's uniform came up to whisper something in the captain's ear. He was tall and thin, with dark eyes set in even darker sockets. Britton nodded and he stepped back, glancing around the table. His easy, fluid movements reminded McFarlane of a large predator.

Britton gestured toward him with an upraised palm. "I'd like to introduce the *Rolvaag*'s chief mate, Victor Howell."

There were murmured greetings, and the man nodded, then moved away to take his position at the head of a nearby table. Glinn spoke quietly. "May I complete the introductions?"

"Of course," the captain said. She had a clear, clipped voice, with the faintest trace of an accent.

"This is the Lloyd Museum meteorite specialist, Dr. Sam McFarlane."

The captain grasped McFarlane's hand across the table. "Sally Britton," she said, her hand cool and strong. And now McFarlane identified the accent as a Scottish burr. "Welcome aboard, Dr. McFarlane."

"And this is Dr. Rachel Amira, the mathematician on my team," Glinn continued, continuing around the table. "And Eugene Rochefort, chief engineer."

Rochefort glanced up with a nervous little nod, his intelligent, obsessive eyes darting about. He was wearing a blue blazer that might have looked acceptable if it had not been made of polyester that shined under the dining room lights. His eyes landed on McFarlane's, then darted away again. He seemed ill at ease.

"And this is Dr. Patrick Brambell, the ship's doctor. No stranger to the high seas."

Brambell flashed the table a droll smile and gave a little Japanese bow. He was a devious-looking old fellow with sharp features, fine parallel wrinkles tracing a high brow, thin stooped shoulders, and a head as glabrous as a piece of porcelain.

"You've worked as a ship's doctor before?" Britton inquired politely.

"Never set foot on dry land if I can help it," said Brambell, his voice wry and Irish.

Britton nodded as she slipped her napkin out of its ring, flicked it open, and laid it across her lap. Her movements, her fingers, her conversation all seemed to have an economy of motion, an unconscious efficiency. She was so cool and poised it seemed to McFarlane a defense of some kind. As he picked up his own napkin, he noticed a card, placed in the center of the table in a silver holder, with a printed menu. It read: *Consommé Olga, Lamb Vindaloo, Chicken Lyonnaise, Tiramisu.* He gave a low whistle.

"The menu not to your liking, Dr. McFarlane?" Britton asked.

"Just the opposite. I was expecting egg salad sandwiches and pistachio ice cream."

"Good dining is a shipboard tradition," said Britton. "Our chief cook, Mr. Singh, is one of the finest chefs afloat. His father cooked for the British admiralty in the days of the Raj."

"Nothing like a good vindaloo to remind you of your mortality," said Brambell.

"First things first," Amira said, rubbing her hands and looking around. "Where's the bar steward? I'm desperate for a cocktail."

"We'll be sharing that bottle," Glinn said, indicating the open bottle of Chateau Margaux that stood beside the floral display.

"Nice wine. But there's nothing like a dry Bombay martini before dinner. Even when dinner's at midnight." Amira laughed.

Glinn spoke up. "I'm sorry, Rachel, but there are no spiritous liquors allowed on board the ship."

Amira looked at Glinn. "Spiritous liquors?" she repeated with a brief laugh. "This is new, Eli. Have you joined the Christian Women's Temperance League?"

Glinn continued smoothly. "The captain allows one glass of wine, taken before or with dinner. No hard liquor on the ship."

It was as if a lightbulb came on over Amira's head. The joking look was replaced by a sudden flush. Her eyes darted toward the captain, then away again. "Oh," she said.

Following Amira's glance, McFarlane noticed that Britton's face had turned slightly pale under her tan.

Glinn was still looking at Amira, whose blush continued to deepen. "I think you'll find the quality of the Bordeaux makes up for the restriction."

Amira remained silent, embarrassment clear on her face.

Britton took the bottle and filled glasses for everyone at the table except herself. Whatever the mystery was, McFarlane thought, it had passed. As a steward slipped a plate of consommé in front of him, he made a mental note to ask Amira about it later.

The noise of conversation at the nearest tables rose once again, filling a brief and awkward silence. At the nearest table, Manuel Garza was buttering a slab of bread with his beefy paw and roaring at a joke.

"What's it like to handle a ship this big?" McFarlane asked. It was not simply a polite question to fill the silence: something about Britton intrigued him. He wanted to see what lay under that lovely, perfect surface.

Britton took a spoonful of consommé. "In some ways, these new tankers practically pilot themselves. I keep the crew running smoothly and act as troubleshooter. These ships don't like shallow water, they don't like to turn, and they don't like surprises." She lowered her spoon. "My job is to make sure we don't encounter any."

"Doesn't it go against the grain, commanding—well—an old rust bucket?"

Britton's response was measured. "Certain things are habitual at sea. The ship won't remain this way forever. I intend to have every spare hand working cleanup detail on the voyage home."

She turned toward Glinn. "Speaking of that, I'd like to ask you a favor. This expedition of ours is rather . . . unusual. The crew have been talking about it."

Glinn nodded. "Of course. Tomorrow, if you'll gather them together, I'll speak to them."

Britton nodded in approval. The steward returned, deftly replacing their plates with fresh ones. The fragrant smell of curry and tamarind rose from the table. McFarlane dug into the vindaloo, realizing a second or two later that it was probably the most fiery dish he had ever eaten.

"My, my, that's fine," muttered Brambell.

"How many times have you been around the Horn?" McFarlane asked, taking a large swig of water. He could feel the sweat popping out on his brow.

"Five," said Britton. "But those voyages were always at the height of the southern summer, when we were less likely to encounter bad weather."

Something in her tone made McFarlane uneasy. "But a vessel this big and powerful has nothing to fear from a storm, does it?"

Britton smiled distantly. "The Cape Horn region is like no place else on earth. Force 15 gales are commonplace. You've heard of the famed williwaws, no doubt?"

McFarlane nodded.

"Well, there's another wind far more deadly, although less well known. The locals call it a *panteonero*, a 'cemetery wind.' It can blow at over a hundred knots for several days without letup. It gets its name from the fact that it blows mariners right into their graves."

"But surely even the strongest wind couldn't affect the *Rolvaag*?" McFarlane asked.

"As long as we have steerage, we're fine, of course. But cemetery winds have pushed unwary or helpless ships down into the Screaming Sixties. That's what we call the stretch of open ocean between South America and Antarctica. For a mariner, it's the worst place on earth. Gigantic waves build up, and it's the only place where both waves and wind can circle the globe together without striking land. The waves just get bigger and bigger—up to two hundred feet high."

"Jesus," said McFarlane. "Ever taken a boat down there?"

Britton shook her head. "No," she said. "I never have, and I never will." She paused for a moment. Then she folded her napkin and gazed across the table at him. "Have you ever heard of a Captain Honeycutt?"

McFarlane thought a moment. "English mariner?"

Britton nodded. "He set off from London in 1607 with four ships, bound for the Pacific. Thirty years before, Drake had rounded the Horn, but had lost five of his six ships in the process. Honeycutt was determined to prove that the trip could be made without losing a single vessel. They hit weather as they approached the Strait of Le Maire. The crew pleaded with Honeycutt to turn back. He insisted on pushing on. As they rounded the Horn, a terrible gale blew up. A giant breaking wave—the Chileans call them *tigres*—sank two of the ships in less than a minute. The other two were dismasted. For several days the hulks drifted south, borne along by the raging gale, past the Ice Limit."

"The Ice Limit?"

"That's where the waters of the southern oceans meet the subfreezing waters surrounding Antarctica. Oceanographers call it the Antarctic Convergence. It's where the ice begins. At any rate, in the night, Honeycutt's ships were dashed against the side of an ice island."

"Like the *Titanic*," Amira said quietly. They were the first words she had spoken for several minutes.

The captain looked at her. "Not an iceberg. An ice *island*. The berg that wrecked the *Titanic* was an ice cube compared to what you get below the Limit. The one that crushed Honeycutt's ships probably measured twenty miles by forty."

"Did you say forty *miles?*" McFarlane asked.

"Much larger ones have been reported, bigger than some states. They're visible from space. Giant plates broken off the Antarctic ice shelves."

"Jesus."

"Of the hundred-odd souls still alive, perhaps thirty managed to crawl up onto the ice island. They gathered some wreckage that had washed up, and built a small fire. Over the next two days, half of them died of exposure. They had to keep shifting the fire, because it kept sinking into the ice. They began to hallucinate. Some claimed a huge shrouded creature with silky white hair and red teeth carried away members of the crew."

"Goodness gracious," said Brambell, arrested in the vigorous act of eating, "that's straight out of Poe's *Narrative of Arthur Gordon Pym*."

Britton paused to look at him. "That's exactly right," she said. "In fact, it's where Poe got the idea. The creature, it was said, ate their ears, toes, fingers, and knees, leaving the rest of the body parts scattered about the ice."

As he listened, McFarlane realized that conversation at the closest tables had fallen away.

"Over the next two weeks, the sailors died, one by one. Soon their numbers had been reduced to ten by starvation. The survivors took the only option left."

Amira made a face and put down her fork with a clatter. "I think I know what's coming."

"Yes. They were forced to eat what sailors euphemistically call 'long pig.' Their own dead companions."

"Charming," Brambell said. "I understand it's better than pork, if cooked properly. Pass the lamb, please."

"Perhaps a week later, one of the survivors spotted the remains of a vessel approaching them, bobbing in the heavy seas. It was the stern of one of their own ships that had broken in two during the storm. The men began to argue. Honeycutt and some others wanted to take their chances on the wreck. But it was lying low in the water, and most did not have the stomach to take to the seas on it. In the end only Honeycutt, his quartermaster, and one common seaman braved the swim. The quartermaster died of the cold before he could clamber aboard the hulk. But Honeycutt and the seaman made it. Their last view of the massive ice island came that evening, as it turned southward in the swells, heading slowly for Antarctica and oblivion. As it faded into the mists, they thought they saw a shrouded creature, tearing apart the survivors.

"Three days later, the wreck they were on struck the reefs around Diego Ramirez Island, southwest of the Horn. Honeycutt drowned, and only the seaman made it ashore. The man lived off shellfish, moss, cormorant guano, and kelp. He kept up a constant fire of turf, on the remote chance some vessel would pass by. Six months later, a Spanish ship saw the signal and brought him aboard."

"He must've been glad to see that ship," said McFarlane.

"Yes and no," said Britton. "England was at war with Spain at the time. He spent the next ten years in a dungeon in Cádiz. But in time he was released, and he returned to his native Scotland, married a lass twenty years his junior, and lived out a life as a farmer far, far from the sea."

Britton paused, smoothing the thick linen with the tips of her fingers. "That common seaman," she said quietly, "was William McKyle Britton. My ancestor."

She took a drink from her water glass, dabbed at her mouth with the napkin, and nodded to the steward to bring on the next course.

Rolvaag,
June 27, 3:45 P.M.

McFarlane leaned against the maindeck railing, enjoying the lazy, almost imperceptible roll of the ship. The *Rolvaag* was "in ballast"—its secondary holds partially filled with seawater to compensate for a lack of cargo—and consequently rode high in the water. To his left rose the ship's aft superstructure, a monolithic white slab relieved only by rheumy windows and the distant bridge wings. A hundred miles to the west, over the horizon, lay Myrtle Beach and the low coastline of South Carolina.

Assembled on the deck around him were the fifty-odd souls who made up the crew of the *Rolvaag*, a small group, considering the vastness of the ship. What struck him most was the diversity: Africans, Portuguese, French, English, Americans, Chinese, Indonesians, squinting in the late-afternoon sunlight and murmuring to each other in half a dozen languages. McFarlane guessed they would not take well to bullshit. He hoped Glinn had also registered that fact.

A sharp laugh cut across the group, and McFarlane turned to see Amira. The only EES staffer in attendance, she was sitting with a group of Africans who were stripped to the waist. They were talking and laughing animatedly.

The sun was dropping into the semitropical seas, sinking into a line of peach-colored clouds that stood like mushrooms on the distant horizon. The sea was oily and smooth, with only the suggestion of a swell.

A door in the superstructure opened and Glinn emerged. He walked slowly out along the central catwalk that ran, arrow straight, over a thousand feet to the *Rolvaag*'s bows. Behind him came Captain Britton, followed by the first mate and several other senior officers.

McFarlane watched the captain with renewed interest. A somewhat abashed Amira had told him the full story after dinner. Two years earlier, Britton had run a tanker onto Three Brothers' Reef off Spitsbergen. There had been no oil in the hold, but the damage to the ship had been considerable. Britton had been legally intoxicated at the time. Though there was no proof that her drinking caused the accident—it appeared to be an operational error by the helmsman—she had been without a command ever since. *No wonder she agreed to this assignment*, he thought, watching her step forward. And Glinn must have realized that no captain in good standing would have taken it. McFarlane shook his head curiously. Glinn would have left nothing to chance, especially the captaincy of the *Rolvaag*. He must know something about this woman.

Amira had joked about it in a way that made McFarlane a little uncomfortable. "It doesn't seem fair, punishing the whole ship for the weakness of one person," she'd said to McFarlane. "You can bet the crew is none too pleased. Can't you just see them in the crew's mess, sipping a glass of wine with dinner? *Lovely, with just a touch of oak, wouldn't you say?*" She had finished by making a wry face.

Overhead, Glinn had now reached the assembly. He stopped, hands behind his back, gazing down at the maindeck and the upturned faces.

"I am Eli Glinn," he began in his quiet, uninflected voice. "President of Effective Engineering Solutions. Many of you know the broad outlines of our expedition. Your captain has asked me to fill in some of the details. After doing so, I'll be happy to take questions."

He glanced down at the company.

"We are heading to the southern tip of South America, to retrieve a large meteorite for the Lloyd Museum. If we're correct, it will be the largest meteorite ever unearthed. In the hold, as many of you know, there is a special cradle built to receive it. The plan is very simple: we anchor in the Cape Horn islands. My crew, with the help of some of you, will excavate the meteorite, transport it to the ship, and place it in the cradle. Then we will deliver it to the Lloyd Museum."

He paused.

"Some of you may be concerned about the legality of the operation. We have staked mining claims to the island. The meteorite is an ore body, and no laws will be broken. There is, on the other hand, a potential *practical* problem in that Chile does not know we are retrieving a meteorite. But let me assure you this is a remote possibility. Everything has been worked out in great detail, and we do not anticipate any difficulties. The Cape Horn islands are uninhabited. The nearest settlement is Puerto Williams, fifty miles away. Even if the Chilean authorities learn what we are doing, we are prepared to pay a reasonable sum for the meteorite. So, as you can see, there is no cause for alarm, or even anxiety."

He paused again, then looked up. "Are there any questions?"

A dozen hands shot up. Glinn nodded to the closest man, a burly oiler wearing greasy overalls.

"So what is this meteorite?" the man boomed. There was an immediate murmur of assent.

"It will probably be a mass of nickel-iron weighing some ten thousand tons. An inert lump of metal."

"What's so important about it?"

"We believe it to be the largest meteorite ever discovered by man."

More hands went up.

"What happens if we get caught?"

"What we are doing is one hundred percent legal," Glinn replied.

A man in a blue uniform stood up, one of the ship's electricians.

"I don't like it," he said in a broad Yorkshire accent. He had a mass of red hair and an unruly beard.

Glinn waited politely.

"If the bloody Chileans catch us making off with their rock, anything could happen. If everything's one hundred percent legal, why not just buy the bloody stone from them?"

Glinn looked at the man, his pale gray eyes unwavering. "May I ask your name?"

"It's Lewis," came the reply.

"Because, Mr. Lewis, it would be politically impossible for the Chileans to sell it to us. On the other hand, they don't have the technological expertise to get it out of the ground and off the island, so it would just sit there, buried—probably forever. In America, it will be studied. It will be exhibited at a museum for all to see. It will be held in trust for mankind. This is not Chilean cultural patrimony. It could have fallen anywhere—even in Yorkshire."

There was a brief laugh from Lewis's mates. McFarlane was glad to see that Glinn seemed to be gaining their confidence with his straightforward talk.

"Sir," said one slight man, a junior ship's officer. "What about this dead man's switch?"

"The dead man's switch," Glinn said smoothly, his voice steady, almost mesmerizing, "is a distant precaution. In the unlikely event that the meteorite comes loose from its cradle—in a huge storm, say—it is merely a way for us to lighten our ballast by releasing it into the ocean. It's no different from the nineteenth-century mariners who had to throw their cargo overboard in severe weather. But the chances of having to jettison it are vanishingly small. The idea is to protect the ship and the crew above all, even at the expense of losing the meteorite."

"So how do you throw this switch?" another shouted out.

"I know the key. So does my chief engineer, Eugene Rochefort, and my construction manager, Manuel Garza."

"What about the captain?"

"It was felt advisable to leave that option in the hands of EES personnel," said Glinn. "It is, after all, our meteorite."

"But it's our bloody ship!"

The murmuring of the crew rose above the sound of the wind and the deep thrum of the engines. McFarlane glanced up at Captain Britton. She was standing behind Glinn, arms at her sides, stony-faced.

"The captain has agreed to this unusual arrangement. We built the dead man's switch, and we know how to operate it. In the unlikely event that it is used, it must be done with great care, with precise timing, by those who are trained for it. Otherwise, the ship could sink with the rock." He looked around. "Any more questions?"

There was a restless silence.

"I realize this is not a normal voyage," Glinn went on. "Some uncertainty—even anxiety—is natural. As with any sea journey, there are risks involved. I told you what we are doing is completely legal. However, I would be deluding you if I said the Chileans would feel the same way. These are the reasons each of you will receive a fifty-thousand-dollar bonus if we are successful."

There was a collective gasp from the crew, and an eruption of talk. Glinn held up his hand and silence again descended.

"If anyone feels uneasy about this expedition, you are free to go. We will arrange passage back to New York, with compensation." He looked pointedly at Lewis, the electrician.

The man stared back, then broke into a broad grin. "You sold me, mate."

"We all have much to do," Glinn said, addressing the group. "If you have anything else to add—or anything else to ask—do so now."

His eyes ranged enquiringly over them. Then, seeing the silence was absolute, he nodded, turned, and made his way back along the catwalk.

Rolvaag, 4:20 P.M.

The crew had broken up into small groups, talking quietly among themselves as they began to move back toward their stations. A sudden breeze tugged at McFarlane's windbreaker. As he turned toward the shelter of the ship, he saw Amira. She was standing by the starboard railing, still talking to the group of deckhands. She made some comment, and the small knot around her suddenly erupted into laughter.

McFarlane made his way to the officers' dayroom. Like most of the other ship's compartments he had seen, it was large and expensively, if sparsely, appointed. But it housed one great attraction for him: a coffeepot that was never empty. He poured himself a cup and sipped at it with a contented sigh.

"Some cream with that?" came a woman's voice from behind him. He turned to see Captain Britton. She closed the door to the dayroom, then walked toward him with a smile. The wind had loosened the severe braid of hair beneath her officer's hat, and a few errant strands hung down, framing a long and elegant neck.

"No thanks, I prefer it black." McFarlane watched as Britton helped herself to a cup, adding a single teaspoon of sugar. They sipped together in silence for a moment.

"I have to ask you," McFarlane said, more to make conversation than anything else. "This pot always seems to be full. And it always tastes perfectly fresh. Just how do you achieve that miracle?"

"It's no miracle. The stewards bring a new pot every thirty minutes, needed or not. Forty-eight pots a day."

McFarlane shook his head. "Remarkable," he said. "But then, it's a remarkable ship."

Captain Britton took another sip of coffee. "Care for a tour?" she asked.

McFarlane looked at her. Surely the master of the *Rolvaag* had better things to do. Still, it would be a nice break. Life on board ship had quickly settled into a routine. He took a final swig of coffee and set down the cup. "Sounds great," he said. "I've been wondering what kind of secrets are hiding inside this big old hull."

"Not many secrets," Britton said, opening the door to the dayroom and ushering him out into the wide hallway. "Just lots and lots of places to put oil."

The door to the maindeck opened and the slight figure of Rachel Amira appeared. Seeing them, she paused. Britton gave her a cool nod, then turned away and started down the corridor. As they rounded the corner, McFarlane glanced backward. Amira was still watching them, a smirk on her lips.

Opening a huge set of double doors, Britton led him into the ship's galley. Here, Mr. Singh held sway over stewards, assistant chefs, and banks of gleaming ovens. There were massive walk-in freezers, full of sides of lamb, beef, chickens, ducks, and a row of red-and-white-marbled carcasses McFarlane thought must be goats. "You've got enough to feed an army here," he said.

"Mr. Singh would probably say you scientists eat like one." Britton smiled. "Come on, let's leave him to it."

They passed the billiards room and swimming pool, then descended a level, where Britton showed him the crew's game room and mess. Down another staircase and they arrived at the crew's quarters: large rooms with individual baths, sandwiched between galleries that ran up the port and starboard sides of the ship. They paused at the end of the port passageway. Here, the noise of the engine was noticeably louder. The corridor seemed to stretch forward forever, portholes on the left, cabin doors on the right.

"Everything's built to a giant's scale," McFarlane said. "And it's so empty."

Britton laughed. "Visitors always say that. The fact is, the ship's basically run by computers. We navigate by geophysical satellite data, course is maintained automatically, even collision detection is monitored electronically. Thirty years ago, ship's electrician was a lowly position. Now, electronics specialists are critical."

"It's all very impressive." McFarlane turned toward Britton. "Don't get me wrong, but I've always wondered why Glinn chose a tanker for this job. Why go to the trouble of disguising a tanker as an ore carrier? Why not just get a dry bulk carrier to begin with? Or a big container ship? God knows it would have been cheaper."

"I think I can explain that. Follow me."

Britton opened a door and ushered McFarlane forward. The carpeting and wood veneer gave way to stamped metal and linoleum. They descended yet another set of stairs to a door labeled CARGO CONTROL ROOM. The room beyond was dominated by a vast electronic schematic of the ship's maindeck, mounted on the far bulkhead. Countless small points of light blinked red and yellow across its surface.

"This is the ship's mimic diagram," Britton said, motioning McFarlane toward the schematic. "It's the way we keep track of how and where cargo is loaded. We control the ballast, pumps, and cargo valves directly from the mimic area." She pointed to a series of gauges and switches arrayed beneath the diagram. "These controls regulate the pump pressures."

She led the way across the room, where a single seaman watched an array of computer screens. "This computer calculates cargo distribution. And these computers are the ship's automatic gauging system. They monitor pressure, volume, and temperature throughout the ship's tanks."

She patted the beige case of the nearest monitor. "*This* is why Glinn chose a tanker. This meteorite of yours is heavy. Loading it will be exceedingly tricky. With our tanks and computers, we can shift seawater ballast around from tank to tank, maintaining even trim and list no matter what weird lopsided thing goes inside. We can keep everything level. I don't think anybody would be happy if we turned belly-up the moment you drop that thing in the tank."

Britton moved to the far side of the ballast control equipment. "Speaking of the computers, do you have any idea what this is?" She pointed to a tall, freestanding tower of black steel, featureless except for a keyhole and a small logo reading SECURE DATAMETRICS. It looked very different from the rest of the ship's electronics. "Glinn's people installed it back in Elizabeth. There's another, smaller one like it, up on the bridge. None of my officers can figure out what the thing does."

McFarlane ran a curious hand over its beveled front. "No idea. Could it have something to do with the dead man's switch?"

"That's what I assumed at first." She led him out of the room and along the metal-floored corridor to a waiting elevator. "But it seems to be tied in to more than one of the ship's key systems."

"Would you like me to ask Glinn?"

"No, don't bother. I'll ask him sometime myself. But here I am, going on and on about the *Rolvaag*," she said, punching an elevator button. "I'm curious how exactly one becomes a meteorite hunter."

McFarlane looked at her as the elevator began to sink. She was a very poised woman; her shoulders were straight, her chin held high. But it was not a military kind of stiffness; rather, he thought, it was a kind of quiet pride. She knew he was a meteorite hunter: he wondered if she knew about Masangkay and the Tornarssuk meteorite fiasco. *You and I have a lot in common,* he thought. He could only imagine how tough it must have been for her to put on a uniform again and walk a bridge, wondering what people were saying behind her back.

"I got caught in a meteorite shower in Mexico."

"Incredible. And you survived."

"Only once in recorded history has a meteorite ever struck anyone," McFarlane said. "A woman with a history of hypochondria, lying in bed. The rock had been slowed by going through the upper stories of her house, so it only made a massive bruise. Sure got her out of bed, though."

Britton laughed: a lovely sound.

"So I went back to school and became a planetary geologist. But I was never very good at playing the sober scientist."

"What does a planetary geologist study?"

"A long list of boring subjects, before you get to the really good stuff. Geology, chemistry, astronomy, physics, calculus."

"Sounds more interesting than studying for a master's license. And the good stuff?"

"My high point was getting to study a Martian meteorite in graduate school. I was looking at the effect of cosmic rays on its chemical composition—trying to find a way to date it, basically."

The elevator door opened and they stepped out. "A real Martian rock," Britton said, opening a door and stepping out into yet another endless corridor.

McFarlane shrugged. "I liked finding meteorites. It was a bit like treasure hunting. And I liked *studying* meteorites. But I didn't like rubbing elbows at faculty sherry hour, or going to conferences and chatting with rock jocks about collisional ejection and cratering mechanics. I guess the feeling was mutual. Anyway, my academic career lasted all of five years. Got denied tenure. I've been on my own ever since."

He held his breath, thinking of his ex-partner, realizing this was a poor choice of words. But the captain did not pursue it, and the moment passed.

"All I know about meteorites is that they're rocks that fall out of the sky," Britton said. "Where do they come from? Other than Mars, of course."

"Martian meteorites are extremely rare. Most of them are chunks of rock from the inner asteroid belt. Small bits and pieces from planets that broke up soon after the formation of the solar system."

"The thing you're after isn't exactly small."

"Well, *most* of them are small. But it doesn't take a whole lot to make a big impact. The Tunguska meteorite, which hit Siberia in 1908, had an impact energy equal to a ten-megaton hydrogen bomb."

"Ten megatons?"

"And that's small potatoes. Some meteoroids hit the earth with a kinetic energy greater than one hundred million megatons. That's the kind of blast that tends to end an entire geologic age, kill off the dinosaurs, and generally ruin everybody's day."

"Jesus." Britton shook her head.

He laughed dryly. "Don't worry. They're pretty rare. One every hundred million years."

They had worked their way through another maze of corridors. McFarlane felt hopelessly lost.

"Are all meteorites the same?"

"No, no. But most of the ones that hit the earth are ordinary chondrites."

"Chondrites?"

"Basically, old gray stones. Pretty boring." McFarlane hesitated. "There are the nickel-iron types—probably like the one we're snagging. But the most interesting type is called CI chondrites." He stopped.

Britton glanced over at him.

"It's hard to explain. It might be boring for you." McFarlane remembered, more than once, putting a glaze over everyone's eyes at a dinner party in his younger, enthusiastic, innocent years.

"I'm the one that studied celestial navigation. Try me."

"Well, CI chondrites are clumped directly out of the pure, unadulterated dust cloud the solar system formed from. Which makes them very interesting. They contain clues to how the solar system formed. They're also very old. Older than the Earth."

"And how old is that?"

"Four and a half billion years." He noticed a genuine interest shining in her eyes.

"Amazing."

"And it's been theorized that there's a type of meteorite even more incredible—"

McFarlane fell silent abruptly, checking himself. He did not want the old obsession to return; not now. He walked on in the sudden stillness, aware of Britton's curious gaze.

The corridor ended in a dogged hatch. Undogging the cleats, Britton pulled it open. A wall of sound flew out at them: the huge roar of endless horsepower. McFarlane followed the captain out onto a narrow catwalk. About fifty feet below, he could see two enormous turbines roaring in tandem. The huge space seemed completely deserted; apparently it, too, was run by computer. He gripped a metal pole for support, and it vibrated wildly in his hand.

Britton looked at him with a small smile as they continued along the catwalk. "Tankers are driven by steam boilers, not diesel motors like other ships," she said, raising her voice over the roar. "We do have an emergency diesel for electricity, though. On a modern ship like this, you can't afford to lose power. Because if you do, you've got nothing: no computers, no navigation, no fire-fighting equipment. You're a drifting hulk. We call it DIW: dead in the water."

They passed through another heavy door at the forward end of the engine space. Britton dogged it shut, then led the way down a hallway that ended at a closed elevator door. McFarlane followed, grateful for the quiet.

The captain stopped at the elevator, looking back at him calculatingly. Suddenly, he realized she had more on her mind than a tour of the jolly old *Rolvaag*.

"Mr. Glinn gave a good talk," Britton said at last.

"I'm glad you think so."

"Crews can be a superstitious lot, you know. It's amazing how fast rumor and speculation can turn into fact belowdecks. I think that talk went a long way toward squelching any rumors."

There was another brief pause. Then she spoke again.

"I have the feeling Mr. Glinn knows a lot more than he said. Actually, no—that isn't the right way to put it. I think maybe he knows *less* than he let on." She glanced sidelong at McFarlane. "Isn't that right?"

McFarlane hesitated. He didn't know what Lloyd or Glinn had told the captain—or, more to the point, what they had withheld. Nevertheless, he felt that the more she knew, the better off the ship would be. He felt a sense of kinship with her. They'd both made big mistakes. They'd both been dragged behind the motorcycle of life a little longer than the average Joe. In his gut, he trusted Sally Britton.

"You're right," he said. "The truth is, we know almost nothing about it. We don't know how something so large could have survived impact. We don't know why it hasn't rusted away. What little electromagnetic and gravitational data we have about the rock seem contradictory, even impossible."

"I see," said Britton. She looked into McFarlane's eyes. "Is it dangerous?"

"There is no reason to think so." He hesitated. "No reason to think not, either."

There was a pause.

"What I mean is, will it pose a hazard to my ship or my crew?"

McFarlane chewed his lip, wondering how to answer. "A hazard? It's heavy as hell. It'll be tricky to maneuver. But once it's safely secured in its cradle, I have to believe it'll be less dangerous than a hold full of inflammable oil." He looked at her. "And Glinn seems to be a man who never takes chances."

For a moment, Britton thought about this. Then she nodded. "That was my take on him, too: cautious to a fault." She pressed the button for the elevator. "That's the kind of person I like on board. Because the next time I end up on a reef, I'm going down with the ship."

Rolvaag,
July 3, 2:15 P.M.

As the good ship *Rolvaag* crossed the equator, with the coast of Brazil and the mouth of the Amazon far to the west, a time-honored ritual began on the ship's bow, as it had on oceangoing vessels for hundreds of years.

Thirty feet below deck and almost nine hundred feet aft, Dr. Patrick Brambell was unpacking his last box of books. For almost every year of his working life he had crossed the line at least once, and he found the concomitant ceremonies—the "Neptune's tea" made from boiled socks, the gauntlet of fish-wielding deckhands, the vulgar laughter of the shellbacks—distasteful in the extreme.

He had been unpacking and arranging his extensive library ever since the *Rolvaag* left port. It was a task he enjoyed almost as much as reading the books themselves, and he never allowed himself to hurry. Now he ran a scalpel along the final seam of packing tape, pulled back the cardboard flaps, and looked inside. With loving fingers, he removed the topmost book, Burton's *Anatomy of Melancholy*, and caressed its fine half-leather cover before placing it on the last free shelf in his cabin. *Orlando Furioso* came next, then Huysmans's *À rebours*, Coleridge's lectures on Shakespeare, Dr. Johnson's *Rambler* essays, Newman's *Apologia pro Vita Sua*. None of the books was about medicine; in fact, of the thousand-odd eclectic books in Brambell's traveling library, only a dozen or so could be considered professional references—and those he segregated in his medical suite, to remove the vocational stain from his cherished library. For Dr. Brambell was first a reader, and second a doctor.

The box empty at last, Brambell sighed in mingled satisfaction and regret and stepped back to survey the ranks of books standing in neat rows on every surface and shelf. As he did so, there was the clatter of a distant door, followed by the measured cadence of footsteps. Brambell waited motionless, listening, hoping it was not for him but knowing it was. The footsteps stopped, and a brief double rap came from the direction of the waiting room.

Brambell sighed again; a very different sigh from the first. He glanced around the cabin quickly. Then, spying a surgical mask, he picked it up and slipped it over his mouth. He found it very useful in hurrying patients along. He gave the books a last loving glance, then slipped out of the cabin, closing the door behind him.

He walked down the long hallway, past the rooms of empty hospital beds, past the surgical bays and the pathology lab, to the waiting room. There was Eli Glinn, an expandable file beneath one arm.

Glinn's eyes fastened on the surgical mask. "I didn't realize you were with someone."

"I'm not," Brambell said through the mask. "You're the first to arrive."

Glinn glanced at the mask a moment more. Then he nodded. "Very well. May we speak?"

"Certainly." Brambell led the way to his consultation room. He found Glinn to be one of the most unusual creatures he had ever met: a man with culture who took no delight in it; a man with conversation who never employed it; a man with hooded gray eyes who made it his business to know everyone's weaknesses, save his own.

Brambell closed the door to his consultation room. "Please sit down, Mr. Glinn." He waved a hand at Glinn's folder. "I assume those are the medical histories? They are late. Fortunately, I've had no need to call on them yet."

Glinn slipped into the chair. "I've set aside some of the folders that might require your attention. Most are routine. There are a few exceptions."

"I see."

"We'll start with the crew. Victor Howell has testicular cryptorchidism."

"Odd that he hasn't had it corrected."

Glinn looked up. "He probably doesn't like the idea of a knife down there."

Brambell nodded.

Glinn leafed through several more folders. There were the usual complaints and conditions to be found in any random sampling of the population: a few diabetics, a chronic slipped disk, a case of Addison's disease.

"Fairly healthy crew, there," said Brambell, hoping faintly that the session was over. But no—Glinn was taking out another set of folders.

"And here are the psychological profiles," Glinn said.

Brambell glanced over at the names. "What about the EES people?"

"We have a slightly different system," said Glinn. "EES files are available on a need-to-know basis only."

Brambell didn't respond to that one. No use arguing with a man like Glinn.

Glinn took two additional folders out of his briefcase and placed them on Brambell's desk, then casually leaned back in the chair. "There's really only one person here I'm concerned about."

"And who might that be?"

"McFarlane."

Brambell tugged the mask down around his chin. "The dashing meteorite hunter?" he asked in surprise. The man did carry around a faint air of trouble, it was true.

Glinn tapped the top folder. "I will be giving you regular reports on him."

Brambell raised his eyebrows.

"McFarlane is the one key figure here not of my choosing. He's had a dubious career, to say the least. That is why I would like you to evaluate this report, and the ones to follow."

Brambell looked at the file with distaste. "Who's your mole?" he asked. He expected Glinn to be offended, but he was not.

"I would rather keep that confidential."

Brambell nodded. He pulled the file toward him, leafing through it. " 'Diffident about expedition and its chances for success,' " he read aloud. " 'Motivations unclear. Distrustful of the scientific community. Extremely uncomfortable with managerial role. Tends to be a loner.' " He dropped the folder. "I don't see anything unusual."

Glinn nodded at the second, much larger folder. "Here's a background file on McFarlane. Among other things, it contains a report here about an unpleasant incident in Greenland some years ago."

Brambell sighed. He was a most incurious man, and this was, he suspected, a major reason why Glinn had hired him. "I'll look at it later."

"Let's look at it now."

"Perhaps you could summarize it for me."

"Very well."

Brambell sat back, folded his hands, and resigned himself to listening.

"Years ago, McFarlane had a partner named Masangkay. They first teamed up to smuggle the Atacama tektites out of Chile, which made them infamous in that country. After that, they successfully located several other small but important meteorites. The two worked well together. McFarlane had gotten in trouble at his last museum job and went freelance. He had an instinctive knack for finding meteorites, but rock hunting isn't a full-time job unless you can get backers. Masangkay, unlike McFarlane, was smooth at museum politics and lined up several excellent assignments. They grew very close. McFarlane married Masangkay's sister, Malou, making them brothers-in-law. However, over the years, their relationship began to fray. Perhaps McFarlane envied Masangkay's successful museum career. Or Masangkay envied the fact that McFarlane was by nature the better field scientist. But most of all it had to do with McFarlane's pet theory."

"And that was?"

"McFarlane believed that, someday, an *interstellar* meteorite would be found. One that had traveled across vast interstellar distances from another star system. Everyone told him this was mathematically impossible—all known meteorites came from inside the solar system. But McFarlane was obsessed with the idea. It gave him the faint odor of quackery, and that didn't sit well with a traditionalist like Masangkay.

"In any case, about three years ago there was a major meteorite fall near Tornarssuk, Greenland. It was tracked by satellites and seismic sensors, which allowed for good triangulation of its impact site. Its trajectory was even captured on an amateur videotape. The New York Museum of Natural History, working with the Danish government, hired Masangkay to find the meteorite. Masangkay brought in McFarlane.

"They found the Tornarssuk, but it took a lot more time and cost a lot more money than they anticipated. Large debts were incurred. The New York Museum balked. To make matters worse, there was friction between Masangkay and McFarlane. McFarlane extrapolated the orbit of the Tornarssuk from the satellite data, and became convinced that the meteorite was following a hyperbolic orbit, which meant it must have come in from far beyond the solar system. He thought it was the interstellar meteorite he had been looking for all his life. Masangkay was worried sick over the funding, and this was the last thing he wanted to hear. They waited, guarding the site, for days, but no money came. At last, Masangkay went off to resupply and meet with Danish officials. He left McFarlane with the stone—and, unfortunately, a communications dish.

"As best I understand it, McFarlane had a kind of psychological break. He was there, alone, for a week. He became convinced that the New York Museum would fail to provide the extra funding, and that in the end the meteorite would be spirited off by somebody, broken up, and sold on the black market, never to be seen or studied again. So he used the satellite dish to contact a rich Japanese collector who he knew could buy it whole and keep it. In short, he betrayed his partner. When Masangkay returned with the supplies—and, as it happened, the extra funding—the Japanese were already there. They wasted no time at all. They took it away. Masangkay felt betrayed, and the scientific world was furious at McFarlane. They've never forgiven him."

Brambell nodded sleepily. It was an interesting story. Might make for a good, if somewhat sensational, novel. Jack London could have done it justice. Or better yet, Conrad . . .

"I worry about McFarlane," Glinn said, intruding on his thoughts. "We can't have anything like that happening here. It would ruin everything. If he was willing to betray his own brother-in-law, he would betray Lloyd and EES without a second thought."

"Why should he?" Brambell yawned. "Lloyd has deep pockets, and he seems perfectly happy to write checks."

"McFarlane is mercenary, of course, but this goes beyond money. The meteorite we're after has some very peculiar properties. If McFarlane grows obsessed with it as he did with the Tornarssuk . . ." Glinn hesitated. "For example, if we ever have to use the dead man's switch, it would be in a time of extreme crisis. Every second would count. I don't want anybody trying to prevent it."

"And my role in this?"

"You have a background in psychiatry. I want you to review these periodic reports. If you see any cause for concern—in particular, any incipient signs of a break like his last one—please let me know."

Brambell flipped through the two files again, the old one and the new. The background file was strange. He wondered where Glinn had gotten the information—very little, if any, was standard psychiatric or medical stuff. Many of the reports had no reporting doctors' names or affiliations—indeed, some had no names at all. Whatever the source, it had a very expensive whiff about it.

He finally looked up at Glinn and slapped the folder shut. "I'll look this over, and I'll keep an eye on him. I'm not sure my take on what happened is the same as yours."

Glinn rose to leave, his gray eyes as impenetrable as slate. Brambell found it unaccountably irritating.

"And the Greenland meteorite?" Brambell asked. "*Was* it from interstellar space?"

"Of course not. It turned out to be an ordinary rock from the asteroid belt. McFarlane was wrong."

"And the wife?" Brambell asked after a moment.

"What wife?"

"McFarlane's wife. Malou Masangkay."

"She left him. Went back to the Philippines and remarried."

In a moment, Glinn was gone, his carefully placed footfalls fading down the corridor. For a moment, the doctor listened to the dying cadence, thinking. Then a line of Conrad's came to mind. He spoke it aloud: "No man ever understands quite his own artful dodges to escape from the grim shadow of self-knowledge."

With a sigh of returning contentment, he put aside the files and went back into his private suite. The torpid equatorial climate, as well as something about Glinn himself, made the doctor think of Maugham—the short stories, to be exact. He ran his fingers over the nubbed spines—each rekindling a universe of memory and emotion as it passed by—found what he was looking for, settled into a large wing chair, and opened the cover with a shiver of delight.

Rolvaag, July 11, 7:55 A.M.

McFarlane advanced onto the parquet deck and looked around curiously. It was his first time on the bridge, and this was without question the most dramatic space on the *Rolvaag*. The bridge was as wide as the ship itself. Three sides of the room were dominated by large square windows, slanting outward from bottom to top, each equipped with its own electric wiper. On either end, doors led out to the bridge wings. Other doors to the rear were labeled CHART ROOM and RADIO ROOM in brass letters. Beneath the forward windows, a bank of equipment stretched the entire length of the bridge: consoles, rows of telephones, links to control stations throughout the ship. Beyond the windows, a predawn squall lay across stormy deserts of ocean. The only light came from the instrument panels and screens. A smaller row of windows gave a view aft, between the stacks and past the stern of the ship to the white double lines of the wake, vanishing toward the horizon.

In the center of the room stood a command-and-control station. Here, McFarlane saw the captain, a dim figure in the near-darkness. She was speaking into a telephone, occasionally leaning over to murmur to the helmsman beside her, the hollows of his eyes illuminated a cold green by his radar screen.

As McFarlane joined the silent vigil, the squall began to break up and a gray dawn crept over the horizon. A single deckhand moved antlike across the distant forecastle, bound on obscure business. Above the creamy bow-wake, a few persistent seabirds wheeled and screamed. It was a shocking contrast to the torrid tropics, which they had left behind less than a week before.

After the *Rolvaag* had crossed the equator, in sultry heat and heavy rains, a lassitude had fallen over the ship. McFarlane had felt it, too: yawning over games of shuffleboard; lolling in his suite, staring at the butternut walls. But as they continued south, the air had grown crisper, the ocean swells longer and heavier, and the pearlescent sky of the tropics had given way to brilliant azure, flecked with clouds. As the air freshened, he sensed that the general malaise was being replaced by a mounting excitement.

The door to the bridge opened once again, and two figures entered: a third officer, taking the morning eight-to-twelve, and Eli Glinn. He came silently up to McFarlane's side.

"What's this all about?" McFarlane asked under his breath.

Before Glinn could answer, there was a soft click from behind. McFarlane glanced back to see Victor Howell step out of the radio room and look on as the watch was relieved.

The third officer came over and murmured something in the captain's ear. In turn, she glanced at Glinn. "Keep an eye off the starboard bow," she said, nodding out toward the horizon, which lay like a knife edge against the sky.

As the sky lightened, the swells and hollows of the heaving sea became more clearly defined. A spear of dawn light probed through the heavy canopy of clouds off the ship's starboard bow. Stepping away from the helmsman, the captain strolled to the forward wall of windows, hands clasped behind her back. As she did so, another ray of light clipped the tops of the clouds. And then, abruptly, the entire western horizon lit up like an eruption of fire. McFarlane squinted, trying to understand what it was he was staring at. Then he made it out: a row of great snowcapped peaks, wreathed in glaciers, ablaze in the dawn.

The captain turned and faced the group. "Land ho," she said dryly. "The mountains of Tierra del Fuego. Within a few hours, we'll pass through the Strait of Le Maire and into the Pacific Ocean." She passed a pair of binoculars to McFarlane.

McFarlane stared at the range of mountains through the binoculars: distant and forbidding, like the ramparts of a lost continent, the peaks shedding long veils of snow.

Glinn straightened his shoulders, turned away from the sight, and glanced at Victor Howell. The chief mate strolled over to a technician at the far end of the bridge, who quickly stood up and disappeared out the door onto the starboard bridge wing. Howell returned to the command station. "Give yourself fifteen for coffee," he said to the third officer. "I'll take the con."

The junior officer looked from Howell to the captain, surprised by this break from procedure. "Do you want me to enter it in the log, ma'am?" he asked.

Britton shook her head. "Unnecessary. Just be back in a quarter of an hour."

Once the man had disappeared from the bridge, the captain turned to Howell. "Is Banks ready with the New York hookup?" she asked.

The chief mate nodded. "We've got Mr. Lloyd waiting."

"Very well. Patch him through."

McFarlane stifled a sigh. *Isn't once a day enough?* he thought. He had almost grown to dread the noon videoconference calls he made daily to the Lloyd Museum. Lloyd was always talking a mile a minute, desperate to learn of the ship's progress down to the nautical mile, grilling everyone at length, hatching schemes and questioning every plan. McFarlane marveled at Glinn's patience.

There was a crackling noise in a loudspeaker bolted to a bulkhead, then McFarlane heard Lloyd's voice, loud even in the spacious bridge. "Sam? Sam, are you there?"

"This is Captain Britton, Mr. Lloyd," Britton said, motioning the others toward a microphone at the command station. "The coast of Chile is in sight. We're a day out of Puerto Williams."

"Marvelous!" Lloyd boomed.

Glinn approached the microphone. "Mr. Lloyd, it's Eli Glinn. Tomorrow we clear Chilean customs. Dr. McFarlane, myself, and the captain will take a launch into Puerto Williams to present ship's papers."

"Is that necessary?" Lloyd asked. "Why must you all go?"

"Let me explain the situation. The first problem is that the customs people will probably want to come on board the ship."

"Jesus," came Lloyd's voice. "That could give the whole game away."

"Potentially. That is why our first effort will be to *prevent* a visit. The Chileans will be curious to meet the principals—the captain, the chief mining engineer. If we sent underlings, they will almost certainly insist on coming aboard."

"What about me?" McFarlane asked. "I'm persona non grata in Chile, remember? I'd just as soon keep a low profile."

"Sorry, but you're our ace in the hole," Glinn replied.

"And why is that?"

"You're the only one of us who has actually been in Chile. You've got more experience in situations like this. In the very remote chance that events play out along an unexpected path, we need your instincts."

"Great. I don't think I'm being properly compensated for taking such a risk."

"Oh yes you are." Lloyd's voice sounded testy. "Look, Eli. What if they want to board her anyway?"

"We've prepared a special reception room for the occasion."

"*Reception* room? The last thing we want is them hanging about."

"The room will not encourage any lingering. If they do come aboard, they will be escorted to the forward tank-washing control room. It's not a very comfortable place. We've fitted it with some metal chairs—not enough—and a Formica table. The heat's been turned off. We've painted parts of the deck with a chemical wash smelling faintly of excrement and vomit."

Lloyd's laugh, amplified and metallic, rang across the bridge. "Eli, God forbid you should ever direct a war. But what if they want to see the bridge?"

"We have a strategy for that as well. Trust me, Palmer, when we get through with the customs people in Puerto Williams, it will be highly unlikely they will want to come aboard, and even less likely they will want to see the bridge." He turned. "Dr. McFarlane, from now on you speak no Spanish. Just follow my lead. Let me and Captain Britton do all the talking."

There was a momentary silence. "You said that was our first problem," Lloyd spoke up at last. "Is there another one?"

"There's an errand we must run while we're in Puerto Williams."

"Dare I ask what that might be?"

"I'm planning to engage the services of a man named John Puppup. We'll have to find him and get him on board."

Lloyd groaned. "Eli, I'm beginning to think you enjoy springing these surprises on me. Who is John Puppup, and why do we need him?"

"He's half Yaghan, half English."

"And what the hell is a Yaghan?"

"The Yaghan Indians were the original inhabitants of the Cape Horn islands. They are now extinct. Only a few mestizos are left. Puppup is old, perhaps seventy. He basically witnessed the extinction of his people. He's the last to retain some local Indian knowledge."

The overhead speaker fell silent a moment. Then it cracked back into life. "Eli, this scheme sounds half-baked. You said you *planned* to engage his services? Does he know about this?"

"Not yet."

"What if he says no?"

"When we get to him, he won't be in any condition to say no. Besides, haven't you heard of the time-honored naval tradition of 'impressment'?"

Lloyd groaned. "So now we're going to add kidnapping to our list of crimes."

"This is a high-stakes game," said Glinn. "You knew it when we began. Puppup will go home a rich man. We will have no trouble from that quarter. The only trouble will be locating him and getting him aboard."

"Any more surprises?"

"At customs, Dr. McFarlane and myself will present counterfeit passports. This is the path with the highest certainty of success, although it entails some minor breaking of Chilean law."

"Wait a minute," McFarlane said. "Traveling with fake passports is breaking *American* law."

"It will never be known. I have arranged for the passport records to be lost in transit between Puerto Williams and Punta Arenas. We will retain your real passports, of course, which have been marked with the correct visas, arrival, and departure stamps. Or so it will seem."

He looked around, as if asking for objections. There were none. The chief officer was at the helm, steering the ship impassively. Captain Britton was looking at Glinn. Her eyes were wide, but she remained silent.

"Very well," Lloyd said. "But I have to tell you, Eli, this scheme of yours makes me very nervous. I want an immediate update when you get back from customs."

The speaker abruptly went dead. Britton nodded to Victor Howell, who disappeared into the radio room.

"Everyone who goes into port is going to have to look the part," Glinn said. "Dr. McFarlane can go as he is"—Glinn gave him a rather dismissive once-over—"but Captain Britton will need to be several degrees less formal."

"You said we'll have fake passports," McFarlane said. "I assume we'll have fake names to go with them?"

"Correct. You'll be Dr. Sam Widmanstätten."

"Cute."

There was a short silence. "And yourself?" Britton asked.

For the first time McFarlane could remember, Glinn laughed—a low, small sound that seemed to be mostly breath.

"Call me Ishmael," he said.

Chile,
July 12, 9:30 A.M.

The following day, the great ship *Rolvaag* lay at rest in the Goree Roads, a broad channel between three islands rising out of the Pacific. A chill sunlight bathed the scene in sharp relief. McFarlane stood at the rail of the *Rolvaag*'s launch, a decrepit vessel almost as rust-stained as its parent, and stared at the tanker as they slowly pulled away. It looked even bigger from sea level. Far above, on the fantail, he could see Amira, swaddled in a parka three sizes too large. "Hey, boss!" she cried faintly as she waved, "don't come back with the clap!"

The boat swung around in the chop and turned toward the desolate landscape of Isla Navarino. It was the southernmost inhabited landmass on earth. Unlike the mountainous coast they had passed the prior afternoon, the eastern flanks of Navarino were low and monotonous: a frozen, snow-covered swamp descending to broad shingled beaches pounded by Pacific rollers. There was no sign of human life. Puerto Williams lay some twenty miles up the Beagle Channel, in protected waters. McFarlane shivered, drawing his own parka more tightly around him. Spending time on Isla Desolación—remote even by the standards of this godforsaken place—was one thing. But hanging around a Chilean harbor made him nervous. A thousand miles north of here there were still plenty of people who would remember his face—and would be happy to acquaint him with the business end of a cattle prod. There was always a chance, however small, that one of them would now be stationed down here.

There was a movement by his side as Glinn joined him at the rail. The man was wearing a greasy quilted jacket, several layers of soiled woolen shirts, and an orange watchcap. He clutched a battered briefcase in one hand. His face, fastidiously clean-shaven under normal conditions, had been allowed to roughen. A bent cigarette dangled from his lips, and McFarlane could see he was actually smoking it, inhaling and exhaling with every indication of pleasure.

"I don't believe we've met," McFarlane said.

"I'm Eli Ishmael, chief mining engineer."

"Well, Mr. Mining Engineer, if I didn't know better I'd say you were actually enjoying yourself."

Glinn pulled the cigarette from his mouth, gazed at it a moment, then tossed it toward the frozen seascape. "Enjoyment is not necessarily incompatible with success."

McFarlane gestured at his shabby clothes. "Where'd you get all this, anyhow? You look like you've been stoking coal."

"A couple of costume consultants flew in from Hollywood while the ship was being fitted," Glinn answered. "We've got a few sea lockers full, enough to cover any contingency."

"Let's hope it doesn't come to that. So what exactly are our marching orders?"

"It's very simple. Our job is to introduce ourselves at customs, handle any questions about the mining permits, post our bond, and find John Puppup. We're a wildcatting outfit, here to mine iron ore. The company is teetering on bankruptcy, and this is our last shot. If someone speaks English and questions you, insist belligerently that we are a first-class outfit. But as much as possible, don't speak at all. And if something untoward happens at customs, react as you would naturally."

"Naturally?" McFarlane shook his head. "My natural instinct would be to run like hell." He paused. "How about the captain? You think she's up to this?"

"As you may have noticed, she's not your typical sea captain."

The launch cut through the chop, the carefully detuned diesels hammering violently from below. The door to the cabin thumped open and Britton approached them, wearing old jeans, a pea jacket, and a battered cap with gold captain's bars. Binoculars swung from her neck. It was the first time McFarlane had seen her out of a crisp naval uniform, and the change was both refreshing and alluring.

"May I compliment you on your outfit?" Glinn said. McFarlane glanced at him in surprise; he did not remember ever hearing Glinn praise anybody before.

The captain flashed Glinn a smile in return. "You may not. I loathe it."

As the boat rounded the northern end of Isla Navarino, a dark shape appeared in the distance. McFarlane could see it was an enormous iron ship.

"God," said McFarlane. "Look at the size of that. We'll have to give it a wide berth, or its wake will sink us."

Britton raised her binoculars. After a long look, she lowered them again, more slowly. "I don't think so," she replied. "She's not going anywhere fast."

Despite the fact that the ship's bow was toward them, it seemed to take an eternity to draw nearer. The twin masts, gaunt and spidery, listed slightly to one side. Then McFarlane understood: the ship was a wreck, lodged on a reef in the very middle of the channel.

Glinn took the binoculars Britton offered. "It's the *Capitán Praxos*," he said. "A cargo vessel, by the looks of it. Must have been driven on a shoal."

"It's hard to believe a ship that size could be wrecked in these protected waters," said McFarlane.

"This sound is only protected during northeasterly winds, like we have today," said Britton, her voice cold. "When they shift to the west, they'd turn this place into a wind tunnel. Perhaps the ship had engine trouble at the time."

They fell silent as the hulk drew nearer. Despite the brilliant clarity of the morning sun, the ship remained oddly out of focus, as if surrounded in its own cloak of mist. The vessel was coated, stem to stern, in a fur of rust and decay. Its iron towers were broken, one hanging off the side and caught among heavy chains, the other lying in a tangle on the deck. No birds perched on its rotting superstructure. Even the waves seemed to avoid its scabrous sides. It was spectral, surreal: a cadaverous sentinel, giving mute warning to all who passed.

"Somebody ought to speak to Puerto Williams Chamber of Commerce about that," McFarlane said. The joke was greeted without laughter. A chill seemed to have fallen on the group.

The pilot throttled up, as if eager to be past the wreck, and they turned into the Beagle Channel. Here, knife-edged mountains rose from the water, dark and forbidding, snowfields and glaciers winking in their folds. The boat was buffeted by a gust of wind, and McFarlane pulled his parka tighter around him.

"To the right is Argentina," Glinn said. "To the left, Chile."

"And I'm heading inside," said Britton, turning toward the pilothouse.

An hour later, Puerto Williams rose out of the gray light off the port bow: a collection of shabby wooden buildings, yellow with red roofs, nestled in a bowl between hills. Behind it rose a range of hyperborean mountains, white and sharp as teeth. At the foot of the town stood a row of decaying piers. Wooden draggers and single-masted gaff sloops with tarred hulls were moored in the harbor. Nearby, McFarlane could see the Barrio de los Indios: a crooked assortment of planked houses and damp huts, tendrils of smoke rising from makeshift chimneys. Beyond them lay the naval station itself, a forlorn row of corrugated metal buildings. What looked like two naval tenders and an old destroyer were moored nearby.

Within the space of a few minutes, it seemed, the bright morning sky had darkened. As the launch pulled up to one of the wooden piers, a smell of rotting fish, shot through with odors of sewage and seaweed, washed over them. Several men appeared from nearby huts and came shambling down gangplanks. Shouting and gesturing, they tried to entice the launch to land at any of half a dozen places, each holding up a hawser or pointing at a cleat. The boat slid into the dock and a loud argument ensued between the two nearest men, quieted only when Glinn passed out cigarettes.

The three climbed out on the slippery dock and looked up at the dismal town. Stray flakes of snow dusted the shoulders of McFarlane's parka.

"Where is the office of customs?" Glinn asked one of the men in Spanish.

"I will take you there," said three simultaneously. Now women were arriving, crowding around with plastic buckets full of sea urchins, mussels, and *congrio colorado*, jostling one another aside and shoving the ripe shellfish into their faces.

"Sea urchin," said one woman in broken English. She had the wizened face of a septuagenarian and sported a single, remarkably white tooth. "Very good for man. Make hard. *Muy fuerte*." She gestured with a stiff upraised arm to indicate its results, while the men roared with laughter.

"No gracias señora," Glinn said, shoving his way through the crowd to follow his self-appointed guides.

The men led the way up the pier and along the waterfront in the direction of the naval station. Here, beside another pier only slightly less shabby, they stopped at a low planked building. Light streamed from its sole window into the darkening air, and the fragrant smoke of a wood fire billowed from a tin pipe in the far wall. A faded Chilean flag hung beside the door.

Glinn tipped their guides and pushed open the door, Britton following behind him. McFarlane came last. He took a deep breath of the ripe, chill air, reminding himself it was very unlikely anyone here would recognize him from the Atacama business.

The inside was what he expected: the scarred table, the potbellied stove, the dark-eyed official. Walking voluntarily into a Chilean government office—even one as remote and provincial as this—made him nervous. His eyes strayed involuntarily to the tattered-looking sheaf of wanted posters hanging from a wall by a rusted metal clamp. *Cool it,* he told himself.

The customs official had carefully slicked-back hair and an immaculate uniform. He smiled at them, revealing an expanse of gold teeth. "Please," he said in Spanish. "Sit down." He had a soft, effeminate voice. The man radiated a kind well-being that seemed extravagantly out of place in such a forlorn outpost.

From a back room of the customs office, voices that had been raised in argument were suddenly hushed. McFarlane waited for Glinn and Britton to sit down, then followed their lead, lowering himself gingerly into a scuffed wooden chair. The potbellied stove crackled, giving off a wonderful glow of heat.

"Por favor," the official said, pushing a cedar box full of cigarettes at them. Everyone declined except Glinn, who took two. He stuck one between his lips and popped the other into his pocket. "Mas tarde," he said with a grin.

The man leaned across the table and lit Glinn's cigarette with a gold lighter. Glinn took a deep drag on the unfiltered cigarette, then leaned over to spit a small piece of tobacco off his tongue. McFarlane glanced from him to Britton.

"Welcome to Chile," the official said in English, turning the lighter over in his delicate hands before slipping it back in his jacket pocket. Then he switched back to Spanish. "You are from the American mining ship *Rolvaag,* of course?"

"Yes," said Britton, also in Spanish. With seeming carelessness, she slipped some papers and a wad of passports out of a battered leather portfolio.

"Looking for iron?" the man asked with a smile.

Glinn nodded.

"And you expect to find this iron on Isla Desolación?" His smile held a touch of cynicism, McFarlane thought. Or was it suspicion?

"Of course," Glinn answered quickly, after stifling a wet cough. "We are equipped with all the latest mining equipment and a fine ore carrier. This is a highly professional operation."

The slightly amused expression on the official's face indicated that he had already received information about the big rust bucket parked beyond the channel. He drew the papers toward him and flipped through them casually. "It will take some time to process these," he said. "We will probably want to visit your ship. Where is the captain?"

"I am the master of the *Rolvaag*," said Britton.

At this the official's eyebrows shot up. There was a shuffling of feet from the back room of the customs house, and two more officials of indistinct rank came through the door. Heading to the stove, they sat down on a bench beside it.

"*You* are the captain," the official said.

"Sí."

The official grunted, looked down at the papers, casually leafed through them, and looked up at her again. "And you, señor?" he asked, swiveling his gaze to McFarlane.

Glinn spoke. "This is Dr. Widmanstätten, senior scientist. He speaks no Spanish. I am the chief engineer, Eli Ishmael."

McFarlane felt the official's gaze linger on him. "Widmanstätten," the man repeated slowly, as if tasting the name. The two other officials turned to look at him.

McFarlane's mouth went dry. His face hadn't been in the Chilean newspapers for at least five years. And he'd had a beard at the time. *Nothing to worry about,* he told himself. Sweat began to form at his temples.

The Chileans stared at him curiously, as if detecting his agitation with some kind of professional sixth sense.

"No speak Spanish?" the official said to him. His eyes narrowed as he stared.

There was a brief silence. Then, involuntarily, McFarlane blurted out the first thing that came to mind: "Quiero una puta."

There was sudden laughter from the Chilean officials. "He speaks well enough," said the man behind the table. McFarlane sat back and licked his lips, exhaling slowly.

Glinn coughed again, a hideous racking cough. "Pardon me," he said, pulling out a grimy handkerchief, wiping his chin, scattering yellow phlegm with a savage shake, and returning it to his pocket.

The official glanced at the handkerchief, then rubbed his delicate hands together. "I hope you are not coming down with something in this damp climate of ours."

"It is nothing," said Glinn. McFarlane looked at him with growing alarm. The man's eyes were raw and bloodshot: he looked ill.

Britton coughed delicately into her hand. "A cold," she said. "It's been going around ship."

"A mere cold?" asked the official, his eyebrows assuming an uneasy arch.

"Well . . ." Britton paused. "Our sick bay is overflowing—"

"It's nothing serious," Glinn interrupted, his voice thready with mucus. "Perhaps a touch of influenza. You know what it is like on board ship, everyone confined to small spaces." He let out a laugh that devolved into another cough. "Speaking of that, we would be delighted to receive you aboard our vessel today or tomorrow, at your convenience."

"Perhaps that won't be necessary," said the official. "Provided these papers are in order." He leafed through them. "Where is your mining bond?"

With a mighty clearing of the throat, Glinn leaned over the desk and pulled an embossed, sealed set of papers from his jacket. Receiving them with the edges of his fingers, the official scanned the top sheet, then flipped to the next with a jerk of his wrist. He laid the sheets on the worn tabletop.

"I am desolated," he said with a sad shake of his head. "But this is the wrong form."

McFarlane saw the other two officials glance covertly at each other.

"It is?" asked Glinn.

There was a sudden change in the room; an air of tense expectation.

"You will need to bring the correct form from Punta Arenas," the official said. "At that time, I can stamp it approved. Until then, I will hold your passports for safekeeping."

"It *is* the correct form," said Britton, her voice taking a hard edge.

"Let me take care of this." Glinn spoke to her in English. "I think they want some money."

Britton flared. "What, they want a *bribe?*"

Glinn made a suppressing motion with one hand. "Easy."

McFarlane looked at the two, wondering if what he was seeing between them was real, or an act.

Glinn turned back to the customs official, whose face was wreathed in a false smile. "Perhaps," Glinn said in Spanish, "we could purchase the correct bond here?"

"It is a possibility," said the official. "They are expensive."

With a loud sniff, Glinn hefted his briefcase and laid it on the table. Despite its dirty, scuffed appearance, the officials glanced at it with ill-concealed anticipation. Glinn flicked open the latches and raised the top, pretending to hide its contents from the Chileans. Inside were more papers and a dozen bundles of American twenties, held together by rubber bands. Glinn removed half of the bundles and laid them on the table. "Will that take care of it?" he asked.

The official smiled and settled back in his chair, making a tent of his fingers. "I'm afraid not, señor. Mining bonds are expensive." His eyes were fastidiously averted from the open briefcase.

"How much, then?"

The official pretended to do a quick mental calculation. "Twice that amount should be sufficient."

There was a silence. Then, wordlessly, Glinn reached into the briefcase, removed the rest of the bundles, and placed them on the table.

To McFarlane, it was as if the tense atmosphere had suddenly dissipated. The official at the table gathered up the money. Britton looked annoyed but resigned. The two officials sitting on the bench beside the stove were smiling widely. The only exception was a new arrival; a striking figure who had slipped in from the back room at some point during the negotiation and was now standing in the doorway. He was a tall man with a brown face as sharp as a knife, keen black eyes, thick eyebrows, and pointed ears that gave him an intense, almost Mephistophelean aura. He wore a clean but faded Chilean naval uniform with a bit of gold thread on the shoulders. McFarlane noted that, while the man's left arm lay at his side with military rigidity, the right was held horizontally across his stomach, its atrophied hand curled into an involuntary brown comma. The man looked at the officials, at Glinn, at the money on the table, and his lips curled into a faint smile of contempt.

The stacks of money had now been gathered into four piles. "What about a receipt?" asked Britton.

"Unfortunately, that is not our way . . ." The customs official spread his hands with another smile. Moving back quickly, he slipped one of the piles of money into his desk, then handed two of the other piles to the men on the bench. "For safekeeping," he said to Glinn. Finally, the official picked up the remaining pile and offered it to the uniformed man. The man, who had been peering closely at McFarlane, crossed his good hand over the bad but made no gesture for the money. The official held it there for a moment, and then spoke to him in a rapid undertone.

"Nada," answered the uniformed man in a loud voice. Then he stepped forward and turned to the group, his eyes glittering with hatred. "You Americans think you can buy everything," he said in clear, uninflected English. "You cannot. I am not like these corrupt officials. Keep your money."

The customs official spoke sharply, waggling the wad of bills at him. "You *will* take it, fool."

There was a distinct click as Glinn carefully closed his briefcase.

"No," said the uniformed man, switching to Spanish. "This is a farce, and all of you know it. We are being robbed." He spat toward the stove. In the dread silence that followed, McFarlane clearly heard the smack and sizzle as the gobbet hit the hot iron.

"Robbed?" the official asked. "How do you mean?"

"You think Americans would come down here to mine iron?" the man said. "Then *you* are the fool. They are here for something else."

"Tell me, wise Comandante, why they are here."

"There is no iron ore on Isla Desolación. They can only be here for one thing. Gold."

After a pause, the official began to laugh—a low-throated, mirthless laugh. He turned to Glinn. "Gold?" he said, a little more sharply than before. "Is that why you are here? To steal gold from Chile?"

McFarlane glanced at Glinn. To his great dismay, he saw a look of guilt and naked fear writ large across Glinn's face; enough to arouse suspicion in even the dullest official.

"We are here to mine iron ore," Glinn said, in a singularly unconvincing way.

"I must inform you that a *gold* mining bond will be much more expensive," said the official.

"But we are here to mine iron ore."

"Come, come," said the official. "Let us speak frankly to each other and not create unnecessary trouble. This story of *iron* . . ." He smiled knowingly.

There was a long, expectant silence. Then Glinn broke it with another cough. "Under the circumstances, perhaps a royalty might be in order. Provided that all paperwork is taken care of expeditiously."

The official waited. Again Glinn opened the briefcase. He removed the papers and placed them in his pocket. Then he ran his hands across the base of the now-empty briefcase, as if searching for something. There was a muffled click and a false bottom sprang loose. A yellow radiance emerged, reflecting off the official's surprised face.

"Madre de dios," the man whispered.

"This is for you—and your associates—now," said Glinn. "On our disembarkation, when we clear customs—*if* all has gone well—you will receive twice that amount. Of course, if false rumors of a gold strike on Isla Desolación get back to Punta Arenas, or if we receive unwelcome visitors, we won't be able to complete our mining operation. You will receive nothing more." He sneezed unexpectedly, spraying the back of the case with saliva.

The official hastily shut it. "Yes, yes. Everything will be taken care of."

The Chilean comandante responded savagely. "Look at the lot of you, like dogs sniffing around a bitch in heat."

The two officials rose from the bench and approached him, murmuring urgently and gesturing toward the briefcase. But the comandante broke free. "I am ashamed to be in the same room. You would sell your own mothers."

The customs official turned in his seat and stared behind him. "I think you had better return to your vessel, Comandante Vallenar," he said icily.

The uniformed man glared at each person in the room in turn. Then, erect and silent, he walked around the table and out the door, leaving it to bang in the wind.

"What of him?" Glinn asked.

"You must forgive Comandante Vallenar," the official said, reaching into another drawer and pulling out some papers and an official stamp. He inked the stamp, then quickly impressed the papers, seemingly anxious to have the visitors gone. "He is an idealist in a land of pragmatists. But he is nothing. There will be no rumors, no interruption of your work. You have my word." He handed the papers and the passports back across the desk.

Glinn took them and turned to go, then hesitated. "One other thing. We have hired a man named John Puppup. Do you have any idea where we might find him?"

"Puppup?" The official was clearly startled. "That old man? Whatever for?"

"It was represented to us that he has an intimate knowledge of the Cape Horn islands."

"I cannot imagine who told you such a thing. Unfortunately for you, he received money from somewhere a few days ago. And that means only one thing. I would try El Picoroco first. On Callejon Barranca." The official rose, flashing his gilded smile. "I wish you luck finding *iron* on Isla Desolación."

Puerto Williams, 11:45 A.M.

Leaving the customs office, they turned inland and began climbing the hill toward the Barrio de los Indios. The graded dirt road quickly gave way to a mixture of snow and icy mud. Wooden corduroys had been placed stairwise along the makeshift track to hold back erosion. The small houses lining the path were a ragtag assortment made with unmatched lumber, surrounded by crude wooden fences. A group of children followed the strangers, giggling and pointing. A donkey carrying an enormous faggot of wood passed them on the way downhill, almost jostling McFarlane into a puddle. He regained his balance with a backward curse.

"Exactly how much of that little dog-and-pony show was planned?" he asked Glinn in a low tone.

"All except for Comandante Vallenar. And your little outburst. Unscripted, but successful."

"Successful? Now they think we're illegally mining gold. I would call it a disaster."

Glinn smiled indulgently. "It couldn't have gone better. If they gave it some thought, they would never believe that an American company would send an ore carrier to the ends of the earth to mine iron. Comandante Vallenar's flare-up was well timed. It saved me from having to plant the idea in their heads myself."

McFarlane shook his head. "Think of the rumors it will start."

"There already are rumors. The amount of gold we gave them will shut them up for life. Now our good customs people are going to scotch those rumors and order the island out of bounds. They're much more suited for the job than we are. And they have excellent incentive to do it."

"What about that comandante?" asked Britton. "He didn't look like he was getting with the program."

"Not everyone can be bribed. Fortunately, he has no power or credibility. The only naval officers who end up down here are the ones that have been convicted of crimes or disgraced in one way or another. Those customs officials will be extremely anxious to keep him in line. That will undoubtedly mean a payoff to the commanding officer of the naval base. We gave those officials more than enough to go around." Glinn pursed his lips. "Still, we should learn a little more about this Comandante Vallenar."

They stepped over a runnel of soapy water as the grade lessened. Glinn asked directions of a passerby, and they turned off into a narrow side street. A dirty noon mist was settling on the village, and along with it came a hard freezing of the damp air. A dead mastiff lay swollen in the gutter. McFarlane breathed in the smell of fish and raw earth, noticed the flimsy wooden tienda advertising Fanta and local beers, and was irresistibly brought back five years in time. After twice trying unsuccessfully to cross into Argentina, burdened by the Atacama tektites, he and Nestor Masangkay had ended up crossing into Bolivia near the town of Ancuaque: so unlike this town in appearance, and yet so like in spirit.

Glinn came to a halt. At the end of the alley before them was a sagging, red-shingled building. A blue bulb blinked above a sign that read EL PICOROCO. CERVEZA MAS FINA. From an open door beneath, the faint throb of ranchera music spilled into the street.

"I think I'm beginning to understand some of your methods," said McFarlane. "What was that the customs man said about somebody sending Puppup money? Was that you, by any chance?"

Glinn inclined his head but did not speak.

"I think I'll wait out here," said Britton.

McFarlane followed Glinn past the door and into a dim space. He saw a scuffed bar made out of deal, several wooden tables covered with bottle rings, and an English dartboard, its numbers faded. The smoke-laden air tasted as if it had hung there for years. The bartender straightened up as they walked in, and the level of conversation dropped as the few patrons turned to stare at the newcomers.

Glinn sidled up the bar and ordered two beers. The bartender brought them over, warm and dripping with foam.

"We are looking for Señor Puppup," said Glinn.

"Puppup?" The bartender broke into a broad, scant-toothed grin. "He is in the back."

They followed the man through a beaded curtain, into a little snug with a private table and an empty bottle of Dewar's. Stretched out on a bench along the wall was a skinny old man in indescribably dirty clothes. A pair of wispy Fu Manchu–style mustaches drooped from his upper lip and chin. A thrumcap that looked like it had been sewn together from bits of old rags had slid from his head to the bench.

"Sleeping or drunk?" asked Glinn.

The bartender roared with laughter. "Both."

"When will he be sober?"

The man leaned down, rummaged through Puppup's pockets, and pulled out a small wad of dirty bills. He counted them, then shoved them back.

"He will be sober on Tuesday next."

"But he has been hired by our vessel."

The bartender laughed again, more cynically.

Glinn thought a moment, or at least gave the appearance of doing so. "We have orders to bring him on board. May I trouble you for the hire of two of your customers to help us?"

The bartender nodded and walked back to the bar, returning with two burly men. A few words were spoken, money was exchanged, and the two lifted Puppup from the bench and slung his arms around their shoulders. His head lolled forward. In their grasp, he looked as light and fragile as a dry leaf.

McFarlane took a deep, grateful breath of air as they stepped outside. It stank, but it was better than the stale atmosphere of the bar. Britton, who had been standing in the shadows on a far corner, came forward. Her eyes narrowed at the sight of Puppup.

"He's not much to look at now," Glinn said. "But he'll make an excellent harbor pilot. He's been traversing the waters of the Cape Horn islands by canoe for fifty years; he knows all the currents, winds, weather, reefs, and tides."

Britton raised her eyebrows. "This old man?"

Glinn nodded. "As I told Lloyd this morning, he's half Yaghan. They were the original inhabitants of the Cape Horn islands. He's practically the last one left who knows the language, songs, and legends. He spends most of his time roaming the islands, living off shellfish, plants, and roots. If you asked him, he'd probably tell you the Cape Horn islands are his."

"How picturesque," said McFarlane.

Glinn turned to McFarlane. "Yes. And he also happens to be the one who found your partner's body."

McFarlane stopped dead.

"That's right," Glinn continued in an undertone. "He's the one who collected the tomographic sounder and the rock samples and sold them in Punta Arenas. On top of everything else, his *absence* in Puerto Williams will be most helpful to us. Now that we have attracted attention to Isla Desolación, he won't be around to gossip and spread rumor."

McFarlane looked again at the drunk. "So he's the bastard who robbed my partner."

Glinn laid a hand on McFarlane's arm. "He's extremely poor. He found a dead man with some valuable things. It's understandable, and forgivable, that he'd look to make a small profit. There was no harm in it. If not for him, your old friend might still be lying undiscovered. And you would not have the opportunity to finish his work."

McFarlane pulled away, even as he was forced to admit to himself that Glinn was right.

"He will be most useful to us," Glinn said. "I can promise you that."

Silently McFarlane followed the group as they made their way down the murky hillside toward the harbor.

Rolvaag, 2:50 P.M.

By the time the launch exited the Beagle Channel and approached the *Rolvaag*, a heavy, bitter fog had enveloped the sea. The small group remained inside the wheelhouse, huddled on flotation cushions, barely speaking. Puppup, who was propped upright between Glinn and Sally Britton, showed no signs of regaining consciousness. However, several times he had to be prevented from nodding to one side and snuggling himself against the captain's pea coat.

"Is he shamming?" the captain asked, as she plucked the old man's frail-looking hand from her lapel and gently pushed him away.

Glinn smiled. McFarlane noticed that the cigarettes, the racking cough, the rheumy eyes had all vanished; the cool presence had returned.

Ahead, the ghostly outline of the tanker now appeared above the heavy swell, its sides rising, rising above them, only to disappear again into the soupy atmosphere. The launch came alongside and was hoisted into its davits. As they went aboard, Puppup began to stir. McFarlane helped him shakily to his feet in the swirling fog. *Couldn't weigh more than ninety pounds*, he thought.

"John Puppup?" Glinn said in his mild voice. "I am Eli Glinn."

Puppup took his hand and gave it a silent shake. He then

solemnly shook hands with everyone else around him, including the launch tender, a steward, and two surprised deckhands. He shook the captain's hand last and longest of all.

"Are you all right?" Glinn asked.

The man looked around with bright black eyes, stroking his thin mustache. He seemed to be neither surprised nor perturbed by the strange surroundings.

"Mr. Puppup, you're probably wondering what you're doing here."

Puppup's hand suddenly dove into his pocket and removed the wad of soiled money; he counted it, grunted with satisfaction that he hadn't been robbed, and replaced it.

Glinn gestured toward the steward. "Mr. Davies here will see you to your cabin, where you can get washed up and put on a fresh change of clothes. Does that suit you?"

Puppup looked at Glinn curiously.

"Maybe he doesn't speak English," McFarlane murmured.

Puppup's eyes swiftly fixed on him. "Speaks the king's own, I does." His voice was high and melodious, and through it McFarlane heard a complex fugue of accents, Cockney English strongly predominating.

"I'll be happy to answer all your questions once you've had a chance to settle in," Glinn said. "We will meet in the library tomorrow morning." He nodded to Davies.

Without another word, Puppup turned away. All eyes followed him as the steward led the way into the rear superstructure.

Overhead, the ship's blower rasped into life. "Captain to the bridge," came the metallic voice of Victor Howell.

"What's up?" McFarlane asked.

Britton shook her head. "Let's find out."

The bridge looked out into an all-enveloping cloud of gray. Nothing, not even the deck of the ship, was visible. As he stepped through the door, McFarlane caught the tense atmosphere within. Instead of the normal skeleton complement, there were half a dozen ship's officers on the bridge. From the radio room, he could hear the high-speed clatter of a computer keyboard.

"What do we have, Mr. Howell?" Britton asked calmly.

Howell looked up from a nearby screen. "Radar contact."

"Who is it?" McFarlane asked.

"Unknown. They're not responding to our hails. Given its speed and radar cross-section, it's probably a gunboat." He peered back, throwing some switches. "Too far to get a good look on the FLIR."

"Where away?" Britton asked.

"They seem to be circling, as if searching for something. Wait a moment, the course has steadied. Eight miles, bearing one six zero true, and closing. The ESM's picking up radar. We're being painted."

The captain joined him quickly and peered into the radar hood. "They're CBDR. Estimated time to CPA?"

"Twelve minutes, at current speed and heading."

"What does all that alphabet soup mean?" McFarlane asked.

Britton glanced at him. "CBDR—constant bearing and decreasing range."

"Collision course," Howell murmured.

Britton turned to the third officer, who was manning the command station. "Are we under way?"

The officer nodded. "Steam's up, ma'am. We're on dynamic positioning."

"Tell the engine room to goose it."

"Aye, aye." The officer picked up a black-handled telephone.

There was a low shudder as the ship's engines revved. Anticollision alarms began to sound.

"Taking evasive action?" McFarlane asked.

Britton shook her head. "We're too big for that, even with engine steering. But we're going to give it a shot."

From far above on the radar mast, the ship's foghorn gave a deafening blast.

"Course unchanged," Howell said, head glued to the radar hood.

"Helm's answering," said the third officer.

"Rudder amidships." Britton walked toward the radio room and opened the gray metal door. "Any luck, Banks?"

"No response."

McFarlane walked to the forward bank of windows. The line of wipers was clearing the film of mist and sleet that seemed to constantly renew itself. Sunlight struggled to break through the heavy gauze beyond. "Can't they hear us?" he asked.

"Of course they can," Glinn said quietly. "They know perfectly well we're here."

"Course unchanged," Howell murmured, peering into the radar hood. "Collision in nine minutes."

"Fire flares in the direction of the ship," Britton said, back at the command station.

Howell relayed the order, and Britton turned to the watch officer. "How's she steer?"

"Like a pig, ma'am, at this speed."

McFarlane could feel a heavy strain shuddering through the ship.

"Five minutes and closing," Howell said.

"Fire some more flares. Fire them *at* the ship. Put me on ICM frequency." Britton picked up a transmitter from the command station. "Unidentified vessel three thousand yards off my port quarter, this is the tanker *Rolvaag*. Change your course twenty degrees to starboard to avoid collision. Repeat, change your course twenty degrees to starboard." She repeated the message in Spanish, then turned up the gain on the receiver. The entire bridge listened silently to the wash of static.

Britton replaced the transmitter. She looked at the helmsman, then at Howell.

"Three minutes to collision," Howell said.

She spoke into the blower. "All hands, this is the master speaking. Prepare for collision at the starboard bow."

The foghorn ripped once again through the thinning veils of mist. A claxon was going off, and lights were blinking on the bridge.

"Coming up on the starboard bow," Howell said.

"Get damage and fire control ready," Britton replied. Then she pulled a bullhorn from the bulkhead, raced toward the door leading onto the starboard bridge wing, tore it open, and vanished outside. As if at a single thought, Glinn and McFarlane followed.

The moment he stepped outside, McFarlane was soaked by the frigid, heavy haze. Below, he could hear confused sounds of running and shouting. The foghorn, even louder here on the exposed deck, seemed to atomize the thick air that surrounded them. Britton had run to the far end of the wing and was leaning over the railing, suspended a hundred feet above the sea, bullhorn poised.

The fog was beginning to break up, streaming across the maindeck. But off the starboard bow, it seemed to McFarlane that the mist was thickening, growing darker again. Suddenly, a forest of antennas solidified out of the gloom, forward anchor lights glowing dull red and green. The foghorn once again blasted its warning, but the vessel came unrelentingly toward them at full speed, a creamy, snarling wake of foam cutting across its gray bows. Its outlines became clearer. It was a destroyer, its sides pitted and scarred and streaked with rust. Chilean flags fluttered from its superstructure and fantail. Four-inch guns, stubby and evil-looking, sat in housings on the fore and aft decks.

Britton was screaming into the bullhorn. Collision alarms sounded, and McFarlane could feel the bridge wing shaking beneath him as the engines tried to pull away. But it was impossible to turn the big ship quickly enough. He planted his feet, grasping the railing, preparing for impact.

At the last moment, the destroyer sheered to port and cut its power, gliding past the tanker with no more than twenty yards to spare. Britton lowered the bullhorn. All eyes followed the smaller vessel.

Every gun of the destroyer—from the big deck turrets to the 40-millimeter cannon—was trained on the bridge of the *Rolvaag*. McFarlane stared at the ship in mingled perplexity and horror. And then his eyes fell on the destroyer's flying bridge.

Standing alone, in full uniform, was the naval comandante they had met that morning in customs. Wind tugged at the gold bars on his officer's cap. He was passing so close beneath them that McFarlane could see the beads of moisture on his face.

Vallenar paid them no mind. He was leaning against a .50-caliber machine gun mounted to the rail, but it was a posture of false ease. The barrel of the gun, its perforated snout heavy with sea salt and rust, was aimed directly at them, an insolent promise of death. His black eyes skewered them one at a time. His withered arm was clutched against his chest at a precise angle to his body. The man's gaze never wavered, and as the destroyer slid by, both he and the machine gun rotated slowly, keeping them in view.

And then the destroyer fell astern of the *Rolvaag*, slipping back into the mist, and the specter was gone. In the chill silence that remained, McFarlane heard the destroyer's engines rumble up to full speed once again, and felt the faintest sensation of rocking as its wake passed beneath the tanker. It had the gentle up-and-down motion of a baby's cradle, and, if it had not been terrifying, would have been distinctly comforting.

Rolvaag,
July 13, 6:30 A.M.

McFarlane stirred in the predawn darkness of his stateroom. The bedsheets were twisted around him in a cyclone of linen, and the pillow beneath his head was heavy with sweat. He rolled over, still half asleep, instinctively reaching for Malou's comforting warmth. But save for himself, the bed was empty.

He sat up and waited for his pounding heart to find its normal rhythm as the disconnected images of a nightmare—a ship, tossed on a stormy sea—receded from his mind. As he passed a hand across his eyes, he realized that not everything had been a dream: the motion of the water was still with him. The ship's movement had changed; instead of the usual gentle roll, it felt shuddery and rough. Throwing aside the sheets, he walked to the window and pulled the curtain back. Sleet splattered against the Plexiglas, and there was a thick coating of ice along its lower edge.

The dark set of rooms seemed oppressive and he dressed hurriedly, eager for fresh air despite the nasty conditions. As he trotted down the two flights of stairs to the maindeck, the ship rolled and he was forced to steady himself on the railing for support.

As he opened the door leading out of the superstructure a blast of icy wind buffeted his face. It was bracing, and it drove the last vestiges of the nightmare from his mind. In the half-light he could see the windward vents, davits, and containers plastered with ice, the deck awash in slush. McFarlane could now hear clearly the boom of a heavy sea running the length of the ship. Out here, the roll of the vessel was more pronounced. The dark, moiling seas were periodically whitened with great combing waves, the faint hiss of the breaking water coming to his ears over the moaning of the wind.

Someone was leaning up against the starboard railing, head sunk forward. As he approached, he saw it was Amira, bundled once again in the ridiculously oversized parka.

"What are you doing here?" he asked.

She turned toward him. Deep within the furred hood of the parka, he made out a green-tinged face. A few tendrils of black hair escaped, whipped back by the wind.

"Trying to puke," she said. "What's your excuse?"

"Couldn't sleep."

Amira nodded. "I'm hoping that destroyer comes by again. I'd like nothing better than to unload the contents of my stomach on that ugly little comandante."

McFarlane did not answer. The encounter with the Chilean vessel, and speculation about Comandante Vallenar and his motives, had dominated dinner-table talk the previous night. And Lloyd, when he heard of the incident, had become frantic. Only Glinn seemed unconcerned.

"Will you look at this?" Amira said. Following her gaze, McFarlane saw the dark form of a jogger, clad only in gray warm-ups, making its way along the port rail. As he stared, he realized it was Sally Britton.

"Only *she* would be man enough to go jogging in this weather," Amira said sourly.

"She's pretty tough."

"More like crazy." Amira snickered. "Look at that sweatshirt bouncing around."

McFarlane, who had been looking at it, said nothing.

"Don't get me wrong. I take a purely scientific interest. I'm thinking how one would calculate an equation of state for those rather impressive breasts."

"An equation of state?"

"It's something we physicists do. It relates all the physical properties of an object—temperature, pressure, density, elasticity—"

"I get the picture."

"Look," Amira said, abruptly changing the subject. "There's another wreck."

In the bleak winter distance, McFarlane could see the outline of a large ship, its back broken on a rock.

"What is that, four?" Amira asked.

"Five, I think." As the *Rolvaag* headed south from Puerto Williams toward Cape Horn, the sightings of giant shipwrecks had grown more frequent. Some were almost as large as the *Rolvaag*. The area was a veritable graveyard of shipping, and the sight no longer brought any surprise.

Britton had by now rounded the bow and was heading in their direction.

"Here she comes," said Amira.

As Britton drew up to them, she slowed, jogging in place. Britton's warm-up suit was damp with sleet and rain, and it clung to her body. *Equation of state*, McFarlane thought to himself.

"I wanted to let you know that, at nine o'clock, I'm going to issue a deck safety-harness order," she said.

"Why's that?" McFarlane asked.

"A squall is coming."

"Coming?" Amira said with a bleak laugh. "It looks like it's already here."

"As we head out of the lee of Isla Navarino, we're going to be heading into a gale. Nobody will be allowed on deck without a harness." Britton had answered Amira's question, but she was looking at McFarlane.

"Thanks for the warning," McFarlane said. Britton nodded to him, then jogged away. In a minute she was gone.

"What is it you have against her?" McFarlane said.

Amira was silent a moment. "Something about Britton bugs me. She's too perfect."

"I think that's what they call an air of command."

"And it seemed so unfair, the whole ship suffering because of her booze problem."

"It was Glinn's decision," said McFarlane.

After a moment, Amira sighed and shook her head. "Yeah, that's vintage Eli, isn't it? You can bet there's an unbroken line of impeccable logic leading up to that decision. He just hasn't told anybody what it is."

McFarlane shivered under a fresh blast of wind. "Well, I've had enough sea air to last awhile. Shall we get some breakfast?"

Amira let out a groan. "You go ahead, I'll wait here awhile longer. Sooner or later, something's bound to come up."

After breakfast, McFarlane headed to the ship's library, where Glinn had asked to meet him. The library, like everything about the vessel, was large. Windows, streaked with sleet, covered one wall. Beyond and far below, he could see snow driving almost horizontally, whirling into the black water.

The shelves contained a wide assortment of books: nautical texts and treatises, encyclopedias, *Reader's Digest* condensations, forgotten best-sellers. He browsed through them, waiting for Glinn, feeling unsettled. The closer they got to Isla Desolación—to the spot where Masangkay died—the more restless he became. They were very close now. Today, they would round the Horn and anchor in the Horn Islands at last.

McFarlane's fingers stopped at the slender volume: *The Narrative of Arthur Gordon Pym of Nantucket*. This was the Edgar Allan Poe title Britton mentioned at dinner that first night at sea. Curious, he took it to the nearest sofa. The dark leather felt slippery as he settled into it and cracked the book. The pleasant smell of buckram and old paper rose to his nostrils.

My name is Arthur Gordon Pym. My father was a respectable trader in sea stores at Nantucket, where I was born. My maternal grandfather was an attorney in good practice. He was fortunate in everything, and had speculated very successfully in stocks of the Edgarton New-Bank, as it was formerly called.

This was a disappointingly dry beginning, and it was with relief that he saw the door open and Glinn enter. Behind him followed Puppup, ducking and smiling, barely recognizable from the drunk they had brought on board the previous afternoon. His long gray hair was braided back from his forehead, and the neatly groomed but still wispy mustache drooped from his pendulous lip.

"Sorry to have kept you waiting," Glinn said. "I've been speaking to Mr. Puppup. He seems content to assist us."

Puppup grinned and shook hands all around again. McFarlane found his hand curiously cool and dry.

"Come to the windows," Glinn said. McFarlane strolled over and gazed out. Through the torn and roiling mists he could now make out, to the northeast, a barren island rising from the water, little more than the jagged top of a drowned mountain, white surf clawing and leaping at its base.

"That," murmured Glinn, "is Isla Barnevelt."

A distant squall line passed, like the drawing of a curtain from the storm-wracked horizon. Another island came into view: black, rugged, its mountainous heights whirling with snow and fog.

"And that is Isla Deceit. The easternmost of the Cape Horn islands."

Beyond it, the fresh light exposed another wilderness of drowned mountaintops poking from the sea. As they watched, the light was extinguished as quickly as it had come. Midnight seemed to close around the vessel, and another squall struck them full on, its fury battering the windows, hail rattling off the ship like machine gun fire. McFarlane felt the big ship lean.

Glinn withdrew a folded piece of paper. "I received this message half an hour ago." He handed it to McFarlane.

McFarlane unfolded it curiously. It was a brief cable: *On no account are you to make landfall on the target island without further instructions from me. Lloyd.*

McFarlane handed it back to Glinn, who returned it to his pocket. "Lloyd's told me nothing about his plans. What do you think it means? And why not simply telephone or e-mail?"

"Because he may not be near a telephone." Glinn drew himself up. "The view from the bridge is even nicer. Care to come along?"

Somehow, McFarlane did not think the EES head was interested in the view. He followed. Glinn was correct, however: from the bridge, the fury of the seas was even more awe-inspiring. Angry black waves broke and fought among themselves, and the wind worried at their tops and ran deep runnels through their troughs. As McFarlane watched, the *Rolvaag*'s forecastle nodded downward into a massive sea, then struggled up again, sheets of seawater cascading from its flanks.

Britton turned toward them, her face spectral in the artificial glow. "I see you've brought the pilot," she said, glancing a little dubiously toward Puppup. "Once we round the Horn, we'll see what advice he can give us for the approach."

At her side, Victor Howell stirred. "There it is now," he said. Far ahead of the ship, a break in the storm threw a gleam of light upon a fissured crag, taller and darker than the others, rising from the frantic seas.

"Cabo de Hornos," said Glinn. "Cape Horn. But I've come about something else. We should expect a visitor momentarily—"

"Captain!" the third officer interrupted, bent over a screen. "The Slick 32 is picking up radar. I've got an air contact, approaching from the northeast."

"Bearing?"

"Zero four zero true, ma'am. Directly for us."

The air on the bridge grew tense. Victor Howell walked quickly to the third officer and peered over his shoulder at the screen.

"Range and speed?" Britton asked.

"Forty miles, and approaching at about one hundred and seventy knots, ma'am."

"Reconnaissance aircraft?"

Howell straightened up. "In this weather?"

A wild gust of wind sent rain rattling against the windows.

"Well, it sure isn't some hobbyist in a Cessna," Britton murmured. "Could it be a commercial aircraft, straying off course?"

"Unlikely. The only things that fly down here are chartered puddle-jumpers. And they'd never be up in something like this."

"Military?"

Nobody answered. Except for the howl of the wind and the crash of the sea, the bridge remained completely silent for the space of a minute.

"Bearing?" the captain asked again, more quietly.

"Still dead on, ma'am."

She nodded slowly. "Very well. Sound stations, Mr. Howell."

Suddenly, the communications officer, Banks, leaned out of the radio room. "That bird out there? It's a Lloyd Holdings helicopter."

"Are you sure?" Britton asked.

"I've verified the call sign."

"Mr. Banks, contact that chopper."

Glinn cleared his throat. As McFarlane watched, he replaced the folded sheet into his jacket. Throughout the sudden excitement he had shown neither alarm nor surprise. "I think," he said quietly, "you had better prepare a landing area."

The captain stared at him. "In this weather?"

Banks stepped back out of the radio room. "They're requesting permission to land, ma'am."

"I don't believe it," Howell cried. "We're in the middle of a Force 8 gale."

"I don't believe you have a choice," Glinn said.

Over the next ten minutes, there was an explosion of activity as preparations were made for a landing. When McFarlane arrived at the hatchway leading out onto the fantail, Glinn at his side, a stern-looking crewman wordlessly issued them safety harnesses. McFarlane tugged the bulky thing on and snapped it into place. The crewman gave it a quick tug, grunted his approval, then undogged the hatch.

As McFarlane stepped through, the blast of wind threatened to carry him over the railing. With an effort, he snapped his harness to the external railing and moved toward the landing pad. Crewmen were stationed along the deck, their harnesses securely strapped to the metal railings. Even though the ship had throttled back her engines to just enough power to claw a steerageway through the seas, the deck pitched. A dozen flares were snapped on and placed around the perimeter, fitful sprays of crimson against the driving sleet and snow.

"There it is!" somebody cried.

McFarlane squinted into the storm. In the distance, the huge form of a Chinook helicopter hung in the air, running lights glowing. As he watched, the helicopter approached, yawing from left to right as gusts of wind hit it. An alarm suddenly screamed nearby, and a series of orange warning lights lit up the *Rolvaag*'s superstructure. McFarlane could hear the beat of the chopper's engines straining against the fury of the storm. Howell shouted directions through a bullhorn even as he kept the radio plastered to his face.

Now the chopper was banking into hover position. McFarlane could see the pilot in the nose, struggling with the controls. The sleet pelted them with the redoubled blast from the blades. The chopper's belly bucked from side to side as it gingerly approached the swaying deck. A violent gust sent it shearing to one side, and the pilot quickly banked away, coming around for a second attempt. There was a desperate moment where McFarlane felt sure the pilot would lose control, but then its tires settled onto the pad and crewmen rushed to place wooden chocks beneath its wheels. The cargo door rolled open. A flurry of men, women, machines, and equipment tumbled out.

And then McFarlane saw the unmistakable figure of Lloyd drop to the wet surface of the pad, larger than life in foul-weather gear and boots. He jogged from the underside of the aircraft, the sou'wester on his head whipping back in the storm. Catching sight of McFarlane and Glinn, he gave an enthusiastic wave. A crewman raced to secure a safety belt and harness to him, but Lloyd motioned him away. He walked up, wiping the rain from his face, and grasped McFarlane and Glinn by the hands.

"Gentlemen," he boomed over the storm, a huge smile on his face. "The coffee's on me."

Rolvaag,
11:15 A.M.

Glancing at his watch, McFarlane entered the elevator and punched a button for the middle bridge deck. He'd passed this empty deck many times, wondering why Glinn had always kept it off-limits. Now, as the elevator rose smoothly, he realized what it had been reserved for. It was as if Glinn had known all along that Lloyd would be dropping in.

The elevator doors opened to a scene of frantic activity: the ringing of phones, the whirr of faxes and printers, and the bustle of people. There were several secretaries at desks ranged along one wall, men and women taking calls, typing at workstations, scuttling about on Lloyd Holdings business.

A man in a light-colored suit approached him, threading his way through the hubbub. McFarlane recognized the oversized ears, drooping mouth, and fat pursed lips as belonging to Penfold, Lloyd's personal assistant. Penfold never seemed to walk toward anything, but instead approached from an angle, as if a direct approach would be too brazen.

"Dr. McFarlane?" Penfold said in his high, nervous voice. "This way, please."

He led McFarlane through a door, down a corridor, and into a small sitting room, with black leather sofas arranged around a glass- and gold-leafed table. A door opened into yet another office, and from it McFarlane could hear Lloyd's basso profundo voice.

"Please sit down," said Penfold. "Mr. Lloyd will be with you shortly." He vanished, and McFarlane settled back into the creaking leather sofa. There was a wall of television sets tuned to various news channels from around the world. The latest magazines lay on the table: *Scientific American*, the *New Yorker*, and the *New Republic*. McFarlane picked one up, began flipping through it absently, then put it down again. Why had Lloyd come down so abruptly? Had something gone wrong?

"Sam!" Looking up, he saw the huge man standing in the doorway, filling it with his bulk, radiating power, good humor, and boundless self-confidence.

McFarlane rose. Lloyd moved toward him, beaming, arms outstretched. "Sam, it's fine to see you again." He squeezed McFarlane's shoulders between his beefy palms and examined him, still gripping his shoulders. "I can't tell you how exciting it is to be here. Come in."

McFarlane followed Lloyd's broad back, beautifully draped in Valentino. Lloyd's inner office was spare: a row of windows, the cold light of the Antarctic regions flooding in, two simple wing chairs, a desk with a phone, a laptop computer—and two wineglasses beside a freshly opened bottle of Chateau Margaux.

Lloyd gestured at the wine. "Care for a glass?"

McFarlane grinned, and nodded. Lloyd poured the ruby liquid into a glass, filling another for himself. He settled his bulk into a chair, and held his glass up. "Cheers."

They clinked and McFarlane sipped the exquisite wine. He wasn't much of a connoisseur, but even the grossest palate could appreciate this.

"I hate Glinn's habit of keeping me in the dark," Lloyd said. "Why wasn't I told about this being a dry ship, Sam? Or about Britton's history? I can't fathom Glinn's thinking on this one. He should have briefed me back in Elizabeth. Thank God there's been no problem."

"She's an excellent captain," McFarlane said. "She's handled the ship with great skill. Knows it inside and out. Crew respects the hell out of her. Doesn't take guff from anybody, either."

Lloyd listened, frowning. "That's good to know." The phone buzzed. Lloyd picked it up. "Yes?" he said impatiently. "I'm in a meeting."

There was a pause while Lloyd listened. McFarlane watched him, thinking that what Lloyd had said about Glinn was true. Secretiveness was a habit with Glinn—or, perhaps, an instinct.

"I'll call the senator back," Lloyd said after a moment. "And no more calls." He strode over to the window and stood, hands clasped behind his back. Although the worst of the storm had passed, the panoramic windows remained streaked with sleet. "Magnificent," Lloyd breathed, something like reverence in his voice. "To think we'll be at the island within the hour. Christ, Sam, we're almost there!"

He swiveled away from the window. The frown was gone, replaced by a look of elation. "I've made a decision. Eli needs to hear it, too, but I wanted you to know first." He paused, exhaled. "I'm going to plant the flag, Sam."

McFarlane looked at Lloyd. "You're going to what?"

"This afternoon, I'm taking the launch to Isla Desolación."

"Just you?" McFarlane felt a strange sensation in the pit of his stomach.

"Just me. And that crazy old Puppup, of course, to guide me to the meteorite."

"But the weather—"

"The weather couldn't be better!" Lloyd stepped away from the windows and paced restlessly between the wing chairs. "This kind of moment, Sam, isn't given to many."

McFarlane sat in his chair, the strange feeling growing. "Just you?" he repeated. "You won't share the discovery?"

"No, I won't. Why the hell should I? Peary did the same thing on his last dash to the Pole. Glinn's got to understand. He may not like it, but it's my expedition. I'm going in alone."

"No," McFarlane said quietly. "No, you're not."

Lloyd stopped pacing.

"You're not leaving me behind."

Lloyd turned in surprise, his piercing eyes on McFarlane. "You?"

McFarlane said nothing, maintaining eye contact.

After a moment, Lloyd began to chuckle. "You know, Sam, you're not the man I first met hiding behind a bush in the Kalahari Desert. It never occurred to me you'd care about something like this." His smile suddenly vanished. "What would you do if I said no?"

McFarlane stood up. "I don't know. Something rash and ill-advised, probably."

Lloyd's whole frame seemed to swell. "Are you threatening me?"

McFarlane held his eyes. "Yeah. I guess I am."

Lloyd continued looking at him steadily. "Well, well."

"You sought me out. You knew what I'd dreamed of my entire life." McFarlane carefully watched Lloyd's expression. This was a man unused to being challenged. "I was out there trying to put the past behind me. And you arrived, *dangling* it, like a carrot on a stick. You knew I'd bite. And now I'm here, and you can't leave me out. I *won't* miss this."

There was a tense silence in which McFarlane could hear the distant clatter of keys, the ringing of phones. Then, abruptly, Lloyd's hard features softened. He placed a hand on his bald head and smoothed his shiny pate. Then he ran his fingers down through his goatee. "If I bring you, then what about Glinn? Or Amira? Or Britton? Everyone's going to want a piece of this."

"No. It'll be just us two. I've earned it; you've earned it. That's all. You have the power to make it happen."

Lloyd continued to stare at him. "I think I like the new Sam McFarlane," he said at last. "I never fully bought that tough-guy cynic act anyway. But I have to tell you, Sam: this interest of yours had better be healthy. Do I have to speak more plainly? I don't want a repeat of that Tornarssuk business."

McFarlane felt a stab of anger. "I'll just pretend I didn't hear that."

"You heard it. Let's not play coy."

McFarlane waited.

Lloyd dropped his hand with a deprecating smile. "It's been years since someone stood up to me like that. It's bracing. God damn you, Sam, all right. We'll do it together. But you realize Glinn's going to try to scotch everything." He walked back toward the bank of windows, checking his watch as he did so. "He's going to be an old woman about this."

As if he had timed the moment—and later, McFarlane realized he probably had—Glinn came gliding into the office. Behind followed Puppup, silent and wraithlike, rapidly becoming a fixture in Glinn's shadow, his alert black eyes filled with some private amusement. Puppup covered his mouth, bowing and genuflecting in the strangest fashion.

"Right on time, as always," Lloyd boomed, turning toward Glinn and taking his hand. "Listen, Eli, there's something I've decided. I'd like your blessing, but I know I'm not going to get it. So I want to warn you in advance, there's no power on heaven or earth that's going to prevent me from carrying it out. Is that clear?"

"Very clear," said Glinn, settling comfortably into one of the wing chairs and crossing his legs.

"There's no use arguing with me about this. The decision's made."

"Wonderful. I wish I could go along."

For an instant, Lloyd appeared to be dumbfounded. Then his look turned into fury. "You son of a bitch, you've got the ship wired."

"Don't be ridiculous. I knew from the very beginning you would insist on making the first visit to the meteorite."

"But that's impossible. Even *I* didn't know—"

Glinn waved his hand. "Don't you think that, in analyzing every possible path of failure and success, we had to take your psychological profile into account? We knew what you were going to do even before you knew yourself." He glanced at McFarlane. "Did Sam here insist on going along, too?"

Lloyd simply nodded.

"I see. The port stern launch will be your best bet. It's the smallest and most maneuverable. I've arranged for Mr. Howell to take you in. I've also ordered haversacks with food, water, matches, fuel, flashlights, and so forth—and, of course, a GPS unit and two-way radios. I assume you'll want Puppup to guide you?"

"Delighted to be of assistance," sung out Puppup.

Lloyd glanced from Glinn to Puppup and back again. After a moment, he gave a rueful chuckle. "Nobody likes to be predictable. Does anything surprise you?"

"You didn't hire me to be surprised, Mr. Lloyd. You're only going to have a few hours of daylight, so you need to push off as soon as the ship arrives in the Franklin Channel. You might want to consider waiting until tomorrow morning."

Lloyd shook his head. "No. My time is short here."

Glinn nodded, as if he had expected as much. "Puppup tells me of a small half-moon beach on the lee end of the island. You can run the motor launch right up on the shingle. You'll need to be in and out of there fairly quickly."

Lloyd sighed. "You really know how to take the romance out of life."

"No," said Glinn, standing up. "I only take out the uncertainty." He nodded out the windows. "If you want romance, come take a look out there."

They stepped forward. McFarlane could see a small island, just coming into view, even darker than the black water around it.

"That, gentlemen, is Isla Desolación."

McFarlane looked at it, mingled curiosity and trepidation quickening within him. A single shaft of light moved across the brutal rocks, vanishing and reappearing at the caprice of the enshrouding fogs. Immense seas tore at its rocky shore. At its northern end, he made out a cloven volcanic plug: a double spire of rock. Snaking through the central valley was a deep snowfield, its icy center exposed and polished by the wind: a turquoise jewel in the monochromatic seascape.

After a moment, Lloyd spoke: "By God, there it is," he said. "Our island, Eli, at the edge of the world. Our island. And my meteorite."

There was a strange, low giggle behind them. McFarlane turned to see Puppup, who had remained silent throughout the entire conversation, covering his mouth with narrow fingers.

"What is it?" Lloyd asked sharply.

But Puppup did not answer, and continued to giggle as he backed and bowed and scraped his way out of the office, unwavering black eyes fixed on Lloyd.

Isla Desolación, 12:45 P.M.

Within an hour, the tanker had eased its bulk into Franklin Channel, which was less a channel than an irregular bay, circled by the craggy peaks of the Cape Horn islands. Now, McFarlane sat in the center of the open launch, his hands gripping the gunwales, aware of the awkward bulk of the life preserver strapped over his heavy jacket and slicker. The seas that caused the *Rolvaag* to roll uncomfortably were now tossing the launch around like a child's paper boat. The chief mate, Victor Howell, stood at the helm, his face furrowed with concentration as he fought to keep his heading. John Puppup had scrambled into the bow and was flopped down like an excited boy, each hand gripping a cleat. Over the last hour, he had acted as an impromptu harbor pilot for the *Rolvaag*, and his infrequent murmured words had turned what would have been a harrowing approach into one that was merely nail-biting. Now his face was turned to the island, light snow settling on his narrow shoulders.

The launch bucked and twisted, and McFarlane clung tighter.

The chop eased as the launch approached the lee of Isla Desolación. The island reared up before them, true to its name: black rocks poking up like broken knuckles through windblown patches of snow. A cove came into sight, dark under the shadow of a ledge. Following Puppup's signal, Howell turned the launch toward it.

At ten yards out he cut the engine, raising the propeller shaft simultaneously. The boat glided in, crunching lightly onto the shingle beach. Puppup sprang out like a monkey, and McFarlane followed. He turned to offer Lloyd a hand.

"I'm not that old, for chrissakes," Lloyd said as he grabbed a pack and hopped out.

Howell backed the boat off with a roar. "I'll be back at three o'clock," he called.

McFarlane watched the boat slap its way from shore. Beyond, he could make out a zinc-colored wall of bad weather coming toward them. McFarlane hugged himself against the cold. Although he knew the *Rolvaag* was less than a mile away, he nevertheless wished it was within eyesight. *Nestor was right,* he thought. *This is the very edge of the world.*

"Well, Sam, we've got two hours," Lloyd said with a broad grin. "Let's make the best of it." He dug into his pocket and pulled out a small camera. "Let's get Puppup to take a picture of our first landfall." He glanced around. "Now where did he get to?"

McFarlane looked around the small beach. Puppup was nowhere to be seen.

"Puppup!" Lloyd cried.

"Up here, guv!" came a faint cry from above. Looking up, McFarlane made out his silhouette at the top of the ledge, framed by the darkening sky. One skinny arm was waving, the other pointing at a nearby ravine that bisected the cliff face.

"How'd he get up there so fast?" McFarlane asked.

"He's a queer little fellow, isn't he?" Lloyd shook his head. "I hope to hell he remembers the way."

They walked up the shingles to the base of the ledge. Chunks of ice, washed ashore by storms, littered the strand. The air smelled sharply of moss and salt. McFarlane squinted at the black basalt cliff. He took a deep breath, then started up the narrow crevasse. It was a tougher climb than it looked: the ravine was slick with packed snow, and the last fifteen feet was a treacherous scramble over icy boulders. Beneath him, he could hear Lloyd puffing as he followed. But he kept a good pace, fit for a man of sixty, and they soon found themselves clambering onto the top of the cliff.

"Good!" cried Puppup, bowing and applauding. "Very good!"

McFarlane bent forward, resting his palms on his knees. The cold air seared his lungs, while the rest of him sweated beneath the parka. Beside him, he could hear Lloyd catching his breath. Nothing more was said about the camera.

Straightening up, McFarlane saw they were standing on a rock-strewn plain. A quarter mile beyond lay the long snowfield that stretched back into the center of the island. Clouds now covered the sky, and the falling snow grew heavier.

Without a word, Puppup turned and set off at a brisk pace. Lloyd and McFarlane scrambled to keep up as they climbed the steady rise. With remarkable speed, the snow developed into a flurry, shutting their world down into a circle of white. Puppup was barely visible twenty feet ahead, a bobbing specter. As they gained altitude the wind picked up, driving the snow horizontally across McFarlane's field of vision. Now he was glad that Glinn had insisted on the subzero boots and Arctic parkas.

They crested the rise. The snow flurries swept aside, giving McFarlane a glimpse into the valley beyond. They were on the edge of a saddle overlooking the snowfield. It looked much larger from up here: a great blue-white mass, almost glacial in its irresistibility. It ran down the center of the valley, surrounded by low hills. Beyond, the twin volcanic peaks thrust up like fangs. McFarlane could see another snowsquall boiling up toward them from the valley: an unrelieved wall of white that swallowed the landscape as it approached.

"Grand view up here, eh?" said Puppup.

Lloyd nodded. The fringe of his parka was dusted with snow, and his goatee was flecked with ice. "I've been wondering about that large central snowfield. Does it have a name?"

"Oh, yes," said Puppup, bobbing his head several times, his wispy mustache swaying in time. "They call it the Vomit of Hanuxa."

"How picturesque. And those two peaks?"

"The Jaws of Hanuxa."

"Makes sense," said Lloyd. "Who is Hanuxa?"

"A Yaghan Indian legend," Puppup replied. He did not offer more.

McFarlane looked sharply at Puppup. He remembered the mention of the Yaghan legends in Masangkay's journal. He wondered if this was the legend that had led Masangkay down there.

"I'm always interested in old legends," he said casually. "Will you tell us about it?"

Puppup shrugged, nodding his head again cheerfully. "I don't believe any of those old superstitions," he said. "I'm a Christian."

Once again, he turned suddenly and began walking, setting a rapid pace down the hillside toward the snowfield. McFarlane almost had to jog to keep up. He could hear Lloyd laboring behind him.

The snowfield lay in a deep fold of the land, mounds of broken boulders and debris lining its edges. As they came up to it, the fresh squall fell about them. McFarlane bowed under the wind.

"Come on, you lot!" cried Puppup out of the storm.

They walked parallel to the snowfield, which rose steeply above them like the flank of a huge beast. Now and then, Puppup stopped to examine it more closely. "Here," he said at last, kicking at the vertical wall to make a toehold, pulling himself up, and kicking again. Cautiously, McFarlane crawled up behind him, using Puppup's toeholds, keeping his face turned away from the wind.

The steep sides of the snowfield gradually leveled out, but the wind swirled around them ever more violently. "Tell Puppup to slow down!" Lloyd shouted from behind. But if anything, Puppup walked faster.

"Hanuxa," he suddenly began in his strange, singsong accent, "was the son of Yekaijiz, god of the night sky. Yekaijiz had two children: Hanuxa and his twin brother, Haraxa. Haraxa was always the favorite of the father. The apple of his eye, like. As time went on, Hanuxa grew more and more jealous of his brother. And he wanted his brother's power for himself."

"Aha, the old story of Cain and Abel," Lloyd said.

The snow in the center of the field had been scoured away, leaving blue ice. It seemed impossibly strange somehow, McFarlane thought, to be trudging through the center of this nothingness, this child's snow globe of white, toward a huge mysterious rock and the grave of his former partner—while listening to this old man relate the legend of Isla Desolación.

"The Yaghans believe that blood is the source of life and power," Puppup continued. "So one day, Hanuxa killed his brother. Slit Haraxa's throat and drank his blood, he did. And his own skin turned the color of blood, and he got the power. But Yekaijiz, the father, found out. He imprisoned Hanuxa inside the island, entombing him below the surface. And sometimes, if people approach too close to the island after dark, on windy nights when the surf is up, they can see flashes of light, and hear howls of rage, when Hanuxa tries to escape."

"Will he ever escape?" Lloyd asked.

"Dunno, guv. Bad news if he does."

The snowfield began to slope downward, ending at last in a six-foot cornice. One at a time, they lowered themselves over the edge, sliding down onto harder ground. The wind was gradually abating and the snow falling more softly now, big fat flakes that spun and fluttered to earth like ash. Even so, the wind kept the barren plain scoured almost clean. A few hundred yards ahead, McFarlane could see a large boulder. He watched as Puppup began to jog toward it.

Lloyd strode over, McFarlane following more slowly. A wrinkled piece of hide lay in the lee of the boulder. Nearby was a scattering of animal bones and two skulls, a rotting halter still wrapped around one of them. A frayed halter rope was tied around the boulder. There were some scattered tin cans, a large piece of canvas, a sodden bedroll, and two broken packsaddles. Something was underneath the canvas. McFarlane felt a sudden chill.

"My God," said Lloyd. "These must be your old partner's mules. They starved to death right here, tied to this rock."

He began to reach forward, but McFarlane raised a gloved hand

and stayed him. Then, he slowly approached the boulder himself. He leaned over and gently grasped the edge of the frozen piece of canvas. He gave it a shake to clear it of snow, then tossed it aside. But it did not uncover Masangkay's body, only a welter of decaying belongings. He could see old packs of ramen noodles and tin cans of sardines. The tins had burst, spewing pieces of fish across the frozen surface. *Nestor always did favor sardines*, he thought with a pang.

Suddenly, an old memory came back. It was five years earlier, and several thousand miles to the north. He and Nestor had been crouched in a deep culvert next to a dirt road, their packs stuffed to bursting with the Atacama tektites. Armored trucks passed by just a few feet away, showering the culvert with pebbles. And yet they were giddy with success, slapping each other and chortling. They were ravenous, but did not dare light a fire for fear of being discovered. Masangkay had reached into his pack and, pulling out a tin of sardines, offered it to McFarlane. "Are you kidding?" McFarlane had whispered. "That stuff tastes even worse than it smells."

"That's why I like it," Masangkay whispered back. "Amoy ek-ek yung kamay mo!"

McFarlane had given him a blank look. But instead of explaining, Masangkay began to laugh: softly at first, and then more and more violently. Somehow, in the supercharged atmosphere of danger and tension, his laughter was irresistibly infectious. And without knowing why, McFarlane, too, dissolved into silent convulsions of laughter, clutching the precious bags, as the very trucks that hunted them crossed and recrossed overhead.

Then McFarlane was back in the present, crouching in the snow, the frozen tins of food and rags of clothing scattered around his feet. A queer sensation had come over him. It seemed like such a pathetic collection of trash. This was a horrible place to die, all alone. He felt a tickling at the corners of his eyes.

"So where's the meteorite?" he heard Lloyd ask.

"The what?" said Puppup.

"The *hole*, man, where's the hole Masangkay dug?"

Puppup pointed vaguely into the swirling snow.

"Damn it, take me there!"

McFarlane looked first toward Lloyd, then at Puppup, who was already trotting ahead. He rose and followed them through the falling snow.

Half a mile, and Puppup stopped, pointing. McFarlane took a few steps forward, staring at the scooped-out depression. Its sides were slumped in, and a drift of snow lay at its bottom. Somehow, he had thought the hole would be bigger. He felt Lloyd grip his arm, squeezing it so tightly it was painful even through the layers of wool and down.

"Think of it, Sam," Lloyd whispered. "It's right here. Right beneath our feet." He tore his eyes away from the hole and looked at McFarlane. "I wish to hell we could see it."

McFarlane realized that he should be feeling something other than a profound sadness and a creeping, eerie silence.

Lloyd slipped off his pack, unfastened the top, and pulled out a thermos and three plastic cups. "Hot chocolate?"

"Sure."

Lloyd smiled wistfully. "That goddamned Eli. He should have supplied a bottle of cognac. Well, at least it's hot." He unscrewed the cap and poured out the steaming cups. Lloyd held his up, and McFarlane and Puppup followed suit.

"Here's to the Desolation meteorite." Lloyd's voice sounded small and muffled in the silent snowfall.

"Masangkay," McFarlane heard himself say, after a brief silence.

"I'm sorry?"

"The Masangkay meteorite."

"Sam, that's not protocol. You always name the meteorite after the place where—"

The empty feeling inside McFarlane vanished. "Screw protocol," he said, lowering his cup. "He found it, not you. Or me. He *died* for it."

Lloyd looked back at him. *It's a little too late now for an attack of ethics*, his gaze seemed to say. "We'll talk about this later," he said evenly. "Right now, let's drink to it, whatever the hell its name."

They tapped their plastic cups and drank the hot chocolate

down in a single gulp. A gull passed by unseen, its forlorn cry lost in the snow. McFarlane felt the welcome creep of warmth in his gut, and the sudden anger eased. Already the light was beginning to dim, and the borders of their small world were ringed with a graying whiteness. Lloyd retrieved the cups and placed them and the thermos back in his pack. The moment had a certain awkwardness; perhaps, McFarlane thought, all such self-consciously historic moments did.

And there was another reason for awkwardness. They still hadn't found the body. McFarlane found himself afraid to lift his eyes from the ground, for fear of making the discovery; afraid to turn to Puppup and ask where it was.

Lloyd took another long look at the hole before his feet, then glanced at his watch. "Let's get Puppup to take a picture."

Dutifully, McFarlane stepped up beside Lloyd as the older man passed his camera to Puppup.

As the shutter clicked, Lloyd stiffened, his eyes focusing in the near distance. "Look over there," he said, pointing over Puppup's shoulder toward a dun-colored jumble, up a small rise about a hundred yards from the hole.

They approached it. The skeletal remains lay partially covered in snow, the bones shattered, almost unrecognizable save for a grinning, lopsided jaw. Nearby was a shovel blade, its handle missing. One of the feet was still wearing a rotten boot.

"Masangkay," Lloyd whispered.

Beside him, McFarlane was silent. They had been through so much together. His former friend, former brother-in-law, reduced now to a cold jumble of broken bones at the bottom of the world. How had he died? Exposure? Freak heart attack? Clearly, it hadn't been starvation: there was plenty of food back at the mules. And what had broken up and scattered the bones? Birds? Animals? The island seemed devoid of life. And Puppup had not even bothered to bury him.

Lloyd swiveled toward Puppup. "Do you have any idea what killed him?"

Puppup simply sniffed.

"Let me guess. Hanuxa."

"If you believe the legends, guv," Puppup said. "And as I said, I don't."

Lloyd looked hard at Puppup for a moment. Then he sighed, and gave McFarlane's shoulder a squeeze. "I'm sorry, Sam," he said. "This must be tough for you."

They stood in silence a moment longer, huddled over the pathetic remains. Then Lloyd stirred. "Time to get moving," he said. "Howell said three P.M. and I'd rather not spend the night on this rock."

"In a moment," McFarlane said, still staring down. "We need to bury him first."

Lloyd hesitated. McFarlane steeled himself, waiting for the protest. But the big man nodded. "Of course."

While Lloyd collected the bone fragments into a small pile, McFarlane hunted up boulders in the deepening snow, prying them loose from the frozen ground with numb fingers. Together, they made a cairn over the remains. Puppup stood back, watching.

"Aren't you going to help?" Lloyd asked.

"Not me. Like I said, I'm a Christian, I am. It says in the Book, let the dead bury the dead."

"Weren't too Christian to empty his pockets, though, were you?" McFarlane said.

Puppup folded his arms, a silly, guilty-looking smile on his face.

McFarlane went back to work, and within fifteen minutes they were done. He fashioned a rough cross from two sticks and planted it carefully atop the low pile of rocks. Then he stepped back, dusting the snow from his gloves.

"Canticum graduum de profundis clamavi ad te Domine," he said under his breath. "Rest easy, partner."

Then he nodded to Lloyd and they turned east, heading for the white bulk of the snowfield as the sky grew still darker and another squall gathered at their backs.

Isla Desolación,
July 16, 8:42 A.M.

McFarlane looked out over the new gravel road, cut through the brilliant expanse of fresh snow like a black snake. He shook his head, smiling to himself in grudging admiration. In the three days since his first visit, the island had been transformed almost beyond recognition.

There was a rough lurch, and half of McFarlane's coffee splashed from his cup onto his snowpants. "Christ!" he yelped, holding the cup at arm's length and swatting at his pants.

From inside the cab, the driver, a burly fellow named Evans, smiled. "Sorry," he said. These Cats don't exactly ride like Eldorados."

Despite its massive yellow bulk, and tires almost twice as tall as a man, the Cat 785's cab held only one person, and McFarlane had ended up sitting, cross-legged, on the narrow platform beside it. Directly beneath him, the huge diesel engine snarled. He didn't mind. Today was the day. Today they were going to uncover the meteorite.

He thought back over the last seventy-two hours. The very night they arrived, Glinn had initiated an astonishing process of unloading. It had all happened with ruthless speed and efficiency. By morning, the most incriminating equipment had been moved by heavy equipment to prefab hangars on the island. At the same time, EES workers under Garza and Rochefort had blasted and leveled the beach site, built jetties and breakwaters with riprap and steel, and graded a broad road from the landing site around the snowfield to the meteorite area—the road he was now on. The EES team had also offloaded some of the portable container labs and workspaces and moved them to the staging area, where they had been arranged among rows of Quonset huts.

But as the Caterpillar 785 Hauler rounded the snowfield and approached the staging area, McFarlane saw that the most astonishing change of all had taken place on an escarpment about a mile away. There, an army of workers with heavy equipment had begun gouging out an open pit. A dozen huts had sprouted up along its verge. Periodically, McFarlane could hear an explosive shudder, and clouds of dust would rise into the sky over the pit. A tailings pile was growing to one side, and a leachpond had been built nearby.

"What's going on over there?" McFarlane shouted to Evans over the roar of the engine, pointing to the escarpment.

"Mining."

"I can see that. But what are they mining?"

Evans broke into a grin. "Nada."

McFarlane had to laugh. Glinn was amazing. Anyone looking at the site would think the activity on the escarpment was their real business; the staging area around the meteorite looked like a minor supply dump.

He turned his gaze from the ersatz mine back to the road that lay ahead. The Hanuxa snowfield coruscated, seeming to grab the light and draw it into its depths, turning it to infinite hues of blue and turquoise. The Jaws of Hanuxa stood beyond, their grimness softened by a dusting of fresh snow.

McFarlane hadn't slept at all the night before, and yet he felt almost too wakeful. In less than an hour, they would know. They would see it. They would *touch* it.

The truck lurched again, and McFarlane tightened his grip on the metal railing with one hand while quickly downing his coffee with the other. It might be sunny for a change, but it was also hellishly cold. He crushed the foam cup and slid it into a pocket of his parka. The big Cat was only slightly less shabby-looking than the *Rolvaag* itself, but McFarlane could see that this, too, was an illusion: the interior of the cab was brand-new.

"Quite a machine," he yelled over to Evans.

"Oh, yeah," the man replied, his breath smoking.

The roadbed grew smoother and the Cat sped up. As they trundled along, they passed another hauler and a bulldozer headed back toward the shore, and the drivers waved cheerfully at Evans. McFarlane realized he knew nothing about the men and women wielding all the heavy equipment—who they were, what they thought about such a strange project. "You guys work for Glinn?" he asked Evans.

Evans nodded. "To a man." He seemed to wear a perpetual smile on his craggy face, overhung with two bristly eyebrows. "Not full-time, though. Some of the boys are roughnecks on oil rigs, some build bridges, you name it. We even have a crew from the Big Dig in Boston. But when you get the call from EES, you drop everything and come running."

"Why's that?"

Evans's smile widened. "The pay is five times scale, that's why."

"Guess I'm working the wrong end of the job, then."

"Oh, I'm sure you're doing all right for yourself, Dr. McFarlane." Evans throttled down to let a grader pass them, its metal blades winking in the brilliant sunshine.

"Is this the biggest job you've seen EES take on?"

"Nope." Evans goosed the engine and they lurched forward once again. "Small to middling, actually."

The snowfield fell behind them. Ahead, McFarlane could now see a broad depression, covering perhaps an acre, that had been scraped into the frozen earth. An array of four huge infrared dishes surrounded the staging area, pointing down. Nearby stood a row of graders, lined up as if at attention. Engineers and other workers were scattered around, huddled together over plans, taking measurements, speaking into radios. In the distance, a snowcat—a large, trailerlike vehicle with monstrous metal treads—was crawling toward the snowfield, wielding high-tech instruments held out on booms. Off to one side, small and forlorn, was the cairn he and Lloyd had built over Nestor Masangkay's remains.

Evans came to an idle at the edge of the staging area. McFarlane hopped off and made for the hut marked COMMISSARY. Inside, Lloyd and Glinn sat at a table near a makeshift kitchen, deep in discussion. Amira was standing by a griddle, loading a plate with food. Nearby, John Puppup was curled up, napping. The room smelled of coffee and bacon.

"About time you got here," Amira said as she returned to the table, her plate heaped with at least a dozen slices of bacon. "Wallowing in bed until all hours. You should be making an example for your assistant." She poured a cup of maple syrup over the mound of bacon, stirred it around, picked up a dripping piece, and folded it into her mouth.

Lloyd was warming his hands around a cup of coffee. "With your eating habits, Rachel," he said good-humoredly, "you should be dead by now."

Amira laughed. "The brain uses more calories per minute thinking than the body does jogging. How do you think I stay so svelte and sexy?" She tapped her forehead.

"How soon until we uncover the rock?" McFarlane asked.

Glinn sat back, slid out his gold pocket watch, and flicked it open. "Half an hour. We're just going to uncover enough of the surface to allow you to perform some tests. Dr. Amira will assist you with testing and analyzing the data."

McFarlane nodded. This had already been carefully discussed, but Glinn always went over everything twice. *Double overage*, he thought.

"We'll have to christen it," Amira said, thrusting another piece of bacon into her mouth. "Anybody bring the champagne?"

Lloyd frowned. "Unfortunately, it's more like a Temperance meeting around here than a scientific expedition."

"Guess you'll have to break one of your thermoses of hot chocolate over the rock," McFarlane said.

Glinn reached down, drew out a satchel, removed a bottle of Perrier-Jouët and placed it carefully on the table.

"Fleur de Champagne," Lloyd whispered almost reverentially. "My favorite. Eli, you old liar, you never told me you had bottles of champagne aboard."

Glinn's only reply was a slight smile.

"If we're going to christen this thing, has anybody thought up a name?" Amira asked.

"Sam here wants to call it the Masangkay meteorite," Lloyd said. He paused. "I'm inclined to go with the usual nomenclature and call it the Desolación."

There was an awkward silence.

"We've got to have a name," Amira said.

"Nestor Masangkay made the ultimate sacrifice finding this meteorite," said McFarlane in a low voice, looking hard at Lloyd. "We wouldn't be here without him. On the other hand, you financed the expedition, so you've won the right to name the rock." He continued gazing steadily at the billionaire.

When Lloyd spoke, his voice was unusually quiet. "We don't even know if Nestor Masangkay would have wanted the honor," he said. "This isn't the time to break with tradition, Sam. We'll call it the Desolación meteorite, but we'll name the hall it's in after Nestor. We'll erect a plaque, detailing his discovery. Is that acceptable?"

McFarlane thought a moment. Then he gave the briefest of nods.

Glinn passed the bottle to Lloyd, then rose. They all went out into the brilliant morning sun. As they walked, Glinn came up to McFarlane's side. "Of course, you realize that at some point we're going to have to exhume your friend," he said, nodding in the direction of the stone cairn.

"Why?" McFarlane asked, surprised.

"We need to know the cause of death. Dr. Brambell must examine the remains."

"What for?"

"It's a loose end. I'm sorry."

McFarlane began to object, then stopped. As usual, there was no arguing with Glinn's logic.

Soon they were standing along the edge of the graded area. Nestor's old hole was gone, filled in by the graders.

"We've scraped the earth down to within about three feet of the top of the rock," Glinn said, "taking samples of each layer. We'll grade off most of the rest, and then switch to trowels and brushes for the last foot. We don't want to so much as even bruise the meteorite."

"Good man," Lloyd answered.

Garza and Rochefort were standing together by the line of graders. Now Rochefort came over to join them, his face purple with windburn.

"Ready?" Glinn asked.

Rochefort nodded. The graders were manned and idling, their exhausts sending up plumes of smoke and steam.

"No problems?" Lloyd asked.

"None."

Glinn glanced over toward the graders and gave a thumbs-up to Garza. The engineer, wearing his usual athletic warm-ups, turned, held up his fist and cranked it in a circle, and the graders rumbled to life. They moved forward slowly, diesel smoke fouling the air, lowering their blades until they bit into the ground.

Behind the lead grader, several white-jacketed workers walked, sample bags in their hands. They picked up pebbles and dirt exposed by the graders and dropped them in the bags for later examination.

The line of graders made a pass over the area, removing six inches of dirt. Lloyd grimaced as he watched. "I hate to think of those big blades passing so close to my meteorite."

"Don't worry," Glinn said. "We've factored in elbow room. There's no chance of them damaging it."

The graders made another pass. Then Amira came slowly through the center of the graded area, wheeling a proton magnetometer across the ground. At the far end, she stopped, punched some buttons on the machine's front panel, and tore off the narrow piece of paper that emerged. She came up to them, trundling the magnetometer behind her.

Glinn took the paper. "There it is," he said, handing it to Lloyd.

Lloyd grasped the paper and McFarlane leaned over to look. A faint, erratic line represented the ground. Beneath, much darker, was the top edge of a large, semicircular shape. The paper shook in Lloyd's powerful hands. McFarlane thought, *God, there really is something down there*. He hadn't quite believed it, not until now.

"Fifteen inches to go," said Amira.

"Time to switch to archaeological mode," Glinn said. "We're sinking our hole in a slightly different place from where Masangkay dug, so we can sample undisturbed earth above."

The group followed him across the freshly exposed gravel. Amira took some more readings, tapped a few stakes into the ground, gridded it off, and snapped some chalk strings to make a square two meters on a side. The group of laborers came forward and began carefully troweling dirt from the square.

"How come the ground's not frozen?" asked McFarlane.

Glinn nodded upward at the four towers. "We've bathed the area in far infrared."

"You've thought of everything," said Lloyd, shaking his head.

"You're paying us to do just that."

The men proceeded to trowel out a neat cube, descending bit by bit, occasionally taking samples of minerals, gravel, and sand as they went. One of them stopped and held up a jagged object, sand adhering to its surface.

"That's interesting," said Glinn, stepping forward quickly. "What is it?"

"You got me," said Amira. "Strange. Looks almost like glass."

"Fulgurite," said McFarlane.

"What?"

"Fulgurite. It's what happens when a powerful bolt of lightning hits wet sand. It fuses a channel through the sand, turning it to glass."

"That's why I hired him," said Lloyd, looking around with a grin.

"Here's another," said a workman. They carefully dug around it, leaving it sticking up in the sand like a tree branch.

"Meteorites are ferromagnetic," McFarlane said, dropping down and carefully plucking it from the sand with his gloved hands. "This one must have attracted more than its share of lightning."

The men continued to work, uncovering several more fulgurites, which were wrapped in tissue and packed in wooden crates. Amira swept her instrument over the ground surface. "Six more inches," she said.

"Switch to brushes," said Glinn.

Two men now crouched around the hole, the rest of the workers taking up positions behind them. At this depth, McFarlane could see that the dirt was wet, almost saturated with water, and the workers were not so much sweeping away sand as they were brushing mud. A hush fell on the group as the hole deepened, centimeter by centimeter.

"Take another reading," murmured Glinn.

"One more inch," Amira said.

McFarlane leaned forward. The two laborers were using stiff plastic brushes to carefully whisk the mud into pans, which they passed to the men behind them.

And then a brush swept across a hard surface. The two workmen stepped out of the hole and gingerly troweled away the heavy mud, leaving a shallow layer covering the hard surface below.

"Rinse it off," said Glinn. McFarlane thought he heard a note of anticipation in the voice.

"Hurry, man!" Lloyd cried.

One of the workmen came running up, unrolling a thin hose. Glinn himself took the nozzle, aimed it toward the mud-covered meteorite, and squeezed. For several seconds, there was no sound except the gentle hiss of water as the last of the mud was rinsed from the surface.

Then Glinn jerked the nozzle shut. The water drained away from the naked surface of the meteorite. A sudden paralysis, an electric moment of suspension, gripped the company.

And then there was the sound of the champagne bottle, heedlessly dropped, landing on the damp earth with a heavy thud.

Isla Desolación,
9:55 A.M.

Palmer Lloyd stood at the edge of the precise cut in the earth, his eyes locked on the naked surface of the meteorite. For a moment, his mind went blank at the astonishing sight. And then, gradually, he became aware of himself again: felt the blood pounding in his temples, the air filling his chest, the cold air freezing his nose and cheeks. And yet the overpowering surprise remained. He was looking at it, he was seeing it, but he couldn't believe it.

"Margaux," he murmured, his voice small in the snowy vastness.

The silence around him was complete. Everyone had been shocked mute.

Lloyd had made pilgrimages to most of the great iron meteorites in the world—the Hoba, the Ahnighito, the Willamette, the Woman. Despite their widely varying shapes, they all had the same pitted, brownish-black surface. All iron meteorites looked alike.

But this meteorite was *scarlet*. But no, he thought, as his brain began to pick up speed again: the word "scarlet" did not do it justice. It was the deep, pure velvety color of polished carnelian, yet even richer. It was, in fact, precisely the color of a fine Bordeaux wine, like the parsimonious drams of Chateau Margaux with which he had been forced to content himself on the *Rolvaag*.

Now one voice cut through the shocked silence. It had a note of authority that Lloyd recognized as Glinn's. "I would like everyone to please step back from the hole."

Distantly, Lloyd was aware that nobody was moving.

"*Step back,*" Glinn repeated, more sharply.

This time, the tight circle of onlookers reluctantly shuffled back a few steps. As the shadows fell away, sunlight lanced through the crowd, illuminating the pit. Once more, Lloyd felt the breath snatched from him. In the sunlight, the meteorite revealed a silky, metallic surface that resembled nothing so much as gold. Like gold, this scarlet metal seemed to collect and trap the ambient light, darkening the outside world while giving itself an ineffable, interior illumination. It was not only beautiful, but unutterably strange.

And it was *his*.

He felt flooded by a sudden, powerful joy: for this amazing thing that lay at his feet and for the astonishing trajectory of his life that had given him the opportunity to find it. Bringing the largest meteorite in human history back to his museum had always seemed goal enough. But now the stakes were higher. It was no accident that he—perhaps the only person on earth with the vision and the resources—would be here, at this time and in this place, staring at this ravishing object.

"Mr. Lloyd," he heard Glinn say. "I said step back."

Instead, Lloyd leaned forward.

Glinn raised his voice. "Palmer, do *not* do it!"

But Lloyd had already dropped into the hole, his feet landing squarely on the surface of the meteorite. He immediately fell to his knees, allowing the tips of his gloved fingers to caress the smoothly rippled metallic surface. On impulse, he leaned down and placed his cheek against it.

Above, there was a brief silence.

"How does it feel?" he heard McFarlane ask.

"Cold," Lloyd replied, sitting up. He could hear the quaver in his voice as he spoke, feel the tears freezing on his numb cheek. "It feels very cold."

Isla Desolación,
1:55 P.M.

McFarlane stared at the laptop on his knees. The cursor blinked back, reproachfully, from a nearly blank screen. He sighed and shifted in the metal folding chair, trying to get comfortable. The lone window of the commissary hut glittered with frost, and the sound of wind came through the walls. Outside, the clear weather had given way to snow. But within the hut, a coal stove threw out a wonderfully intense heat.

McFarlane moused a command, then closed the laptop with a curse. On a nearby table, a printer began to hum. He shifted again, restlessly. Once again, he replayed the events of the morning. The moment of awestruck silence, Lloyd jumping so impulsively into the hole, and Glinn calling out to him—by his Christian name, for the first time McFarlane remembered. The triumphant christening, the torrent of questions that followed. And—overlaying everything—an overpowering sense of incomprehension. He felt that the breath had been knocked out of him, that he was struggling for air.

He, too, had felt a sudden urge to jump in; to touch the thing, to reassure himself that it was real. But he was also slightly afraid of it. It had such a rich color, so out of place in the monochromatic landscape. It reminded him of an operating table, a vast expanse of snowy white sheets with a bloody incision at their center. It repelled and fascinated simultaneously. And it excited in him a hope that he thought had been dead.

The door to the hut opened, admitting a howl of snow. McFarlane glanced up as Amira stepped in.

"Finish the report?" she asked, removing her parka and shaking off the snow.

In response, McFarlane nodded toward the printer. Amira walked to it and grabbed the emerging sheet. Then she barked a laugh. " 'The meteorite is red,' " she read aloud. She tossed the sheet into McFarlane's lap. "Now that's what I like in a man, succinctness."

"Why fill up paper with a lot of useless speculations? Until we get a piece of it for study, how can I possibly say what the hell it is?"

She pulled up a chair and sat down beside him. It seemed to McFarlane that, beneath a forced casualness, she was eyeing him very carefully. "You've been studying meteorites for years. I doubt your speculations would be useless."

"What do *you* think?"

"I'll show you mine if you show me yours."

McFarlane glanced down at the pattern of ripples on the plywood table, tracing his finger along them. It had the fractal perfection of a coastline, or a snowflake, or a Mandelbrot set. It reminded him how complicated everything was: the universe, an atom, a piece of wood. Out of the corner of his eye he saw Amira draw a metal cigar tube from her parka and upend it, letting a half-burnt stogie drop into her hand.

"Please don't," he said. "I'd rather not be driven out into the cold."

Amira replaced the cigar. "I know *something* is running through that head of yours."

McFarlane shrugged.

"Okay," she said. "You want to know what I think? You're in denial."

He turned to look at her again.

"That's right. You had a pet theory once—something you

believed in, despite the razzing of your peers. Isn't that right? And when you thought you'd finally found evidence for that theory, it got you into trouble. In all the excitement you lost your usual good judgment and shafted a friend. And in the end, your evidence turned out to be worthless."

McFarlane looked at her. "I didn't know you had a degree in psychiatry, along with everything else."

She leaned closer, pressing. "Sure, I heard the story. The point is, now you've got what you've been looking for all these years. You've got more than evidence. You've got *proof*. But you don't want to admit it. You're afraid to go down that road again."

McFarlane held her gaze for a minute. He felt his anger drain away. He slumped in his chair, his mind in turmoil. *Could she be right?* he wondered.

She laughed. "Take the color, for example. You know why no metals are deep red?"

"No."

"Objects are a certain color because of the way they interact with photons of light." Amira shoved a hand in her pocket and took out a crumpled paper bag. "Jolly Rancher?"

"What the hell's a Jolly Rancher?"

She tossed him a candy and shook another one into her hand. She held the green lozenge up between thumb and forefinger. "Every object, except for a perfect blackbody, absorbs some wavelengths of light and scatters others. Take this green candy. It's green because its scatters the green wavelengths of light back at our eye, while absorbing the rest. I've run a few pretty little calculations, and I can't find a single theoretical combination of alloyed metals that will scatter red light. It seems to be *impossible* for any known alloy to be deep red. Yellow, white, orange, purple, gray—but not red." She popped the green candy in her mouth, bit down with a loud crunch, and began to chew.

McFarlane placed his candy on the table. "So what are you saying?"

"You know what I'm saying. I'm saying it's made of some weird element we've never seen before. So stop being coy. I know that's what you've been thinking: *This is it: this is an interstellar meteorite*."

McFarlane raised his hand. "All right, it's true, I *have* been thinking about it."

"And?"

"All the meteorites ever found have been made from known elements—nickel, iron, carbon, silicon. They all formed here, in our own solar system, out of the primordial cloud of dust that once surrounded our sun." He paused, choosing his words carefully. "Obviously, you know I used to speculate about the possibility of meteorites coming from *outside* the solar system. A chunk of something that just happened to wander past and get caught in the sun's gravitational field. An *interstellar* meteorite."

Amira smiled knowingly. "But the mathematicians said it was impossible: a quintillion to one."

McFarlane nodded.

"I ran some calculations back on the ship. The mathematicians were wrong: they were working from faulty assumptions. It's only about a billion to one."

McFarlane laughed. "Yeah. Billion, quintillion, what's the difference?"

"It's a billion to one *for any given year*."

McFarlane stopped laughing.

"That's right," said Amira. "Over billions of years, there's a better than even chance that one *did* land on Earth. It's not only possible, it's *probable*. I resurrected your little theory for you. You owe me, big time."

A silence fell in the commissary hut, broken only by the rattle of wind. Then McFarlane began to speak. "You mean you really believe this meteorite is made of some alloy or metal that doesn't exist anywhere in the solar system?"

"Yup. And you believe it, too. That's why you haven't written your report."

McFarlane went on slowly, almost to himself. "If this metal did exist somewhere, we'd have found at least some trace of it. After all, the sun and the planets formed from the same dust cloud. So it *must* have come from beyond." He looked at her. "It's inescapable."

She grinned. "My thoughts exactly."

He fell silent and the two sat, absorbed for the moment.

"We need to get our hands on a piece of it," Amira said at last. "I've got the perfect tool for the job, too, a high-speed diamond corer. I'd say five kilos would be a nice chunk to start with, wouldn't you?"

McFarlane nodded. "But let's just keep our speculations to ourselves for now. Lloyd and the rest are due here any minute."

As if on cue, there was a stomping outside the hut, and the door opened to reveal Lloyd, even more bearlike than usual in a heavy parka, framed against the dim blue light. Glinn followed, then Rochefort and Garza. Lloyd's assistant, Penfold, came last, shivering, his thick lips blue and pursed.

"Cold as a witch's tit out there," Lloyd cried, stamping his feet and holding his hands near the stove. He was bubbling over with good humor. The men from EES, on the other hand, simply sat down at the table, looking subdued.

Penfold took up a position in the far corner of the room, radio in hand. "Mr. Lloyd sir, we have to get to the landing site," he said. "Unless the helicopter leaves within the hour, you'll never get back to New York in time for the shareholders' meeting."

"Yes, yes. In a minute. I want to hear what Sam here has to say."

Penfold sighed and murmured into the radio.

Glinn glanced at McFarlane with his gray, serious eyes. "Is the report ready?"

"Sure." McFarlane nodded at the piece of paper.

Glinn glanced at it. "I'm not much in the mood for drollery, Dr. McFarlane."

It was the first time McFarlane had seen Glinn show irritation, or any strong emotion, for that matter. It occurred to him that Glinn, too, must have been shocked by what they found in the hole. *This is a man who hates surprises*, he thought. "Mr. Glinn, I can't base a report on speculation," he said. "I need to study it."

"I'll tell you what we need," Lloyd said loudly. "We need to get it the hell out of the ground and into international waters, before the Chileans get wind of this. You can study it later." It seemed to McFarlane that this was the latest salvo in a continuing argument between Glinn and Lloyd.

"Dr. McFarlane, perhaps I can simplify matters," Glinn said. "There's one thing I'm particularly interested in knowing. Is it dangerous?"

"We know it's not radioactive. It might be poisonous, I suppose. Most metals are, to one degree or another."

"How poisonous?"

McFarlane shrugged. "Palmer touched it, and he's still alive."

"He'll be the last one to do that," Glinn replied. "I've given orders that nobody is to come into direct contact with the meteorite, under any circumstances." He paused. "Anything else? Could it be harboring viruses?"

"It's been sitting there for millions of years, so any alien microbes would have dispersed long ago. It might be worth taking soil samples and collecting moss, lichen, and other plants from the area, to see if anything's unusual."

"What would one look for?"

"Mutations, perhaps, or signs of low-level exposure to toxins or teratogens."

Glinn nodded. "I'll speak to Dr. Brambell about it. Dr. Amira, any thoughts on its metallurgical properties? It is a metal, isn't it?"

There was another crunch of candy. "Yes, very likely, since it's ferromagnetic. Like gold, it doesn't oxidize. However, I can't figure out how a metal can be *red*. Dr. McFarlane and I were just discussing the need to take a sample."

"Sample?" Lloyd asked. The room fell silent at the change in his voice.

"Of course," said McFarlane after a moment. "It's standard procedure."

"You're going to cut a piece off my meteorite?"

McFarlane looked at Lloyd, and then at Glinn. "Is there a problem with that?"

"You're damn right there's a problem," Lloyd said. "This is a museum specimen. We're putting it on display. I don't want it chopped up or drilled."

"There isn't a major meteorite found that hasn't been sectioned. We're only talking about coring out a five-kilogram piece. That'll be enough for all the tests anyone could conceivably think of. A piece that large could be worked on for years."

Lloyd shook his head. "No way."

"We *must* do it," McFarlane said with vehemence. "There's no way to study this meteorite without vaporizing, melting, polishing, etching. Given the size of this thing, the sample would be a drop in the bucket."

"It ain't the Mona Lisa," Amira murmured.

"That's an ignorant comment," Lloyd said, rounding on her. Then he sank back with a sigh. "Cutting it up seems like such a—well, a sacrilege. Couldn't we just leave it a mystery?"

"Absolutely not," said Glinn. "We need to know more about it before I'll authorize moving it. Dr. McFarlane is right."

Lloyd stared at him, his face reddening. "Before *you'll* authorize moving it? Listen to me, Eli. I've gone along with all your little rules. I've played your game. But let's get one thing straight: I'm paying the bills. This is *my* meteorite. You signed a contract to get it for me. You like to brag that you've never failed. If this ship returns to New York without that meteorite, *you will have failed.* Am I right?"

Glinn looked at Lloyd. Then he spoke calmly, almost as one might speak to a child. "Mr. Lloyd, you will get your meteorite. I merely want to see you have it without anyone getting unnecessarily hurt. Isn't that what you want, too?"

Lloyd hesitated. "Of course it is."

McFarlane was amazed at how quickly Glinn had put the man on the defensive.

"Then all I am asking is that we proceed with care."

Lloyd licked his lips. "It's just that everything's come to a grinding halt. Why? The meteorite's *red.* So I ask you, what's wrong with red? I think it's great. Has everybody forgotten about our friend in the destroyer? Time is the *one* thing we don't have here."

"Mr. Lloyd!" Penfold said, holding up the radio appealingly, like a beggar might hold up an alms cup. "The helicopter. *Please!*"

"God *damn* it!" Lloyd cried. After a moment, he spun away. "All right, for chrissakes, take your sample. Just cap the hole so it isn't visible. And do it fast. By the time I get back to New York, I want that son of a bitch on the *move*."

He stomped out of the hut, Penfold at his heels. The door banged shut behind them. For a minute, maybe two, the room was still. Then Amira rose to her feet.

"Come on, Sam," she said. "Let's drill this sucker."

Isla Desolación, 2:15 P.M.

After the warmth of the hut, the wind felt keen as a knife. McFarlane shivered as he followed Amira to tech stores, thinking longingly of the dry heat of the Kalahari.

The container was longer and wider than the rest, dingy on the outside, clean and spacious on the inside. Monitors and rack-mounted diagnostic tools, powered by the central generator in a neighboring hut, glowed in the dim light. Amira made for a large metal table, which held a collapsed tripod and a high-speed portable mining drill. If it weren't for the leather sling around the drill, McFarlane would never have suspected it of being particularly "portable." It looked like a twenty-first-century bazooka.

Amira patted the drill affectionately. "Don't you just love high-tech toys that break things? Look at this mother. Ever seen one of these before?"

"Not one so big." McFarlane watched as she expertly broke the drill down and examined its components. Satisfied, she slapped it back together, plugged the end of a heavy cord into a socket, and ran the machine through its diagnostics.

"Check this out." She hefted a long, cruel-looking shaft of metal, one end bulbous and pocked like a club, with a hollow core. "Ten carats of industrial diamond in the bit alone." She pressed a button and the electronic chuck loosened with a snap.

She slung the drill over her shoulder with a grunt and pressed its trigger, filling the room with a deep-throated growl. "Time to make a hole," she said, grinning.

They left the equipment hut and headed out into the gloom, McFarlane playing out the electrical cord behind them. A shoddy-looking maintenance shack had been erected over the exposed meteorite, concealing it from view. Inside, banks of halogen lights bathed the shallow cut in a cool glow. Glinn was already standing at the edge of the hole, peering down, radio in one hand, his small frame set into sharp relief by the light.

They joined Glinn at the edge of the hole. In the white light, the meteorite below their feet glowed almost purple, like a fresh bruise. Pulling off her gloves, Amira took the tripod from McFarlane, quickly set its legs, and fitted the drill into its housing. "This thing has a terrific vacuum system," she said, pointing to a narrow manifold that curved beneath the bit. "Sucks up every particle of dust. If the metal's poisonous, it won't matter."

"Even so, I'm evacuating the area," said Glinn, who raised the radio and spoke rapidly into it. "And remember, keep well back. Do *not* touch it." He motioned for the workmen to leave.

McFarlane watched as Amira snapped on the power switch, checked the indicator lights along the drill's flank, and deftly positioned the bit above the meteorite. "Looks like you've done this before," he said.

"Damn right. Eli here put me through this a dozen times."

McFarlane looked at Glinn. "You rehearsed this?"

"Every step," Amira said as she pulled a large remote from her pocket and began calibrating it. "And not just this. Everything. He plans all our projects like an invasion. D-Day. You practice your ass off, because you only get one shot at the real thing." She stepped back and blew on her hands. "Man, you should've seen the big ball of iron Eli made us dig up and schlepp all over creation, again and again. We called it Big Bertha. I really learned to hate that damn rock."

"Where did you do this?"

"Up at the Bar Cross Ranch near Bozeman, Montana. You didn't really think this was a first run, did you?"

With the remote calibrated and the drill fixed into position over the naked surface of the meteorite, Amira turned to a nearby case and snapped its hinges open. Pulling out a small metal can, she tore off its lid and—keeping well back—upended it over the meteorite. A black, gluey substance poured out, spreading over the red surface in a viscous layer. With a small brush, she applied the remainder to the end of the diamond bit. Then, reaching into the case again, she pulled out a thin sheet of rubber and gingerly pressed it down over the sealant.

"We'll give that a moment to get tacky," she explained. "We don't want even the slightest speck of meteorite dust escaping into the air." She fumbled in her parka, extracted the cigar tube, glanced at the expressions on Glinn's and McFarlane's faces, sighed, and began cracking peanuts instead.

McFarlane shook his head. "Peanuts, candy, cigars. What else do you do that your mother would disapprove of?"

She looked at him. "Hot monkey sex, rock and roll, extreme skiing, and high-stakes blackjack."

McFarlane laughed. Then he asked, "Are you nervous?"

"Not so much nervous as incredibly excited. You?"

McFarlane thought about this for a moment. It was almost as if he was *allowing* himself to become excited; to grow used to the idea that this was, after all, the very thing he had hunted for all those years.

"Yeah," he said. "Excited."

Glinn pulled out his gold pocket watch, flicked open its cover, and glanced at its face. "It's time."

Amira returned to the drill and adjusted a dial. A low rumble began to fill the close air of the shack. She checked the position of the bit, then took a step back, making an adjustment with the remote. The rumble rose to a whine. She maneuvered a small hat switch on the remote, and the whirling bit obediently descended, then retracted.

"Five by five," she said, glancing at Glinn.

Glinn reached into the open case, pulled out three respirators, and tossed two of them to McFarlane and Amira. "We'll step outside now and work from the remote."

McFarlane snugged the respirator onto his head, seating the cold rubber around his jaws, and stepped outside. Without a hood, the wind cut cruelly around his ears and the nape of his neck. From inside, the angry, hornetlike whine of the idling drill was still clearly audible.

"Farther," Glinn said. "Minimum distance one hundred feet."

They stepped back from the building. Snow was tumbling into the air, turning the site into a filmy sea of white.

"If this turns out to be a spaceship," Amira said, her voice muffled, "somebody inside's gonna be mighty pissed when Mr. Diamond Head pokes through."

The shack was barely visible through the snow, the open door a dim rectangle of white in the swirling gray. "All ready."

"Good," Glinn replied. "Cut through the sealant. We'll pause at one millimeter below the surface of the meteorite to scan for outgassing."

Amira nodded and aimed the remote, fingering the hat switch. The whine grew louder for a moment, then suddenly became muffled. A few seconds went by.

"Funny, I'm not making any progress," said Amira.

"Raise the drill."

Amira pulled back on the hat, and the whine grew louder again, settling down quickly to a steady pitch. "Seems fine."

"RPM?"

"Twelve thousand."

"Raise it to sixteen and lower again."

The whine increased in pitch. As McFarlane listened, it grew muffled once again. There was a sharp grinding noise, then nothing.

Amira glanced at a small LED readout on the remote, its red numbers stark against the black casing. "It stopped," she said.

"Any idea why?"

"Seems to be running hot, maybe there's something wrong with the motor. But the internals all checked out."

"Retract and let it cool. Then double the torque, and lower again."

They waited while Amira fiddled with the remote. McFarlane kept his eyes on the open door of the shack. After a few moments, Amira grunted to herself and nosed the hat switch forward. The whine returned, throatier now. Suddenly, the note grew lower as the drill labored.

"Heating up again," Amira said. "*Damn* this thing." Her jaw set, and she gave the hat switch a jab.

The pitch changed abruptly. There was a sharp ripping sound, and a dull flicker of orange light burst from the doorway. It was followed by a loud crackle, then another, much quieter. And then all was silent.

"What happened?" Glinn asked sharply.

Amira peered out, frowning through her respirator. "I don't know."

She took an impulsive step toward the shack, but Glinn put out a hand to stop her. "No. Rachel, *determine* what happened first."

With a heavy sigh, Amira turned back to the remote. "There's a lot of gibberish I've never seen before," she said, scrolling back through the LED readout. "Wait, here's something. It says 'Failure Code 47.' " She looked up and snorted. "That's just great. And the manual's probably back in Montana."

A small booklet appeared, as if by sleight of hand, in Glinn's right glove. He turned the pages. Then he stopped short. "Failure Code 47, you said?"

"Yup."

"Impossible."

There was a pause. "Eli, I don't think I've ever heard you use that word before," Amira replied.

Glinn looked up from the manual, alien in his parka and goon-like respirator. "The drill's burned out."

"Burned out? With the kind of horsepower that thing's sporting? I don't believe it."

Glinn slipped the manual back into the folds of his parka. "Believe it."

They looked at each other as the snowflakes curled around them.

"But that could only happen if the meteorite was harder than diamond," Amira said.

In answer, Glinn simply moved toward the hut.

Inside, the air was thick with the smell of burnt rubber. The drill was half obscured by smoke, the LED lights along its flank dark, its underside scorched. "It's not responding at all," Amira said, manipulating its controls by hand.

"Probably tripped the circuit breakers," said Glinn. "Retract the bit manually."

McFarlane watched as, inch by inch, the huge bit rose out of the acrid smoke. When the tip at last came into view, he saw that its serrated end was now an ugly, circular scar of metal, fused and burnt.

"Jesus," said Amira. "That was a five-thousand-dollar diamond-carborundum bit."

McFarlane looked over at Glinn, half hidden by the curls of smoke. The man's eyes were not on the drill bit; instead, they seemed to be contemplating something in the distance. As McFarlane watched, he unclipped his respirator and pulled it free.

The wind rose suddenly, slamming the door shut, rattling its hinges and worrying the knob.

"What now?" Amira asked.

"We take the bit back to the *Rolvaag* for a thorough examination," Glinn said.

Amira turned to the drill, but Glinn's expression had lost none of its distance. "And it's time we took something else back with us as well," he added quietly.

Isla Desolación, 3:05 P.M.

Outside the shack, McFarlane pulled off the respirator and snugged the hood of his parka tightly around his face. Wind gusted through the staging area, sending skeins of snow whirling across the frozen ground. By now, Lloyd must be well on his way back to New York. Already, what little light the heavy clouds permitted was fading from the sky. It would be dark in half an hour.

There was a crunch of snow, and Glinn and Amira appeared, returning from the stores hut. Amira held a fluorescent storm lantern in each hand, and Glinn was pulling a long, low aluminum sled behind him.

"What's that?" McFarlane asked, pointing to a large blue trunk of molded plastic that lay on the sled.

"Evidence locker," Glinn said. "For the remains."

McFarlane felt a mounting queasiness in his gut. "Is this absolutely necessary?"

"I know it can't be easy for you," Glinn replied. "But it's an unknown. And at EES, we dislike unknowns."

As they approached the pile of rocks that marked Masangkay's grave, the snow flurries began to draw away. The Jaws of Hanuxa came into view, dark against an even darker sky. Beyond, McFarlane caught the merest patch of storm-flecked bay. On the distant horizon, the sharp peaks of Isla Wollaston clawed their way skyward. It was incredible how quickly the weather changed down here.

Already the wind had stuffed snow and ice into the crevices of the makeshift cairn, mortaring the grave in white. Without ceremony, Glinn pulled out the cross, laid it down, and began prying frozen rocks from the pile and rolling them aside. He glanced back at McFarlane. "It's fine if you'd rather hang back a bit."

McFarlane swallowed. There were very few things he could imagine less pleasant than this particular job. But if it had to be done, he wanted to be part of it. "No," he said. "I'll help."

It was much easier to pull the grave apart than it had been to assemble it. Soon, Masangkay's remains began to come into view. Glinn slowed his pace, working more gingerly. McFarlane stared at the broken bones; the split skull and broken teeth; the ropy pieces of gristle, the partly mummified flesh. It was hard to believe that this had once been his partner and friend. He felt his gorge rise, his breath come fast.

Darkness was falling quickly. Putting aside the last of the rocks, Glinn lit the lanterns and placed one on either side of the grave. With a pair of forceps he began placing the bones into the plastic-lined compartments of the locker. A few of the bones still adhered to each other, held together by strips of cartilage, skin, and desiccated gristle, but most looked as if they had been violently torn asunder.

"I'm no forensic pathologist," said Amira, "but this guy looks like he had a close encounter with a Peterbilt."

Glinn said nothing, forceps moving again and again from the ground to the locker, his face hidden by the folds of his hood. Then he stopped.

"What is it?" Amira asked.

Reaching out with the forceps, Glinn carefully pried something out of the frozen dirt. "This boot isn't just rotten," he said. "It's been burned. And some of these bones appear to have been burned, too."

"Do you suppose he was murdered for his equipment?" Amira

asked. "And they burned the body to conceal the crime? It would be a hell of a lot easier than digging a grave in this soil."

"That would make Puppup a murderer," said McFarlane, feeling the hardness in his own voice.

Glinn held up a distal phalanx, examining it in the light like a small jewel. "Very unlikely," he said. "However, that's a question for the good doctor to answer."

"About time he had something to do," Amira said. "Instead of reading his books and wandering around the ship like a ghoul."

Glinn placed the bone into the evidence locker. Then he turned back to the gravesite and picked up something else with his forceps.

"This was underneath the boot," he said. He held the object up to the light, brushed off the clinging ice and dirt, and held it up again.

"A belt buckle," said Amira.

"What?" McFarlane asked. He pushed his way forward, staring.

"It's some kind of purple gemstone, placed in a silver setting," Amira said. "But look, it's been melted."

McFarlane sank back.

Amira looked at him. "Are you all right?" McFarlane merely passed a gloved hand across his eyes and shook his head. *To see that here, of all places . . .* Years ago, after they had scored big with the Atacama tektites, he had had a pair of belt buckles made, each with a sectioned tektite, to celebrate their coup. He'd lost his long ago. But despite everything, Nestor had still been wearing his at his death. It surprised McFarlane how very much that meant to him.

Without speaking, they gathered up the prospector's meager effects. Then Glinn fastened the locker, Amira gathered up the lights, and the two began trudging back. McFarlane remained a moment longer, staring at the cold jumble of rocks. Then he turned to follow.

Punta Arenas, July 17, 8:00 A.M.

Comandante Vallenar stood over the tiny metal sink in his cabin, smoking the bitter end of a *puro* and lathering his face with sandalwood-scented shaving cream. He detested the fragrant shaving cream, just like he detested the razor that lay on the basin: a two-bladed disposable of bright yellow plastic. Typical American throwaway trash. Who else would build such a wasteful thing, two blades when just a single blade would do? But naval stores were capricious, especially for ships that spent most of their time in the far south. He stared at the little disposable in disgust, one of a pack of ten that the quartermaster had issued him that morning. It was either that or a straight razor. And on board ship, straight razors could be dangerous.

He rinsed the blade, then raised it to his left cheekbone. He always started with the left side of his face: he had never been comfortable shaving with his left hand, and this side was easier somehow.

At least the shaving cream hid the smell of the ship. *Almirante Ramirez* was the oldest destroyer in the fleet, purchased from the U.K. in the fifties. Decades of poor sanitation, vegetable peelings rotting in bilgewater, chemical solvents, faulty sewage disposal, and spilled diesel fuel had suffused the vessel with a stench that nothing short of sinking would eradicate.

The sudden blat of an airhorn chased away the noise of crying birds and distant traffic. He glanced through the rusted porthole toward the piers and the city beyond. It was a brilliant day, with crystal skies and a brisk cold wind from the west.

The comandante returned to his shaving. He never liked anchoring in Punta Arenas; it was a poor place for a ship, especially in a westerly wind. He was surrounded, as usual, by fishing boats taking advantage of the destroyer's lee. It was typical South American anarchy; no discipline, no sense of the dignity due a military vessel.

There was a rap on the door. "Comandante," came the voice of Timmer, the signal officer.

"Enter," the comandante said without turning. In the mirror, he could see the door open and Timmer enter with another man in tow: a civilian, well-fed, prosperous, satisfied with himself.

Vallenar ran the blade a few times along his chin. Then he rinsed the blade in the metal basin and turned. "Thank you, Mr. Timmer," he said with a smile. "You may go. If you would be so kind as to post a man outside."

After Timmer left, Vallenar took a moment to examine the man before him. He stood before the desk, a slight smile on his face, no trace of apprehension. *And why should he be afraid?* Vallenar thought, without malice. Vallenar was a commander in name only. He had the oldest warship in the fleet, with the worst posting. So who could blame the man who stood here before him now for sticking out his chest ever so slightly, for feeling like a big man who could stare down the powerless comandante of a rusting vessel?

Vallenar took one last, deep drag on the *puro*, then flicked it out the open porthole. He laid down the razor and pulled a cigar box from a desk drawer with his good hand, offering the box to the stranger. The man glanced at the cigars with disdain and shook his head. Vallenar took one for himself.

"I apologize for the cigars," the comandante said, replacing the box. "They are of very poor quality. Here in the navy, you must take what you are given."

The man smiled condescendingly, staring at his withered right arm. Vallenar eyed the heavy sheen of pomade in the man's hair and the clear polish on his fingernails. "Sit down, my friend," he said, placing the cigar in his mouth. "Forgive me if I continue shaving while we talk."

The man took a seat in front of the desk, daintily propping one leg over the other.

"I understand you are a dealer in used electronic equipment—watches, computers, photocopiers, that sort of thing." Vallenar paused while drawing the razor across his upper lip. "Yes?"

"*New* and used equipment," the man said.

"I stand corrected," Vallenar said. "About four or five months ago—it would have been in March, I believe—you purchased a certain piece of equipment, a tomographic sounder. It is a tool used by prospectors, a set of long metal rods with a keyboard at its center. Did you not?"

"*Mi Comandante*, I have a large business. I cannot remember every piece of junk that crosses my door."

Vallenar turned. "I did not say it was junk. You said you sell new and used equipment, did you not?"

The merchant shrugged, raised his hands, and smiled. It was a smile that the comandante had seen countless times before from petty bureaucrats, officials, businessmen. It was a smile that said, *I won't know anything, and I won't help you, until I get* la mordida, *the bribe*. It was the same smile he had seen on the faces of the customs officials in Puerto Williams, a week before. And yet today, instead of rage, he felt only a great pity for this man. A man like this wasn't born polluted. He had been corrupted by degrees. It was a symptom of a greater sickness; a sickness that manifested itself all around him.

Sighing deeply, Vallenar came around the desk and perched on the edge closest to the merchant. He smiled at the man, feeling the shaving cream drying on his skin. The merchant nodded his head with a conspiratorial wink. As he did so, he rubbed his thumb and forefinger together in the universal gesture, laying the other manicured palm on the table.

As quick as a striking snake, the comandante's hand shot forward. With a sharp, digging movement, he sank the twin blades of the razor into the moon end of the merchant's middle fingernail. The man drew in his breath sharply. Terrified eyes stared up at the comandante, who met his gaze with perfect impassivity. Then the comandante gave a brutal tug and the man shrieked as the fingernail was torn away.

Vallenar shook the razor, flicking the bloody nail out the porthole. Then he turned to the mirror and resumed shaving. For a moment, the only sounds in the small cabin were the scrape of the blades against skin and the loud moaning of the merchant. Vallenar noticed, with faint interest, that the razor was leaving an unshaven stripe on his face; a piece of matter must have remained stuck between the blades.

He rinsed the blade again and finished shaving. Then, patting and drying his face, he turned to the merchant. The man had risen to his feet and was standing before the desk, swaying and moaning, and clutching his dripping finger.

Vallenar leaned over the desk, tugged a handkerchief out of his pocket, and gently wrapped it around the man's wounded finger. "Please, sit down," he said.

The merchant sat, whimpering softly, his jowls quivering with fright.

"You will do us both a service if you answer my questions quickly and precisely. Now, did you purchase a device such as I described?"

"Yes, I did," the man said instantly. "I did have an instrument like that, Comandante."

"And who bought it from you?"

"An American artist." He cradled his wounded finger.

"An artist?"

"A sculptor. He wanted to make a modern sculpture out of it to show in New York. It was rusted, useless for anything else."

Vallenar smiled. "An American sculptor. What was his name?"

"He did not give me his name."

Vallenar nodded, still smiling. The man was now so very eager to tell the truth. "Of course not. And now tell me, señor—but I realize I have not asked your name. How inconsiderate of me."

"Tornero, *mi Comandante*. Rafael Tornero Perea."

"Señor Tornero, tell me, from whom did you purchase the instrument?"

"A mestizo."

Vallenar paused. "A mestizo? What was his name?"

"I am sorry . . . I do not know."

Vallenar frowned. "You don't know his name? There are very few mestizos left, and fewer still come to Punta Arenas."

"I can't remember, Comandante, truly I can't." The man's eyes grew frantic as he searched his memory in desperation. Sweat trickled from the pomaded brow. "He was not from Punta Arenas, he was from the south. It was a strange name."

Suddenly, a flash came over Vallenar. "Was it Puppup? Juan Puppup?"

"Yes! Thank you, thank you, Comandante, for refreshing my memory. Puppup. That was the name."

"Did he say where he found it?"

"Yes. He said he found it on las Islas de Hornos. I didn't believe him. Why would anything of value be found down there?" The man was babbling urgently now, speaking as if he could not get the words out fast enough. "I thought he was trying to get a better price." His face brightened. "And now, I remember, there was a pick, and a strange-looking hammer, too."

"A strange-looking hammer?"

"Yes. One end was long and curved. And there was a leather bag of rocks. The American bought all those things, too."

Vallenar leaned eagerly across the desk. "Rocks? Did you look at them?"

"Yes, sir, I certainly did. I looked at them."

"Were they gold?"

"Oh, no. They had no value."

"Ah. And you must be a geologist, of course, to know that they had no value?"

Though Vallenar's tone was mild, the man cringed in the chair.

"Comandante, I showed them to Señor Alonso Torres, who owns the rock shop on Calle Colinas. I thought they might be valuable ores. But he said they were worthless. He said I should throw them away."

"And how would he know?"

"He knows, Comandante. He is an expert in rocks and minerals."

Vallenar walked toward the single porthole, limed and rusted from years of salt water. "Did he say what they were?"

"He said they were nothing."

Vallenar turned back to the merchant. "What did they look like?"

"They were just rocks. Ugly rocks."

Vallenar closed his eyes, trying hard to stem the anger rising within him. It would be unseemly to lose his temper, here in front of a guest on his own ship.

"I may have one more in my shop, Comandante."

Vallenar opened his eyes again. "You *may?*"

"Señor Torres kept one to do further tests. I got it back after the American bought the instrument. For a time, I used it as a paperweight. I, too, hoped it might be valuable, despite what Señor Torres said. Perhaps I can still locate it."

Comandante Vallenar suddenly smiled. He removed the unlit cigar from his mouth, examined the tip, and lit it from a box of wooden matches on his desk. "I should like to purchase this rock you mention."

"You are interested in this rock? It would be my privilege to give it to you. Let us not talk of purchase, Comandante."

Vallenar bowed slightly. "Then I would be pleased to accompany you, señor, to your place of business, to accept this kind gift." Then he took a deep drag on the cigar and, with the greatest of courtesy, ushered the merchant out of the cabin and into the foul central corridor of the *Almirante Ramirez*.

Rolvaag,
9:35 A.M.

The drill bit was laid out on an examination table, its scorched head resting on a bed of white plastic. A bank of overhead lights bathed the hulk in blue. Sampling instruments were lined up beside it, individually sealed in plastic. McFarlane, dressed in scrubs, fitted a surgical mask into position over his head. The channel was unusually calm. In the windowless lab, it was hard to believe they were on board a ship.

"Scalpel, doctor?" Amira asked, her voice muffled by her mask.

McFarlane shook his head. "Nurse, I think we lost the patient."

Amira clucked in sympathy. Behind her, Eli Glinn watched, arms folded.

McFarlane moved to an electronic stereozoom microscope and swiveled it into position over the table. A highly magnified picture of the drill head flickered into view on a nearby workstation screen: a landscape of Armageddon, fused canyons and melted ridges. "Let's burn one," he said.

"Sure thing, doc," Amira said, sliding a writeable CD into the drive bay of the machine.

McFarlane pulled a swivel chair toward the table, sat down at the microscope, and snugged the twin eyepieces to his head. Slowly, he moved the eyepieces, scanning the crevasses, hoping the drill bit might have removed something, no matter how small, from the surface of the meteorite. But no telltale particles of red gleamed in the lunar landscape, even when he switched to UV light. As he searched, he was aware that Glinn had come forward and was staring at the video screen.

After several fruitless minutes, McFarlane sighed. "Go to 120x."

Amira adjusted the machine. The landscape leapt forward, looking even more grotesque. Again McFarlane scanned it, sector by sector.

"I can't believe it," said Amira, staring at the screen. "It should have picked up *something*."

McFarlane sat back with a sigh. "If it did, it's beyond the power of this microscope to see it."

"That suggests the meteorite must be one tenacious crystal lattice."

"It sure as hell isn't a normal metal." McFarlane slapped the two eyepieces together and folded them back into the machine.

"What now?" said Glinn, his voice low.

McFarlane swiveled in his chair. He pulled down the mask and thought for a moment. "There's always the electron microprobe."

"And that is . . . ?"

"The planetary geologist's favorite tool. We've got one here. You put a sample of material in a vacuum chamber, shoot a high-speed beam of electrons at it. Normally, you analyze the X rays it produces, but you can heat up the electron beam to the point where it'll vaporize a tiny amount of the material, which will condense as a thin film on a gold plate. Voilà, your sample. Small, but viable."

"How do you know the electron beam will be able to vaporize a bit of the rock?" Glinn asked.

"The electrons are ejected from a filament at extremely high speed. You can ramp it up almost to the speed of light and focus it down to a micrometer. Believe me, it'll knock off at least a few atoms."

Glinn was silent, clearly weighing in his mind the possible danger against the need for more information. "Very well," he said.

"Proceed. But remember, no one is to touch the meteorite directly."

McFarlane frowned. "The tricky part is *how* to do it. Normally, you bring the sample to the microprobe. This time we'll have to bring the microprobe to the sample. But the thing isn't portable—it weighs about six hundred pounds. And we'll have to jury-rig some sort of vacuum chamber over its surface."

Glinn removed a radio from his belt. "Garza? I want eight men up on the maindeck immediately. We'll need to get a sling and vehicle big enough to move a six-hundred-pound instrument on the first morning transport."

"Tell him we need a major power source, too," McFarlane added.

"And have a cable with a ground-fault interrupt able to carry up to twenty thousand watts."

McFarlane gave a low whistle. "That'll do it."

"You have one hour to get your samples. We have *no more time*." These words were spoken very slowly, and very clearly. "Garza will be here shortly. Be ready."

Glinn rose abruptly and left the lab, the door sucking in a gust of frigid air as it shut behind him.

McFarlane looked at Amira. "He's getting touchy."

"He *hates* not knowing," said Amira. "Uncertainty drives him around the bend."

"It must be hard to live life like that."

A distant look of pain crossed her face. "You haven't any idea."

McFarlane looked at her curiously, but Amira merely pulled down her mask and removed her gloves. "Let's break down the microprobe for transport," she said.

Isla Desolación,
1:45 P.M.

By early afternoon, the staging area had been prepped for the test. Inside the little shack, the light was brilliant, the air suffocatingly warm. McFarlane stood over the hole, looking down on the rich, deep red surface. Even in the harsh light it had a soft luster. The microprobe, a long cylinder of stainless steel, lay on a padded cradle. Amira was arranging the other equipment McFarlane had ordered: an inch-thick bell jar containing a filament and plug, a set of gold disks sealed in plastic, and an electromagnet for focusing the electron beam.

"I need one square foot of the meteorite cleaned to absolute perfection," McFarlane said to Glinn, who was standing nearby. "Otherwise we'll get contaminants."

"We'll make it happen," said Glinn. "Once we get the samples, what's your plan?"

"We'll run a series of tests on them. With any luck, we'll be able to determine its basic electrical, chemical, and physical properties."

"How long will that take?"

"Forty-eight hours. More, if we eat and sleep."

Glinn's lips compressed together. "We can't afford more than twelve hours. Confine yourself to the most essential tests." He checked his massive gold pocket watch.

* * *

Another hour, and all was in readiness. The bell jar had been tightly sealed to the surface of the meteorite—an excruciatingly cautious operation. Inside the bell jar, ten tiny sample disks lay on pieces of glass, arrayed in a circle. A ring of electromagnets surrounded the jar. The electron microprobe lay nearby, partially open, its complex guts exposed. Multicolored wires and tubes streamed from it.

"Rachel, please turn on the vacuum pump," McFarlane said.

There was a whir as air was sucked from the bell jar. McFarlane monitored a screen on the microprobe. "What do you know. The seal's holding. Vacuum's down to five microbars."

Glinn moved closer, watching the small screen intently.

"Turn on the electromagnets," McFarlane said.

"You've got it," said Amira.

"Douse the lights."

The room went dark. The only light came from cracks in the walls of the ill-made shack and from the LEDs arranged along the microprobe's controls.

"I'm turning the beam on at low power," McFarlane whispered.

A faint bluish beam appeared in the bell jar. It flickered and rotated, casting a spectral light across the meteorite's surface, turning the crimson surface almost black. The walls of the shack danced and wavered.

McFarlane carefully turned two sets of dials, altering the magnetic fields around the jar. The beam stopped rotating and began to narrow, becoming brighter. Soon it looked like a blue pencil, its point resting on the meteorite's surface.

"We're there," he said. "Now I'm going to bring it to full power for five seconds."

He held his breath. If Glinn's concerns were justified—if the meteorite was somehow dangerous—this was when they might find out.

He pressed the timer. There was a sudden, much brighter, beam inside the jar. Where it touched the meteorite's surface, there was an intense violet pinpoint of light. Five seconds ticked off, and then everything went dark again.

McFarlane felt himself relax involuntarily. "Lights."

As the lights came on, McFarlane knelt above the meteorite's surface, staring eagerly at the gold disks. He caught his breath. Each disk was now marked with the faintest blush of red. Not only that, but at the spot where the electron beam had touched the meteorite, he saw—or thought he saw—the tiniest pit, a gleaming speck on the smooth surface.

He straightened up.

"Well?" asked Glinn. "What happened?"

McFarlane grinned. "This baby isn't so tough, after all."

Isla Desolación, July 18, 9:00 A.M.

McFarlane crunched across the staging area, Amira at his side. The site looked the same—the same rows of containers and Quonset huts; the same raw, frosted earth. Only *he* was different. He felt bone tired yet exhilarated. As they walked in silence, the crisp air seemed to magnify everything: the sound of his boots creaking in the fresh snow, the clatter of distant machinery, the rasp of his own breath. It helped clear his head of all the strange speculations that the night's experiments had aroused.

Reaching the bank of containers, he approached the main lab and held open the door for Amira. Inside, in the dim light, he could see Stonecipher, the project's second engineer, working on an open computer box, disks and circuit boards spread out fan-wise. Stonecipher straightened up his short, narrow body at their arrival.

"Mr. Glinn wants to see you, on the double," he said.

"Where is he?" asked McFarlane.

"Underground. I'll take you."

Not far from the shack that covered the meteorite, a second shack had been erected, even more dilapidated than its cousin. The door to this shack opened and Garza emerged, wearing a hard hat beneath his hood and carrying several others in his hands. He tossed one to each of them.

"Come on in," he said, ushering them into the smaller shack. McFarlane looked around the dim space, wondering what was going on. The shack held nothing but some old tools and several nail kegs.

"What's this?" McFarlane asked.

"You'll see," said Garza with a grin. He rolled the nail kegs away from the center of the shack, exposing a steel plate, which he hooked open.

McFarlane drew in his breath in astonishment. The open trapdoor revealed a descending staircase in a tunnel, cut into the ground, and heavily reinforced with steel. White light blazed upward. "Pretty cloak-and-dagger," he said.

Garza laughed. "I call it the King Tut method. They hid the tunnel into King Tut's treasure chamber by locating it beneath the shack of an insignificant worker."

They descended the narrow staircase, single file, to a narrow tunnel illuminated by dual lines of fluorescent lights. The tunnel was so massively cribbed with I-beams that it seemed made entirely of steel. The group proceeded single file, their breath leaving fog trails in the frosty air. Icicles hung from the overhead struts, and hoarfrost grew in sheets and spikes along the walls. McFarlane caught his breath as he saw a patch of unmistakable color ahead of them, bright red against the shine of ice and steel.

"You're looking at a small section of the meteorite's underside," Garza said, stopping beside it.

Underneath the lustrous red surface, a row of jacks, each a foot in diameter, sat like squat pillars on fat, clawlike feet, bolted to the metal cribbing on the floor and walls.

"There they are," said Garza affectionately. "The bad boys who'll be doing the lifting." He patted the closest with a gloved hand. "At go-ahead, we'll lift the rock exactly six centimeters. Then we'll wedge it, reposition the jacks, and lift again. As soon as we get enough clearance, we'll start building the cradle underneath. It'll be cramped, and cold as hell, but it's the only way."

"We've placed fifty percent more jacks than we need," added Rochefort. His face had turned mottled in the cold, and his nose was blue. "The tunnel was designed to be stronger than the matrix of the earth itself. It's completely safe." He spoke very rapidly, his thin lips compressed in a disapproving frown, as if he felt any questioning of his work would be a waste of time as well as an affront.

Garza turned away from the meteorite and led the group down a tunnel that branched away at right angles. Several smaller tunnels curved away from its right-hand wall, heading to other exposed areas of the meteorite's underside and additional banks of jacks. After about a hundred feet, the tunnel opened into a huge subterranean storage room. It had a packed dirt floor and was roofed with caisson plates. Inside, I-beams, laminated timbers, and structural steel were stacked in orderly rows, along with a variety of construction equipment. Glinn stood at the far end of the space, talking quietly to a technician.

"Jesus," breathed McFarlane. "This place is huge. I can't believe you built it in a couple of days."

"We don't want anyone nosing around our warehouse," said Garza. "If an engineer saw all this, he'd know immediately we weren't mining iron. *Or* gold. This will be used to build the cradle, bit by bit, as we jack up the meteorite and get a better understanding of its contours. Over there are precision arc welders, acetylene torches, hot riveting equipment, and some good old-fashioned woodworking tools."

Glinn came over, nodding first at McFarlane, then at Amira. "Rachel, please sit down. You look tired." He indicated a pile of I-beams as a seat.

"Tired." She gave a wan smile. "And amazed."

"I'm eager to hear your report."

McFarlane squeezed his eyes shut, then opened them again. "Nothing's written up yet. If you want a briefing, you'll have to settle for a verbal one."

Glinn tented his gloved fingers together, nodding as McFarlane removed a dog-eared lab notebook from his jacket. Every breath was sending up a plume of frost. He opened it and flipped briefly through many pages of scribbled notes.

"I want to say up front that this is just the beginning. Twelve hours gave us barely enough time to scratch the surface."

Glinn nodded again, silently.

"I'll describe the results of the tests, but I warn you: they don't make a whole lot of sense. We started by trying to determine the metal's basic properties—melting point, density, electrical resistance, atomic weight, valence—that sort of thing. First off, we heated a sample to find its melting point. We brought it up to over fifty thousand degrees K, vaporizing the gold substrate. It still remained solid."

Glinn's eyes were half-lidded. He murmured, "So that's how it survived the impact."

"Exactly," said Amira.

"Then we tried to use a mass spectrometer to find its atomic weight. Because of the high melting point, the experiment didn't fly. Even with the microprobe, we couldn't get it to remain a gas long enough to run the test."

McFarlane flipped some pages. "Likewise with specific gravity. The microprobe didn't give us a large enough sample to determine that. It appears to be chemically inactive—we hit it with every solvent, acid, and reactive substance we could find in the lab at room temperature and pressure, as well as at high temperatures and pressures. Totally inert. It's like a noble gas, except it's solid. No valence electrons."

"Go on."

"Then we wired it up to test its electromagnetic properties. And that's when we hit pay dirt. Basically, the meteorite seems to be a room-temperature superconductor: it conducts electricity without resistance. You put a current into it, and it will circulate forever unless something breaks it out."

If he was surprised at this, Glinn did not show it.

"Then we hit it with a beam of neutrons. It's a standard test on an unknown material: the neutrons cause the material to emit X rays, which tell you what's inside it. But in this case, the neutrons just disappeared. Swallowed up. Gone. It did the same thing with a beam of protons."

Now Glinn raised his eyebrows.

"That would be like shooting a forty-four magnum at a piece of paper, and having the bullet vanish into the paper," said Amira.

Glinn looked at her. "Any explanation?"

She shook her head. "I tried to do a quantum mechanical analysis of what might be happening. No luck. It appears to be impossible."

McFarlane continued to flip through his notes. "The last test we did was X-ray diffraction."

"Explain," Glinn murmured.

"You shine X rays through the material, then you make a picture of the diffraction pattern that results. A computer reverse-engineers those patterns and tells you what kind of crystal lattice generated them. Well, we got a seriously weird diffraction pattern—virtually fractal. Rachel wrote a program that tried to calculate what kind of crystal structure would produce such a pattern."

"It's still trying," Amira said. "It's probably gagged on it by now. It's one hell of a computation, if it can be done at all."

"One other thing," said McFarlane. "We used fission-track analysis to date the coesite from the staging area. We've now got a date on when the meteorite struck: thirty-two million years ago."

As he listened, Glinn's gaze had slowly dropped to the frozen dirt floor. "Conclusions?" he said at last, very quietly.

"They're very preliminary," McFarlane said.

"Understood."

McFarlane took a deep breath. "Have you heard of the hypothetical 'island of stability' on the periodic table?"

"No."

"For years, scientists have been searching for heavier and heavier elements higher on the periodic table. Most of the ones they've found are very short-lived: they last only a few billionths of a second before they decay into some other element. But there's a theory that way, way up on the periodic table might be a group of elements that *are* stable—that don't decay. An island of stability.

Nobody knows what kind of properties these elements would have, but they would be extremely strange, and very, very heavy. You couldn't synthesize them even with the largest of today's particle accelerators."

"And you think this might be such an element?"

"I'm fairly sure of it, actually."

"How would such an element be created?"

"Only in the most violent event in the known universe: a hypernova."

"A hypernova?"

"Yes. It's much bigger than a supernova. It occurs when a giant star collapses into a black hole, or when two neutron stars collide to form a black hole. For about ten seconds, a hypernova produces as much energy as the rest of the known universe put together. Such a thing just might have enough energy to create these strange elements. It also might have had enough energy to accelerate this meteorite into space at a speed that would carry it across the vast distances between stars, to land on Earth."

"An interstellar meteorite," Glinn said in a flat tone.

McFarlane noticed, with surprise, a brief but significant exchange of glances between Glinn and Amira. He tensed immediately, but Glinn merely nodded.

"You've given me more questions than answers."

"You gave us only twelve hours."

There was a brief silence.

"Let's return to the most basic question," Glinn said. "Is it dangerous?"

"We don't have to worry about it poisoning anybody," said Amira. "It's not radioactive or reactive. It's totally inert. I believe it's safe. I wouldn't, however, mess around with it electrically. Being a room-temperature superconductor, it has powerful and strange electromagnetic properties."

Glinn turned. "Dr. McFarlane?"

"It's a mass of contradictions," McFarlane said, keeping his voice neutral. "We haven't discovered anything specifically dangerous. But then again, we haven't shown it to be completely safe, either. We've got a second set of tests running now, and if that sheds any more light we'll let you know. But it will take years to really answer these questions, not twelve hours."

"I see." Glinn sighed, a small hissing sound that in anybody else would have been irritation. "As it happens, *we* have discovered something about the meteorite that may be of interest to you."

"What's that?"

"We'd originally estimated it to be about twelve hundred cubic meters in size, or about forty-two feet in diameter. Garza and his crew have been mapping the external contours of the meteorite as they prepare these tunnels. It turns out the meteorite is a lot smaller than we believed. It's only about *twenty* feet in diameter."

McFarlane's mind tried to fit this fact in. In an odd way, he felt disappointment. It wasn't much bigger than the Ahnighito, at the museum in New York.

"It's difficult to measure its mass at this point," Glinn said. "But all indications are that the meteorite still weighs at least ten thousand tons."

McFarlane suddenly forgot his disappointment. "That means it has a specific gravity of—"

"Jesus, at *least* seventy-five," said Amira.

Glinn raised an eyebrow. "And what does that signify?"

"The two heaviest known elements are osmium and iridium," Amira said. "They each have a specific gravity of around twenty-two. With a specific gravity of seventy-five, this meteorite is more than *three times* denser than any known element on Earth."

"There's your proof," murmured McFarlane. He felt his heart pounding.

"I'm sorry?" said Glinn.

It was as if a weight was suddenly plucked from McFarlane's shoulders. He looked Glinn in the face. "There can't be any doubt now. It's interstellar."

Glinn remained inscrutable.

"There's no *way* anything that dense originated in our solar system. It must have come from somewhere else. A place in the universe *very* different from our own. The region of a hypernova."

There was a very long moment of silence. McFarlane could hear workmen shouting in the distant tunnels, and the muffled sound of jackhammers and welding. Finally Glinn cleared his throat. "Dr. McFarlane," he began quietly. "Sam. I apologize if I seem doubtful. Understand that we're operating outside the parameters of any conceivable model. There's no precedent to guide us. I realize you haven't had adequate time for your tests. But our window of opportunity is about to close. I want your best guess—as a scientist, and as a human being—whether it's safe to proceed, or whether we should close down the operation and go home."

McFarlane took a deep breath. He understood what Glinn was asking. But he also knew, quite clearly, what Glinn had left unsaid. *As a scientist, and as a human being* . . . Glinn was asking him to look at the question objectively—not as the man who betrayed his friend over this precise thing five years before. Several pictures flashed through his mind: Lloyd, pacing before his pyramid; the glittering black eyes of the destroyer comandante; the broken, weathered bones of his dead partner.

McFarlane began slowly. "It's been lying here for thirty-two million years without apparent problems. But the truth is, we *don't* know. All I can say is, this is a scientific discovery of the highest importance. Are the risks worth it? Nothing truly great is ever accomplished without risk."

Glinn's eyes seemed to go very far away. His expression was as unreadable as always, but McFarlane sensed he had articulated the man's own thoughts.

Glinn pulled out his pocket watch, opening it with a smart snap of his wrist. He had made a decision. "We'll lift the rock in thirty minutes. Rachel, if you and Gene will test the servo connections, we'll be ready."

McFarlane felt a sudden flood of emotion—excitement or anticipation, he couldn't be precisely sure.

"We have to be topside for those tests," Garza said, glancing at his watch. "Nobody is allowed down here."

The feeling ebbed quickly. "I thought you said it was completely safe," McFarlane said.

"Double overage," Glinn murmured. Then, leading the way, he walked out of the storage vault and led the way down the narrow tunnel.

Rolvaag,
9:30 A.M.

Dr. Patrick Brambell lay snug in his bunk, reading Spenser's *The Faerie Queen*. The tanker rode peacefully in the sound, and the mattress was delightfully soft. The temperature in the medical suite had been cranked up to eighty-six degrees: exactly the way he liked it. Everyone but a skeleton crew was ashore, preparing to lift the meteorite, and the ship was quiet. He was aware of no discomfort, no annoyance in the world—save perhaps that his arm, which had been propping up the book in front of his nose for the last half hour, had begun to fall asleep. And that was a problem easily remedied. With a sigh of contentment, he transferred the book to his other hand, turned the page, and immersed himself again in Spenser's elegant dactyls.

Then he stopped. There was, in fact, one other annoyance. His glance fell reluctantly through the open doorway, past the hall and into the medical laboratory beyond. On a gleaming metal gurney sat the blue evidence locker, clasps loosened but lid unopened. There was something forlorn, almost reproachful, about it. Glinn wanted the examination by the end of the day.

Brambell stared at it for a moment. Then he laid the book aside, rose regretfully from his bunk, and straightened his surgical smock. Though he rarely practiced medicine, and even more rarely performed surgery, he delighted in wearing a surgical smock and never took one off while awake. As a uniform, he found it vastly more intimidating than a policeman's and only a little less so than the grim reaper's. Surgical smocks, especially when flecked with blood, tended to hurry office visits along and speed unnecessary conversations.

He stepped out of his cabin and paused in the long hallway of the medical suite, surveying the parallel lines of open doorways. Nobody in the waiting room. Ten beds, all empty. It was most satisfactory.

Entering the medical laboratory, he washed his hands in the oversized sink, then flicked the water from his fingers while turning in a small circle, in an irreverent imitation of a priest. Nudging the hot-air dryer with his elbow, he rubbed his knobbed old hands before the gush of air. As he did so, he gazed around at the neat rows of well-worn books: overflow from his cabin. Above them he had hung two pictures: a depiction of Jesus Christ, with the fire and thorns of the sacred heart; and a small, faded photograph of two identical babies in sailor suits. The picture of Christ reminded him of many things, some self-contradictory but always interesting. The picture of himself and his twin brother, Simon, who had been murdered by a mugger in New York City, reminded him of why he had never married or had children.

He pulled on a pair of latex gloves, snapped on the ring light, and swiveled the magnifying glass into place over the gurney. Then he opened the evidence locker and stared disapprovingly at the jumble of bones. He could see right away that several were missing, and the rest had been tossed in higgledy-piggledy, with no regard for anatomy. He shook his wizened head at the general incompetence of the world.

He began removing the bones, identifying them, and arranging them in their proper places on the gurney. Not much sign of animal damage, beyond the nibblings of rodents. Then his brow furrowed. The number of perimortem breaks was unusual, even remarkable. He paused, a nugget of bone suspended halfway between locker and gurney. Then, more slowly, he placed it on the metal surface. There was a stillness in the medical suite as Brambell stepped back, folded his green-suited arms, and stared at the remains.

Ever since his Dublin childhood, his mother had entertained dreams of her twin lads growing up to be doctors. Ma Brambell had been an irresistible natural force, and so, like his brother Simon, Patrick had gone to medical school. While Simon had relished the job and gone on to great acclaim as a medical examiner in New York, Patrick found himself resenting the time away from literature. Over the years, he had gravitated to ships, most recently to large tankers, where the crews were small and the accommodations comfortable. And so far, the *Rolvaag* had lived up to his expectations. No parade of broken bones, raging fevers, or dripping cases of clap. Aside from a few bouts of seasickness, a sinus infection, and of course Glinn's preoccupation with the meteorite hunter, he had been left to read his books. Until now.

But as he stared at the collection of broken bones, Brambell felt an uncharacteristic curiosity stirring within him. The silence of the medical lab was broken by the whistled strains of "The Sprig of Shillelagh."

More quickly now, Brambell, whistling merrily, finished laying out the skeleton. He examined the effects: buttons, bits of clothing, an old boot. Of course there was only one boot; the daft beggars had missed the other. Along with the right clavicle, a piece of the ilium, the left radius, carpals and intercarpals . . . He made a mental list of the missing bones. At least the skull was there, if in several pieces.

He bent closer. It, too, was webbed with perimortem fractures. The rim of the orbit was heavy; the mandible robust; definitely a male. From the state of the sutural closing he would be about thirty-five, maybe forty. A small man, no more than five foot seven, but powerfully built, with well-developed muscle attachments. Years of fieldwork, no doubt. This fit the profile of the planetary geologist Nestor Masangkay that Glinn had given him.

Many of the teeth were snapped off at the root. It looked like the poor man had convulsed so hard in his death throes that he had broken all his teeth, and even split his jaw.

Still whistling, Brambell turned his attention to the postcranial skeleton. Virtually every bone that could be broken was broken. He wondered what could have caused such massive trauma. It was apparently a blow to the front, striking simultaneously from toe to crown. He was reminded of a poor skydiver he had autopsied in medical school; the man had packed his chute wrong and fallen three thousand feet onto the middle of I-95.

Brambell caught his breath, "The Sprig of Shillelagh" suddenly dying on his lips. He had been so caught up by the fracturing of the bones that he had not stopped to examine their other characteristics. But now, as he did so, he could see that the proximal phalanges showed flaking and crumbling characteristic of high heat—or severe burning. Almost all of the distal phalanges were missing, probably completely burned up. Toes *and* fingers. He bent closer. The broken teeth were scorched, the brittle enamel spalling off.

His eyes made a circuit of the remains. The parietal showed heavy burn damage, the bone soft and crumbling. He bent down, sniffed. Ah, yes: he could even smell it. And what was this? Brambell picked up a belt buckle. The bloody thing was *melted*. And the single boot wasn't just rotten—it too had burned. The bits of cloth were also scorched. That devil, Glinn, hadn't mentioned a word of this, although he surely must have noticed.

Then Brambell rocked back on his feet. It was with a twinge of regret that he realized there was no mystery here, after all. He now knew exactly how the prospector had died.

In the dim light of the medical spaces, "The Sprig of Shillelagh" started up once again, the merry tune now sounding a little mournful, as Brambell carefully closed up the evidence locker and returned to his bunk.

Isla Desolación, 10:00 A.M.

McFarlane stood at the frosted window of the communications center, melting a hole with his hand. Clouds hung heavy over the Jaws of Hanuxa, casting a pall of darkness over the Cape Horn islands. Behind him, Rochefort, more tense than usual, was typing at a Silicon Graphics workstation.

The last half hour had seen a frenzy of activity. The corrugated-metal shack that shielded the meteorite from view had been moved to one side, and the area above the rock had been freshly bladed down to dirt, a dark brown scar on the white fairyland of snow. A small army of workers swarmed about, each at some obscure task. The radio traffic had been a perfect Babel of technical incomprehension.

Outside, a deep-throated whistle blew. McFarlane felt his pulse quicken.

The door to the hut banged open and Amira entered, a wide smile on her face. Coming in behind, Glinn closed the door carefully, then went to stand behind Rochefort. "Lift sequence ready?" he asked.

"Check."

Glinn lifted a radio and spoke into it. "Mr. Garza? Five minutes to lift. Please monitor this frequency." He dropped the radio and glanced at Amira, who had taken a seat at a nearby console and was fitting an earphone. "Servos?"

"On line," she replied.

"So what will we see?" McFarlane asked. Already, he could anticipate Lloyd's barrage of questions during the next videoconference.

"Nothing," said Glinn. "We're only raising it six centimeters. There might be a little crackling of the earth above." He nodded to Rochefort. "Bring the jacks up to sixty tons each."

Rochefort's hands moved across the keyboard. "Jacks are uniformly engaging. No slippage."

There was a faint, subaudible vibration in the ground. Glinn and Rochefort bent close to the screen, examining the data that scrolled past. They seemed perfectly calm and unconcerned. Typing, waiting, typing some more. It seemed so routine. Not exactly the kind of meteorite hunting McFarlane was used to: digging in some sheikh's backyard by moonlight, heart in mouth, muffling every bite of the shovel.

"Bring the jacks up to seventy," said Glinn.

"Done."

There was a long, boring wait.

"Damn," Rochefort muttered. "I'm getting no movement. Nothing."

"Bring them up to eighty."

Rochefort tapped on some keys. There was a pause, then he shook his head.

"Rachel?" Glinn asked.

"Nothing wrong with the servos."

There was another silence, longer this time.

"We should have seen movement at sixty-seven tons per jack." Glinn waited a moment, then spoke again. "Raise it to one hundred."

Rochefort tapped the keyboard. McFarlane glanced at the two faces illuminated in the gleam of Rochefort's monitor. Suddenly, the tension in the hut had risen dramatically.

"Nothing?" asked Glinn, something like concern in his voice.

"It's still sitting there." Rochefort's face was even more pinched than usual.

Glinn straightened up. He slowly walked to the window, his fingers squeaking on the glass as he cleared a hole through the frost.

Minutes crawled by while Rochefort remained glued to the computer and Amira monitored the servos. Then Glinn turned.

"All right. Let's lower the jacks, examine the settings, and try again."

Suddenly a strange keening seemed to fill the room, coming from everywhere and nowhere at once. It was almost ghostly. McFarlane felt his skin crawl.

Rochefort was suddenly intent on the monitor. "Slumping in sector six," he said, his fingers flying over the keyboard.

The sound subsided.

"What the hell was that?" McFarlane asked.

Glinn shook his head. "It looks like we might have lifted the meteorite just a millimeter in sector six, but then it subsided and pushed the jacks back."

"Getting another shift," Rochefort said suddenly, a note of alarm in his voice.

Glinn strode over and peered at the screen. "It's asymmetrical. Lower the jacks to ninety, quickly."

A patter of keystrokes, and Glinn stepped back, frowning. "What's with sector six?"

"The jacks seemed to have locked at a hundred tons," Rochefort said. "They won't go down."

"Your analysis?"

"The rock may be settling toward that sector. If so, a lot of weight has just shifted onto them."

"Zero out all the jacks."

To McFarlane, the scene seemed almost surreal. There was no sound, no dramatic subterranean rumbling; just a group of tense people gathered around flickering monitors.

Rochefort stopped typing. "All of sector six has locked up. The jacks must have frozen under the weight."

"Can we zero the rest?"

"If I do that, the meteorite might destabilize."

"Destabilize," McFarlane repeated. "You mean, as in tilt?"

Glinn's eyes glided toward him, then returned to the computer screen. "Suggestions, Mr. Rochefort?" he asked coolly.

The engineer leaned back, licked the tip of his left index finger, and placed it against his right thumb. "Here's what I think. We leave the jacks as is. Keep them in position. Then we release the fluid from the emergency hydraulic valves on the sector six jacks. Unfreeze them."

"How?" Glinn asked.

After a moment, Rochefort replied, "Manually."

Glinn held up his radio. "Garza?"

"Roger."

"You follow this?"

"Roger that."

"Your opinion?"

"I agree with Gene. We must've seriously underestimated the weight of this baby."

Glinn swiveled his gray eyes back to Rochefort. "And who do you suggest should drain the jacks?"

"I wouldn't ask anyone to do it but myself. Then we'll let the meteorite settle back down to a stable resting place, set additional jacks, and try again."

"You're going to need a second person," came Garza's voice over the radio. "That would be me."

"I'm not going to send both my chief engineer and my construction manager underneath that rock," said Glinn. "Mr. Rochefort, analyze the risk."

Rochefort did some calculations on a pocket calculator. "The jacks are rated to stand maximum pressure for sixteen hours."

"What about higher-than-maximum? Assume one hundred percent above maximum."

"The time-failure rate gets shorter." Rochefort made another series of calculations. "However, the chance of failure in the next thirty minutes is less than one percent."

"That's acceptable," said Glinn. "Mr. Rochefort, take a crew member of your choice along." He glanced at his pocket watch. "You have thirty minutes from this moment, not one second more. Good luck."

Rochefort stood up and looked at them, his face pale. "Remember, sir, we don't believe in luck," he said. "But thank you all the same."

Isla Desolación, 10:24 A.M.

Rochefort opened the door to the decrepit hut and moved the nail kegs aside, exposing the access tube and its halo of bright fluorescent light. He gripped the rungs of the ladder and began to descend, palmtop computer and radio jiggling on his belt. Evans followed behind, humming an off-key variant of "Muskrat Ramble."

The main emotion Rochefort felt was embarrassment. Brief as it was, the walk from the communications hut had taken an eternity. Although the staging area was deserted, he had nevertheless sensed dozens of eyes trained directly—and no doubt reproachfully—on his back.

He had set fifty percent more jacks than deemed necessary. It was within EES operating guidelines, and it had seemed like a safe margin. But he had miscalculated. He should have invoked double overage, set two hundred jacks. But the time pressure had always been there, hovering over everything, flowing from Lloyd to Glinn and infecting everything they did. So Rochefort had suggested a hundred and fifty, and Glinn had not questioned his decision. The fact was, *nobody* had said anything to him about the mistake—or even hinted one was made. But that did not negate the fact that he had been wrong. And Rochefort could not bear to be wrong. He felt saturated by bitterness.

Reaching the bottom, he moved quickly along the tunnel, ducking his head instinctively below the lines of fluorescent lights. Chains of ice crystals, formed from the condensed breath of the workers, stuck like feathers to the spars and trusses. Evans, coming up behind, dragged a finger through them as he whistled.

Rochefort was humiliated, not worried. He knew that even if the jacks in sector six failed—a minuscule possibility—it was unlikely the meteorite would do anything except settle back down into place. It had sat there for untold millennia, and the forces of mass and inertia dictated it would probably stay that way. The worst-case scenario meant they'd be back where they started from.

Back where they started from . . . His mouth set in a hard line. It meant setting more jacks, perhaps even digging a few more tunnels. He had strongly recommended to Glinn that all Lloyd Museum personnel be left behind; that it should be strictly an EES expedition; that Lloyd's only personal involvement should be to take final possession of the meteorite and pay the bill. For some unknown reason of his own, Glinn had allowed Lloyd to get daily updates. This was the sort of thing that resulted.

The tunnel reached sector one, then veered left at a ninety-degree angle. Rochefort followed the main tunnel another forty feet, then took one of the side branches that curved around toward the far side of the meteorite. The radio burbled and he pulled it from his belt. "Approaching sector six," he said.

"Diagnostics indicate that all jacks in that sector, with the exception of four and six, need to be unlocked," said Glinn. "We estimate you can complete the task in sixteen minutes."

Twelve, thought Rochefort, but he responded, "Affirmative."

The side tunnel angled around the front of the meteorite and split into three access tubes. Rochefort chose the center tube. Ahead, he could see the jacks of sector six, yellow against the bloodred meteorite. They ran ahead in a long line from the end of the access tube. Walking forward, he examined all fifteen in turn. They looked perfectly secure, their claw feet firmly anchored to the base of the wall struts, servo cables running away in rivers of wire and cable. The jacks did not appear to have moved in the slightest. It was hard to believe they were each frozen under a hundred tons of strain.

With a sigh of irritation, he crouched by the first jack. The belly of the meteorite curved above him, ribbed as smoothly and as regularly as if worked by a machine. Evans came forward with a small cami-tool for unlocking the hydraulic valves. "Looks like a great big bowling ball, doesn't it?" he said cheerfully.

Rochefort grunted and pointed toward the valve stem of the first jack. Evans knelt beside it, gripped the stem with his cami, and began to turn it gingerly.

"Don't worry, it's not going to break," Rochefort snapped. "Let's move. We've got another twelve waiting."

More rapidly, Evans spun the stem through a ninety-degree twist. With a small hammer, Rochefort adroitly tapped out the manual slide on the rear of the jack, exposing the safety plate. A red light went on, indicating the valve was unlocked and ready to open.

After the first jack, Evans grew less hesitant, and they began to work quickly in tandem, moving down the line, skipping the jacks numbered four and six. At the last jack, number fifteen, they stopped. Rochefort looked at his watch. It had taken only eight minutes. All that was left was to go back down the line, punching the release buttons on each valve. Although the fluid was under intense pressure, an internal regulator would ensure even drainage, slowly easing the load off the jack. Meanwhile, the controlling computer back in the communications hut would be lowering in tandem the hydraulic pressure on all the other jacks. The situation would return to normal, and then all they needed to do was set more jacks and try again. He'd do Glinn one better, set *three* hundred jacks. But they would need at least a day to ferry them over from the ship, get them in place, wire the servos, run diagnostics. They would need more tunnels, too . . . He shook his head. He should have started with three hundred the first time.

"Feels hot in here," said Evans, tugging back his hood.

Rochefort didn't answer. Heat and cold were one and the same to him. The two men turned and began walking down the line of jacks, stopping at each to raise the safety plate and push the emergency fluid release button.

Halfway down the line, a faint, mouselike sound brought Rochefort to a halt.

Although it was important to begin releasing fluid from all the jacks together, the sound was so unusual that Rochefort glanced down the row of jacks, trying to determine its source. It seemed to have come from the front of the row of jacks. As he looked in that direction, the sound came again: a kind of whispered, agonized creak. He narrowed his eyes. Jack number one didn't look right; it seemed oddly crooked.

He didn't need time to think. "Get out!" he shouted. "*Now!*"

He rose to his feet and sprinted for the access tube, Evans at his heels. He knew that there must be more weight on those jacks than they had guessed in even their most pessimistic assumptions: a *lot* more weight. Just how much more would determine whether they would get out in time.

He could hear Evans running behind him, feet thudding, grunting with each step. But even before they reached the access tube the first jack gave with a terrifying crack, followed by a second crack, and then a third, as the jacks failed in sequence. There was a pause, then a stuttering series of pops, like a burst of machine gun fire, as the rest of the jacks failed. Instantly, Rochefort was surrounded by blinding sprays of hydraulic fluid. There was a sound like a whirr of a vast sewing machine as the tunnel's struts and braces began to unravel. He ran desperately through the spray, the intense force of the pressurized fluid tearing his coat to ribbons and searing his flesh. He calculated that the probability of survival was dropping fast.

He knew it was exactly zero when the meteorite tipped toward him with a great hollow boom, buckling steel as it came, squirting dirt and mud and ice, looming into his field of vision until all he saw was a shining, inexorable, pitiless red.

Rolvaag,
Noon

When McFarlane arrived at the *Rolvaag*'s library, he found a hushed group scattered among the chairs and couches. Shock and discouragement hung in the air. Garza stared, unmoving, out of the wall of windows, across the Franklin Channel toward Isla Deceit. Amira sat in a corner, knees huddled beneath her chin. Britton and First Mate Howell were speaking in low tones. Even the reclusive Dr. Brambell was on hand, drumming his fingers on the arms of his chair and glancing impatiently at his watch. Of the major players, only Glinn was absent. As McFarlane took a seat, the library door opened again and the head of EES slipped in, a slim folder beneath one arm. On his heels was John Puppup, his smile and sprightly step out of place among the somber group. McFarlane was not surprised to see him: though Puppup was disinclined to go ashore, while Glinn was on board the *Rolvaag* the Yaghan seemed perpetually at his side, following him around like a faithful dog.

All eyes turned to Glinn as he stepped into the middle of the room. Privately, McFarlane wondered just how hard the man was taking all this: two of his men, including his chief engineer, dead. But he seemed, as usual, calm, neutral, unaffected.

Glinn's gray eyes flickered over the group. "Gene Rochefort had been with Effective Engineering Solutions from the beginning.

Frank Evans was a relatively new employee, but his death is no less regretted. This is a tragedy for all of us in this room. But I'm not here to eulogize. Neither Gene nor Frank would have wanted that. We made an important discovery, but we made it the hard way. The Desolación meteorite is a great deal heavier than any of us predicted. Careful analysis of the failure data from the jacks, along with some highly sensitive gravimetric measurements, have given us a new and more accurate estimate of mass. And that mass is twenty-five thousand tons."

Despite his lingering sense of shock, McFarlane felt himself go cold at these words. He made a quick calculation: that gave it a specific gravity of about 190. One hundred and ninety times denser than water. A cubic foot of it would weigh . . . *Good Lord. Almost six tons*.

But two men were dead. Two *more* men, McFarlane corrected himself, thinking of the pathetic litter of bones that had been his ex-partner.

"Double overage is our policy," Glinn was saying. "We planned as if everything would be twice our best estimate—twice the expense, twice the effort—and *twice the mass*. That means we already planned for a rock that weighed almost this much. So I'm here to tell you that we can proceed on schedule. We still have the means at our disposal to retrieve it, bring it to the ship, and load it into the holding tank."

It seemed to McFarlane as if, mingled among Glinn's cool tones, there was an odd note: of something almost like triumph.

"Just a minute," McFarlane said. "Two men just *died*. We have a responsibility—"

"You are not responsible," Glinn interrupted smoothly. "*We* are. And we're fully insured."

"I'm not talking about insurance. I'm talking about two people's lives. Two people were *killed* trying to move this meteorite."

"We took every reasonable precaution. The probability of failure was less than one percent. Nothing is free of risk, as you yourself so recently pointed out. And in terms of casualties, we're actually on schedule."

"On schedule?" McFarlane could hardly believe what he heard. He glanced at Amira, and then at Garza, failing to see in their faces the outrage he felt. "What the hell does that mean?"

"In any complex engineering situation, no matter how much care is taken, casualties occur. By this stage, we had *expected* two casualties."

"Jesus, that's a heartless calculation."

"On the contrary. When the Golden Gate Bridge was being designed, it was estimated that three dozen men would lose their lives during construction. That was neither cold-blooded nor heartless—it was just part of the planning process. What *is* heartless is bringing people into danger *without* calculating the risk. Rochefort and Evans knew those risks, and accepted them." Glinn looked straight at McFarlane, speaking almost in a monotone. "I assure you, I'm grieving in ways you will never know. But I was hired to retrieve this meteorite, and that's what I intend to do. I can't afford to let personal feelings cloud my judgment or weaken my resolve."

Suddenly Britton spoke up. McFarlane could see outrage glittering in her eyes. "Tell me, Mr. Glinn. Just how many others have you calculated need to die before we bring the Desolación meteorite home?"

For the briefest of moments, Glinn's neutral veneer seemed to slip at this salvo from an unexpected direction. "None, if I can help it," he said more coldly. "We will do *everything* in our power to prevent anyone from getting hurt or killed. And your implication that I find a certain number of deaths acceptable only shows your ignorance of risk assessment. The point is this: no matter how careful we are, there may be casualties. It's like flying: despite everyone's best efforts, planes crash. You can calculate the probable death rate for any particular flight. But we still continue to fly. That decision to keep flying doesn't make the deaths any more acceptable. Do I make myself understood?"

Britton stared fixedly at Glinn but said nothing further.

Then Glinn's voice suddenly became gentle. "Your concerns are genuine, and understandable. I appreciate that." He turned, and his voice hardened slightly. "But Dr. McFarlane, we can't retrieve this meteorite by half measures."

McFarlane flushed. "I don't want anyone else getting hurt. That's not the way I operate."

"I can't make that promise," Glinn said. "You, of all people, know how unique this meteorite is. You can't assign it a value in dollars, and you can't assign it a value in human life. It all boils down to the one question, which I will direct to you as the representative of the Lloyd Museum—*do you still want it?*"

McFarlane glanced around the room. All eyes had turned toward him. In the silence that followed, he realized he could not bring himself to answer the question.

After a moment, Glinn nodded slowly. "We'll recover the bodies and give them a heroes' burial when we return to New York."

Dr. Brambell cleared his throat, and his querulous Irish voice sang out. "I'm afraid, Mr. Glinn, there won't be anything more to bury than, ah, two boxes of wet dirt."

Glinn darted Brambell an icy look. "Do you have anything else of substance to add, Doctor?"

Brambell crossed one green-smocked leg over the other and tented his fingers. "I can tell you how Dr. Masangkay died."

There was a sudden hush.

"Go on," said Glinn finally.

"He was struck by a bolt of lightning."

McFarlane struggled to absorb this. His old partner, at the very moment of making the discovery of a lifetime—struck and killed by lightning? It seemed like something out of a bad novel. And yet in hindsight, it made sense. The fulgurites he'd seen at the site were a tip-off. On top of everything else, the meteorite was a gigantic lightning rod.

"Your evidence?" Glinn asked.

"The bones were burned in a pattern that suggested lightning—a massive charge of electricity passing through the body. I've seen it before. And only an electrical blast on the order of lightning could cause the kind of scaling and shattering those bones evidenced. Lightning, you see, not only *burns* bones and instantly boils the blood, causing an explosive release of steam, but it also triggers sudden muscle contractions that *shatter* bones. In some cases, it strikes the body with such force that it mimics, say, being hit by a truck. Dr. Masangkay's body virtually exploded."

The doctor dawdled over the word "exploded," lingering on each syllable with a loving drawl. McFarlane shuddered.

"Thank you, Doctor," said Glinn dryly. "I will also be eager to hear your analysis of the biota found in the eighty bags of sample earth we removed from the vicinity of the meteorite. I'll have them sent down to the medical lab right away."

Glinn opened his folder. "If the meteorite attracts lightning, that's yet another reason to keep it covered. Let's move on. A moment ago, I said we could proceed on schedule. There will, however, have to be some adjustments. For example, the weight of the meteorite is so great that we are now forced to take the absolute shortest path from the impact site to the ship. That means bringing the meteorite *through* the snowfield, rather than around it. The meteorite can only be moved in a straight line, along a slope of constant descent. It won't be easy, and it will mean a lot of cutting and filling, but it can be done. Also, Captain Britton has advised me that a winter storm is moving in our direction. If it stays on course, we will have to factor it into our plans. To a certain extent, the cover will be welcome." He stood up. "I'll be preparing letters for the family of Gene Rochefort and for the widow of Frank Evans. If any of you would like to include a personal note, please get it to me before we dock in New York. And now, one final thing."

He glanced at McFarlane. "You told me that the coesite and impactite around the meteorite was formed thirty-two million years ago."

"Yes," said McFarlane.

"I want you to collect samples of the basalt flows and volcanic plug beyond the camp and date them as well. We clearly need to know more about the geology of this island. Did your second series of tests bring about any fresh conclusions?"

"Only fresh puzzles."

"In that case, island geology will be your next project." He looked around. "Anything else before we get back to work?"

"Yes, guv," came the reedy voice from the corner of the library. It was Puppup, forgotten by all. He was sitting in a straight-backed chair, hair disheveled, raising his hand and waving it like a schoolboy.

"Yes?" Glinn asked.

"You said that two people died."

Glinn did not answer. McFarlane, watching, noticed that Glinn did not meet Puppup's eyes in the way he met everyone else's.

"You said that maybe some more people are going to die."

"I said nothing of the sort," said Glinn crisply. "Now, if we're finished here—"

"What happens if *everybody* dies?" Puppup asked, his voice suddenly loud.

There was an awkward moment.

"Damn lunatic," Garza muttered under his breath.

Puppup merely pointed out the grimy window. All eyes turned.

Just beyond the rocky outline of Isla Deceit, dark against the failing sky, the gaunt prow of a destroyer was easing into view, its guns trained on the tanker.

Rolvaag,
12:25 P.M.

Glinn slipped a hand into his pocket, withdrew a pair of miniature binoculars, and examined the ship. He had expected Vallenar to make another move; and this, apparently, was it.

Britton leapt out of her seat and strode to the window. "He looks like he's about to blow us out of the water," she said.

Glinn first examined the masts, and then the four-inch guns. He lowered the binoculars. "It's a bluff."

"How do you know that?"

"Check your Slick 32."

Britton turned to Howell.

"Slick shows no fire-control radar active along that line of bearing."

Britton glanced back at Glinn with a curious expression in her face.

Glinn handed her the binoculars. "He's pointing the guns at us, but he has no intention of firing them. You'll notice the fire-control radars aren't rotating."

"So I see." Britton returned the binoculars. "Stations fore and aft, Mr. Howell."

"Mr. Garza, will you make sure our reception room is ready, just in case?" Glinn pocketed the binoculars and glanced at Puppup. The mestizo had slumped back in his chair and was stroking his long, drooping mustaches. "Mr. Puppup, I would like to take a turn with you on deck, if you please."

Puppup's expression did not change. He stood and followed Glinn out of the library and down the wide corridor.

Outside, a bitter wind blew across the bay, raising dancing whitecaps. Pieces of ice skittered across the deck. Glinn walked ahead, the little old man at his heels, until they reached the great bulbous curve of the bow. Here, Glinn stopped and leaned against an anchor windlass, gazing out at the distant destroyer. Now that Vallenar had made his move, the problem would be to anticipate his future actions. Glinn glanced covertly at Puppup. The only person on board who could shed light on Vallenar was the one he understood least. He had found himself unable to predict or control Puppup's actions. And the man dogged him like a shadow. It had proved surprisingly unsettling.

"Got a cigarette?" Puppup asked.

Glinn slid a new pack out of his pocket—Marlboros, worth their weight in gold—and handed it to Puppup. The man tore it open and tapped out a cigarette. "Match?"

Glinn lit his cigarette with a lighter.

"Thank, guv." Puppup took a deep drag on the cigarette. "Bit parky out today, eh?"

"Yes it is." There was a pause. "Where did you learn your English, Mr. Puppup?"

"From the missionaries, didn't I? The only bit of schooling I had was from them."

"Did one of them come from London, by chance?"

"Both of them as did, sir."

Glinn waited a moment while Puppup smoked. Even considering the cultural differences, the man was remarkably difficult to read. In fact, Glinn had never met such an opaque individual.

He began slowly. "That's a nice ring," he said, pointing offhandedly at a little gold ring on the mestizo's pinkie.

Puppup held it up with a grin. "That it is. Pure gold, a pearl, two rubies, and all."

"A gift from Queen Adelaide, I presume?"

Puppup started, the cigarette jiggling in his mouth. But he recovered quickly. "Right you are."

"And what happened to the queen's bonnet?"

Puppup looked at him curiously. "Buried with the missus. Looked a fair old treat in it, too."

"Was Fuegia Basket your great-great-great-grandmother, then?"

"In a manner of speaking." Puppup's eyes remained veiled.

"You come from a distinguished family." As Glinn spoke, he looked very closely at Puppup's eyes. When they flicked away, he knew the comment had had its intended effect. Still, it was essential that this be handled with the greatest finesse. He would have only one chance to unlock John Puppup.

"Your wife must have died a long time ago."

Puppup still didn't answer.

"Smallpox?"

Puppup shook his head. "Measles."

"Ah," Glinn said. "My grandfather died of measles, also." This was, in fact, true.

Puppup nodded.

"We have something else in common," said Glinn.

Puppup looked at him sideways.

"My great-great-great-grandfather was Captain Fitzroy." Glinn spoke the lie very carefully, keeping his eyes unmoving.

Puppup's own eyes slid back out to sea, but Glinn could see the uncertainty in them. The eyes betrayed, every time. Unless, of course, you trained them.

"Strange how history repeats itself," he went on. "I have an engraving of your great-great-great-grandmother, when she was a little girl, meeting the queen. It hangs in my parlor." For the Yaghan, establishing the family connection was everything, if Glinn's reading of the ethnographic literature was correct.

As he listened, Puppup grew tense.

"John, may I see the ring again?"

Without looking at him, Puppup raised his brown hand. Glinn took it gently in his own, applying a warm pressure to the palm. He had noticed the ring the first time he had seen him, drunk in the snug in Puerto Williams. It had taken his people back in New York a few days to determine what it was, and where it had come from.

"Fate is a strange thing, John. My great-great-great-grandfather, Captain Fitzroy, of the HMS *Beagle*, kidnapped your great-great-great-grandmother, Fuegia Basket, and took her to England to meet the queen. And now I have kidnapped you," he added with a smile. "Ironic, isn't it? Except that I won't be taking you to England. Soon, you'll be home again." It was popular in those days to bring "primitives" back from the farthest reaches of the earth to display at court. Fuegia Basket had gone back to Tierra del Fuego on the *Beagle* several years later, with the bonnet and ring given her by the queen. Another passenger on that voyage had been Mr. Charles Darwin.

Although Puppup did not look at him, the opacity seemed to be fading from his eyes.

"What will happen to the ring?" Glinn asked.

"It'll stay with me into the grave."

"No children?" Glinn already knew that Puppup was the last of the Yaghan, but he wanted to gauge the answer.

Puppup shook his head.

Glinn nodded, still holding the hand. "Are there no others left at all?"

"A few mestizos, but I'm the last one to speak the lingo."

"That must make you sad."

"There's an ancient Yaghan legend, and the older I get the more I think it was meant for me."

"What is that?"

"When the time comes for the last Yaghan to die, Hanuxa himself will draw him down into the earth. From his bones, a new race will grow."

Glinn let go of Puppup's hand. "And how would Hanuxa take the last Yaghan?"

Puppup shook his head. "It's a bloody superstition, isn't it then? I don't remember the details."

Glinn didn't push. This was the old Puppup talking again. He realized there was no way to know if he had been successful in reaching him. "John, I need your help with Comandante Emiliano Vallenar. His presence here is a threat to our mission. What can you tell me about him?"

Puppup shook another cigarette out of the pack. "Comandante Emiliano came down here twenty-five years ago. After the Pinochet coup."

"Why?"

"His father fell out of a helicopter while being questioned. An Allende man. So was the son. He was posted down here to keep him at arm's length, like."

Glinn nodded. That explained a great deal. Not only his disgrace in the Chilean navy, but his hatred of the Americans, possibly even his self-loathing as a Chilean. "Why is he still commanding a destroyer?"

"He knows certain things about certain people, don't he? He's a good officer. And Comandante Emiliano is very stubborn. And very careful."

"I see," said Glinn, noting the shrewdness of Puppup's insights. "Is there anything else about him that I should know? Is he married?"

Puppup licked the end of a new cigarette and placed it between his lips. "The comandante is a double murderer."

Glinn stifled his surprise by lighting the cigarette.

"He brought his wife to Puerto Williams. It's a bad place for a woman. There's nothing to do, no dances, no fiestas. During the Falklands War, the comandante was put on a long tour of duty in the Estrecho de Magallanes, keeping the Argentinian fleet pinned down for the British. When he came back, he discovered his wife had taken a lover." Puppup took a deep drag. "The comandante was clever. He waited until he could walk in on them, doing it, like. He cut her throat. As I heard it, he did something even worse to the man. He bled to death on the way to the hospital in Punta Arenas."

"Why wasn't he put in prison?"

"Down here, you don't just tell your rival to sod off. Chileans have old notions of honor, don't they?" Puppup spoke very clearly, very matter-of-factly. "If he had killed them outside the bedroom, it would have been different. But . . ." He shrugged. "Everyone understood why a man who saw his wife *like that* would do what he did. And that's another reason why the comandante kept his command so long."

"Why is that?"

"He's a man who might do anything."

Glinn paused a moment, looking out across the channel at the destroyer. It hung there, motionless, dark. "There's something else I must ask you," he said, his eyes still on the warship. "That merchant in Punta Arenas, the one you sold the prospector's equipment to. Would he remember you? Would he be able to identify you, if asked?"

Puppup seemed to think for a minute. "Can't say," he answered at last. "It was a big shop. Then again, there aren't many Yaghan Indians in Punta Arenas. And we had quite a bargaining session."

"I see," said Glinn. "Thank you, John. You've been very helpful."

"Speak nothing of it, guv'nor," said Puppup. He looked sidelong at Glinn, eyes sparkling with shrewdness and amusement.

Glinn thought quickly. Sometimes it was best to confess a lie immediately. If done properly, it could breed a perverse kind of trust.

"I'm afraid I haven't been entirely honest with you," he said. "I know a lot about Captain Fitzroy. But he isn't actually my ancestor."

Puppup cackled unpleasantly. "Of course not. No more than Fuegia Basket was mine."

A gust of bitter wind tore at Glinn's collar. He glanced over at Puppup. "How did you get the ring then?"

"With us Yaghans, so many died that the last one left inherited the lot. That's how I got the bonnet and the ring, and just about everything else." Puppup continued gazing at Glinn in a bemused way.

"What happened to it all?"

"Sold most of it. Drank the proceeds."

Glinn, startled again at the directness of the response, realized he hadn't even begun to understand the Yaghan.

"When this is over," the old man added, "you'll have to take me with you, wherever you're going. I can't go back home again."

"Why not?" But even as he asked the question, Glinn realized he already knew the answer.

Rolvaag, 11:20 P.M.

McFarlane walked down the blue-carpeted corridor of the lower bridge deck. He was bone tired, yet he could not sleep. Too much had happened for one day: the long string of bizarre discoveries, the deaths of Rochefort and Evans, the reappearance of the destroyer. Having given up on sleep, he found himself roaming the decks of the *Rolvaag* like a restless apparition.

Now he paused before a stateroom door. His feet, unbidden, had brought him to Amira's cabin. He realized, with surprise, that he wanted her company. Her cynical laugh might be just the bracing tonic he needed. Time spent with her would be mercifully free of chitchat or exhaustive explanations. He wondered if she'd be interested in a cup of coffee in the wardroom, or a game of pool.

He knocked on the door. "Rachel?"

There was no response. She couldn't be sleeping—Amira claimed she had never gone to bed before 3 A.M. in the last ten years.

He knocked again. The unlatched door eased open under the pressure of his knuckles.

"Rachel? It's Sam." He stepped inside, curious despite himself; he had never been inside Amira's cabin. Instead of the disarray, the confused riot of sheets and cigar ash and clothes he expected, the place looked fastidiously clean. The sofa and chairs were neatly arranged, the shelves of scientific manuals carefully ordered. For a moment he wondered if she was even living there, until he saw a litter of broken peanut shells, lying in a semicircle underneath the computer table.

He smiled fondly as he stepped toward the table. His eyes strayed to the screen and were arrested by the sight of his own last name.

A two-page document stood in the nearby printer. Snatching the top page, he began to read.

EES CONFIDENTIAL
From: R. Amira
To: E. Glinn
Subject: S. McFarlane

Since the last report, the subject has become increasingly engrossed with the meteorite and its incomprehensibility. He is still ambivelent about the project, and about Lloyd himself, he has also been drawn in, almost against his will, by the problems the meteorite poses. There is little talk between us of anything else—at least, until what happened at the site this morning. I am not sure he is being completely forthright with me, but I'm not comfortable pressing the issue any farther.

After the meteorite was first uncovered, I initiated a conversation about his earlier theory about the existence of interstellar meteorites. While reluctant at first, he soon became enthusiastic, explaining how the theory fits the Desolación meteorite. However, he felt a need for secrecy and asked me not to share his suspicions with anyone. As you must know from this morning's discussion, his belief in its interstellar nature is, if anything, growing.

There was a closing of a door, the sharp intake of breath. McFarlane turned. Amira stood with her back to the cabin door. She was still dressed for dinner in a knee-length black dress, but she had thrown her parka over her shoulders for the trip to the commissary. She was in the act of pulling a newly purchased bag of peanuts from one of the pockets. She glanced at him, then at the paper in his hand, and became still.

For a moment, they simply looked at each other. Slowly, as if by its own accord, the bag of peanuts dropped back into the pocket of the parka.

More than anything else, McFarlane felt a bleakness spread through him. It was as if, after all the recent shocks, he could find no more reserves of emotion to draw on.

"Well," he said finally. "Looks like I'm not the only Judas on this boat."

Amira returned his gaze, her face pale. "You always break into other people's rooms and read their private papers?"

McFarlane smiled coldly. He flipped the paper onto the desk. "Sorry, but this work is unsatisfactory. 'Ambivalent' is misspelled. Eli's not going to paste a star by your name today." He stepped toward the door that was still blocked by her body. "Please step aside."

Amira faltered, dropped her eyes, but she did not step away. "Wait," she said.

"I *said*, step aside."

She nodded toward the printer. "Not until you read the rest."

A flush of rage coursed through him at this, and he raised his hand to brush her aside. Then, mastering himself, he willed his hand back down. "I've read quite enough, thanks. Now get the hell out of my way."

"Read the rest. Then you can go." Amira blinked, licked her lips. She stood her ground.

He held her gaze for a minute, perhaps two. Then he turned, reached for the rest of the report, and read.

As it happens, I agree with him. The evidence is strong, if not irrefutable, that this meteorite came from far beyond the solar system. Sam's theory has been vindicated. Furthermore, I see no evidence of obsession in Sam, or anything else that could pose a threat to the expedition. Just the opposite: the meteorite seems to be awakening the scientist in him. I've seen less of the sarcastic, defensive, and sometimes mercenary side of him that was so evident in the beginning; this has been replaced by a voracious curiosity, a profound desire to understand this bizarre rock.

And so this will be my third, and final, report. I can't in good conscience continue to provide these reports. If I sense problems, I'll report them. I'd do that in any case as a loyal EES employee. The fact is, this meteorite is stranger than any of us could have possibly foreseen. It may even be dangerous. I can't both watch him and work with him. You asked me to be Sam's assistant. And that's just what I plan to be—for his good, my good, and the good of the mission.

McFarlane pulled the chair away from the computer table and eased down into it, the paper crackling in his hand. He felt his anger draining away, leaving a confused welter of feelings.

For what seemed like a long time, neither one spoke. McFarlane could hear the distant rush of water, feel the faint thrumming of the engines. Then he looked up at her.

"It was Eli's idea," she said. "You were Lloyd's man, not his. You had a questionable history. And at that first meeting, that thing with the sandwich, you showed yourself to be a bit unpredictable. Unpredictable people make him nervous. So he told me to keep an eye on you. Write regular reports."

McFarlane sat, watching her in silence.

"I didn't like the idea. At first it was being your assistant that really got to me most, though. I just thought the reports would be a pain. But I had no idea—*no* idea—how hard they would actually be. I felt like a real shit every time I sat down to write one." She sighed deeply, a catch sounding in her throat. "These last couple of days . . . I don't know." She shook her head. "And then, writing this one . . . I just realized I couldn't do it anymore. Not even for him."

She abruptly fell silent. She dropped her eyes from his face to the carpet. Despite her efforts, he saw her chin tremble. A single tear charted an erratic course down her cheek.

Quickly, McFarlane rose from his chair and came to her. He

drew the tear away. She put her hands around his neck and drew him toward her, burying her face in his neck.

"Oh, Sam," she whispered. "I'm so sorry."

"It's all right."

A second tear began to furrow down her cheek. He bent to brush it away, but she turned her face to meet his and their lips joined instead.

With a soft moan, she pulled him more tightly to her. McFarlane, drawn forward over the sofa, felt the pressure of her breasts against him, felt her calves sliding past his hips. For a moment, he hesitated. Then he felt her hands tease the back of his neck and her thighs lock around him, and he yielded to a flood of passion. He slid his hands beneath her dress and pulled her to him, raising her legs, pressing the palms of his hands against the insides of her knees. He kissed her ardently as her hands traced caressing lines down his back.

"Oh, Sam," she said again. And then she pressed her mouth to his.

Isla Desolación, July 19, 11:30 A.M.

McFarlane eyed the towers of black lava that reared before him. The immense fangs were even more impressive close up. Geologically, he recognized them as classic "volcanic plugs"—the remnants of a twin volcano, in which the slopes had eroded away, leaving behind the two basalt-filled throats.

He turned around, glancing over his shoulder. Several miles behind and far below them, the landing area was a sprinkling of black dots on a white landscape, threadlike roads leading away across the island. In the wake of Rochefort's and Evans's deaths, recovery work had resumed immediately. It was being directed by Garza and the second engineer, Stonecipher, a humorless man who seemed to have inherited Rochefort's personality along with his duties.

Rachel Amira came up beside him, her breath frosty. She gazed up at the peaks, frowning. "How far do we have to go?"

"I want to reach that stripe of darker material about halfway up. That's probably a remnant of the last eruption, so we'd want to use that to date the flow."

"No problem," she said, rattling her gear with a show of bravado.

She had been in high spirits since meeting up for the climb, speaking little but humming and whistling to herself. McFarlane, on the other hand, felt restless, impatient.

His eyes traveled up the possible routes, looking for obstacles, cornices, loose rock. Then he started off again, snowshoes biting into the freshly fallen snow. They moved slowly, hiking up the talus slope. Near the base of the plug, McFarlane stopped at an unusual rock that poked out from the snow. He gave it a sharp rap with his rock hammer, slipped two chips into his sample pouch, and jotted a quick note.

"Playing with rocks," said Rachel. "How like a boy."

"That's why I became a planetary geologist."

"Bet you had a rock collection as a kid."

"Actually, no. What did you collect? Barbie dolls?"

Rachel snorted. "I had a rather eclectic collection. Bird's nests, snakeskins, dried tarantulas, bones, butterflies, scorpions, a dead owl, unusual roadkill—that sort of thing."

"Dried *tarantulas?*"

"Yeah. I grew up in Portal, Arizona, at the foot of the Chiricahua Mountains. In the fall, the big male tarantulas would come out onto the roads, looking to get laid. I had about thirty of them, mounted on a board. Goddamn dog ate my whole collection one day."

"Did the dog die?"

"Unfortunately, no. She threw them up all over my mom's bed, though. In the middle of the night. That was pretty funny." She giggled at the recollection.

They paused. The slope beyond grew steeper. Here the constant wind had given the snow a thick crust.

"Let's ditch the snowshoes," McFarlane said.

Despite the subzero weather, he felt overheated and tugged down the zipper of his parka. "We'll head for the saddle between the two peaks," he said, fitting crampons to his boots and moving forward again. "What kind of roadkill?"

"Herps, mostly."

"Herps?"

"Herpetological specimens. Amphibians and reptiles."

"Why?"

Rachel smiled. "Because they were interesting. Dry, flat, easy to sort and store. I had some pretty unusual species."

"I bet your mom loved that."

"She didn't know about it."

They lapsed into silence, their breath leaving white trails behind them. A few minutes brought them to the saddle, and McFarlane stopped for another rest. "Three weeks on that damn ship has put me out of shape," he gasped.

"You did all right last night, mister." A grin began to spread across her face. Then she suddenly flushed, turning her face away.

He did not respond. Rachel had been a good partner, and he felt that he could trust her now, despite the duplicity. But what had happened last night was an unexpected complication. The last thing he wanted now were complications.

They rested for a few minutes, sharing a canteen of water. Far to the west, McFarlane could see a dark streak lying across the horizon: a harbinger of the storm.

"You seem different from the rest of Glinn's team," he said. "Why's that?"

"I *am* different. That's no accident. Everyone at EES is super cautious, including Glinn. He needed somebody who took risks. And, in case you hadn't noticed, I'm brilliant."

"I had noticed," said McFarlane, taking out a candy bar and handing it to her.

They chewed in silence. Then McFarlane stuffed the empty wrappers back into the pack and swung it over his shoulder, casting an appraising eye at the slope above them. "It looks a little tricky from here. I'll go—"

But Rachel already began scrambling up the icy snowfield ahead of him. It rose to the bottom of the rock, getting bluer—icier—as it became steeper.

"Take it easy," he called up, looking out from the face. The view out over the rugged islands of the Horn group was spectacular. Far beyond, over the horizon, he could just see the tops of the Fuegian mountains. The *Rolvaag*, for all its bulk, looked like a child's bathtub toy in the black water of the bay. The destroyer could just be seen, mostly hidden by a rugged island. At the limit of vision, he could see the line of storm eating into the crystalline sky.

Looking back up, he was alarmed to see how quickly Rachel had climbed. "Slow down!" he called, more urgently this time.

"Slow*poke!*" was the taunting reply.

And then a rock clattered past, followed by another, larger, inches from his ear. With a crumpling sound, a small part of the talus slope slid away from Rachel's feet, exposing a dark scar beneath the snow. She dropped heavily onto her stomach, legs dangling into space. A strangle of fear escaped her as she twisted, scrabbling for a purchase.

"Hold on!" McFarlane cried, scrambling upward.

In a moment he was on a broad ledge directly beneath her. He edged closer, cautious now, planting his feet carefully in the hard surface. He reached out and grasped her forearm. "I've got you," he panted. "Let go."

"I can't," she said between clenched teeth.

"It's okay," he repeated quietly. "I've got you."

She gave a small groan, then relaxed her grip. He felt her weight coming down on him and he twisted, guiding her feet to the broad ledge below him. She landed hard and collapsed, shaking, onto her knees.

"Oh, my God," she said, her voice quavering. "I almost fell." She put an arm around him.

"It's okay," he said. "You would've fallen all of five feet. Into a snowdrift."

"Really?" She looked down and made a wry face. "It felt like the whole mountain was falling away in a landslide. I was going to say you saved my life, but I guess you didn't. Thanks anyway."

She raised her head to his, giving him a quick light kiss on the mouth. She paused a moment, then kissed him again, more deliberately this time. Then, sensing resistance, she pulled back, regarding him intently with her dark eyes. They stared at each other in silence for a moment, the world spread out a thousand feet below them.

"You still don't trust me, Sam?" she asked quietly.

"I trust you."

She drew closer to him again, her eyebrows knitting in a look of consternation. "Then what's wrong? Is there somebody else? Our gallant captain, perhaps? Even Eli seems—" She stopped abruptly, her eyes cast downward, hugging her knees closely to herself.

Half a dozen responses came to McFarlane's mind, but each one seemed either frivolous or patronizing. For want of a better reply, he simply reshouldered the pack and shook his head, smiling foolishly.

"There's a good sampling spot maybe twenty feet up the slope," he said after a moment.

Rachel's eyes were still on the ground. "You go get your sample. I think I'll wait here."

It was the work of a few minutes to reach the site, hack half a dozen pieces of the darker basalt from the rock face, and return to Rachel. She stood up as he approached, and they climbed back down to the saddle in silence.

"Let's take a breather," McFarlane said at last, as casually as he could. His eyes were on Rachel. They would be working together closely for the rest of the expedition; the last thing he needed was to have an awkwardness between them. He put his hand on her elbow and she turned toward him expectantly.

"Rachel," he said. "Listen. Last night was wonderful. But let's leave it like that. At least for now."

Her look sharpened. "Meaning?"

"Meaning we have a job to do. Together. And it's complicated enough as it is. So let's not push things, okay?"

She blinked quickly, then nodded, a brief smile covering the disappointment, even hurt, that had flashed across her face. "Okay," she said, looking away.

McFarlane put his arms around her. With her heavy parka, it was like embracing the Michelin man. With a gloved finger, he gently raised her face toward his.

"Is it okay?" he asked.

She nodded again. "It's not the first time I've heard it," she said. "It gets easier."

"What does that mean?"

She shrugged. "Nothing. I guess I'm just not very good at this kind of thing, that's all."

They held each other as the cold wind eddied around them. McFarlane looked down at the stray hairs curling away from the hood of Rachel's parka. And then, on impulse, he asked a question he'd been wondering about since the first night on the fly deck. "Was there ever anything between you and Glinn?"

She looked at him, then pulled away, her expression becoming guarded. Then she sighed, relaxing. "Oh, why the hell not tell you. It's true. Once upon a time, Eli and I had a thing. Just a little thing, I suppose. It was . . . very nice." A smile rose on her lips, then slowly faded. She turned away and sat down in the snow, legs kicked out before her, gazing out over the white vista beneath them.

McFarlane sat down beside her. "What happened?"

She glanced over. "Do I really need to spell it out? Eli broke it off." She smiled coldly. "And you know what? Everything was going great. There was nothing wrong. I'd never been happier in my life." She paused. "I guess that's what spooked him. He couldn't bear the thought that it wouldn't always stay that great. So when things couldn't get any better, he cut it off. Just like that. Because if things can't get any better, they can only get worse. That would be a failure. Right? And Eli Glinn is a man who can't fail." She laughed mirthlessly.

"But you two still think alike, in some ways," said McFarlane. "Like yesterday, in the library. I kind of figured you'd speak up. About what happened to Rochefort and Evans, I mean. But you didn't. Does that mean their deaths are okay with you, too?"

"Please, Sam. No death is okay. But almost every project I've worked on with EES has seen casualties. It's the nature of this business."

They sat a moment, looking away from each other. Then Rachel rose to her feet.

"Come on," she said quietly, dusting herself off. "Last one back has to clean the test tubes."

Almirante Ramirez, 2:45 P.M.

Comandante Emiliano Vallenar stood on the destroyer's *puente volante*, the flying bridge, scanning the enormous tanker with his field binoculars. Slowly, carefully, his eyes traveled from the bow, along the maindeck, on and on and on, until at last he reached the superstructure. As always, it was an interesting journey. He had lingered on it so long, and so carefully, that he felt he knew every rusted porthole, every davit, every smear of oil. There were certain things on this so-called ore carrier that he found suspicious: those antennas, hidden low, that looked distinctly as if they belonged to some passive electronic surveillance measuring device. And a very tall antenna at the top of the mast, despite its broken appearance, looked like an air-search radar.

He lowered the binoculars, reached into his coat with a gloved hand, and pulled out the letter from the geologist in Valparaiso.

Estimable Sir,

The rock which you so kindly furnished me is a somewhat unusual type of striated quartz—specifically, silicon dioxide—with microscopic inclusions of feldspar, hornblende, and mica. However, I am sorry to tell you that it is of no value whatsoever, either for commercial purposes or to mineral collectors. In response to your specific query, there are no traces of gold, silver, or any other valuable ores, minerals, or compounds present. Nor is this type of mineral found in association with deposits of oil, gas, oil shale, or other commercial hydrocarbon products.

Once again, I am humbly sorry to convey this information to you, as it must surely discourage any pursuit of your great-uncle's mining claim.

Vallenar traced the embossed seal at the top of the letter with his hand. Then, in a spasm of disgust, he balled it in his fist and shoved it into his pocket. The analysis was not worth the paper it was written on.

Once again, he raised the binoculars in the direction of the foreign vessel. No ship of its size should be moored here. In the Horn islands there was only one known anchorage, Surgidero Otter, and that was on the far side of Isla Wollaston. In the Franklin Channel, there was no decent holding ground at all, with the exception of an uncharted ledge that he, alone, had discovered. The currents were strong. Only a very ignorant captain would try to moor here. And then he would have surely run mooring cables to shore.

But this vessel had dropped anchor in bad ground, and had been sitting there for a number of days, swinging back and forth with the tide and wind, as if it had found the finest holding ground in the world. At first, Vallenar had been astonished by this. It seemed miraculous. But then he had noticed small, infrequent swirls of water at the vessel's stern, and he realized that its auxiliary propellers were running. *Always* running. They were adjusting their thrust to keep the ship stationary in the ever-changing currents of the channel, except at the change of tide, when he could see they were being used to swing the ship around.

And that could mean only one thing: the anchor cables were a deception. The ship was equipped with a dynamic positioning system. This required a link to a geopositioning satellite and a powerful computer operating the ship's engines, working together to maintain an exact position on the surface of the earth. It was the very latest technology. Vallenar had read about it, but never seen it. No ship in the Chilean navy was equipped with DPS. Even in a small vessel, it was extremely costly to install and burned a tremendous amount of fuel. And yet here it was, on this alleged shabby converted tanker.

He breathed deeply, swiveling the binoculars from the ship to the island beyond. He took in the equipment shed, the road leading inland to the mine. There was a large scar on a hillside where heavy equipment was at work, beside what might be leaching pools. But there was also a deception here. There were no hydraulic nozzles or sluicing work to indicate placer mining. Except for the pools, it was a neat operation. Too neat, in fact. He had grown up in a mining camp in the north, and he knew what they were like.

In his heart, the comandante now knew the Americans were not digging for gold. And any fool could see they were not digging iron ore. It looked more like a diamond pipe operation than anything else. But if the Americans were mining diamonds, why then had they brought such a huge vessel with them? The whole operation, from start to finish, carried a strong odor of duplicity.

He wondered if the work had anything to do with the legends about the island, the old myths of the Yaghans. He vaguely remembered the *borracho*, Juan Puppup, rambling on about some legend in the bar one evening. He tried to remember what it was: something about an angry god and his fratricidal son. When he got his hands on Puppup, he would make sure the mestizo's last earthly act would be to tell him everything he knew.

Footsteps approached, then the *oficial de guardia*, the officer of the deck, appeared at his side. "Comandante," the man said, snapping a salute. "Engine room reports all engines on line."

"Very well. Make your course zero nine zero. And please send Mr. Timmer to me."

The officer saluted again, then turned and left the flying bridge. Vallenar scowled as he watched the man retreat down the metal stairway. New orders had come in; as usual, they amounted to more worthless patrolling in desolate waters.

With his good hand, he reached into the pocket of his jacket and found the chunk of rock that had been returned with the letter. It was barely larger than a prune. And yet he was convinced it held the secret to what the Americans were doing. They had learned something from the prospector's machine and the sack of rocks. Something important enough to bring a vast amount of money and equipment to this remote, dangerous place.

Vallenar clutched the rock tightly. He needed to know what the Americans knew. If the moronic geologist at the university could not help him, he would find somebody who could. He knew that Australia had some of the best geologists in the world. That was where he would send it, by urgent express. They would unlock the pebble's secret. Then he would know what they were after. And how to respond.

"Sir!" The voice of Timmer intruded on his thoughts.

Vallenar glanced over at the man's trim figure, standing at rigid attention; glanced over his blue eyes and sun-bleached hair, his spotless uniform. Even in a crew that had been drilled for instant, instinctive obedience, Oficial de Comunicaciones Timmer stood out. His mother had come to Chile from Germany in 1945; a beautiful woman, cultivated, sensual. Timmer had been raised with discipline. And he was no stranger to the use of force.

"At ease," said Vallenar, his tone softening. Timmer relaxed almost imperceptibly.

Vallenar clasped his hands behind his back and gazed out at the flawless sky. "We are heading east," he said, "but we will return here tomorrow. Bad weather is expected."

"Yes, sir." Timmer continued staring straight ahead.

"On that day, I will have an assignment for you. It will involve a degree of risk."

"I look forward to it, sir."

Comandante Vallenar smiled. "I knew you would," he said, the faintest touch of pride in his voice.

Rolvaag,
2:50 P.M.

McFarlane paused just inside the outer door of the *Rolvaag*'s sick bay. He'd always had a morbid fear of doctors' offices and hospitals—any place with intimations of mortality. The *Rolvaag*'s waiting room was devoid even of the false sense of tranquillity such places ordinarily tried to project. The well-thumbed magazines, the shabby Norman Rockwell reproductions, were missing. The only decoration was a large medical school poster detailing, in full color, various diseases of the skin. The place smelled so strongly of rubbing alcohol and iodine that McFarlane believed the strange old doctor must be using them for rug cleaner.

He hesitated a moment, feeling a little foolish. *This errand can wait*, he thought. But then, with a deep breath, he found himself walking across the room and into a long hallway. He stopped at the last door and rapped on the frame.

Captain Britton and the doctor were inside, quietly discussing a chart that lay open on the table between them. Brambell sat back in his chair, casually closing the folder as he did so. "Ah, Dr. McFarlane." The dry voice held no surprise. He stared at McFarlane, eyes unblinking, waiting.

This can wait, he thought again. But it was too late; they were both looking at him expectantly. "Masangkay's effects," he said aloud. "Those things with the body? Now that you've completed the tests, can they be released?"

Brambell continued to look at him. It was a stare not of human compassion but of clinical interest. "There was nothing of value among them," he answered.

McFarlane leaned against the doorframe and waited, refusing to betray anything to the watchful eyes. At last, the doctor sighed. "Once they've been photographed, I see no reason to keep them. What precisely are you interested in?"

"Just let me know when they're ready, will you?" McFarlane pushed himself away from the frame, nodded to Britton, and turned back toward the waiting room. As he pulled open the outer door, he heard quick footsteps behind him.

"Dr. McFarlane." It was Captain Britton. "I'll walk topside with you."

"Didn't mean to break up the party," McFarlane said, swinging out into the hall.

"I have to get back up to the bridge anyway. I'm expecting an update on that approaching storm."

They moved down the wide corridor, dark except for the regular stripes of sunlight that slanted inward from the round portholes.

"I'm sorry about your friend Masangkay, Dr. McFarlane," she said with unexpected kindness.

McFarlane glanced at her. "Thanks." Even in the dim corridor, her eyes were bright. He wondered if she was going to probe his nostalgic desire for Nestor's effects, but she remained silent. Once again, he was struck by an indefinable feeling of kinship. "Call me Sam," he said.

"Okay, Sam."

They stepped out of the stairwell onto the maindeck.

"Take a turn around the deck with me," Britton said.

Surprised, McFarlane followed her back through superstructure to the fantail. Something in her stately bearing, in the sway of her walk, reminded him of his ex-wife, Malou. A pale golden light lay over the ship's stern. The water of the channel shone a rich, deep blue.

Britton walked past the landing pad and leaned against the rail, squinting into the sun. "Sam, I have a dilemma. I frankly don't like what I'm hearing about that meteorite. I fear it will endanger the ship. A seaman always trusts her gut. And I *really* don't like seeing that out there." She motioned toward the low, slender line of the Chilean destroyer lying in the waters beyond the channel. "On the other hand, from what I've seen of Glinn, I have every reason to expect success." She glanced at him. "You see the paradox? I can't trust Eli Glinn and my own instincts both. And if I need to act, I need to act now. I'm not going to put anything in the hold of my ship that isn't safe."

In the pitiless sunlight, Britton looked older than her years. *She's thinking of aborting the mission*, he thought in surprise.

"I don't think Lloyd would be very happy if you balked now," he said.

"Lloyd isn't the master of the *Rolvaag*. I'm speaking to you, as I did before, because you're the only one I *can* speak to."

McFarlane looked at her.

"As captain, I can't confide in any of my officers or crew. And I certainly can't speak to EES personnel about these concerns. That leaves you, the meteorite expert. I need to know if you think that meteorite will endanger my ship. I need *your* view, not Mr. Lloyd's."

McFarlane held her gaze a moment longer. Then he turned back toward the sea.

"I can't answer your question," he said. "It's dangerous enough—we've learned that the hard way. But will it specifically endanger the ship? I don't know. But I think maybe it's too late for us to stop, even if we wanted to."

"But in the library, you spoke up. You had concerns. Just as I did."

"I'm very concerned. But it isn't that simple. That meteorite is as deep a mystery as any in the universe. What it represents is so important that I think we've got no choice but to continue. If

Magellan had soberly taken into account all the risks, he never would have begun his voyage around the world. Columbus would never have discovered America."

Britton was silent, studying him intently. "You think this meteorite is a discovery on a par with Magellan or Columbus?"

"Yes," he said finally. "I do."

"In the library, Glinn asked you a question. You didn't answer it."

"I *couldn't* answer it."

"Why?"

He turned and looked into her steady green eyes. "Because I realized—despite Rochefort, despite everything—I *want* that meteorite. More than I've ever wanted anything."

After a pause, Britton drew herself up. "Thank you, Sam," she said. Then, turning smartly, she headed for the bridge.

Isla Desolación, July 20, 2:05 P.M.

McFarlane and Rachel stood at the edge of the staging area, in the cold afternoon sun. The eastern sky was clear and bright, the landscape below painfully sharp in the crisp air. But the sky to the west looked very different: a vast, dark cloak that stretched across the horizon, tumbling low, moving in their direction, blotting out the mountain peaks. A gust of wind swirled old snow around their feet. The storm was no longer just a blip on a screen: it was almost on top of them.

Garza came toward them. "Never thought I'd like the look of a storm as ugly as that one," he said, smiling and pointing westward.

"What's the plan now?" McFarlane asked.

"Cut and cover, from here to the shore," said Garza with a wink.

"Cut and cover?"

"Instant tunnel. It's the simplest engineered tunnel, a technique that's been used since Babylon. We dig a channel with a hydraulic excavator, roof it over with steel plates, and throw dirt and snow on top to hide it. As the meteorite is dragged toward the shore, we backfill the old tunnel and dig new tunnel ahead."

Rachel nodded toward the hydraulic excavator. "That baby makes Mike Mulligan's steam shovel look like a Tonka toy."

McFarlane thought back to all that had been accomplished in the two days since the meteorite crushed Rochefort and Evans. The tunnels had been cleared and reshored, and double the number of jacks positioned under the rock. The meteorite had been raised without a hitch, a cradle built underneath it, and the dirt cleared away. A gigantic steel flatbed cart had been brought up from the ship and positioned next to it. Now it was time to drag the meteorite and its cradle onto the cart. Garza had made it all look so easy.

The engineer grinned again. He was garrulous, in high spirits. "Ready to see the heaviest object ever moved by mankind get moved?"

"Sure," said McFarlane.

"The first step is positioning it on the cart. We'll have to uncover the meteorite for that. Briefly. That's why I like the look of that storm. Don't want those damn Chileans getting a gander at our rock."

Garza stepped back and spoke into his radio. Farther away, Stonecipher made a motion with his hands to the crane operator. As McFarlane watched, the crane operator began removing the steel roofing plates off the cut that held the meteorite and stacking them nearby. The wind was picking up, whistling about the huts and whipping snow along the ground. The final metal plate twisted wildly in the air as the crane operator fought to hold the boom steady against the gusts. "To the left, to the left!" Stonecipher called into his radio. "Now, boom down, boom down, boom down . . . Cut." After a tense moment, it, too, was set safely aside. McFarlane gazed into the open trench.

For the first time, McFarlane saw the meteorite exposed in its entirety. It lay in its cradle, a bloodred, lopsided egg atop a nest of timbers and metal I-beams. It was a breathtaking sight. Dimly, he was aware that Rachel was speaking.

"What did I tell you," she said to Garza. "He's got the look."

"The look" was a term she had coined for the way almost anybody—technicians, scientists, construction workers—tended to stop what they were doing and stare at the meteorite, as if mesmerized.

With an effort, McFarlane pulled his gaze from the meteorite to her. The infectious twinkle of merriment—so evidently missing for the last twenty-four hours—had returned to her eyes.

"It's beautiful," he said.

He glanced back down the length of the exposed tunnel to the cart that would carry the rock. It was a remarkable-looking thing, a honeycombed flatbed of steel and ceramic-carbon composite a hundred feet long. Although he could not see them from above, McFarlane knew that beneath the cart was an array of heavy-duty aircraft tires: thirty-six axles, with forty tires on each axle, to bear the staggering weight of the meteorite. At the far end, a massive steel capstan rose from a socket in the tunnel bed.

Glinn was calling out orders to dark figures in the tunnel, raising his voice above the increasing fury of the wind. The front now loomed above them, a cliff of dark weather that ate away daylight as it approached. He broke off and came over to McFarlane.

"Any new results from the second set of tests, Dr. McFarlane?" he asked as he watched the men work beneath them.

McFarlane nodded. "On several fronts." He fell silent. It was only a small satisfaction, he knew: making Glinn ask. It continued to rankle him, Glinn's monitoring his actions. But he had decided not to make an issue of it—at least not now.

Glinn inclined his head, as if perceiving the thought. "I see. May we hear them, please?"

"Sure thing. We have its melting point now. Or rather, I should say vapor point, since it goes directly from a solid to a gas."

Glinn raised his eyebrows inquiringly.

"One point two million degrees Kelvin."

Glinn breathed out. "Good Lord."

"We've also made some progress on its crystalline structure. It's an extremely complicated, asymmetrical fractal pattern built from nested isosceles triangles. The patterns repeat themselves at different scales from the macroscopic all the way down to individual atoms. A textbook fractal. Which explains its extreme hardness. It appears to be elemental, not an alloy."

"Any more information about its place on the periodic table?"

"Very high up, above one seventy-seven. A superactinide element, probably. The individual atoms appear to be gigantic, each with hundreds of protons and neutrons. It's most definitely an element in the 'island of stability' we talked about earlier."

"Anything else?"

McFarlane took a breath of frosty air. "Yes. Something very interesting. Rachel and I dated the Jaws of Hanuxa. The volcanic eruptions and lava flows date almost precisely to the time of the meteorite's impact."

Glinn's eyes flickered toward him. "Your conclusion?"

"We always assumed that the meteorite landed near a volcano. But now it looks as if the meteorite *made* the volcano."

Glinn waited.

"The meteorite was so heavy and dense, and traveling so fast, that it punched deep into the earth's crust, like a bullet, triggering the volcanic eruption. That's why Isla Desolación, alone among the Cape Horn islands, is volcanic. In his journal, Nestor talked about the 'weird coesite' of the region. And when I reexamined the coesite with the X-ray diffractor, I realized he was right. It *is* different. The meteorite's impact was so severe that the surrounding rock that wasn't vaporized underwent a phase change. The impact chemically changed the material into a form of coesite never seen before."

He gestured in the direction of the Jaws of Hanuxa. "The force of the eruption, the turbulence of the magma and the explosive release of gases, carried the meteorite back up, where it froze into position several thousand feet down. Over millions of years, in the uplift and erosion of the southern Cordillera, it gradually moved closer and closer to the surface, until it finally eroded out of the island valley. At least, that's what seems to fit the facts."

There was a thoughtful silence. Then Glinn looked over at Garza and Stonecipher. "Let's proceed."

Garza shouted out orders. McFarlane watched as some of the

figures in the tunnel below gingerly attached a webbing of thick Kevlar straps to the cradle and the meteorite. Others pulled more straps over the top of the sled and into position around the capstan. Then the group stood back. There was a metallic cough, then a throaty rumble, and the ground beneath McFarlane's feet came alive with vibration. Two massive diesel generators began turning the steel capstan. As it turned, the webbing of Kevlar straps slowly began to wind up, taking out the slack, tightening around the rock. The generators stopped: the meteorite was now ready to move.

McFarlane's eyes returned to the meteorite. The shadow of the storm fell across the staging area, and the meteorite looked duller, as if some internal fire had been quenched.

"Jesus," Rachel said, glancing at the wall of wind and snow that was boiling toward them. "Here it comes."

"Everything's in position," Garza said.

Glinn turned, the wind tugging at his parka. "We stop at the first sign of lightning," he said. "Move it."

There was a sudden rising darkness, a muffled howl, and pellets of snow came blasting horizontally through the air. In an instant, McFarlane's view was reduced to monochromatic shadows. Over the fury of the wind came the roar of heavy machinery as the generators came up to speed. The ground was shaking harder now, and a low, subauditory rumble—a pressure on the ear and gut—went through him. The generators climbed, whining louder as they strained to move the rock.

"It's a historic moment," Rachel wailed, "and I can't see a damn thing."

McFarlane pulled the hood of his parka tight around his face and crouched forward. He could see the Kevlar was drawn tight now, the straps like bars of iron, singing under the strain. Creaks and strange twanging noises rose up, audible even over the wind. The rock did not move, and the tension began to mount. The twanging noises rose in pitch; the generators roared; and still the rock remained stationary. And then, at the height of the cacophony, McFarlane thought he saw the meteorite move. But with the wind shrieking in his ears and the snow obscuring his vision, he could not be sure.

Garza looked up, smiled crookedly, and gave them a thumbs-up.

"It's moving!" Rachel cried.

Garza and Stonecipher shouted orders to the workers below. Beneath the cradle, the steel runners squealed and smoked. Workers pumped a continuous slurry of graphite on the runners and the surface of the cart. The acrid smell of burning steel rose to McFarlane's nostrils.

And then it was over. With a tremendous, decaying groan, the meteorite and its cradle settled onto the waiting cart. The Kevlar straps loosened, and the generators powered down.

"We did it!" Rachel pressed her index fingers to her lips and gave a piercing whistle.

McFarlane gazed down at the meteorite, now safely mounted on the cart. "Ten feet," he said. "Ten thousand miles to go."

Beyond the Jaws of Hanuxa, there was a brilliant flash of lightning, then another. A monstrous clap of thunder rolled past them. The wind rose in strength, tearing at the snow, sending sheets of white across the ground and into the trench.

"That's it!" Glinn called out to the group. "Mr. Garza, please cover the tunnel."

Garza turned toward the crane operator, one gloved hand keeping his hood secure against the wind. "Can't do it!" he shouted back. "The wind's too strong. It'll topple the boom."

Glinn nodded. "Then pull the tarps and ribbing over it until the storm passes."

As McFarlane watched, a group of workers ran down both sides of the trench, unrolling a tarp as they went, struggling to keep it in place against the rising fury of the wind. It was streaked with mottled white and gray, camouflaged to resemble the bleak surface of the island. McFarlane was impressed once again by Glinn's ability to anticipate every possibility, to have a contingency plan always waiting in the wings.

Another flash of lightning, closer this time, gave a strange illumination to the snow-heavy air.

Satisfied that the tarp had been properly secured, Glinn nodded to McFarlane. "Let's get back to the huts." He looked over at Garza. "I want the area cleared of personnel until the storm passes. Post a guard at four-hour shifts."

Then he motioned to McFarlane and Rachel and they began to make their way across the staging area, leaning into the howling wind.

Isla Desolación, 10:40 P.M.

Adolfo Timmer waited behind a large snowdrift, motionless in the dark. He had lain, watching, until he was almost completely buried by the storm. Down below, he could see the faint glow of lights, fading in and out of the snow. It was now after midnight, and he had seen no activity. The cleared area was deserted, the workers no doubt sheltering in the huts. It was time to act.

Timmer raised his head against the still-intensifying blast. He rose, the wind whipping the accumulated snow from his limbs. Around him, the storm had shaped the snow into long, diagonal fins, some more than ten feet high. It was perfect cover.

He moved forward on his snowshoes, shielded by the drifts. He stopped near the edge of the cleared area. Ahead lay a pool of dirty light. Crouching behind a snowbank, he waited, then raised his head and looked around. Perhaps fifty yards away, a lone shack stood, the wind moaning through gaps in its corrugated roof. On the far side of the cleared area, across from the shack, he could make out the long row of Quonset huts, their windows small squares of yellow. Beside them were other structures and some containers. As he stared, Timmer's eyes narrowed. The leaching ponds and tailing piles across the island had proved to be a ruse, a cover for something else.

But what?

He tensed. From around the corner of the shack, a man in a heavy parka appeared. He opened the door of the shack, looked inside, closed it again. Then he walked slowly along one edge of the cleared area, rubbing his mittens together, ducking his head against the wind and snow.

Timmer watched carefully. The man was not out for an evening smoke. He was doing guard duty.

But why post a guard over an old shack and a barren patch of ground?

He crept forward, slowly, until he reached another drift. He was much closer to the shack now. He waited, motionless, as the man returned to its door, stamped warmth into his feet, then walked away again. Unless there was somebody else posted inside the shack, the guard was alone.

Timmer came around the side of the drift and approached the building, keeping it between him and the guard. He stayed close to the ground, letting the darkness and the storm conceal him, careful to expose only the white nylon of his snowsuit to the circle of light.

Before he left the *Almirante Ramirez*, the comandante had told him to take no unnecessary risks. He had said it more than once: *Be very careful, Mr. Timmer. I want you back in one piece*. There was no way to know if the guard was armed: Timmer would assume he was. Crouching in the shadow of the shack, he reached into his snowsuit. His hand closed around the handle of his knife and slid it out of the scabbard, making sure it had not frozen in place. Tugging off one glove, he felt the blade: ice cold and razor sharp. Excellent. *Yes, my Comandante*, he thought: *I will be very, very careful*. He clasped it tightly, ignoring the cold that bit into his fingers. He wanted the blade warm enough to cut through flesh without freezing and snagging.

He waited as the storm grew even stronger. The wind whipped around the bare sides of the shack, howling and crying. He pulled his hood from his head, listening with his naked ear. Then he heard it again: the soft swish and crush of footsteps approaching through the snow.

A faint shadow came into view around the edge of the hut, barely visible in the dim light. Timmer pressed against the shack as it approached. There was the sound of breathing, the thumping of arms as the man hugged himself against the cold.

Timmer spun around the corner, lashing out low with his foot. The figure fell facedown in the snow. In a flash Timmer was on top of him, knee digging into his back, dragging the man into shadow while wrenching back his head. The knife came forward, scoring deeply across the man's neck. Timmer felt the blade grating against the cervical vertebrae. There was a soft gurgle, then a rush of hot blood. Timmer continued to hold the man's head back, letting his life drain into the snow. Then he relaxed his grip and eased the body forward.

Timmer turned the man over and examined his face. He was white, not the mestizo the comandante had told him to watch for. He patted the man's pockets quickly, finding a two-way radio and a small semiautomatic weapon. He slipped them into his pocket, then concealed the body in a nearby drift, sweeping snow over it and smoothing over the area. He cleaned his knife in the snow and carefully buried the bloody mush. The fact that he had seen only one guard did not mean there could not be another.

Moving around the rear of the shack and keeping out of the light, he crept along the edge of the cleared area, following the path the guard had walked. It was most curious: there was nothing here but snow. As he stepped forward again, the ground yielded suddenly beneath one of his snowshoes, and he scrambled backward in surprise. Exploring cautiously, on his hands and knees now, he felt something strange beneath the thin covering of snow. It was not earth, it was not a crevasse; there was a hollow beneath the ground, with some kind of cloth stretched tight across it, held up by spacers.

Carefully, Timmer made his way back to the shadows behind the shack. Before he explored further, he would have to make sure there were no surprises inside. Keeping his knife poised, he crept around to the front, opened the door a crack, and glanced within. It was deserted. He slipped inside and closed the door behind him.

He pulled out a small flashlight and swept it around. The beam illuminated nothing but kegs full of nails.

Why would somebody post a guard in front of a useless, empty shack?

Then he noticed something. Quickly, he turned out his light. A faint line of light was coming from the edge of a steel plate *beneath* one of the kegs.

Moving it aside, Timmer saw a trapdoor of banded metal. He knelt beside it, listening intently for a moment. Then he grasped the door and lifted it gingerly.

After the hours of waiting and watching in the winter night, the fluorescence that streamed up was blinding. He closed the trapdoor again and crouched in the darkness, thinking. Then he removed his snowshoes, concealed them in the far corner of the hut, and opened the door again, waiting a moment for his eyes to adjust. Then, knife in hand, he descended the ladder.

Thirty feet down, he stepped off the ladder into the tunnel. He paused. It was warmer down here, but at first Timmer barely noticed: in the glare of the light he felt exposed and vulnerable. He moved rapidly along the tunnel, keeping low. This was like no gold mine he had ever heard of. In fact, it was like no mine at all.

Reaching a junction, he paused to look around. There was nobody: no sound, no movement. He licked his lips, wondering what to do next.

Then he paused. Up ahead, the tunnel widened. There was an open space ahead, with something very large in it. He crept to the edge of the open area and shined his light around. A giant cart.

Timmer approached it cautiously, creeping along the wall. It was a huge steel flatbed trailer, perhaps a hundred feet long. Mounted to its underside were big tires: hundreds of them, on gleaming titanium axles. His eyes traveled slowly upward. Built on the cart was a complex pyramid of wooden struts and members. And nestled in that was something Timmer had never seen or imagined before. Something huge and red. Something that gleamed with impossible richness in the artificial light of the tunnel.

He looked around again, then approached the cart. Setting one foot on the closest tire, he pulled himself onto the platform, breathing heavily. He was quickly overheating in his heavy snowsuit, but he ignored the discomfort. Overhead, a large tarp was stretched tightly across the open roof: the tarp onto which he had stepped. But Timmer had no interest in this. His eyes were on the thing resting in the huge cradle.

Very carefully, he climbed the wooden struts toward it. There was no doubt about it: this, *this* was what the Americans had come for. But what was it?

There was no time to waste; there was no time even to hunt for the little mestizo. Comandante Vallenar would want to know about this right away. And yet still Timmer hesitated, balanced on the wooden cradle.

The thing was almost ethereal in its beauty. It was as if it had no surface; as if he could put his hand forward and thrust it right into its ruby depths. As he stared, he thought he could see subtle patterns within, shifting and changing, coruscating in the light. He almost imagined a coldness emanating from it, cooling his overheated face. It was the most beautiful, otherworldly thing he had ever seen.

Without taking his eyes away, Timmer slipped the knife into a pocket, pulled off his glove, and held his hand forward, slowly, almost reverently, toward the rich and shining surface.

Isla Desolación, 11:15 P.M.

Sam McFarlane jerked awake, heart pounding. He would have thought it a nightmare, if the sound of the explosion was not still reverberating across the landscape. He stood bolt upright, the chair falling to the floor behind him. From the corner of his eye he saw that Glinn, too, was on his feet, listening. As they met each other's gaze, the lights in the hut winked out. There was a moment of pitch-blackness, and then an emergency light snapped on over the door, bathing the room in pale orange.

"What the hell was that?" McFarlane said. His voice was almost drowned out by a loud gust of wind: the window had been blown out, and snow swirled into the hut, mingling with wooden splinters and shards of glass.

Glinn approached the window and gazed out into the stormy darkness. Then he glanced at Garza. He, too, was on his feet. "Who's got duty?"

"Hill."

Glinn raised a radio. "Hill. This is Glinn. Report." He took his thumb from the transmit button and listened. "Hill!" he called again. Then he switched frequencies. "Forward post? Thompson?" He was answered by a loud hiss of static.

He dropped the radio. "Radio's out, I'm not getting any

responses." He turned back to Garza, who was pulling on his snowsuit. "Where are you going?"

"To the electrical hut."

"Negative. We'll go together."

Glinn's tone had become sharper, military. "Yes, sir," Garza replied briskly.

There was a clattering outside, then Amira tumbled in from the communications hut, snow clinging to her shoulders.

"Power's down everywhere," she gasped. "All we've got is the reserve."

"Understood," Glinn said. A small Glock 17 pistol had appeared in his hand. He checked the magazine, then tucked it into his belt.

McFarlane had turned to reach for his own snowsuit. As he thrust his arms into the sleeves, he saw Glinn look at him.

"Don't even say it," McFarlane began. "I'm coming with you."

Glinn hesitated, and saw his resolve. He turned to Amira. "You stay here."

"But—"

"Rachel, we need you here. Lock the door after we leave. We'll have a guard here shortly."

Within moments, three of Glinn's men, Thompson, Rocco, and Sanders, appeared at the door, powerful torches in their hands and Ingram M10 submachine guns slung over their shoulders.

"Everyone accounted for except Hill, sir," Thompson said.

"Sanders, have guards posted at every hut. Thompson, Rocco, you come with me." Glinn strapped on snowshoes, grabbed a torch, and led the way out into the swirling dark.

McFarlane struggled with the unfamiliar snowshoes. Hours of drowsing by the stove had made him forget how cold it was outside, how sharp the snowflakes felt when the wind drove them against his face.

The electrical hut lay only fifty yards away. Garza unlocked the door and they entered the small space, Thompson and Rocco sweeping it with their torches. The smell of burnt wiring hung in the air. Garza knelt to pull open the gray metal cover of the master control cabinet. As he did so, a cloud of acrid smoke billowed out into the light of the torches.

Garza ran his finger down the panel. "Totally fried," he said.

"Estimated time to repair?" Glinn asked.

"Main switching box, ten minutes, max. Then we can run diagnostics."

"Do it. You men, get outside and guard the door."

The construction chief worked in silence while McFarlane looked on. Glinn tried the radio again; finding it was still broadcasting nothing but noise, he replaced it in his pocket. At length, Garza stepped back and threw a series of switches. There was a click and a hum, but no lights. With a grunt of surprise, Garza opened a nearby metal locker, withdrew a palmtop diagnostic computer, plugged it into a jack on the master control cabinet, and switched it on. A small blue screen flickered into life.

"We've got multiple burnouts, up and down the line," he said after a moment.

"What about the surge suppressors?"

"Whatever it was, it caused one hell of a spike. Over a billion volts in under a millisecond, with a current exceeding fifty thousand amps. No dampeners or surge suppressors could protect against that."

"A billion volts?" McFarlane said in disbelief. "Not even lightning is that powerful."

"That's right," Garza said, pulling the tool from the panel and dropping it into a pocket of his snowsuit. "A burst of this size makes lightning look like static cling."

"Then what was it?"

Garza shook his head. "God knows."

Glinn stood still a moment, gazing at the fused components. "Let's check the rock."

They stepped back out into the storm, moved past the huts, and struggled across the staging area. Even from a distance, McFarlane could see that the tarp had been torn from its tethers. As they drew nearer, Glinn made a suppressing motion with his hand, then instructed Rocco and Thompson to enter the shack and descend into the tunnel. Pulling out his pistol, Glinn moved forward carefully, Garza at his side. McFarlane stepped up to the edge of the trench, the tattered remains of the tarp billowing skyward like ghostly linen. Glinn angled the beam of the torch downward, into the tunnel.

Dirt, rocks, and charred wood were scattered everywhere. Part of the cart was twisted and fused, hissing faintly, sending up clouds of steam. Globs of foamy metal, now resolidified, spattered the tunnel. Beneath the cart, several rows of tires had melted together and were now burning, sending up foul clouds of smoke.

Glinn's eyes moved rapidly around the scene, following his torch. "Was it a bomb?"

"Looks more like a gigantic electrical arc."

Lights wavered at the far end of the tunnel, then Thompson and Rocco approached beneath them, waving away the pall of smoke. They began spraying fire suppressant on the burning tires.

"See any damage to the meteorite?" Glinn called down.

There was a pause as the men below made a visual inspection. "Can't see a scratch on it."

"Thompson," Glinn said, pointing down into the trench. "Over there."

McFarlane followed his arm to a spot beyond the cart. Something was burning fitfully. Nearby, ragged clumps of matter and bone glistened in the flickering light. Thompson shined his torch toward one of them. There was a hand, a piece of what looked like a flayed human shoulder, a twisted length of grayish entrails.

"Christ," McFarlane groaned.

"Looks like we found Hill," said Garza.

"Here's his gun," Thompson said.

Glinn shouted down into the tunnel. "Thompson, I want you to check the rest of the tunnel system. Report anything you find. Rocco, roust up a med team. Let's get those remains gathered up."

"Yes, sir."

Glinn looked back toward Garza. "Get the perimeter secured. Gather all surveillance data and get it analyzed right away. Call back to the ship for a general alert. I want a new power grid up and running in six hours."

"All communications with the ship are down," said Garza. "We're getting nothing but noise on all channels."

Glinn turned back toward the tunnel. "You! Thompson! When you're done here, take a snowcat to the beach. Contact the ship from the landing area. Use Morse if you have to."

Thompson saluted, then turned and made his way down the tunnel. In a moment he disappeared from view in the smoke and darkness.

Glinn turned to McFarlane. "Go get Amira and any diagnostic tools you'll need. I'm going to have a team sweep the tunnels. Once the area's secured, and Hill's body is removed, I want you to examine the meteorite. Nothing elaborate for the time being. Just determine what happened here. And don't touch that rock."

McFarlane looked down. At the base of the cart, Rocco was slipping what looked like a lung onto a folded section of tarp. Above, the meteorite steamed in its wooden bed. He wasn't about to touch it, but he said nothing.

"Rocco," Glinn called out, pointing to an area just to the rear of the damaged cart, where there was a faint flickering. "You've got another small fire over there."

Rocco approached it with the extinguisher, then stopped short. He looked up at them. "I think it's a heart, sir."

Glinn pursed his lips. "I see. Extinguish it, Mr. Rocco, and carry on."

Isla Desolación, July 21, 12:05 A.M.

As McFarlane trudged across the staging area toward the row of huts, the wind pressed rudely at his back, as if trying to force him to his knees. Beside him, Rachel stumbled, then recovered.

"Is this storm ever going to end?" she asked.

McFarlane, his mind a whirlwind of speculation, did not reply.

In another minute they were inside the medical hut. He peeled out of his suit. The air was rich with the smell of roasted meat. He saw that Garza was speaking into a radio.

"How long have you had communications?" he asked Glinn.

"Half an hour, or thereabouts. Still spotty, but improving."

"That's odd. We just tried to contact you from the tunnel and got nothing but radio noise." McFarlane began to speak again, but fell silent, forcing his mind to work through the weariness.

Garza lowered his radio. "It's Thompson, from the beach. He says Captain Britton refuses to send anyone over with the equipment until the storm dies down. It's too dangerous."

"That's not acceptable. Give me that radio." Glinn spoke rapidly. "Thompson? Explain to the captain that we've lost communications, the computer network, and the power grid. We need the generator and the equipment, and we need them *now*. Lives are at risk. If you encounter any more difficulties, let me know and

I'll see to it personally. Get Brambell out here, too. I want him to examine Hill's remains."

Distantly, McFarlane watched Rocco, hands and forearms hidden by heavy rubber gloves, removing charred body parts from a tarp and placing them in a freezer-locker.

"There's something else, sir," Garza said, listening once again to the radio. "Palmer Lloyd's in communication with the *Rolvaag*. He demands to be patched through to Sam McFarlane."

McFarlane felt himself shocked back into the stream of events. "It's not exactly the best time, is it?" he said with a disbelieving laugh, looking at Glinn. But the expression on Glinn's face took him by surprise.

"Can you rig up a squawk box?" Glinn asked.

"I'll grab one from the communications hut," Garza said.

McFarlane spoke to Glinn. "You're not really going to chitchat with Lloyd, are you? Now, of all times?"

Glinn returned the look. "It beats the alternative," he replied.

Only much later did McFarlane realize what Glinn meant.

Within minutes, the hut's transmitter had been jury-rigged with an external speaker. As Garza attached his radio, a wash of static filled the room. It faded into silence, grew louder, then faded again. McFarlane glanced around: at Rachel, huddled near the stove for warmth; at Glinn, pacing in front of the radio; at Rocco, industriously sorting body parts in the back of the room. He had a theory—or the beginnings of one. It was still too raw, too full of holes, to be shared. And yet he knew he had little choice.

There was a squeal of feedback, then a ragged voice emerged from the speaker. "Hello?" it said. "Hello?" It was Lloyd, distorted.

Glinn leaned forward. "This is Eli Glinn, Mr. Lloyd. Can you hear me?"

"Yes! Yes, I can! But you're damned faint, Eli."

"We're experiencing some kind of radio interference. We'll have to be brief. There's a great deal going on at the moment, and our battery power is limited."

"Why? What the hell *is* going on? Why didn't Sam call in for his daily briefing? I couldn't get a straight answer from that bloody captain of yours."

"There's been an accident. One of our men is dead."

"Two men, you mean. McFarlane told me about that incident with the meteorite. Damn shame about Rochefort."

"There's been a new fatality. A man named Hill."

There was a piercing shriek from the speaker. Then Lloyd's voice returned, even fainter now: "—happened to him?"

"We don't know yet," Glinn said. "McFarlane and Rachel Amira have just returned from examining the meteorite." He motioned McFarlane toward the speaker.

McFarlane moved forward with great unwillingness. He swallowed. "Mr. Lloyd," he began. "What I'm about to tell you is theoretical, a conclusion based on what I've observed. But I think we were wrong about how Nestor Masangkay died."

"Wrong?" said Lloyd. "What do you mean? And what does it have to do with the death of this man Hill?"

"If I'm right, it has everything to do with it. I think both men died because they touched the meteorite."

For a moment, the hut was silent save for the pop and stutter of the radio.

"Sam, that's absurd," Lloyd said. "*I* touched the meteorite."

"Bear with me. We thought Nestor was killed by lightning. And it's true, the meteorite is a powerful attractor. But Garza can tell you that the blast in the tunnel was on the order of a billion volts. No lightning bolt could produce that kind of power. I examined the cart and meteorite. The pattern of damage shows definite signs that the meteorite threw out a massive blast of electricity itself."

"But I laid my damn cheek against it. And I'm still here."

"I know that. I don't have an answer yet to why you were spared. But nothing else fits. The tunnel was deserted, the meteorite was shielded from the elements. No other force was acting upon it. It looks like a bolt of electricity came out of the rock, passed through part of the cart and cradle, spraying molten metal outward. And beneath the cart, I found a glove. It was the only piece of Hill's clothing not burned. I think he dropped the glove so he could touch the meteorite."

"Why would he do something like that?" Lloyd asked impatiently.

This time, it was Rachel who spoke up. "Why did *you?*" she asked. "That's one mighty strange-looking rock. You can't always predict what someone's going to do the first time they see it."

"Jesus, this is unbelievable," Lloyd said. There was a moment of silence. "But you can proceed. Right?"

McFarlane darted a look at Glinn.

"The cart and the cradle have been damaged," Glinn said. "But Mr. Garza tells me they can be repaired within twenty-four hours. The meteorite remains a question, however."

"Why?" Lloyd asked. "Was it damaged?"

"No," Glinn continued. "It appears to be unscathed. I'd given standing orders from the beginning to treat this thing as if it was dangerous. Now—if Dr. McFarlane's right—we *know* that it is. We must take additional precautions to load that rock onto the ship. But we have to move fast: it's also dangerous to remain here any longer than absolutely necessary."

"I don't like it. You should have figured out these precautions before we ever left New York."

It seemed to McFarlane that Glinn's eyes narrowed almost imperceptibly. "Mr. Lloyd, this meteorite has confounded all our expectations. We're now outside the parameters of the original EES analysis. That has never happened before. Do you know what that normally means?"

Lloyd did not reply.

"We abort the project," Glinn finished.

"That is *not* a goddamn option!" Lloyd was suddenly shouting, but the reception had grown so poor that McFarlane had to strain to hear. "I don't want that kind of talk. You hear me? Glinn, you *get* the goddamn rock on the boat and you *bring* it home."

Abruptly, the radio cut out.

"He terminated the transmission," said Garza.

The hut was silent; all eyes were on Glinn.

Over the man's shoulder, McFarlane could see Rocco, still at his grisly task. He had what looked like a piece of skull in his gloved hands, an eyeball hanging from it, held only by the ocular nerve.

Rachel sighed, shook her head, and rose slowly from her wooden chair. "So what do we do?"

"For now, help us get the plant back on line. Once we have power, you two will tackle that problem." Glinn turned to McFarlane. "Where's Hill's glove?"

"Right here." McFarlane reached wearily for his satchel, pulled out a sealed baggie, and held it up.

"That's a leather glove," Garza said. "The construction team was issued Gore-Tex gloves."

There was a sudden silence.

"Mr. Glinn?"

Rocco's voice was so sharp, the note of surprise so clear, that everyone glanced toward him. He still had the piece of skull in his hand, poised in front of his chin, as if he were about to take a snapshot with it.

"Yes, Mr. Rocco?"

"Frank Hill had brown eyes."

Glinn's face flicked from Rocco to the skull and then back again, the mute question clear on his face.

With an oddly delicate motion, Rocco drew the cuff of his shirt across the dangling eyeball, wiping it clean.

"This isn't Hill," he said. "This eye is blue."

Isla Desolación,
12:40 A.M.

Glinn stopped, arrested by the sight of the eyeball dangling from a strip of nerve. "Mr. Garza?" His voice was unusually calm.

"Sir."

"Get a team together. Find Hill. Use probes, thermal sensors."

"Yes, sir."

"But keep a sharp eye out. Watch for booby traps, snipers. Don't rule out anything."

Garza disappeared into the night. Glinn took the shattered eye from Rocco and began rotating it under his gaze. It seemed to McFarlane that he scrutinized it as one might a piece of fine porcelain. Then he walked over to the table where the body parts lay divided between the tarp and the cold-storage locker.

"Let's see what we've got here," he murmured. As McFarlane watched, he began sorting through them, handling each piece, peering at it critically, setting it down again and moving to the next, like a shopper browsing the meat section of a supermarket.

"Blond," he said, holding up a tiny hair to the light. He began assembling pieces of the head. "High cheekbones . . . close-cropped hair . . . Nordic features . . ." He put them aside and continued rummaging. "Death's head tattoo on the right arm . . . Young, perhaps twenty-five."

His examination lasted fifteen minutes, during which nobody

else spoke. At last, he straightened up and went to wash his hands in the sink. There was no water, so he flicked the excess matter from his hands and wiped them with a towel. Then he paced the length of the hut, turned, walked back.

Suddenly, Glinn went still. He seemed to have come to a decision. He plucked a radio from the table. "Thompson?"

"Yes, sir."

"What's the status on the generator?"

"Britton is bringing it herself; she wouldn't risk her crew. She says Brambell will come as soon as it's safe. The storm is supposed to ease by dawn."

The radio beeped and Glinn switched frequencies. "Found Hill," came Garza's terse voice.

"Yes?"

"He was buried in a snowdrift. Throat cut. Very professional piece of work."

"Thank you, Mr. Garza." Glinn's profile was dully illuminated in the emergency light of the hut. A single bead of sweat stood on his brow.

"And there's a pair of snowshoes hidden in the entrance shack. Like the glove, they're not ours."

"I see. Bring Hill's body to the medical hut, please. We wouldn't want it to freeze before Dr. Brambell arrives; that would be inconvenient."

"So who *was* this other man?" McFarlane asked.

Instead of answering, Glinn turned away and murmured something in Spanish, just loud enough for McFarlane to catch: "*You are not a wise man,* mi Comandante. *Not a wise man at all.*"

Isla Desolación, July 23, 12:05 P.M.

The storm eased, and forty-eight hours passed without further incident. Security was beefed up considerably; guard duty was tripled, additional cameras were installed, and a perimeter of motion-detecting sensors was sunk into the snow around the operation.

Meanwhile, work on the sunken roadway proceeded at a breakneck pace. As soon as one section was built, the meteorite and cart were dragged along, inch by inch, to rest only while the capstan was repositioned, a new section of roadway built, and the previous section filled in. Safety precautions around the meteorite had been redoubled.

At last, the excavators reached the interior of the snowfield. Here, sheltered beneath almost two hundred feet of solid ice, the meteorite waited while digging teams cored through the snowfield from both ends.

Eli Glinn stood inside the mouth of the ice tunnel, watching the progress as the great machines worked. All had gone according to plan, despite the two recent deaths. Half a dozen thick hoses snaked out of the hole in the ice, diesel fumes and soot spewing from their ends: a jury-rigged forced-air system to suck exhaust from the tunnel while the heavy machinery carved through the ice. It was beautiful in its way, Glinn thought, one more engineering marvel in a long list since the project had begun. The walls and ceiling of the tunnel were rough-edged and irregular, fractal in their endless knobs and ridges. A million cracks and fissures ran away in crazy spiderwebs across the walls, white against the shockingly deep blue of the ice. Only the floor was even, covered with the omnipresent crushed gravel over which the cart would travel.

A single row of fluorescent lights lit the tunnel. Peering ahead, Glinn could see the meteorite on its cart, a red blob inside an eerie blue tube. The tunnel echoed with the crashing and grinding of unseen machinery. There was a wink of headlights in the distance, then some kind of vehicle made its way around the meteorite and came toward him. It was a train of ore carts, full of glittering blue shards of ice.

The revelation that the meteorite could kill by touch had startled Glinn more than he cared to admit. Despite that he had instituted orders never to touch the rock directly, he had always considered this merely a judicious precaution. He sensed that McFarlane was right: the touch had caused the explosion. There seemed to be no other possible answer. A strategic recalculation had become necessary. It had caused yet another revision in his failure-success analysis—one that required virtually all of EES's computer capacity back in New York to process.

Glinn looked once again at the red rock, sitting like a huge gemstone on its bed of greenheart oak. This was the thing that killed Vallenar's man, killed Rochefort and Evans, killed Masangkay. Strange that it had not killed Lloyd. It was undeniably deadly . . . but the fact was, they were still ahead of schedule on fatalities. The volcano project had cost fourteen lives, including one meddling government minister who insisted on being where he shouldn't have been. Glinn reminded himself that, despite the strangeness of the rock, despite the problem of the Chilean destroyer, this remained essentially a heavy moving job.

He glanced at his watch. McFarlane and Amira would be on time; they always were. And he could see them now, stepping out of a snowcat at the mouth of the ice tunnel, McFarlane lugging a duffel bag full of instruments. In five minutes they were at Glinn's side. He turned to them. "You've got forty minutes until the tunnel is complete and the meteorite is moved again. Make good use of it."

"We intend to," said Amira.

He watched her pulling gear out of the duffel and setting up instruments, while McFarlane silently took pictures of the rock with a digital camera. She was capable. McFarlane had learned about her reports, as he had expected. This had had the desired effect: it put McFarlane on notice that his behavior was being scrutinized. It also gave Amira an ethical dilemma to occupy herself with, always helpful in distracting her from the thornier moral questions she had a tendency to ask. Moral questions that had no place in a cold-blooded engineering project. McFarlane had taken it better than the profile predicted. A complicated man, and one who had proven himself unusually useful.

Glinn noticed another cat arriving, also with a passenger. Sally Britton stepped out, a long coat of navy blue wool billowing out behind her. Uncharacteristically, there was no officer's cap on her head, and her wheat-colored hair gleamed in the lights of the tunnel. Glinn smiled. He had also been expecting this, ever since the explosion that killed the Chilean spy. Expecting it, even looking forward to it.

As Britton drew near, Glinn turned toward her with a genuinely welcoming smile. He took her hand. "Nice to see you, Captain. What brings you down here?"

Britton looked around, her intelligent green eyes taking in everything. They froze when they saw the meteorite.

"Good God," she said, her step suddenly faltering.

Glinn smiled. "It's always a shock at first sight."

She nodded wordlessly.

"Nothing great can happen in this world, Captain, without some difficulty." Glinn spoke quietly, but with great force. "It's the scientific discovery of the century." Glinn did not particularly care about its value to science; his interest was solely in the engineering aspects. But he was not going to eschew a little drama, if it served his purposes.

Britton continued staring. "They said it was red, but I had no idea . . ."

The roar of heavy machinery echoed down the ice tunnel as she stared: one minute, then two. At last, with obvious effort, she took a breath, pulled her eyes away, and faced him.

"Two more people have been killed. But what news we've had from you has been slow in coming, and rumors are everywhere. The crew are nervous, and so are my officers. I need to know exactly what happened, and why."

Glinn nodded, waiting.

"That meteorite is not coming on board my ship until I'm convinced it's safe." She said it all at once and then stood firm, her slim, small form planted on the gravel.

Glinn smiled. This was one hundred percent Sally Britton. Every day he admired her more.

"I feel exactly the same way," he said.

She looked at him, off balance, obviously having expected resistance.

"Mr. Glinn, we have a dead Chilean naval officer to explain to the authorities. We have a warship out there somewhere, a destroyer that likes to train its guns on us. Three of your people are dead. We have a twenty-five-thousand-ton rock that, when it isn't crushing people, blows them to bits, and you want to put it inside my ship." She paused a moment, then continued, her voice lower. "Even the best crews can get superstitious. There's been a lot of wild talk."

"You are right to be concerned. Let me brief you on what happened. I apologize for not coming to the ship myself, but as you know we've been fighting the clock."

She waited.

"Two nights ago, during the storm, we had an intruder from the Chilean ship. He was killed by an electrical discharge from the meteorite. Unfortunately, not before he murdered one of our men."

Britton looked at him sharply. "So it's true? Lightning shot out of the meteorite? I didn't believe it. And I sure as hell don't understand it."

"It's actually quite simple. It's made of a metal that is a superconductor of electricity. The human body—human skin—has an electrical potential. If you touch the meteorite, the meteorite discharges some of the electricity circulating inside it. Like a blast of lightning, only greater. McFarlane has explained the theory to me. That's what we believe killed the Chilean, as well as Nestor Masangkay, the man who first discovered the meteorite."

"Why does it do that?"

"McFarlane and Amira are working on that question now. But moving the rock is the priority now, and they haven't had time for further analysis."

"So what's to prevent this from happening on my ship?"

"Another good question." Glinn smiled. "We're working on that one too. We're taking great precautions to make sure no one touches it. Indeed, we had instituted such a policy even before we realized that touch could trigger an explosion."

"I see. Where does the electricity come from?"

Glinn's hesitation was very brief. "That's one of the things that Dr. McFarlane is studying right now."

Britton did not respond.

Quite suddenly, Glinn took her hand. He felt a brief, instinctive resistance. Then she relaxed.

"I understand your concerns, Captain," he said gently. "That's why we are taking all possible precautions. But you must believe we will not fail. You must believe in *me*. Just as I believe in you to maintain discipline aboard your ship, despite the nervousness and superstitions of the crew."

She looked at him, but he could see her eyes irresistibly drawn back to the great red rock.

"Stay a while," said Glinn softly, smiling. "Stay and watch us bring the heaviest object ever moved by mankind to your ship."

She looked from the rock toward him, then back to the rock, hesitating.

A radio on her belt chirped. She immediately freed herself and stepped away. "This is Captain Britton," she said.

Watching the change in her face, Glinn knew precisely what she must be hearing.

She replaced the radio. "The destroyer. It's returned."

Glinn nodded. The smile had not left his face. "No surprise," he said. "The *Almirante Ramirez* has lost one of her own. Now she's come to get him back."

Rolvaag,
July 24, 3:45 P.M.

Night was falling over Isla Desolación. Coffee cup in hand, McFarlane watched the twilight gather from the solitude of the fly deck. It was a perfect evening: clear, cold, windless. In the distance, there were some remaining streaks of clouds: mare's tails of pink and peach. The island lay etched in light, unnaturally clear and crisp. Beyond, the glossy waters of Franklin Channel reflected the last rays of the setting sun. Farther still lay Vallenar's destroyer, gray, malevolent, the name *Almirante Ramirez* barely legible on its rust-streaked sides. That afternoon it had moved in closer, nosing into place at the entrance to Franklin Channel—their only route of exit. Now it looked as though it planned to stay.

McFarlane took a sip of coffee, then impulsively poured the rest over the side. Caffeine was the last thing he needed right now. There was already a tremendous tension in his gut. He wondered just how Glinn was planning to deal with the destroyer, on top of everything else. But Glinn had seemed calm that day; exceptionally calm. He wondered if the man was having a nervous breakdown.

The meteorite had been moved—painfully, centimeter by centimeter—through the icefield and down the sunken roadway to the edge of Isla Desolación. It had finally reached a bluff overlooking Franklin Channel. To hide it, another of Glinn's corrugated metal shacks had gone up. McFarlane examined the shack from the deck. As usual, it was a masterpiece of deception: a rusty contraption of secondhand metal that listed dangerously. Bald tires had been piled in front. He wondered how they planned to lower it into the hold; Glinn had been exceptionally cagey. All he knew was, it was going to happen in a single night: *that* night.

The hatch opened and McFarlane turned at the sound. He was surprised to see Glinn, who hadn't been on board the ship, as far as he could tell, for almost a week.

The man sauntered over casually. Although his face remained gray, there was an easiness to his movements. "Evening," he said.

"You seem awfully calm."

Instead of replying, Glinn removed a pack of cigarettes and, much to McFarlane's surprise, slid one into his mouth. He lit it, the match flaring against his sallow face, and took a long drag.

"Didn't know you smoked. Out of costume, anyway."

Glinn smiled. "I allow myself twelve cigarettes a year. It's my one foolishness."

"When was the last time you slept?" McFarlane asked.

Glinn gazed out over the peaceful waters. "I'm not sure. Sleep is like food: after the first few days you stop missing it."

He smoked in silence for a few minutes. "Any fresh insights from your time in the ice tunnel?" he asked at last.

"Tantalizing bits and pieces. It has an atomic number in excess of four hundred, for example."

Glinn nodded.

"Sound travels through it at ten percent the speed of light. It has a very faint internal structure: an outer layer and an inner layer, with a small inclusion in the center. Most meteorites come from the breakup of a larger body. This one is just the opposite: it looks like it grew by accretion, probably in a jet of plasma from a hypernova. Sort of like a pearl around a grain of sand. That's why it's somewhat symmetrical."

"Extraordinary. And the electrical discharge?"

"Still a mystery. We don't know why a human *touch* should trigger it when nothing else seems to. We also don't know why it is that Lloyd, alone, escaped getting blown to bits. We've got more data than we can even begin to analyze, and it's all contradictory."

"What about the way our radios were knocked out after the explosion? Any connection?"

"Yes. It seems that after the discharge, the meteorite was in an excited state, emitting radio waves—long-wavelength electromagnetic radiation. That accounts for the interference with radio communication. Over time, it died down, but in its immediate vicinity—say, inside the tunnel—the meteorite was still throwing off enough radio noise to defeat radio traffic for several hours, at least."

"And now?"

"It's settled down. At least until the next explosion."

Glinn puffed silently, savoring the cigarette as McFarlane watched. Then he gestured toward the shore, and the rickety shack that concealed the meteorite. "In a few hours, that thing will be in the tank. If you have any last reservations, I need to know now. Our lives at sea depend on it."

McFarlane said nothing. He could almost feel the burden of the question settling on his shoulders. "I simply can't predict what's going to happen," he said.

Glinn smoked. "I'm not asking for a prediction, only an educated guess."

"We've had the chance to observe it, under various conditions, for almost two weeks. Except for the electrical discharge apparently caused by human touch, it seems completely inert. It doesn't react to metal touching it, or even a high-powered electron microprobe. As long as our safety precautions are kept rigidly in place, I can't think of any reason why it should act differently in the holding tank of the *Rolvaag*."

McFarlane hesitated, wondering if his own fascination with the meteorite was causing him to lose his objectivity. The idea of leaving it behind was . . . unthinkable. He changed the subject. "Lloyd's been on the satellite phone almost hourly, and he's desperate for news."

Glinn inhaled blissfully, his eyes half closed, like a Buddha. "In thirty minutes, as soon as it's fully dark, we bring the ship up against the bluff and begin loading the meteorite on a tower built out of the tank. It will be in the tank by three A.M., and by dawn we'll be a good way to international waters. You can relate that to Mr. Lloyd. Everything is under control. Garza and Stonecipher will be running the operation. I won't even be needed until the final stage."

"What about *that?*" McFarlane nodded toward the destroyer. "Once you start lowering the rock into the tank, it's going to be exposed for all to see. The *Rolvaag* will be a sitting duck."

"We will work under cover of darkness and a predicted fog. Nevertheless, I will be paying a call on Comandante Vallenar during the critical period."

McFarlane was not sure he had heard correctly. "You'll be doing *what?*"

"It will distract him." Then, more quietly, "And it will serve other purposes as well."

"That's insane. He might arrest you, or even kill you."

"I don't believe so. By all accounts, Comandante Vallenar is a brutal man. But he is not crazy."

"In case you hadn't noticed, he's blocking our only exit."

Night had fallen, and a cloak of darkness had settled over the island. Glinn checked his gold watch, then pulled a radio out of his pocket. "Manuel? You may commence."

Almost instantaneously, the bluff was lit up by banks of brilliant lights, bathing the bleak landscape in a cold illumination. A swarm of workers appeared as if out of nowhere. Heavy machinery growled.

"Jesus, why don't you put up a billboard saying: 'Here it is'?" asked McFarlane.

"The bluff is not visible from Vallenar's ship," Glinn said. "It's blocked by that headland. If Vallenar wants to see what this new activity is about—and he will—he'll have to move the destroyer back up to the northern end of the channel. Sometimes the best disguise is no disguise at all. Vallenar, you see, won't be expecting our departure."

"Why not?"

"Because we will also continue the decoy mining operation all night long. All the heavy equipment, and two dozen men, will remain on the island, working at a feverish pace. There will be occasional explosions, naturally, and lots of radio traffic. Just before dawn, something will be found. Or at least it will look that way to the *Almirante Ramirez*. There will be great excitement. The workmen will take a break to discuss the discovery." He flicked the butt away, watching it sail into the darkness. "The *Rolvaag*'s tender is hidden on the far side of the island. As soon as we depart, the tender will load up the men and meet us behind Horn Island. Everything else will be left behind."

"Everything?" McFarlane let his mind run over the shacks full of equipment, the dozers, the container labs, the huge yellow haulers.

"Yes. The generators will be running, all the lights will be left on. Millions of dollars' worth of heavy equipment will be left on the island in plain view. When Vallenar sees us move, he'll assume we're coming back."

"He won't give chase?"

Glinn did not respond for a moment. "He might."

"What then?"

Glinn smiled. "Every path has been analyzed, every contingency planned for." He raised his radio again. "Bring the vessel in toward the bluff."

After a pause, McFarlane could feel the vibration of the big engines. Slowly, very slowly, the great ship began to turn.

Glinn looked back toward McFarlane. "You have a critical role in this, Sam."

McFarlane looked at him in surprise. "Me?"

Glinn nodded. "I want you to stay in communication with Lloyd. Keep him informed, keep him calm, and, above all, *keep him where he is*. It might be disastrous if he came down now. And now, farewell. I must prepare for my meeting with our Chilean friend." He paused and looked McFarlane steadily in the face. "I owe you an apology."

"What for?" McFarlane asked.

"You know very well what for. I couldn't have wished for a more consistent or reliable scientist. At the conclusion of the expedition, our file on you will be destroyed."

McFarlane didn't quite know what to make of this confession. It seemed sincere; but then, everything about the man was so calculated that he wondered if even this admission was intended to do double, or even triple duty, in Glinn's grand scheme.

Glinn held out his hand. McFarlane took it, and laid his other hand on Glinn's shoulder.

In a moment Glinn was gone.

It was only later that McFarlane realized the thick padding he'd felt under his fingers was not a heavy coat but a flak vest.

Franklin Channel, 8:40 P.M.

Glinn stood at the bow of the small launch, welcoming the frigid air that streamed across his face. The four men who were part of the operation sat on the deck of the dark pilothouse, suited up, silent and out of sight. Directly ahead, the lights of the destroyer wavered in the calm waters of the sound. As he predicted, it had moved up channel.

He glanced back toward the island itself. An immense cluster of lights surrounded the feverish mining activity. Heavy equipment rumbled back and forth. As he watched, the faint crump of a distant explosion rolled through the air. By comparison, the real work taking place on the bluff looked incidental. The movement of the *Rolvaag* had been presented, through radio traffic, as a precaution against another storm—the big ship would be moving into the lee of the island and stringing cables to shore.

He smelled the moisture-laden sea air, breathed in the deceptive calm. A big storm was certainly coming. Its precise nature was a secret shared only by Glinn, Britton, and the on-duty officers of the *Rolvaag;* there had seemed no need to distract the crew or the EES engineers at such a critical moment. But satellite weather analysis indicated it might develop into a *panteonero*, a cemetery wind, kicking up as early as dawn. Such a wind always started out of the southwest and then swung around to the northwest as it gained strength. Such winds could grow to Force 15. But if the *Rolvaag* could get through the Strait of Le Maire by noon, they would be in the lee of Tierra del Fuego before the worst of the wind started. And it would be at their backs: ideal for a large tanker, hellish for a small pursuer.

He knew that Vallenar must now be aware of his approach. The launch moved slowly, its full complement of running lights on. Even without radar it would be conspicuous against the black, moonless night water.

The launch drew within two hundred yards of the ship. Glinn heard a faint splash behind him but did not turn around. As expected, three other splashes quickly followed. He was aware of a preternatural calmness, a sharpening of his senses, that always came before an op. It had been a long time, and the feeling was pleasant, almost nostalgic.

A spotlight on the destroyer's fantail snapped on and swiveled toward the launch, blinding him with its brilliance. He remained motionless in the bow as the launch slowed. If he was going to be shot, this would be the moment. And yet he felt an unwavering conviction that the destroyer's gun would remain silent. He breathed in, then exhaled slowly, once, twice. The critical moment passed.

They met him at the boarding hatch and led him up through a series of foul passageways and slippery metal stairways. At the entrance to the *puente*, the bridge, they paused. Except for the deck officer, Vallenar was alone. He stood at the forward windows, looking out at the island, cigar in his mouth, hands clasped behind his back. It was cold; either the heating system did not work, or it had been turned off. Like the rest of the ship, the bridge smelled of engine oil, bilgewater, and fish.

Vallenar did not turn. Glinn let a very long silence ensue before he began.

"Comandante," he said in polite, measured Spanish, "I have come to pay you my respects."

A faint noise issued from Vallenar, which Glinn took for amusement. The man still did not turn. The atmosphere around

Glinn seemed charged with superhuman clarity; his body felt light, as if made of air.

Vallenar removed a letter from his pocket, unfolded it, and paused. Glinn could see the letterhead of a well-known Australian university. Vallenar spoke at last. "It's a meteorite," he said, his voice flat and dry.

So he knew. It had seemed the most unlikely path of those they had analyzed; but now it became the path they must follow.

"Yes."

Vallenar turned. His heavy woolen coat fell back, displaying an old Luger snugged into his belt.

"You are stealing a meteorite from my country."

"Not stealing," said Glinn. "We are within international law."

Vallenar barked out a laugh, hollow on the nearly deserted bridge. "I know. You are a mining operation, and it is metal. I was wrong after all: you *did* come down here for iron."

Glinn said nothing. With every word of Vallenar's, he was getting priceless information about the man; information that would allow him to make ever more accurate predictions on future behavior.

"But you, señor, are outside *my* law. The law of Comandante Vallenar."

"I do not understand," said Glinn, although he did.

"You will not leave Chile with this meteorite."

"If we find it," said Glinn.

Vallenar paused ever so slightly, and in that pause Glinn saw that he did not, in fact, know they had found it.

"What is to prevent me from simply reporting this to the authorities in Santiago? *They*, at least, have not been bribed."

"You are free to report it to anyone you wish," said Glinn. "We are doing nothing illegal." He knew Vallenar would never report it. Vallenar was the kind of man who would settle things his own way.

Vallenar took a long drag on the cigar, blowing the smoke in Glinn's direction. "Tell me, señor . . . Ishmael, was it not?"

"Actually, my name is Glinn."

"I see. So tell me, Mr. Glinn, why have you come to my ship?"

Glinn knew he had to answer this carefully. "I was hoping, Comandante, that we could work out an arrangement with you."

He saw the expected anger in the captain's face, and pressed on. "I am authorized to give you one million dollars, gold, for your cooperation."

Vallenar suddenly smiled, his eyes veiled. "You have it on you?"

"Of course not."

The comandante lazily puffed on the *puro*. "Perhaps, señor, you think I have a price like the others. Because I am a South American, a dirty Latin, that I am always willing to cooperate in exchange for *la mordida*."

"It has been my experience that no one is incorruptible," said Glinn. "Americans included." He watched the comandante carefully. He knew he would refuse the bribe, but even in the refusal there would be information.

"If that has been your experience, then you have led a corrupt life, surrounding yourself with whores, degenerates, and homosexuals. You will not leave Chile with this meteorite. I request you to take your gold, señor, and fill your mother's whorish *coño* with it."

Glinn did not respond to this strongest of Spanish insults.

Vallenar lowered his cigar. "There is another matter. I sent a man over to make a reconnaissance of the island, and he has not returned. His name is Timmer. He is my oficial de comunicaciones, my signal officer."

Glinn was faintly surprised at this. He did not believe the comandante would bring up the subject, let alone admit the man was on a spying expedition. After all, this man Timmer had failed, and Vallenar was clearly someone to whom failure was contemptible.

"He slit the throat of one of our men. We are holding him."

The comandante's eyes narrowed, and for a moment his control seemed to slip. But he recovered and smiled again. "You will return him to me, please."

"I am sorry," said Glinn. "He committed a crime."

"You will return him to me at once, or I will blow your ship out of the water," Vallenar said, his voice rising.

Again, Glinn felt a twinge of puzzlement. This rash threat was far out of proportion to the situation. A signal officer was easily replaced, not of high rank. There was something more here than met the eye. His mind raced over the possibilities even as he was formulating his answer. "That would be unwise, since your man is in the ship's brig."

The comandante stared hard at Glinn. When he spoke again, his voice was even once more. "Give me back Timmer, and I may consider letting you take the meteorite."

Glinn knew this was a lie. Vallenar would no more let them go if they returned Timmer than they could return the man. The comandante, he understood from Puppup, had a fanatically loyal crew. Now, perhaps, he could understand why: Vallenar returned their loyalty just as fiercely. Glinn had believed the comandante to be a man to whom other people were dispensable. This was a side of Vallenar that he had not anticipated. It didn't fit the profile that his people back in New York had drawn up, or the background dossier he had obtained. Still, it was useful. He would have to reconsider Vallenar. At any rate, he now had the information he needed: he knew now what Vallenar knew. And his own team had had ample time to do what needed to be done.

"I will relay your offer to our captain," he said. "And I think it might be possible to arrange. I will have an answer for you by noon." Glinn bowed slightly. "And now, with your permission, I will return to my ship."

Vallenar smiled, making an almost successful effort to cover up a simmering anger. "You do that, señor. Because if I do not see Timmer with my own eyes by noon, then I will know that he is dead. And your lives will not be worth dog dirt under my heel."

Rolvaag,
11:50 P.M.

McFarlane took the call in Lloyd's suite of deserted offices. Outside the wide span of windows, a breeze had sprung up, and a swell was rolling in from the west. The great ship stood in the lee of the sheer basaltic cliffs, its hawsers strung to the shore, affixed to steel bolts in the bedrock itself. All was in readiness, awaiting the cloaking fog that Glinn said was predicted for midnight.

The phone on Lloyd's desk began to blink angrily, and McFarlane reached for it with a sigh. It would be his third conversation with Lloyd that evening. He hated this new role, a go-between, a secretary. "Mr. Lloyd?"

"Yes, yes, I'm here. Has Glinn returned?" There was that same loud, continuous noise in the background he had heard during their last conversation. Idly, McFarlane wondered where Lloyd was calling from.

"He came back two hours ago."

"What did he say? Did Vallenar take the bribe?"

"No."

"Maybe he didn't offer enough money."

"Glinn seems to think that no amount of money would make a difference."

"Jesus Christ, everyone has a price! I suppose it's too late now, but I'd pay *twenty* million. You tell him that. Twenty million in gold, sent anywhere in the world. And American passports for him and his family."

McFarlane said nothing. Somehow, he didn't think Vallenar would be interested in American passports.

"So what's Glinn's plan?"

McFarlane swallowed. He hated this more by the minute. "He says it's foolproof, but he can't share it with us now. He says confidentiality is critical to its success—"

"What bullshit! Put him on. Now."

"I tried to find him when I heard you were calling. Again. He's not answering his page or radio. No one seems to know where he is."

"Damn him! I knew I shouldn't have put all my—"

His voice was drowned out by a roar of static. It returned, a little fainter than before. "Sam? *Sam!*"

"I'm here."

"Listen. You're the Lloyd representative down there. You tell Glinn to call me immediately, and tell him that's an order, or I'll fire his ass and personally throw him overboard."

"Yes," said McFarlane wearily.

"Are you in my office? Can you see the meteorite?"

"It's still hidden on the bluff."

"When will it be moved onto the ship?"

"As soon as the fog rolls in. I'm told it'll take a few hours to get it into the tank, maybe half an hour to secure it, and then we're off. We're supposed to be out of here no later than five A.M."

"That's cutting it close. And I hear there's another storm coming, bigger than the last."

"Storm?" McFarlane asked.

The only answer was static. He waited, but the line was dead. After a minute he hung up the phone and stared out the window. As he did so, he heard the electronic clock on Lloyd's desk chime out midnight.

I'll personally throw him overboard, he'd said.

And then McFarlane suddenly understood the sound he had heard behind Lloyd's voice: a jet engine.

Lloyd was on a plane.

Almirante Ramirez, July 25, Midnight

Comandante Vallenar stood at the bridge, staring through the binocular scope. His ship lay at the northern end of the channel, where he had an unopposed view of the activity on shore. It was a revealing sight indeed.

The Americans had brought the big tanker in against the bluff and strung hawsers to shore. Clearly, the captain of the *Rolvaag* knew a thing or two about Cape Horn weather. They could not know of the uncharted undersea ledge to which he had anchored the *Almirante Ramirez*. So instead they had tethered the ship in the lee of the island, hoping to protect themselves from the worst fury of the storm. With any luck, the offshore breeze would keep the ship away from the dangerous rocks. Still, it was a very risky maneuver for a vessel that large, particularly a ship using dynamic positioning, if the wind should change suddenly. It would have been much safer to take the ship away from land altogether. Something pressing was keeping them nearby.

And he did not have far to look for it. He swiveled the scope back to the center of the island and the wide-scale mining operation, taking place some two miles from the *Rolvaag*. He had been scrutinizing it even before the American, Glinn, had arrived. A few hours before, there had been a sudden increase in activity: explosions, the frantic grinding of machinery, workmen dashing here and there, huge lights bathing the worksite. The intercepted radio traffic indicated the work crews had found something. Something big.

But they were having great difficulty with this find. First, they broke their most powerful crane trying to lift it. And now they were trying to drag the thing with heavy machinery. But the radio chatter made it clear they were having little or no luck. No doubt the *Rolvaag* was staying nearby in case extra men or equipment was needed. Vallenar smiled: the Americans were not so competent after all. At this rate, it would take them weeks to get the meteorite on board the ship.

Of course, he would never allow that to happen. Once Timmer was safely back, Vallenar would disable the tanker to prevent their leaving, and then communicate the news of their attempted theft. It would preserve the honor of his country. When the politicians saw the meteorite—when they learned how the Americans had tried to steal it—they would understand. With that meteorite, he might even be promoted out of Puerto Williams. It would be the corrupt bastards in Punta Arenas, not he, who would suffer. But the timing was everything . . .

His smile faded as he thought of Timmer, locked in the brig of that tanker. That he had killed someone was no surprise; young Timmer was a quick thinker, eager to impress. What surprised Vallenar was that he had been caught. He looked forward to the debriefing.

He did not allow himself to think about the other possibility: that the American had lied, and Timmer was dead.

There was a rustle, and the *oficial de guardia* came up behind him. "Comandante?"

Vallenar nodded without looking at him.

"We have received a second order to return to base, sir."

Vallenar said nothing. He waited, thinking.

"Sir?"

Vallenar looked back out into the darkness. The expected fog was now rolling in. "Observe radio silence. Acknowledge nothing."

There was a faint flickering in the officer's eyes at this request, but the man was far too well trained to question an order. "Yes, sir."

Vallenar watched the fog. It drifted in like smoke, creeping out of nowhere to shroud the seascape. The lights of the great tanker began flickering in and out, blotted by patches of fog, until they disappeared. In the middle of the island, the brilliant light of the worksite gave way to an indistinct glow, then yielded completely, leaving a wall of darkness before the bridge. He bent his head toward the FLIR scope, where the ship was outlined in a hazy yellow.

Vallenar straightened, then stepped back from the scope. He thought of Glinn. There was something strange about him, something unreadable. His visit to the *Almirante Ramirez* had been brazen. It had taken *cojones*. And yet it bothered him.

He stared out into the fog another moment. Then he turned to the deck officer. "Have the oficial central de informaciones de combate report to the bridge," he said softly but carefully.

Rolvaag, Midnight

When McFarlane arrived on the bridge, he found a troubled-looking group of officers huddled over the command station. A claxon had gone off and all hands had been called to quarters over the ship's PA. Britton, who had sent him an urgent summons, seemed not to notice his arrival. Outside the bank of windows lay a haze of fog. The powerful lights on the ship's forecastle were faint pinpricks of yellow.

"Has he got a lock on us?" Britton asked.

"Affirmative," answered a nearby officer. "With targeting radar."

She drew the back of her hand across her forehead, then glanced up and caught sight of McFarlane. "Where is Mr. Glinn?" she asked. "Why isn't he responding?"

"I don't know. He disappeared soon after returning from the Chilean ship. I've been trying to reach him myself."

Britton turned to Howell.

"He may not be on the ship," the chief mate said.

"He's on the ship. I want two search parties, one forward and one aft. Have them work their way midships. Do a high-order search. Bring him to the bridge immediately."

"That won't be necessary." Glinn, noiseless as ever, had materialized at McFarlane's side. Behind him were two men that McFarlane didn't remember having seen before. Their shirts bore the small circular EES insignia.

"Eli," McFarlane began, "Palmer Lloyd has been on the phone again—"

"Dr. McFarlane, silence on the bridge, if you please!" Britton barked. The note of command in her voice was overwhelming. McFarlane fell silent.

Britton turned toward Glinn. "Who are these men, and why are they on my bridge?"

"They are EES employees."

Britton paused a moment, as if digesting this. "Mr. Glinn, I wish to remind you—and Dr. McFarlane, as the onboard representative of Lloyd Industries—that, as master of the *Rolvaag*, I am the ultimate authority as to the handling and disposition of this vessel."

Glinn nodded. Or, at least, McFarlane thought he did; the gesture was so slight as to be imperceptible.

"I now intend to exercise my prerogative under such authority."

McFarlane noticed that the faces of Howell and the other bridge officers were hard-set. Clearly, something was about to happen. And yet Glinn seemed to receive this stiff announcement without concern.

"And how do you plan to exercise this prerogative?"

"That meteorite is not coming aboard my ship."

There was silence while Glinn looked at her mildly. "Captain, I think it would be better if we discussed this in private."

"No, sir." She turned to Howell. "Begin preparations to vacate the island. We leave in ninety minutes."

"One moment, if you please, Mr. Howell." Glinn's eyes remained on the captain. "May I ask what precipitated this decision?"

"You know my misgivings about that rock. You've given me no assurances, beyond guesswork, that the thing is safe to bring aboard. And just five minutes ago, that destroyer painted us with fire-control radar. We're a sitting duck. Even if the meteorite is safe, the conditions aren't. A severe storm is on its way. You don't load the heaviest object ever moved by man when you're staring down the business end of a four-inch gun."

"He will not fire. At least, not yet. He believes we have his man Timmer in the brig. And he seems remarkably eager to get him back safely."

"I see. And what will he do when he finds Timmer's dead?"

Glinn did not answer this question. "Running away without a proper plan is a guaranteed way to fail. And Vallenar won't let us leave until Timmer is returned."

"All I can say is that I'd rather try running now than with a bellyful of meteorite slowing us down."

Glinn continued to regard her with a mild, almost sad expression.

A technician cleared his throat. "I've got an inbound air contact bearing zero zero nine at thirty-five miles."

"Track it and get me a call sign," Britton said, without shifting position or dropping her gaze from Glinn.

There was a short, tense silence.

"Have you forgotten the contract you signed with EES?" Glinn asked.

"I've forgotten nothing, Mr. Glinn. But there is a higher law which supersedes all contracts: the law and custom of the sea. The captain has the last word on matters pertaining to her vessel. And, under present circumstances, I will not allow that meteorite on board."

"Captain Britton, if you will not speak privately with me, all I can do is assure you there is no need to worry." Glinn nodded to his men. One of them stepped forward, sitting down at an unused computer console of black steel. The words SECURE DATAMETRICS were stamped into its side. The other man took up a position behind him, his back to the console, facing the bridge officers. McFarlane realized this console was a smaller cousin of the mysterious machine Britton had pointed out to him in the cargo control room.

Britton watched the two strangers darkly. "Mr. Howell, remove all EES personnel from the bridge."

"That," said Glinn sorrowfully, "will not be possible."

Something in his tone seemed to make Britton hesitate. "What do you mean?"

"The *Rolvaag* is a marvelous ship, the latest in maritime computerization. As a precaution, EES has used that computerization against a contingency such as this. You see, *our* systems control the main computer. Normally, this control is transparent. But after the *Rolvaag* was brought in to shore, I deactivated the bypass. Now we alone have the authorization codes to control the main engines. You cannot transmit any engine or rudder orders until the correct sequence is punched in."

Britton looked at him, silent fury on her face.

Howell picked up a telephone on the command console. "Security to the bridge, on the double."

Britton turned to the watch officer. "Initiate engine sequence."

There was a pause as the officer entered a series of commands. "No response from the engines, ma'am. I've got a dead board."

"Run a diagnostic," she said.

"Captain," continued Glinn, "I'm afraid you will be required to observe the letter of your contract whether you like it or not."

She wheeled suddenly, her eyes locked on his. She said something to him in a voice too low for McFarlane to hear.

Glinn stepped forward. "No," he almost whispered. "*You* promised to captain this ship back to New York. I merely added a safeguard to prevent a violation of that promise—by you, or by others."

Britton fell silent, her tall frame quivering slightly.

"If we leave now, rashly, without a plan, they *will* sink us." Glinn's voice remained low, persuasive, urgent. "Our very survival now depends on your following my lead. *I know what I am doing*."

Britton continued looking at him. "This will not stand."

"Captain, you *must* believe me when I tell you that, if we are to survive, we have only one course of action. You *must* cooperate with me, or we will all die. It is as simple as that."

"Captain," the watch officer began, "the diagnostics check out . . ." His voice died away as he saw Britton had not heard him.

A group of security officers appeared on the bridge.

"You heard the captain," barked Howell, motioning the security team forward. "Clear all EES personnel from the bridge." At the console, Glinn's operatives stiffened in preparation.

And then Britton slowly held up a hand.

"Captain—" Howell began.

"They may remain."

Howell looked at her incredulously, but Britton did not turn.

There was a long, agonized silence. Then Glinn nodded to his team.

The seated man took a stubby metal key from around his neck and inserted it into the front of the console. Glinn stepped forward, typed a short series of commands, then turned to a numeric keypad and typed again, briefly.

The watch officer glanced up. "Sir, the board's gone green."

Britton nodded. "I hope to God you *do* know what you're doing." She did not look at Glinn as she spoke.

"If you trust anything, Captain, I hope you will trust this. I have made a professional pact—and a personal one—to bring the meteorite to New York. I have thrown tremendous resources into solving any problem we might encounter—including this one. I—*we*—will not fail."

If this had any impact on Britton, McFarlane could not see it. Her eyes remained distant.

Glinn stepped back. "Captain, the next twelve hours will be the most trying of the entire mission. Success now depends on a certain subordination of your authority as captain. For that I apologize. But once the meteorite is safely in the holding tank, the ship will be yours again. And by noon tomorrow, we'll be well on our way back to New York. With a prize beyond price."

As Glinn looked at her, McFarlane saw him smile: faint, tenuous, but there nonetheless.

Banks stepped out of the radio room. "I've got an ID on the bird, ma'am. It's a Lloyd Holdings helicopter, sending an encrypted call sign over the bridge-to-bridge frequency."

The smile vanished from Glinn's face. He darted a look at

McFarlane. *Don't look at me*, McFarlane almost said. *You should have kept him in the loop*.

The officer at the radar console adjusted his headphones. "Captain, he's requesting permission to land."

"ETA?"

"Thirty minutes."

Glinn turned. "Captain, if you don't mind, I have a few matters to attend to. Make any necessary preparations for our departure you see fit. I'll return shortly."

He began walking away, leaving the two EES employees at the console. In the doorway, he paused. "Dr. McFarlane," he said, without looking around. "Mr. Lloyd will be expecting a welcome. Arrange it, if you please."

Rolvaag,
12:30 A.M.

With a depressing sense of déjà vu, McFarlane paced the maindeck, waiting for the helicopter to approach the tanker. For interminable minutes, there was nothing more than a low thud of rotors somewhere out in the murk. McFarlane watched the frenzied activity that had begun the moment the fog concealed their ship from the *Almirante Ramirez*. The bluff loomed beside them, the crags of rock softened by the fog. Atop stood the shack that enclosed the meteorite. Before him, the center tank lay open. A pale light drifted upward. McFarlane watched while, with astonishing speed, swarms of workmen began assembling a tower of gleaming struts. It rose out of the tank, its metal latticework glowing softly in the sodium lights. Now, two derricks swung additional prefabricated pieces of tower into place. At least a dozen welders were at work on the tower, and continuous streams of sparks cascaded downward onto the hard hats and shoulders of the engineers below. Despite its size and bulk, the whole structure looked oddly delicate: a complex spiderweb of three dimensions. For the life of him, McFarlane could not see how the meteorite was going to get into the tank once it was dragged on top of the tower.

The thudding sound grew suddenly louder, and McFarlane trotted back along the superstructure to the fantail. The big Chinook was emerging out of the fog, its rotors sending billows of fine spray up from the deck. A man with coned flashlights in his hands maneuvered the bird into position. It was a routine landing, with none of the excitement of Lloyd's arrival during their stormy rounding of Cape Horn.

Moodily, he watched as the helicopter's oversize tires sank onto the pad. Acting as a gofer between Lloyd and Glinn was a no-win situation. He wasn't a liaison: he was a scientist. This wasn't why he had hired on, and the knowledge made him angry.

A hatchway in the helicopter's belly opened. Lloyd stood within, a long black cashmere coat billowing out behind him, a gray fedora in one hand. Landing lights gleamed off his wet pate. He made the jump, landing gracefully for a man of his size, and then strode across the deck, unbowed, powerful, oblivious to the jumble of equipment and staff that streamed out of the chopper on the hydraulic ramp deployed behind him. He grasped McFarlane's hand in his steel grip, smiled and nodded, and continued walking. McFarlane followed him across the windswept deck and out of the noise of the blades. Near the forward railing, Lloyd stopped, scanning the fantastical tower from bottom to top. "Where's Glinn?" he shouted.

"He should be back on the bridge by now."

"Let's go."

The bridge was alive with tension, faces drawn in the pale illumination. Lloyd paused in the doorway for a moment, drinking it in. Then he stepped heavily forward.

Glinn was standing at the EES console, speaking in hushed tones to his man at the keyboard. Lloyd strode toward him, enfolding Glinn's narrow hand in his own. "The man of the hour," he cried. If he had been angry on the plane, he seemed to have recovered his high spirits. He waved one hand out toward the structure rising out of the tank. "Christ, Eli, that's incredible. Are you sure it's going to hold a twenty-five-thousand-ton rock?"

"Double overage," was Glinn's reply.

"I should have known. How the hell is it supposed to work?"

"Controlled failure."

"What? *Failure?* From your mouth? Heaven forbid."

"We move the rock to the tower. Then we set off a series of explosive charges. These will cause the levels of the tower to fail in sequence, bringing the meteorite down, bit by bit, into the holding tank."

Lloyd gazed at the structure. "Amazing," he said. "Has it ever been done before?"

"Not in quite this way."

"Are you sure it'll work?"

A wry smile appeared on Glinn's thin lips.

"Sorry I asked. All that's your department, Eli, and I'm not going to second-guess you on it. I'm down here for a different reason." He drew himself to his full height and looked around. "I'm not going to mince words. We've got a problem here, and it's not being dealt with. We've come too far to let anything stop us now. So I've come down to kick ass and take names." He pointed out into the dense fog. "There's a warship parked right off our bow. It's sent in spies. They're just waiting for us to make a move. And, goddammit, Eli, you've done nothing about it. Well, there's to be no more chickenshit wavering. Strong action is what's needed here, and from now on I'll be handling it personally. I'm traveling back to New York with you onboard the ship. But first, I'm getting the Chilean navy to recall this damn cowboy." He turned back toward the door. "It'll take my people just a few minutes to get up to speed. Eli, I'll expect you in my office in half an hour. I'm going to make some calls. I've dealt with this kind of tinpot political situation before."

During this brief speech, Glinn kept his deep gray eyes trained steadily on Lloyd. Now he touched his brow with a handkerchief and glanced at McFarlane. As usual, it was almost impossible to read anything into his gaze: Weariness? Disgust? Nothing at all?

Glinn spoke. "I'm sorry, Mr. Lloyd. Did you say you had contacted the Chilean authorities?"

"No, not yet. I wanted to find out exactly what was happening here first. But I've got powerful friends in Chile, including the vice president and the American ambassador."

Casually, Glinn took a step closer to the EES console. "I'm afraid that will not be possible."

"What, exactly, will not be possible?" Surprise mingled with impatience in Lloyd's tone.

"Your involvement in any aspect of this operation. You would have done better to stay in New York."

Lloyd's voice sharpened with anger. "Glinn, don't go telling me what I can and can't do. I'll leave the engineering in your hands, but this is a *political* situation."

"I assure you I am dealing with all aspects of the *political* situation."

Lloyd's voice trembled. "Oh really? And what about that destroyer out there? It's armed to the teeth, and its guns are pointing at us, in case you didn't notice. You've not done a damn thing. *Nothing*."

Hearing this, Captain Britton glanced at Howell, and then—more significantly—at Glinn.

"Mr. Lloyd, I will say this only once. You gave me a job to do. I am doing it. Your role right now is very simple: let me carry out my plan. This is no time for drawn-out explanations."

Lloyd, instead of responding, turned to Penfold, who had been hovering unhappily in the door to the bridge. "Get Ambassador Throckmorton on the horn and conference him into the vice president's office in Santiago. I'll be down in a minute."

Penfold disappeared.

"Mr. Lloyd," said Glinn quietly. "You may remain on the bridge and observe. That is all."

"It's way too late for that, Glinn."

Glinn turned quietly and spoke to his man at the black computer. "Kill the power in the Lloyd Industries suite, and suspend ship-to-shore communications across the board."

There was a shocked silence. "You son of a bitch," Lloyd roared, recovering quickly. He turned to Britton. "I contravene that order. Mr. Glinn is relieved of authority."

It appeared that Glinn hadn't heard. He punched in another frequency on his radio. "Mr. Garza? I'll take that report now."

He listened for a moment, then replied, "Excellent. With the covering fog, let's start an early evacuation of the island. Order all nonessential personnel back on board. But follow the game plan precisely: instruct them to leave the lights on and the equipment running. I've had Rachel set the radio transmission routines to automatic. Bring the tender around the rear of the island, but be careful to always keep it within the radar shadow of the island or the *Rolvaag*."

Lloyd broke in, his voice shaking with rage. "Aren't you forgetting, Glinn, who's ultimately in charge of this operation? On top of firing you, I'm stopping all payments to EES." He turned to Britton. "Restore power to my suite."

It again appeared for several moments as if Glinn had still not heard Lloyd. Britton, also, made no move. Glinn continued speaking calmly into the radio, giving orders, checking on progress. A sudden gust of wind buffeted the bridge windows, sending streamers of rain down the Plexiglas. Lloyd's face flushed a deep purple as he looked around at the captain and the crew. But no one met his eyes. The work of the bridge went on.

"Did any of you hear me?" he cried.

And then at last Glinn turned back. "I am not forgetting that you are ultimately in charge, Mr. Lloyd," he answered, his voice suddenly conciliatory, even friendly.

Lloyd took a deep breath, momentarily thrown off balance.

Glinn continued to speak softly, persuasively, even kindly. "Mr. Lloyd, in any operation, there must be a *single* commander. You know that better than anyone. In our contract, I made you a promise. I'm not going to break that promise. If I seem insubordinate, please know that I am doing it for *you*. If you had contacted the Chilean vice president, all would have been lost. I know him personally: we used to play polo together on his Patagonian ranch. He would like nothing better than to give the Americans a swift poke in the eye."

Lloyd faltered. "You played *polo* with—?"

Glinn went on, speaking rapidly. "I *alone* have all the facts. I *alone* know the path to success. I am not being secretive for the sake of coyness, Mr. Lloyd. There is a vital reason for this: it is essential to prevent second-guessing and freelance decision making. Frankly, the meteorite bears no intrinsic interest for me. But I promised to move this thing from point A to point B, and no one, *no one*, is going to stop me. So I hope you understand now why I am not going to relinquish control of this operation, or share with you explanations and prognostications. As for you withholding payment, we can settle that question like gentlemen once we are back on American soil."

"Look here, Glinn, that's all very well and good—"

"This discussion is over, and now, sir, you *will* obey *me*." Glinn's voice, still soft, suddenly took on a steely edge. "Whether that means staying here quietly, or disappearing into your office, or being escorted to the brig, is a matter of indifference to me."

Lloyd stared at him, dumbfounded. "You think you could put me in the brig, you arrogant bastard?"

The expression on Glinn's face provided the answer.

Lloyd was silent for a moment, his face almost purple with rage. Then he turned to Britton. "And who are *you* working for?"

But Britton's eyes, deep and green as the ocean, were still on Glinn. "I'm working for the man with the keys to the car," she said at last.

Lloyd stood there, swelling in fury. But he did not immediately react. Instead, he made a slow circuit of the bridge, his creaking wingtips leaving a trail of water, until he stopped at the bridge windows. There he stood, breathing heavily a moment, looking out at nothing in particular. "Once again, I order that power and communications be restored to my suite."

There was no sound, no answer. It was clear that no one, not even the lowest officer, intended to obey Lloyd.

Lloyd slowly turned, and his eyes fell square on McFarlane. He spoke in a low voice. "And you, Sam?"

Another hard gust buffeted the windows. McFarlane, standing in suspension, felt the shudder in the air. The bridge had fallen deathly quiet. He had a decision to make—and he found it one of the easiest decisions of his career.

"I'm working for the rock," said McFarlane quietly.

Lloyd continued looking at him, his eyes black, adamantine. Then, all at once, he seemed to crumple. The bull-like power seemed to drain out of his massive frame; his shoulders slumped; his face lost its fiery color. He turned, hesitated, then walked slowly off the bridge and disappeared out the door.

After a moment, Glinn bent once again toward the black computer and murmured to his man at the keyboard.

Rolvaag, 1:45 A.M.

Captain Britton stared straight ahead, betraying nothing of her feelings. She tried to measure her breathing, the rhythm of her heart—everything—to the pulse of the ship. Over the past hours, the wind had been picking up steadily, and it moaned and rattled about the ship. It was raining harder now, fat drops that shot out of the fog like bullets. The *panteonero* was not far away.

She transferred her attention to the spiderwebbed tower that rose out of the ship's tank. It was still well below the level of the bluff, and yet it seemed to be complete. She had no idea what the next step would be. It was uncomfortable, even humiliating, not knowing. She glanced over toward the EES computer and the man operating it. She had thought she knew everyone on board. And yet this man was a stranger who seemed to know a great deal about the operation of a supertanker. She pressed her lips more tightly together.

There were times, of course, when she relinquished command—taking on fuel, say, or when a harbor pilot came aboard. But those were comfortable, familiar patterns of running a ship, established over decades. This was not comfortable: it was a humiliation. Strangers were running the loading process, after lashing the ship to the shore and leaving her a sitting duck three thousand yards from a warship . . . Once again, she struggled to tuck away the feelings of anger and hurt. After all, her own feelings were not important—not when she thought about what waited for them, out there in the murk.

Anger and hurt . . . Her eyes flickered to Glinn, standing beside the black console, occasionally whispering words to his operative. He had just humiliated, even crushed, the world's most powerful industrialist, and yet he looked so slender, so ordinary. She continued looking covertly at him. She could understand her anger. But hurt was something else. More than once she had lain awake at night, wondering what went on in his mind, what made him tick. She wondered how a man who was so physically inconsequential—a man she might pass in the street without a second glance—could take up residence in her imagination so vividly. She wondered how he could be so ruthless, so disciplined. Did he really have a plan, or was he simply good at covering up a series of ad hoc reactions to unexpected events? The most dangerous people were those who knew they were always right. And yet Glinn had been always right. He seemed to know everything in advance, he seemed to understand everybody. He certainly had understood *her*—at least, the professional Sally Britton. *Success now depends on a certain subordination of your authority as captain*, he had said. She found herself wondering if he really knew how she felt about having her command subordinated, even temporarily, or if he even cared. She wondered why she cared that he cared.

She felt a shudder as pumps came on along both sides of the ship. Jets of seawater blasted through discharge pipes into the sea. The ship began to rise almost imperceptibly as the ballast tanks emptied. *Of course:* that's how the squat-looking tower would be raised to the level of the meteorite on the bluff. The whole ship would rise to meet it, bringing the platform flush with the rock. Again she felt humiliated at having control of the tanker taken from her, and yet awed at the audacity of the plan.

She remained stiffly at attention, speaking to no one, as the great ship rose in the water. It was a strange feeling, to see the ship going through the traditional motions of deballasting—lashing the sea suctions, aligning the loading arms, opening the manifold blocks—and yet seeing them as an observer rather than a participant. And to observe it under such circumstances—tethered to shore in the lee of a storm—went against everything she had ever learned in her career.

At last the tower was even with the shed perched on the bluff. She watched Glinn murmur to the console operator. Instantly, the pumps ceased.

A loud crack echoed from the bluff. A cloud of smoke expanded as the metal shed blew apart. The smoke rolled away to merge with the fog, revealing the meteorite, bloodred under the sodium lights. Britton caught her breath. She was aware that all eyes on the bridge had locked on the meteorite. There was a collective gasp.

On the bluff, diesel engines roared into life and a complicated series of pulleys and capstans began to turn. A high-pitched squeal sounded; diesel smoke billowed skyward to mingle with fog. Inch by inch, the meteorite began moving toward the reinforced edge of the bluff. Britton watched, transfixed, the flood of emotions inside her temporarily stilled. There was something regal about the meteorite's progress: stately, slow, regular. It crept past the edge onto the platform atop the tower. Then it stopped. Again she felt the whole ship vibrate as the computer-controlled pumps kept the ship trim, emptying precisely enough ballast to compensate for the growing weight of the meteorite.

Britton watched the process in tense silence. The meteorite would creep a little farther onto the platform, then stop, to an answering shudder from the ballast pumps. The jerky ballet continued for twenty minutes. At last, it was finished: the meteorite was centered atop the tower. She felt the *Rolvaag*'s top-heaviness, the destabilization caused by the meteorite's weight; but she could also sense the ballast tanks now refilling with water, the ship sinking back down into the water for stability.

Glinn spoke again to the computer operator. Then, nodding at Britton, he walked out onto the bridge wing nearest the bluff. The bridge remained silent for another minute. Then she felt Chief Mate Howell come up behind her. She did not turn as he leaned toward her ear.

"Captain," he murmured. "I want you to know that we—I mean, the officers and myself—aren't happy about this. It isn't right, the way you were treated. We're behind you a hundred percent. You just say the word and . . ." There was no need to finish the sentence.

Britton remained rigidly at attention. "I thank you, Mr. Howell," she replied in a quiet voice. "But that will be all."

After a moment, Howell stepped back. Britton took a deep breath. The time for action had passed. Now, they were committed. The meteorite was no longer a land-based problem. It was on the ship. And the only way to get it off was to see the *Rolvaag* docked safely in New York. Once again she thought of Glinn, of the way he had wooed her into commanding the *Rolvaag*, how he had known everything about her, how much he had trusted her in customs at Puerto Williams. They had been a good team. She wondered if she had done the right thing in yielding her command to him, however temporary. But then she had had no choice.

Through all these thoughts, Britton stood rigidly at attention.

Outside, there was another sharp cracking sound; a gleaming row of titanium struts flew away from the top rung of the tower with a dozen puffs of smoke. They spun away, coruscating into the fog, dropping lazily out of sight. The meteorite sank onto the next layer of the tower; the whole ship shuddered again; and the ballast pumps rumbled into life. Then there was another round of explosions; another narrow layer of the tower crumpled into itself, and the meteorite sank a few inches closer to the tank.

A part of Britton realized this was an awesome engineering feat; utterly original, perfectly planned, beautifully executed. But another part of her found no pleasure in it. She glanced down the length of the vessel. The fog was getting patchier, and the sleety rain was now blowing horizontally across the windows. Soon the fog would blow away. Then the game would be up. Because Vallenar was not some engineering problem Glinn could solve with a slide rule. And their only bargaining chip lay deep inside the *Rolvaag*—not in the brig, but in Dr. Brambell's frozen morgue.

Rolvaag, 2:50 A.M.

Lloyd paced his darkened study on the middle bridge deck with the restless fury of a caged beast. The wind had picked up, and every few minutes a gust would strike the ship with such force that the stern windows bowed and rattled in their frames. Lloyd barely noticed.

He paused a moment, then stared out through the open door of his private office into the sitting room beyond. Its surfaces were faintly illuminated in the dull red glow of emergency lights. The wall of television screens, black and featureless, blinked back the silent mockery of a hundred dim reflections of himself.

He spun away, trembling. His body swelled with anger inside his suit, straining the expensive fabric. It was incomprehensible. Glinn—a man *he* was paying three hundred million dollars—had ordered him from the bridge of his own ship. He had cut off the power to his suite, leaving him deaf, dumb, and blind. There were matters to take care of back in New York—*critical* matters. The enforced silence was costing him big money. And there was something else; something that hurt more than money. Glinn had humiliated him in front of the bridge officers and his own people. Lloyd could forgive a lot of things, but that he could never forgive. Palmer Lloyd had faced down presidents, prime ministers, sheikhs, captains of industry, and mob kingpins. But this man was different.

In a paroxysm of rage he kicked out at one of the wing chairs, sending it crashing to the deck. And then suddenly he whirled around, listening intently.

The howl of the wind, the faint grinding of machinery from the bogus worksite, went on as they had before. But there had been another, more regular sound: something that Lloyd, in the full flood of his anger, had not immediately noticed. There it was again: the staccato pop of an explosion. It was very near; on the ship, in fact, because he could feel the deck shuddering faintly beneath his feet.

He waited in the faint light, muscles tense, curiosity now mingling with his outrage. There it was again: the sound, followed by the shudder.

Something was happening on the maindeck.

Quickly, he walked out through the sitting room, down the corridor, and into the central suite. Here, his secretaries and assistants sat awkwardly among the dead phones and darkened computers, talking quietly. The talk fell away as he passed through the long, low space. Noiselessly, Penfold slipped out of the shadows to pluck at his sleeve. Brushing him away, Lloyd moved past the closed elevators and opened the soundproofed door that led to his private apartment. He went through the rooms to the forward bulkhead of the superstructure. He wiped the condensation from a porthole with the cuff of his suit jacket and peered out.

Below, the deck was a hive of activity. Workers were battening down the deck equipment, checking fastenings, tightening hatches, making all the last frenzied preparations for a sea voyage. But what caught his attention was the bizarre tower that reared out of the tank. It was shorter than it had been before; much shorter, in fact. Smoke and steam encircled it, blending with the fog to create clouds that unfurled along the deck in a slow-motion ballet. As he watched, there was another rat-tat-tat of explosions. The meteorite dropped slightly and the ship shuddered again. Groups of workers scurried forward, clearing away the fresh debris before the next set of explosions.

Now he understood precisely what Glinn had meant by a controlled failure of the tower. They were blowing it apart, bit by bit. As he watched, Lloyd grasped that this was the best—probably the only—way of getting something that heavy into the tank. He caught his breath at the brilliance and the audacity of it.

At this thought, a fresh spasm of rage ripped through his body. But Lloyd closed his eyes against it, turning away, taking a deep breath, trying to calm himself.

Glinn had told him not to come; McFarlane had told him not to come. But he had come anyway. Just as he had leapt onto the meteorite when it was first exposed. He thought of what had happened to the man named Timmer, and he shuddered.

Perhaps coming down again, guns blazing, had not been the right thing to do. It was impulsive, and Lloyd knew enough about himself to know he was not normally an impulsive man. He was too close to this: it had become too personal. J. P. Morgan once said, "If you want something too much, you will not succeed in getting it." He had always lived by that philosophy: he had never been afraid to walk away from a deal, no matter how lucrative. The ability to fold a hand, even with four aces, had been his most valuable business asset. Now, for the first time in his life, he had drawn a hand that he could not fold. He was in the game to the finish, win or lose.

Lloyd found himself fighting an unfamiliar battle: a struggle to steady his mind. He considered that he had not made $34 billion by being unreasonable and hot-tempered. He had always avoided second-guessing his hired professionals. In this terrible moment of humiliation, defeat, and self-reflection, he realized that Glinn might, in fact, have been acting in his best interests by sending him from the bridge and cutting him off from the world. But even this thought touched off another wave of anger. Best interests or not, the man had been arrogant and high-handed. Glinn's coolness, his unflappability, his assumption of leadership, enraged Lloyd. He had been humiliated in front of everyone, and he would never forget nor forgive it. When all this was over, there would be a reckoning for Glinn, financial and otherwise.

But first they had to get the meteorite the hell out of there. And Glinn seemed to be the only man who could do it.

Rolvaag,
3:40 A.M.

"Captain Britton, the meteorite will be inside the holding tank within ten minutes. The ship will be yours, and we can depart."

Glinn's words broke the long hush that had fallen over the bridge. Like the others, McFarlane had been staring at the slow, regular progress of the meteorite into the belly of the *Rolvaag*.

For another minute, maybe two, Britton stood unmoving, statuesque, staring out the windows of the bridge as she had ever since Lloyd's departure. At last she turned and looked directly at Glinn. After a significant moment she turned toward the second officer. "Wind speed?"

"Thirty knots from the southwest, gusting to forty, and rising."

"Currents?"

The murmured exchange continued, while Glinn leaned toward his man at the computer console: "Have Puppup and Amira report to me here, please."

There was another rapid series of explosions. The ship lurched, and the ballast pumps rumbled to compensate.

"There's a weather front coming in," Howell murmured. "We're losing our fog."

"Visibility?" Britton asked.

"Rising to five hundred yards."

"Position of the warship?"

"Unchanged at twenty-two hundred yards, zero five one."

A gust of wind hit the ship hard. Then there was a vast, hollow boom, different from anything McFarlane had felt before, and a shudder seemed to run through the very spine of the vessel.

"The hull just hit the bluff," said Britton quietly.

"We can't move yet," replied Glinn. "Will the hull stand it?"

"For a while," Britton answered expressionlessly. "Perhaps."

A door at the far end of the bridge opened and Rachel entered. She looked around, her bright alert eyes quickly sizing up the situation. She came up beside McFarlane. "Garza better get that thing in the tank before we're holed," she muttered.

There was another series of explosions, and the meteorite dropped farther. Its base was now hidden inside the frame of the ship.

"Dr. McFarlane," Glinn said without turning around. "Once the meteorite is secured in the tank, it becomes yours. I want you and Amira to monitor it round the clock. Let me know if there's any change in readings, or in the meteorite's status. I don't want any more surprises from that rock."

"Right."

"The lab is ready, and there's an observation platform above the tank. If you need anything, let me know."

"More lightning now," the second officer broke in. "Ten miles out."

There was a moment of silence.

"Speed this up," Britton said suddenly to Glinn.

"Can't," murmured Glinn, almost absentmindedly.

"Visibility one thousand yards," said the second officer. "Wind speed increasing to forty knots."

McFarlane swallowed. Everything had been moving ahead with such predictable, clockwork precision that he'd almost been lulled into forgetting the danger. He remembered Lloyd's question: *So how are you going to deal with that destroyer out there?* How indeed? He wondered what Lloyd was doing, down in his darkened staterooms. He thought, with surprisingly little regret, about the probable loss of his $750,000 fee, given what he had said to Lloyd. It hardly mattered to him now—now that he had the rock.

Another crackle of explosions, and titanium struts flashed out, bouncing and skidding along the maindeck and ricocheting off the rails. He could hear the thunk of additional struts falling away into the tank. There were occasional ticks of gravel on the bridge windows now, picked off the nearby bluff by the rising wind. The *panteonero* was descending in earnest.

Glinn's radio squawked. "Two more feet and we'll have clearance," came the metallic voice of Garza.

"Stay on this channel. I want you to call out each drop."

Puppup opened the door and entered the bridge, rubbing his eyes and yawning.

"Visibility two thousand yards," said the second officer. "The fog's lifting fast. The warship will have visual contact with us at any moment."

McFarlane heard a rumble of thunder. It was drowned out by another great boom as the vessel made contact with the bluff for a second time.

"Increase RPM on main engines!" barked Britton. A new vibration was added to the mix.

"Eighteen inches to go," came Garza's voice from the maindeck.

"Lightning at five miles. Visibility twenty-five hundred yards."

"Initiate blackout," Glinn said.

Instantly, the brilliantly lit deck was plunged into darkness as the ship went black. The ambient light from the superstructure cast a dull glow over the meteorite, its top now barely visible. The whole ship was shaking—whether from the meteorite's descent, the rollers now crashing along its flank, or the wind, it was impossible for McFarlane to tell. There was another round of explosions, and the meteorite sank still lower. Both Britton and Glinn were calling out commands now; there was an awkward moment in which the ship seemed to have two masters. As the fog rolled back, McFarlane could see that the channel was a turmoil of whitecaps, heaved up and down by combers. His eyes remained glued to the nocturnal seascape beyond the windows, waiting for the sharp prow of the destroyer to materialize.

"Six inches," said Garza over the radio.

"Prepare to close the hatch," Glinn said.

There was a flash of lightning to the southwest, followed shortly by a faint rumble.

"Visibility four thousand yards. Lightning at two miles."

McFarlane became aware of Rachel, gripping his elbow hard. "Jesus, that's too close," she murmured.

And there it was: the destroyer off to the right, a dim cluster of lights, flickering through the storm. As McFarlane stared, the fog peeled away from the destroyer. It was stationary, lights ablaze, as if flaunting its presence. There was another explosion, another shudder.

"She's in," came Garza's voice.

"Close the mechanical doors," Britton said crisply. "Slip cable, Mr. Howell. Smartly. Set course one three five."

There was a fresh set of explosions, and the great hawsers that moored the ship to the cliff dropped away, swinging lazily toward the bluff.

"Right fifteen degrees rudder, steady on course one three five," said Howell.

Almirante Ramirez, 3:55 A.M.

Just over a mile away, Comandante Vallenar paced his own bridge. It was unheated, and, as he preferred, manned with the minimum complement. He stared out the forward windows toward the ship's *castillo*, the forecastle. He could see nothing through the lightening fog. Then, abruptly, he veered toward the *oficial de guardia en la mer,* the conning officer, who was standing in the radar alcove. He leaned over his shoulder to scrutinize the forward-looking infrared radar. The tanker's signature showed him nothing he did not already know, and answered none of his questions. Why was the ship still moored to the shore? In the gathering storm, it had become increasingly dangerous to remain. Could they be attempting to move the meteorite toward the ship? No—before the fog had moved in, he'd watched them struggling ineffectively with it in the island's interior. Even now, he could hear the frantic grinding of machinery. And the chatter of talk over the shore radio was continuing. Still, it seemed foolish to endanger the ship by leaving it strung to shore. And the man Glinn was no fool.

What, then, was going on?

Earlier, the loud thud of propeller blades had sounded over the wind as a helicopter hovered nearby, landed, then departed. There had been the sound of nearby explosions—much smaller than those from the island, but apparently originating from the vicinity of the ship. Or perhaps from the ship itself. Could there have been some accident on board? Were there casualties? Had Timmer commandeered a weapon and tried to escape?

He turned from the ancient green radar screen and gazed intently into the darkness. Through the flickering tatters of fog and sleet, he thought he glimpsed lights. The fog was lifting and he would soon have visual contact with the ship. He blinked hard, then looked again. The lights were gone. Wind whipped against the ship, whistling and crying. Vallenar had heard that cry before. It was a *panteonero*.

He'd already ignored several orders to return to base, each more urgent, more threatening, than the last. It was the corruption, the bribed officials, calling him back. By the Mother of God, they would thank him in the end.

He could feel the movement of his ship in the heavy swell, a corkscrew motion that he did not like. The moorings to the uncharted underwater ledge held—the best anchorage, the *only* anchorage, in the Franklin Channel.

What was going on?

He would not wait for noon to get an answer about Timmer. At first light, he would fire a few four-inch shells high into their bows—nothing that would sink the ship, of course, but enough to disable it and get their attention. Then he would deliver an ultimatum: hand over Timmer or die.

Something flickered through the parting sheets of fog. He stared, face close to the glass. There they were again: lights, no doubt of it. He strained into the darkness. The fog and sleet whipped past, but he saw it again, fleetingly; and then again. Now, the outline of the great ship was becoming visible in the lifting murk. He raised his binoculars—and the ship disappeared. He cursed as he examined the blackness. And then, again, he saw lights: one light now, very faint.

The bastards had darkened ship.

What were they hiding?

He stepped backward, glancing at the FLIR scope, trying to pull some kind of meaning out of the blurry green smear. Something, he sensed, was about to happen. Perhaps the time to act was now.

He turned to the boatswain's mate. "Sound general quarters," he said.

The mate leaned into the IMC. "General quarters, general quarters, all hands man battle stations."

A claxon horn went off. Almost immediately, the *jefe de la guardia en la mer,* the tactical action officer, appeared on the bridge and saluted.

Vallenar opened a stores closet and pulled out a bulky set of Sovietski night-vision goggles. Strapping them in place around his head, he stepped toward the windows and peered out again. The Russian technology was not as good as the ITT devices made by the Americans, but then again they were not nearly as expensive. He glanced out toward the tanker.

With the goggles, he could see more clearly. Figures were scurrying across the deck, clearly making preparations to get under way. But, perplexingly, the greatest activity seemed to center around a large open hatch in the middle of the deck. Something was protruding from the hatchway; something Vallenar could not quite make out.

As he stared, there was a searing flicker of small explosions just above the open tank. The second-generation night goggles, unequipped with safety cutouts, overloaded in the glare. Vallenar staggered backward, clawing at the goggles, pulling them from his face and rubbing his eyes with a curse.

"Target by fire control," he called out to the tactical action officer. "Do not engage with four-inch guns until I so order."

There was a slight hesitation.

Although spots still swayed in front of his eyes, Vallenar turned sharply in the direction of the weapons officer.

"Aye aye, sir," came the reply. "Targeted by fire control. Tracking data transferred to weapons system."

Vallenar turned to the conning officer. "Prepare to raise anchor."

"Aye, preparing to raise anchor."

"How is our fuel?"

"Fifty-five percent, sir."

Vallenar closed his eyes, letting the painful glare subside. He withdrew a cigar from his pocket, and spent a good three minutes lighting it. Then he turned back toward the window.

"The American ship is moving," said the conning officer, leaning over the radar.

Vallenar took a slow puff. High time. Perhaps they were finally going to anchor in safer water, in the lee up the channel. From there, they could ride out the storm.

"It's moving away from the bluff."

Vallenar waited.

"Turning . . . Bearing zero eight five now."

The wrong direction for the lee water up channel. Still Vallenar waited, a sudden, cold dread in his heart. Five minutes passed.

"Still bearing zero eight five, accelerating to four knots."

"Keep tracking," he murmured. The dread gripped him tighter now.

"Target turning, moving five knots, bearing one one five, one two zero, one two five—"

Accelerating fast for a tanker, he thought. But it didn't matter what kind of engines the massive ship sported; outrunning a destroyer was a physical impossibility.

He turned away from the windows. "Aim forward of the king posts, above the waterline. I want the ship crippled, not sunk."

"The target is moving five knots, steadying at one three five."

Heading for open sea, Vallenar thought. That was it, then; Timmer was dead.

Casseo, the tactical action officer, spoke: "Maintaining tracking of target, sir."

Vallenar struggled to keep himself calm, to keep himself strong; to show nothing of himself to the men around him. Now, more than ever, he would need clarity.

He lowered the cigar, licked his dry lips.

"Prepare to fire," he said.

Rolvaag,
3:55 A.M.

Glinn drew in breath slowly, deliberately, feeling the steady rush of air fill his lungs. As always before an action, a preternatural calm settled over him. The ship was rigged for sea and the powerful engines hummed far beneath his feet. The destroyer sat low in the water, a bright spot in the gloom about twenty degrees aft of the port beam.

It would all be over within five minutes. But the timing would be everything.

He turned his gaze toward the corner of the bridge. Puppup was standing in the shadows, hands folded, waiting. Now he came forward at Glinn's nod.

"Yes?"

"I'll need you to stand ready to assist the helmsman. We may have to make abrupt changes to our course, and we'll need your expertise with the currents and underwater topography."

"The underwater what?"

"Where the reefs are, where it's shallow, where it's deep enough to pass safely."

Puppup seemed to accept this. Then he looked up at Glinn, eyes bright.

"Guv?"

"Yes."

"My canoe only draws six inches. I never had to worry about any of that lot."

"I'm aware of that. I'm also aware that the tides here run thirty feet, and it's high tide. You know where the wrecks are and the sunken ledges. Be ready."

"Very well, guv."

Glinn watched as the little man slunk back into the shadows. Then his glance flickered toward Britton, at the command station with Howell and the deck officer. She was indeed a fine woman, a good captain, everything he had known she would be. The way she'd reacted when he temporarily abrogated her authority—that, above all, had impressed him deeply. There was a great dignity and self-control in her bearing, even as she relinquished command. He wondered if it was innate, or the result of her earlier disgrace.

On impulse, he had early on picked up a book of W. H. Auden's poetry from the ship's library. He was not a reader of poetry; it had always seemed a nonproductive pursuit. He'd turned to something called "In Praise of Limestone," with its vague promise of engineering. It had been a revelatory experience. He'd had no idea of the power of poetry: of how much feeling, thought, even wisdom could be imparted in such compact language. It occurred to him that it would be interesting to discuss this with Britton. After all, it had been her Auden quotation during their first meeting that had led him to the book.

All these thoughts occupied Glinn's mind for less than a second. They vanished at the low sound of an alarm.

Britton spoke, her voice distinct but calm: "The warship's painting us with high PRF fire-control radar." She turned to Howell. "Sound stations."

Howell repeated the command. Another siren went off, much louder.

Glinn stepped lightly toward his man at the computer console. "Jam it," he murmured.

He felt Britton's eyes flicker toward him. "Jam it?" she repeated, a trace of sarcasm mingling with the tension in her voice. "May I ask with what?"

"With the McDonnell-Douglas Blackout Series Wide-Band ECM system on your mast. He's going to fire on us with his guns, or perhaps even launch an Exocet. We have chaff and CIWS, to take care of any missile launch."

This time, Howell turned to look at him incredulously. "Close-In Weapons System? There's nothing like that on our ship."

"Under those forward bulkheads." Glinn nodded to his man. "Time to shed our clothes."

The man typed a few commands and there was a sharp crack forward. Glinn watched as the bulkheads peeled off and fell into the sea, just as planned, exposing the six stubby barrels of the Phallanx Gatling guns which, Glinn knew, could fire 20-millimeter rounds of depleted uranium at an incoming missile at a rate in excess of 3,000 rounds per minute.

"Jesus," said Howell, "that's classified hardware."

"Indeed."

"Additional security equipment, I believe he once called it," Britton said with a trace of irony.

Glinn turned back toward her. "At the moment we begin jamming, I suggest you bring her head hard to starboard."

"Evasive action?" Howell said. "With this ship? It takes three miles just to stop."

"I'm well aware of that. Do it anyway."

Britton spoke. "Mr. Howell, bring her head hard to starboard."

Howell turned to the helmsman. "Hard right rudder, starboard engine back emergency full, port engine emergency ahead."

Britton looked at Glinn's man. "Employ all countermeasures. If he fires a missile, deploy chaff, CIWS, as necessary."

There was a delay, then a shudder, as the ship began to slow and turn.

"This isn't going to work," Howell muttered.

Glinn did not bother to answer. He knew that, in fact, the tactic would work. Even if the electronic countermeasures failed, Vallenar would be aiming high at the bow, where it would cause the most excitement with the least damage. He wouldn't try to sink the *Rolvaag*—not yet, at any rate.

A long two minutes passed in the darkness. Then there was an eruption of light along the side of the destroyer as its four-inch guns fired. Some tense seconds later, there was an explosion off the *Rolvaag*'s port bow, and another, and a third, faint geysers of water rising in the darkness and twisting away in the wind. Glinn noted that, as he expected, the shells were going wide.

The officers on the bridge exchanged pale, shocked glances. Glinn watched them with sympathy. He knew that, even in the best of circumstances, coming under fire for the first time was traumatic.

"I'm getting movement on the destroyer," Howell said, staring at the radar.

"May I suggest all ahead flank, steady course one eight zero," Glinn said gently.

The helmsman did not repeat the order, instead glancing over at the captain. "That'll take us out of the main channel, inside the reefs," he said, voice wavering ever so slightly. "They're uncharted . . ."

Glinn motioned to Puppup.

"Yes, guv?"

"We're taking the reef side of the channel."

"Sure thing." Puppup skipped over to stand beside the helmsman.

Britton sighed. "Execute the order."

Surf crashed into the bow, sending foam across the deck. Puppup peered out into the dark.

"Take it a little to the left, there."

"Make it so, Mr. Howell," Britton said tersely.

"Left five degrees rudder," said Howell, "steady on course one seven five."

There was a moment of strained silence. Then the helmsman spoke. "Aye, sir, steady at one seven five."

Howell leaned over the radar. "They're picking up speed, up to twelve knots now to our eight." He stared hard at Glinn. "What the hell's your plan now?" he asked. "You think we can outrun that bastard? You *crazy?* In a few minutes he'll be close enough to sink us with his four-inchers, despite our jamming."

"Mr. Howell!" Britton said sharply. The chief mate fell silent.

Glinn glanced at his man at the computer. "Armed?" he asked.

The man nodded.

"Wait for my signal."

Glinn looked out through the window at the destroyer. He, too, could see it was now moving faster through the water. Even an old warship like that could do thirty-four knots. It was a beautiful sight, in the dark at least: the brilliant cluster of lights, the "bone in the throat," the watery reflections off the underside of the gun turrets. He waited another moment, letting the destroyer build up plenty of headway.

"Fire in the hole."

It was gratifying to see the two sudden geysers of water rip along the destroyer's stern; to see the high wind carry the water right across the flying bridge; and, more gratifying still, to hear the twin reports, barely seven seconds later. He watched as the destroyer began to swing broadside to the swell.

With both screws stripped, Comandante Vallenar would swiftly end up on the rocks. Glinn wondered, with faint amusement, how Vallenar would now explain the loss of his ship. Assuming he survived, of course.

There was a report from the destroyer, and then another: it was firing its four-inch guns again. Then the reports were punctuated with the higher sound of 40-millimeter cannon. In a moment, all the ship's guns were firing in a furious gesture of impotent rage, the cluster of flashes like manic strobes against the velvety darkness of the sea. But with the *Almirante Ramirez*'s radar useless, their steerage gone, their ship wallowing broadside to a heavy sea, and the *Rolvaag* in blackout, slipping away into the dark night on a new course, their shots were, naturally, going wild.

"A touch more to the left there, guv," said Puppup, stroking one mustache, squinting into the darkness.

"Left five degrees rudder," said Britton to the helmsman, without waiting for Howell.

The ship changed course almost imperceptibly.

Puppup peered out intently. The minutes ticked on. Then he bent his head toward Glinn. "We're out of it."

Britton watched him retreat again to the far shadows of the bridge. "Steady as she goes," she said. "All ahead flank."

The massive reports continued to echo crazily among the mountain peaks and silent glaciers, rolling and booming, gradually growing fainter. Soon they were heading into the open ocean.

Thirty minutes later, on the west side of Horn Island, they slowed just long enough to make a running recovery of the tender.

Then Britton spoke: "Take her round the Horn, Mr. Howell."

Cabo de Hornos came dimly into view and the sound of firing finally disappeared, swallowed by the howl of the wind and the thunder of the sea along the hull. It was over. Glinn had never once looked back at Desolation Island—at the bright lights of its works, at the machines that still raced furiously on their imaginary errands. Now, with the op completed, he felt his breathing pick up, his heart rate begin to increase again.

"Mr. Glinn?"

It was Britton. She was looking at him, her eyes luminous and intense.

"Yes?"

"How are you going to explain the sinking of a warship of a foreign nation?"

"They fired first. We acted in self-defense. Besides, our charges only knocked out their steerage. The *panteonero* will sink them."

"That isn't going to cut it. We'll be lucky not to spend the rest of our lives in prison."

"I respectfully disagree, Captain. Everything we've done has been legal. *Everything*. We were a legal mining operation. We recovered an ore body, a meteorite, it so happens, which fell well within the legal language of our mining contract with Chile. From the very beginning, we were harassed, forced to pay bribes, and threatened. One of our men was murdered. Finally, as we departed, we were fired upon by a freelancing warship. And yet, during this entire period, there was no warning to us from the

Chilean government, no official communication whatsoever. I assure you, we're going to lodge the strongest possible protest with the State Department on our return. We've been treated outrageously." He paused, then added with the faintest of smiles, "You don't really think our government will see it any other way, do you?"

Britton continued regarding him, her eyes quite beautifully green, for what seemed a long time. Now she came close and spoke in his ear.

"You know what?" she whispered. "I think you're certifiable."

There was, Glinn thought, a note of admiration in her voice.

Rolvaag,
4:00 A.M.

Palmer Lloyd sat in his study, slouched deep in the lone upright wing chair, his broad back to the door. His custom-made English shoes, now dry, had nudged the useless phone and laptop to one corner of the small table. Outside the bank of windows, a faint phosphorescence lay across the violent surface of the ocean, throwing rippling patterns of green light around the darkened study, giving the impression that the room lay on the bottom of the sea.

Lloyd gazed out motionlessly at that faint light. He had sat motionless through it all: the firing of the guns, the brief chase with the Chilean destroyer, the explosions, the tempestuous trip around the Cape.

With a soft click, the lights in the study came on, instantly turning the stormscape beyond the windows to an indistinct black. In the private office beyond, the wall of television sets lit up, suddenly crowded with dozens of silent talking heads. Further, in the suite of offices, a telephone rang; then another, and another. Still Palmer Lloyd did not move.

Even Lloyd could not say precisely what was going through his mind. Over the dark hours, there had been anger, of course; there had been frustration, humiliation, denial. All these feelings he understood. Glinn had summarily removed him from the bridge, clipped his wings, left him powerless. Such a thing had never happened to him before. What he could not quite understand—what he could not explain—was the growing feeling of joy that shot through all these other feelings, suffusing them like light through a screen. The loading of the rock, the disabling of the Chilean ship, had been a magnificent piece of work.

Under the unexpected glare of self-examination, Lloyd realized that Glinn had been correct to send him away. His own bull-in-a-china-shop methods would have been disastrous alongside such a carefully balanced scheme. And now the lights were back on. Glinn's message to him was crystal clear.

He remained still, a fixed spot at the center of freshly renewed activity, and thought about his past successes. This, too, would be a success. Thanks to Glinn.

And who had hired Glinn? Who had chosen the right man—the only man—for the job? Despite the humiliation, Lloyd congratulated himself on his choice. He had chosen well. He had succeeded. The meteorite was safely aboard. With the destroyer out of action, nothing could stop them. Soon, they would be in international waters. And then it was a straight shot to New York. There would be an uproar, of course, when they returned to the States. But he relished a good fight—especially when he was in the right.

He inhaled deeply, as the feeling of joy continued to swell. The phone on his desk began to ring, but still he ignored it. There was a tapping at the door, no doubt Penfold; he ignored that too. A violent gust shook the windows, splattering them with rain and sleet. And then at last Lloyd stood up, dusted himself off, and squared his shoulders. Not yet, but soon—very soon—it would be time to return to the bridge and congratulate Glinn on his—on *their*—success.

Almirante Ramirez, 4:10 A.M.

Comandante Vallenar stared into the blackness of the Cape Horn night, gripping the engine-room telegraph, steadying himself against the steep rolling of the ship. It was all too clear what had happened . . . and why.

Pushing the fury to the back of his consciousness, he concentrated on a mental calculation. In the sixty-knot *panteonero,* the destroyer's windage would produce a two-knot drift; combine that with the two-knot easterly set of the current, and he had about one hour before his ship was thrust onto the reefs beyond Isla Deceit.

Behind him, he could feel the silence of his officers. They were awaiting the orders to abandon ship. They were going to be disappointed.

Vallenar took a breath, controlling himself with an iron will. When he spoke to the officer of the deck, his voice was steady, without quaver. "Damage assessment, Mr. Santander."

"It is difficult to say, Comandante. Both screws appear to be stripped. Rudder damaged but functional. No hull breach reported. But the ship has lost headway and steerage. We are dead in the water, sir."

"Send two divers over the side. Report specific damage to the screws."

This order was greeted with a deeper silence. Vallenar turned, very slowly, raking the assembled officers with his eyes.

"Sir, it will be death to send anyone overboard in this sea," said the officer of the deck.

Vallenar held him in his gaze. Unlike the others, Santander was relatively new to his command: a mere six months spent here at the bottom of the world. "Yes," said Vallenar, "I see the problem. We cannot have that."

The man smiled.

"Send a team of six. That way, at least one should survive to complete the job."

The smile vanished.

"That's a direct order. Disobey, and you will be leading that team."

"Yes, sir," said the officer of the deck.

"There is a large wooden crate in along the starboard side of Forward Hold C, marked '40 mm ordnance.' Inside is a spare screw." Vallenar had prepared for many emergencies, the loss of a screw included. Hiding spare parts aboard ship was a good way to get around the corrupt officials of the Punta Arenas Navy Yard. "After documenting the damage, you will cut what sections you need from the spare screw. Divers will weld these sections to the damaged screws to give us propulsion. We will be on the shoals of Isla Deceit in less than sixty minutes. There will be no order given to abandon ship. There will be no distress call. You will either give me propulsion, or all hands will go down with the ship."

"Yes, sir," said the officer of the deck in a near whisper. The looks of the other bridge officers betrayed what they thought of this desperate plan. Vallenar ignored them. He did not care what they thought: he cared only that they obeyed. And for now, they were obeying.

Rolvaag, 7:55 A.M.

Manuel Garza stood on a narrow metal catwalk, peering down at the great red rock that lay far below him. From this height it looked almost small: an exotic egg, sitting in a nest of steel and wood. The webbing surrounding it was a fine piece of work: damn fine, perhaps the best thing he had done in his life. Marrying brute strength to pinpoint precision had been remarkably difficult, a challenge that only someone like Gene Rochefort could appreciate. Garza found himself sorry that Rochefort wasn't here to see it; beautiful engineering was one of the few things that had brought a smile to the man's pinched face.

The TIG welding crew had followed him down the access tunnel and were now stepping through the hatchway onto the catwalk, making a racket in their heavy rubber boots. They were a colorful bunch: yellow suits and gloves, welding diagrams with individual jobs colored in red.

"You've got your assignments," Garza said. "You know what to do. We need to lock that son of a bitch into place and we need to do it before the seas get any rougher."

The foreman gave Garza a mock salute. Everyone seemed to be in high spirits; the meteorite was in the hold, the Chilean destroyer was out of the picture, and they were on their way home.

"Oh, and one other thing. Try not to touch it."

The men laughed at the little joke. Someone made a crack about Timmer's ass achieving escape velocity; there was a reference to being mailed home in Tupperware containers. But nobody moved toward the elevator cage leading to the bottom of the tank. Garza could see that, despite the humor and the high spirits, there was a deep nervousness. The meteorite might be safely in the *Rolvaag*, but it had lost none of its ability to inspire dread.

There was only one way to handle this: quickly. "Go to it," Garza said, slapping the foreman on the back with an air of heartiness.

Without further delay, the men began stepping into the cage. Garza almost stayed behind—after all, he could direct the entire operation better from the observation unit at the end of the catwalk—but decided that would be unseemly. He stepped into the cage and slid the grating shut.

"Into the belly of the beast, Mr. Garza?" one man asked.

"Gotta keep you jackasses out of trouble."

They descended to the bottom of the tank, where a series of metal beams had been laid across the keel rider, forming a floor. Buttressing members ran from the cradle in all directions, distributing the weight of the meteorite toward all corners of the ship. Following the directions on their welding diagrams, the men branched out, climbing along struts and disappearing into the complex lattice that surrounded the meteorite. Soon they were all in place, but the tank remained silent for a long moment; it was as if, down here beside the rock, nobody wanted to be the first to begin. And then the bright points of light began popping out in the dim space, casting crazy shadows as the welders fired up their equipment and went to work.

Garza checked the assignment list and the master diagram, satisfying himself that everybody was doing just what he was supposed to. There was a faint chorus of sizzling as the TIG welders bit into the metal, fusing the cradle into place at a host of critical nodes. He ran his gaze over the welders in turn. It was unlikely some cowboy would get too close to the rock, but he made sure nonetheless. Somewhere in the distance he could hear an occasional drip. Searching idly for the source, he glanced at the longitudinal bulkheads rising sixty feet to the top of the tank, ribbed and worked like a metal cathedral. Then he glanced down at the bottom girders. The hull plates were wet. It was natural—all ships took in bilgewater. He could hear the measured boom of surf along the hull, feel the gentle, slow-motion rolling of the ship. He thought of the three membranes of metal that lay between him and the bottomless ocean. It was a disquieting thought, and he pulled his gaze away, looking now at the meteorite itself, inside its webbed prison.

Although from down here it looked more imposing, it was diminished by the vastness of the tank. Once again, he tried to comprehend how something so small could weigh so much. Five Eiffel towers packed into twenty feet of meteorite. Curved, pebbled surface. No scooped-out hollows like a normal meteorite. Stunning, almost indescribable color. He'd love to give his girlfriend a ring made out of that stuff. And then his memory flashed back to the various chunks of the man named Timmer, laid out in the command hut. Nope; no ring.

He glanced at his watch. Fifteen minutes. The work was estimated to take twenty-five. "How's it going?" he called to the crew foreman.

"Almost there," the foreman called back, his voice echoing and distorted in the great tank. Garza stood back and waited, feeling the ship rolling more heavily now. The smell of cooking steel, tungsten, and titanium was strong in the air.

At last the TIG welders began snapping off as the welders finished their work. Garza nodded. Twenty-two minutes: not bad. Just a few more critical welds and they'd be done. Rochefort had designed things to keep those welds to a minimum. Whenever possible, he'd kept things simple. Less likely to fail. He may have been a prig, but he was a damn good engineer. Garza sighed as the ship began to roll again, wishing again Rochefort could have seen his plan become real here in this tank. Someone got killed on almost every job. It was a little like war; better not to make too many friends . . .

He realized that the vessel was still rolling. *This is a big one*, he thought. There was a faint flurry of creaks and groans. "Hold tight!" he called out to the crew as he turned away and grasped the lift railing for support. The ship heeled, more, and still more.

Then he found himself lying on his back, in the pitch-dark, pain coursing through him. How did he get there? A minute could have passed, or an hour; there was no way to tell. His head swirled: there had been an explosion. Somewhere in the blackness, a man was screaming—hideously—and there was a strong smell of ozone and burnt metal in the air, overlaid with a whiff of woodsmoke. Something warm and sticky coated his face, and the pain throbbed in rhythm with the beat of his heart. But then it began to go away—far away—and soon he was able to sleep once again.

Rolvaag, 8:00 A.M.

Palmer Lloyd had taken his time arriving on the bridge. He had to brace himself. He could show no lingering childish resentment.

He was received with polite, even deferential nods. There was a new feeling on the bridge, and it took him a moment to understand. The mission was almost over. He was no longer a passenger, a nuisance at a critical moment. He was Palmer Lloyd, owner of the most important meteorite ever discovered, director of the Lloyd Museum, CEO of Lloyd Holdings, the seventh richest man in the world.

He came up behind Britton. Over the gold bars on her shoulder, he could see a monitor displaying a global positioning diagram. He had seen this screen before. Their ship showed on the screen as a cross, the long axis indicating direction of travel. Its forward end was steadily approaching a red line that arced gently across the diagram. Every few seconds, the screen flickered as the chart information was updated via satellite. When they crossed that line, they would be in international waters. Home free.

"How long?" he asked.

"Eight minutes," Britton replied. Her voice, though cool as ever, had lost the tightness of those harrowing final minutes at the island.

Lloyd glanced over at Glinn. He was standing beside Puppup,

hands clasped behind his back, his face the usual mask of indifference. Still, Lloyd felt sure he could see a smugness lingering in those impassive eyes. As well it should. They were minutes from one of the greatest scientific and engineering achievements of the twentieth century. He waited, not rushing it.

He glanced around the rest of the company: the crew of the watch, tired but satisfied, anticipating their relief. Chief Mate Howell, inscrutable. McFarlane and Amira, standing together silently. Even the crafty old doctor, Brambell, had emerged from his hole belowdecks. It was as if, on some unspoken signal, they had assembled to witness something momentous.

Lloyd straightened up, a small gesture meant to attract attention. He waited until all eyes were on him, then turned to Glinn.

"Mr. Glinn, may I offer you my heartfelt congratulations," he said.

Glinn bowed slightly. Smiles and glances went around the bridge.

At that moment the bridge door opened and a steward came in, wheeling a stainless-steel cart. The neck of a champagne bottle peeked out from an urn of crushed ice. A dozen crystal glasses were racked up beside it.

Lloyd rubbed his hands together delightedly. "Eli, you liar. You may be an old woman about some things, but your timing today has been exquisite."

"I did tell an untruth when I said I'd only brought one bottle along. Actually, I brought a case."

"Marvelous! Let's have at it, then."

"We'll have to make do with this single bottle. This *is* a ship's bridge. Fear not—the moment we reach New York Harbor, I'll uncork the other ten myself. Meanwhile, please do the honors." And he gestured toward the cart.

Lloyd strode over, slid the bottle out of the ice, and held it up with a grin.

"Don't drop it this time, guv," Puppup said, almost inaudibly.

Lloyd looked at Britton. "How much longer?"

"Three minutes."

The wind beat against the windows. The *panteonero* was growing, but—Britton had informed him—they would round Staten Island and be in the lee of Tierra del Fuego long before the southwesterly wind shifted to the more dangerous northwest. He unwired the cork and waited, the bottle cold in his hand.

For a moment, the only sounds on the bridge were the moan of the wind and the distant thundering of the ocean.

Then Britton looked up from the screen and glanced at Howell, who nodded his affirmation.

"The *Rolvaag* has just crossed into international waters," she said quietly.

A small cheer erupted. Lloyd popped the cork and began pouring judicious measures all around.

Suddenly the grinning face of Puppup appeared before Lloyd, his skinny arms holding up two glasses. "Right here, guv. One for me and one for me friend." He ducked his head.

Lloyd emptied the bottle into the glasses. "Who's your friend?" he asked, smiling indulgently. The man's role, though not large, had been crucial. He would find him a good job at the Lloyd Museum, in maintenance perhaps, or even security. Or maybe, as the last surviving Yaghan Indian, there might be something even better. Perhaps he should consider some kind of exhibit, after all. It would be tasteful and correct—a far cry from those nineteenth-century exhibitions of primitive people—but it could be a draw. Especially with Puppup on hand as the last living example. Yes, he would have to think about it . . .

"Hanuxa," Puppup answered, with another duck and grin. Lloyd looked up in time to see his rabbitlike retreat, drinking two-fistedly from both glasses.

The chief mate's voice broke through the hubbub. "I've got a surface contact at thirty-two miles, bearing three one five true at twenty knots."

Instantly, the conversation ceased. Lloyd glanced over at Glinn, eager for assurance, and felt a prickly sensation stir in his gut. The man had an expression on his face he had never seen before: a look of sick surprise.

"Glinn?" he said. "It's some merchant vessel, right?"

Without answering, Glinn turned to his operative at the EES console and spoke a few words in an undertone.

"It's the *Almirante Ramirez,*" said Britton in an undertone.

"What? How can you know that from the radar?" Lloyd asked, the prickly sensation turning into a flush of disbelief.

Britton looked at him. "There's no way to tell for sure, but it's in the right place at the right time. Most shipping would be heading through the Strait of Le Maire, particularly in this weather. But this one's coming after us, with all it's got."

Lloyd watched as Glinn conferred with the man at the computer. There was the faint sound of a dial tone, of high-speed dialing, the hiss of a digital handshake.

"I thought you put that son of a bitch out of action," Lloyd said.

Glinn straightened up, and Lloyd was immediately reassured to see that the collected, confident expression had returned to his face. "Our friend proves unusually resourceful."

"Resourceful?"

"Comandante Vallenar has managed to repair his vessel, at least partly. Quite an achievement. I can scarcely believe it possible. But it makes no difference."

"Why not?" Britton asked.

"It's all in the computer profile. He will not pursue us into international waters."

"That's a rather arrogant prediction, if you ask me. The man's crazy. He might do anything."

"You are in error. Comandante Vallenar, despite everything, is a naval officer at heart. He prides himself on his honor and loyalty, and on a set of abstract military ideals. For all these reasons, he will not pursue us beyond the line. To do so would be to embarrass Chile—and create an unpleasant incident with his country's largest supplier of foreign aid. Furthermore, he will not take a crippled ship too deeply into a building storm."

"So why's he still coming?"

"Two reasons. First, he doesn't know our exact location, and he still hopes to cut us off before we reach international waters. Second, our comandante is a man of the noble gesture. Like a dog running to the end of his chain knowing his quarry is out of reach, he will drive full bore to the edge of his country's waters, then turn back."

"Fancy analysis," said Britton, "but is it right?"

"Yes," said Glinn, "it is right." His voice was serene with conviction.

Lloyd smiled. "I've made the mistake of not trusting you before. I'm satisfied. If you say he won't cross, he won't cross."

Britton said nothing. Glinn turned to her with a personal, almost intimate gesture, and Lloyd was surprised to see him clasp her hands gently. He did not quite catch Glinn's words, but Britton appeared to flush.

"All right," she said, in a voice that was just audible.

Puppup suddenly appeared, both glasses empty, holding them up in a supplicating gesture. Lloyd glanced at him, noticing the way he unconsciously kept his balance despite an unusually heavy roll of the deck. "Any more, then?" the Yaghan asked. "For me and me friend, I mean."

There was no time to answer. There was a sudden vibration, a subsonic boom, that shook the very frame of the tanker. The bridge lights flickered, and the banks of monitors sank into a wash of gray electronic snow. Immediately, Britton and the rest of the officers were at their stations.

"What the hell was that?" Lloyd asked sharply.

No one answered him. Glinn had returned to his operative's side and was conferring with him in low, urgent tones. There was a deep vibration in the ship, almost like a groan. It was followed by another.

And then, as abruptly as it began, the disturbance ceased: the screens returned, the lights brightened and steadied. There was a chorus of chirps and whirrs as devices across the bridge rebooted.

"We don't know what it was," Britton said, finally answering Lloyd's question. Her eyes swept over the instrumentation. "Some kind of general malfunction. An explosion, perhaps. It seems to have affected all ship's systems." She turned to the chief mate. "I want a damage assessment right away."

Howell picked up the telephone and made two quick calls. After the second, he replaced the phone, face ashen. "It's the holding tank," he said, "the one with the meteorite. There's been a serious accident."

"What kind of accident?" Glinn asked.

"A discharge from the rock."

Glinn turned to McFarlane and Amira. "Get on it. Find out what happened and why. And Dr. Brambell, you better get to—"

But Brambell had already disappeared from the bridge.

Almirante Ramirez, 8:30 A.M.

Vallenar stared hard into the murk, as if the act of staring itself would bring the elusive tanker into view.

"Status," he murmured again to the conning officer.

"With the jamming, sir, it's hard to tell. My best estimate is that the target is heading zero nine zero at approximately sixteen knots."

"Range?"

"Sir, I can't tell exactly. Somewhere around thirty nautical miles. We wouldn't even have that close a fix, except their jamming seemed to drop briefly a few minutes ago."

Vallenar could feel a rhythmic surge to his ship: a sickening lifting and dropping of the deck. He had only felt this motion once before, when he had been caught in a storm south of Diego Ramirez during a training mission. He knew what this odd motion meant: the distance between the wave crests had begun to exceed twice the length of the *Almirante Ramirez*. He could see the following sea from the aft windows: long muscular swells, topped with a breaking line of water, coming at his stern and foaming along the hull before disappearing forward into the darkness. Once in a while a giant wave, a *tigre*, would come up from behind, the water piling up against the rudder, giving the helmsman a loose wheel and threatening to shove the destroyer around, causing it to broach to. It would only get worse when they turned south and took the sea on their beam.

Reaching thoughtfully into his pocket, he withdrew a *puro* and examined its soiled outer leaves absently. He thought of the two dead divers, their cold stiff bodies wrapped in tarps and stored in sea lockers aft. He thought of the three others, who never resurfaced, and a fourth, shivering now in the last stages of hypothermia. They had done their duty—no more, and no less. The ship was seaworthy. True, they could make only twenty knots with their damaged propellers. But the tanker was only making sixteen. And the long eastward run toward international waters was giving him the time he needed to achieve his strategy.

He glanced back at the conning officer. The crew was frightened: of this storm, of this chase. That fear was good. Frightened men worked faster. But Timmer had been worth any ten of them.

He bit off the end of the cigar and spat it away. Timmer had been worth the entire complement . . .

Vallenar mastered himself, taking the time to light the cigar carefully, methodically. The glowing red tip reflected back from the inky windows. By now they surely knew he was coming after them once again. This time he would be more careful. He had fallen into their trap once, and he would not allow it to happen again. Initially, his plan had been to cripple the ship. But now it was clear that Timmer was dead. The time for mere crippling was long past.

Five hours, maybe less, would bring them into range of his four-inch guns. In the meantime, if there was even a short respite from jamming, the Exocets were ready to fire at a moment's notice.

This time, there would be no mistake.

Rolvaag,
9:20 A.M.

As McFarlane ran down the center corridor of the medical suite, Rachel on his heels, he almost collided with Brambell, stepping through the operating room door. He was a very different Brambell than the wry, dry man of the dinner table: this Brambell was grim, his movements brusque, his wiry frame tense.

"We're here to see—" McFarlane began, but Brambell was stalking down the hall and disappearing behind another door, paying them not the slightest bit of attention. McFarlane glanced at Rachel.

Following Brambell's path, they entered a brightly lit room. The doctor, who was still wearing a pair of surgical gloves, stood over a gurney, examining a motionless patient. The man's head was swathed in bandages, and the surrounding sheets were soaked in blood. As McFarlane watched, Brambell jerked a sheet over the man's head with a sharp, angry motion. Then he turned to a nearby sink.

McFarlane swallowed hard. "We need to speak with Manuel Garza," he said.

"Absolutely not," Brambell said as he broke scrub, ripping off the pair of bloody gloves and dashing his hands under hot water.

"Doctor, we *must* question Garza about what happened. The safety of the ship depends on it."

Brambell stopped in his tracks, looking at McFarlane for the first time. His face was somber but controlled. He said nothing for a moment, and McFarlane could see behind the mask the racing mind of a doctor making a decision under extreme pressure.

"Room Three," he said as he pulled on a fresh pair of surgical gloves. "Five minutes."

They found Garza in a small room, wide awake. His face was bruised, his eyes blackened, and his head heavily bandaged. When the door opened, he swiveled his dark gaze at them, then looked away immediately. "They're all dead, aren't they?" he whispered, eyes on the bulkhead.

McFarlane hesitated. "All but one."

"But he's also going to die." It was a statement, not a question.

Rachel came over and laid a hand on his shoulder. "Manuel, I know how hard this must be for you. But we need to know what happened in the holding tank."

Garza did not look at her. He pursed his lips, blinked his blackened eyes. "What happened? What do you think happened? That goddamn meteorite went off again."

"Went off?" McFarlane repeated.

"Yeah. It exploded. Just like it did with that guy Timmer."

McFarlane and Rachel exchanged glances.

"Which one of your men touched it?" Rachel asked.

Garza suddenly turned to stare at her. McFarlane wasn't sure if his look was one of surprise, anger, or disbelief; the wide purple moon-holes of his eyes seemed to draw all expression from the rest of his face.

"Nobody touched it."

"Somebody must have."

"I said nobody. I was watching every minute."

"Manuel—" Rachel began.

He rose angrily. "You think my men were crazy? They hated being near that thing, they were scared to death of it. Rachel, I'm telling you, nobody got within *five feet*."

He winced and lay back.

After a moment, McFarlane spoke again. "We need to know

exactly what you saw. Can you tell us what you remember, right before it happened? What was going on? Did you notice anything unusual?"

"No. The men were almost finished with the welding. Some of them *had* finished. The job was virtually done. Everyone was still wearing their protective gear. The ship was heeling. It seemed to be taking a pretty big wave."

"I remember that wave," Rachel said. "Are you sure nobody lost his balance, nobody put out an involuntary hand to steady—"

"You don't believe me, do you?" he asked. "Tough shit, because it's true. *Nobody* touched the rock. Check the tapes yourself if you want."

"Was there anything unusual about the meteorite?" McFarlane asked. "Anything funny?"

Garza thought for a moment. Then he shook his head.

McFarlane leaned closer. "That freak wave that heeled the ship. Do you think tilting the meteorite could have caused the explosion?"

"Why? It was tilted, banged, and shoved all the way from the impact site to the holding tank. Nothing like this happened."

There was a silence.

"It's the rock," Garza murmured.

McFarlane blinked, not sure he had heard correctly. "What?" he asked.

"I said, it's the goddamn rock. It wants us dead. All of us."

And with that, he turned toward the bulkhead and would not speak again.

Rolvaag,
10:00 A.M.

A violent dawn rose beyond the windows of the bridge, revealing a wind-torn sea. A procession of gigantic swells, undulating, remorseless, came out of the storm-wracked western horizon and disappeared into the east. The *panteonero* continued to build, a screaming wind that seemed to rip pieces of sea from the tops of the waves and send them flying, shredding the water into white sheets of foam. The great ship heaved up, heaved down, rolling and pitching in agonizing slow motion.

Eli Glinn stood alone at the windows, hands clasped behind his back. He gazed out at the violence, conscious of an internal serenity he had rarely felt since the project began. It had been a project fraught with unexpected turns and surprises. Even here, on the ship, the meteorite continued to bedevil them: Howell had returned from the sick bay with reports of six dead and Garza injured. Nevertheless, EES had succeeded. It was one of the greatest engineering feats ever.

He would not care to repeat such a project again.

He turned. Britton and the other ship's officers were glued to the surface radar, tracking the *Almirante Ramirez*. Lloyd hovered behind them. It was a tense-looking group. Clearly, his assurances about Comandante Vallenar had not convinced them. A natural, if illogical, position to take. But Glinn's proprietary profiling program had never been wrong in a critical prediction. Besides, he *knew* Vallenar. He had met the man on his own turf. He had seen the iron discipline on his ship. He had seen the man's skill as a naval officer, his overweening pride, his love of country. *The man will not cross the line*. Not for a meteorite. At the last minute he would turn; the moment of crisis would pass; and they would be on their way home.

"Captain," he asked, "what course do you propose to take us out of Drake Passage?"

"As soon as the *Ramirez* turns around, I'll order a three three zero bearing to bring us back into the lee of South America and get us out of this gale."

Glinn nodded approvingly. "That will be soon."

Britton's eyes dropped back to the screen. She said nothing more.

Glinn strolled over and stood with Lloyd behind Captain Britton. On the electronic chart, the green dot that represented Vallenar was fast approaching international waters. Glinn couldn't help but smile. It was like watching a horse race on television for which he alone knew the outcome.

"Any radio contact from the *Ramirez?*"

"No," Britton replied. "They've been maintaining radio silence throughout. Not even making contact with their own base. Banks heard the base CO order him back hours ago."

Naturally, thought Glinn. It fit the profile.

He allowed his gaze to linger on Britton: at the scattering of freckles on her nose, the poise in her bearing. She doubted his judgment now; but later she would see that he had been right. He thought about the courage she had shown, the unerring good sense, the coolness under pressure; the dignity, even while the bridge had been out of her command. This was a woman, he felt, he could finally trust. Perhaps this was the woman he had been looking for. It bore further consideration. He began thinking of the correct strategy to win her, potential avenues of failure, the likeliest path to success . . .

He glanced back at the radar screen. The dot was now just minutes from the line. He felt the faintest twinge of nervousness disturb his serenity. But all factors had been taken into account. The man would turn.

He looked deliberately away from the screen and strolled back to the window. It was an awesome sight. The waves were topping the maindeck, sweeping past in green sheets, streaming through the scuppers back into the sea. The *Rolvaag*, despite its movement, still felt quite stable—it was a following sea, which greatly aided stability. And the mass in the center tank acted as ballast.

He glanced at his watch. Any moment now, Britton would report that the *Ramirez* had turned back.

There was an audible sound, a collective murmur, from the group around the radar.

"The *Ramirez* is changing course," said Britton, glancing up.

Glinn nodded, suppressing a smile.

"Turning northerly to a zero six zero heading."

Glinn waited.

"He just crossed the line," Britton added in a low voice. "Still heading zero six zero."

Glinn hesitated. "Vallenar's navigation is slightly off. His rudder is damaged. He's clearly in the process of turning around."

The minutes ticked off. Glinn left the windows and once again approached the screen. The green dot continued heading east-northeast. It wasn't exactly chasing them now, but it wasn't turning around either. Strange. He felt another twinge.

"He will come around momentarily," murmured Glinn.

The silence lengthened as the *Ramirez* continued on its bearing.

"Maintaining speed," said Howell.

"*Turn*," muttered Lloyd.

The ship did not turn. Instead, it made another slight course correction to zero five zero.

"What's the hell's he doing?" Lloyd suddenly exploded.

Britton straightened up and looked squarely at Glinn. She said nothing, but words were unnecessary: Glinn could read her expression with crystal clarity.

Doubt passed through him like a spasm, to be quickly replaced by reassurance. He knew now what the problem was. "Of course. He's not only having trouble with his rudder, but his primitive navigation systems have been affected by our jamming. The man doesn't know where he is." He turned to his operative at the console. "Turn off the ECM. Let our friend find his bearings."

The operative typed a series of commands.

"He's twenty-five miles distant," said Howell. "We're just within range of his Exocets."

"I'm aware of that," murmured Glinn.

There was a moment in which the entire bridge fell silent. Then Howell spoke again. "We're being illuminated with targeting radar. He's getting our range and bearing."

For the first time since his final op as a Ranger, Glinn felt a certain kind of uneasiness in his gut. "Give him a few more minutes. Let him figure out we're both in international waters."

Again the minutes ticked by.

"For God's sake, bring the ECM back on line!" Britton said sharply.

"Another minute. Please."

"Exocet launched," said Howell.

"CIWS full auto," said Britton. "Prepare to launch chaff."

The minutes passed in frozen dread.

Then there was a sudden rattling of Gatling guns as the CIWS went into action, followed by a harrowing airburst off the starboard side of the ship. A tiny piece of shrapnel ticked off a bridge window, leaving a star.

"Still being painted with radar," said Howell.

"Mr. Glinn!" Britton cried. "Order your man to reemploy ECM!"

"Reemploy electronic countermeasures," Glinn said weakly, leaning on the console for support. He stared at the implacable green point on the screen, his mind racing to find the answers, to see the pattern. Vallenar had stayed true to form by launching a missile at them. This was a gesture Glinn had anticipated. Now, having rattled his saber in impotent rage, the man would turn back. Glinn waited, willing the ship to turn.

But the pulsing green dot continued on its course: not their own course, exactly, but a course that took it ever deeper into international waters.

"Eli?" It was Lloyd. His voice was strangely calm. With an effort, Glinn detached himself from a hundred avenues of speculation and met Lloyd's flinty stare.

"He's not going to turn," Lloyd said. "He's coming after us. For the kill."

Rolvaag,
10:20 A.M.

Sally Britton steeled herself, tuning out extraneous details one at a time, focusing her mind for what was to come. One look at Glinn's pale, shattered face had disarmed her anger and told her all she needed to know about the failure of his prediction. She felt a twinge of sympathy for the man, despite the unforgivable misjudgment which had now put all their lives in extreme danger. She herself had made a misjudgment, on a bridge similar to this one, not all that long ago.

She turned her attention to the rear of the bridge, where a large nautical chart of the Cape Horn region was displayed. As she looked at it, going automatically through the familiar steps, she felt the worst of the tension ease. A few options presented themselves. All might not be lost.

She felt Glinn's presence behind her. She turned to see that the color was returning to his face, and the look of shock and paralysis was leaving his eyes. She realized, with surprise, that this man was still far from beaten.

"Captain," he said, "may I confer with you a moment?"

She nodded.

He took up position beside her, removing a piece of paper from the vest pocket of his suit as he did so. "I have here all the specifications of the *Almirante Ramirez*. The data is accurate as of approximately three weeks ago."

She looked at him. "Where did you get this?"

"From our home office."

"Let's hear it."

"The *Almirante Ramirez* is an Almirante-class destroyer, built for the Chilean navy by Vickers-Armstrong in the U.K. Its keel was laid in 1957 and the ship was commissioned in 1960. It has a complement of 266, with 17 officers. It displaces—"

"I don't need to know how many dinners they serve. Get to the threat systems."

Glinn's eyes flitted downward. "It was retrofitted in the seventies to hold four Aerospatiale 38 Exocet sea-skimming missiles. They have a range of twenty-five nautical miles. Fortunately for us, they use an earlier generation of active radar homing that can't overcome our advanced ECM system. So the Exocets are useless to him, even in visual range."

"What else has he got?"

"Four Vickers four-inch guns, two forward and two aft, that can deliver forty rounds a minute with a range of ten nautical miles. These are normally directed using two SGR 102 fire-control radars, but, if necessary, can also be targeted visually."

"Dear God. Forty rounds a minute *per gun?*"

"There are also four Bofors 40-millimeters with a range of six point five nautical miles. They can throw three hundred shells a minute."

Britton felt the blood leave her face. "Any one of those guns could take us out in a matter of minutes. We can't let him get within range."

"Visual targeting in this heavy sea will be difficult. But you are correct: we wouldn't last long in a barrage. We've got to increase our speed."

Britton didn't answer at first. "You know we're already pushing the limits of the turbines at sixteen knots." She turned to the chief mate. "Mr. Howell, is there any way we can squeeze a little more speed out of her?"

"I might be able to wring out another knot."

"Very well. Do it."

He turned to the helmsman. "All ahead one ninety."

Deep inside the ship, she felt an answering rumble as the engines were brought up to 190 rpms. That would give them—she did a quick mental calculation—four and a half hours, maybe a little less, before they were within range of the Vickers.

She turned back to Glinn and the chart. "I've worked it out," she said. "Our best option is to head northeast into Argentinian national waters as soon as possible. Argentina is a bitter enemy of Chile, and they'd hardly countenance a Chilean destroyer chasing us into their waters. They'd consider it an act of war."

She glanced at Glinn, but his veiled look betrayed nothing.

"Alternatively, we could head for the British naval base on the Falkland Islands. We should also radio our government and report we're under attack by a Chilean warship. We might be able to put some military pressure on that crazy son of a bitch."

She waited for a response.

At last, Glinn spoke. "I understand now what Vallenar's slight course changes were about."

"What?"

"We've been cut off."

Britton looked quickly back at the map. The *Ramirez* was now twenty miles northwest of them, on a true bearing of 300 degrees. Suddenly, she understood.

"Oh shit," she breathed.

"If we change course now to Argentina or the Falklands, he'll overtake us about here." Glinn drew a small circle on the map with his finger.

"We'll head west back to Chile, then," Britton said quickly. "He wouldn't get away with sinking us in the Puerto Williams harbor."

"No doubt. Unfortunately, even if we turn back now, he'll intercept us here." His finger traced another circle on the map.

"Then we'll head for the British scientific station on South Georgia Island."

"Then he'll intercept us here."

She watched the map, a paralyzing chill creeping down her spine.

"You see, Sally—may I call you Sally?—when he made those course changes to the northeast, he had *already* anticipated our possible points of refuge. If we had realized this and acted immediately, we would have had a chance of getting to Argentina, at least. But now even that route is closed to us."

Britton felt a pressure on her chest. "The U.S. Navy—"

"My man's already checked that. There's no effective military help within twenty-four hours."

"But there's a British naval base on the Falklands, armed to the teeth!"

"We considered that, too. Chile was a British ally in the Falklands War. For the U.S. to request military help from the U.K. against its former ally, using the very base they fought for—well, let us just say it is a request that would take more time than we have to expedite, even with Lloyd's and my connections. Unfortunately, the extreme South Atlantic is no place to get into a military scrape. We're on our own."

She looked at Glinn. He returned her gaze with gray eyes that seemed to have deepened until they were almost the color of the surrounding ocean. There was a plan behind those eyes. She was afraid to ask what it was.

"We head south," Glinn said simply. "To the Ice Limit."

Britton could hardly believe it. "Go south into the Screaming Sixties, into the ice, in a storm like this? That's not an option."

"You're right," said Glinn quietly. "It's not an option. It's the *only* option."

Almirante Ramirez,
11:00 A.M.

After dawn, Vallenar noticed that the wind had begun its inevitable shift to the west. His plan had worked. Belatedly, the Americans had realized they were cut off. There was no place for them to go but down into the Sixties. Already, they had changed course to one eight zero—due south. And that's where he would intercept them, where the endgame would play out: at the Ice Limit, in the black freezing waters of the Antarctic Ocean.

He spoke softly, precisely. "From now on, I'll have the deck."

The *oficial de guardia*, the officer of the deck, called out, "Aye, sir, the comandante has the deck!"

"Set heading one eight zero," Vallenar said to the conning officer.

This order would place the violent sea directly on their beam, the most dangerous position for the destroyer. The bridge officers knew this. He waited for the conning officer to repeat the order and call rudder directions. But no orders came.

"Sir?" It was the officer of the deck who spoke.

Vallenar did not turn to look at the officer of the deck. He did not need to; he sensed what was about to happen. Out of the corner of his eye he could see the conning officer and the *timonel*, the helmsman, all rigidly at attention.

So this was it. Better it should happen now than later.

He raised his eyebrows at the officer of the deck. "Mr. Santander, are we having a problem with the chain of command on the bridge?" He spoke as mildly as possible.

"The officers of the *Almirante Ramirez* would like to know our mission, sir."

Vallenar waited, still not looking at the man. Silence, he had long discovered, was more intimidating than words. A minute passed, and then he spoke.

"Is it customary for Chilean naval officers to question their commander?"

"No, sir."

Vallenar took out a *puro*, rolled it between his fingers, bit off the end, and placed it carefully between his lips. He drew air through it.

"Then why are you questioning me?" He spoke gently.

"Sir . . . because of the unusual nature of the mission, sir."

Vallenar removed the cigar and inspected it. "Unusual? How so?"

There was an uncomfortable pause.

"It is our impression, sir, that we were ordered back to base last night. We are not aware of any orders to pursue this civilian ship."

Vallenar took in the word *civilian*. It was a deliberate rebuke, a suggestion that Vallenar was engaged in a cowardly pursuit against an unarmed adversary. He drew more air through the unlit cigar.

"Tell me, Mr. Santander. On board ship, do you take orders from your comandante, or from a base commander on shore?"

"From the comandante, sir."

"Am I your comandante?"

"Yes, sir."

"Then there is nothing more to discuss." Vallenar removed a box of matches from his uniform pocket, opened the box, removed one wax match, drew it slowly across the striker until it flared, and lit his cigar.

"Sir, I beg your pardon, what you have said is insufficient. Men died repairing that screw. We respectfully request information on our mission."

At last, Vallenar turned. He felt the growing rage within him—rage at the arrogant Americans, at the man Glinn who came to chitchat while his divers sabotaged the vessel, at Timmer's death—all channeled now toward this subordinate, who dared to question his decisions. He puffed, drawing the smoke into his lungs, feeling the surge of nicotine in his blood. When he was steady again, he flicked the match toward the damp deck and lowered the cigar. This *oficial de guardia* was a green, foolish man, and the challenge was not unexpected. He looked around at the other officers on the bridge. All of them quickly lowered their eyes.

With one smooth movement, Vallenar withdrew his sidearm and pressed its barrel against the officer's chest. As Santander opened his mouth to protest, he pulled the trigger. The 9-millimeter slug thrust the man back like the blow of a fist, slamming him hard into a bulkhead. The officer of the deck stared down in disbelief at his ruined chest and the small horizontal fountain of blood that pumped its rhythmic stream. Air sucked in and out of the wound, once, then again. The man fell to his knees, then toppled forward onto his elbows, surprised eyes now turning glassy, mouth still open wide.

Vallenar returned the gun to its sling. The only sound on the bridge was Santander's stertorous attempts to breathe and the quiet patter of blood as it rained from his chest onto the deck.

Vallenar glanced at the conning officer. "Mr. Aller. Effective immediately, you are the officer of the deck. And you, Mr. Lomas, are the conning officer. A new course has been ordered. Execute it."

He turned away, drawing on his cigar, looking once again out over the storm-tossed ocean. The heel of his right hand still rested on the Luger. He waited to see if the incipient mutiny would continue. It would be a pity to lose Aller as well.

Aller looked at the new conning officer, and nodded weakly.

"Right standard rudder," said the conning officer, "steady on course one eight zero."

The helmsman answered. "Aye, sir, right standard rudder, coming to course one eight zero."

Vallenar slipped his hand from his weapon. It was over. Cut off the head and the body will die.

The ship began to turn broadside to the sea, helped along by terrifying shoves from each passing wave. As the shuddering and reeling grew worse, the bridge personnel took hold of stanchions, flagbag rails, anything that would help them keep upright.

"Steady on one eight zero," said the helmsman in a quavering voice.

"Very well," the conning officer answered.

Vallenar leaned into the speaking tube. "Radar, estimate when we will be within targeting range of the American ship with the Vickers guns."

After a moment, the response came: "Sir, at present course and speed, estimated range in three hours, thirty minutes."

"Very good." Vallenar leaned away from the tube and flicked a thumb toward the dying man at his feet. "Mr. Sanchez, take this away. And get a cleaning detail up here."

He turned back to the violent sea.

Rolvaag,
11:30 A.M.

Glinn stood next to Britton, motionless beside the helm. As they fled southward toward the sixtieth parallel, the *Rolvaag* had moved squarely into the westerlies that raged around the bottom of the world, endlessly circling, building up the greatest seas on earth. As far as the eye could see, a terrifying progression of Atlantic rollers swept eastward, high as mountains. In the last hour, as the storm grew in intensity, the ocean seemed to have lost a solid surface; there was no longer a sharp line between water and air. The screaming winds and heaving seas joined in a fury of spray and spume. As the tanker sank into the trough between each wave there would come a brief, eerie calm; and then the great ship would shudder and rise back into the howling gale.

But Glinn did not see the storm. For some time his thoughts had been elsewhere. Vallenar had staked everything—his career, his crew, his ship, the honor of his country, his very life—on this chase. He knew they were carrying only a rock; a huge rock, but a rock nonetheless. This chase did not make sense.

He had miscalculated badly. Unforgivably. For the briefest of moments, Glinn contemplated failure; rolled it to and fro on his tongue, as if tasting it. Then, with a spasm, he forced it from his thoughts. There would be, *could be,* no failure here.

The problem did not lie in the computer profile, or in the two-foot file on Vallenar back in New York; it lay in *himself*. There was a crucial piece missing. And this piece was in his own mind, waiting for him to recognize it. If he could understand Vallenar's motivation for this insane pursuit, then he could act upon it . . . How far would Vallenar take it? Would he pursue them past the Ice Limit? He shook his head, as if to shake loose the answer, but there was nothing. Without understanding Vallenar's motivation, he could develop no plan.

He glanced over at Britton. She was staring at the radar, and the wavering green pip that represented the *Almirante Ramirez*.

"The *Ramirez* has matched our course for the last half hour," she said, without looking up. "One eight zero, dead astern, holding at twenty knots, constant bearing and decreasing range."

Glinn said nothing. It was incredible to him that Vallenar would take his ship into a beam sea like this. The giant *Rolvaag* was struggling, and it was far better at handling the storm than a destroyer with scarcely a forty-foot beam. It was truly insane. There was a good chance that the *Almirante Ramirez* would be capsized. But a good chance was still a chance, and Glinn had no idea what kind of seamanship Vallenar could bring to bear. He suspected first-rate.

"At current speed and bearing, he'll catch up with us at the Ice Limit," Britton said. "And he'll come within firing range considerably before then."

"In just over three hours," said Glinn. "Around dusk."

"Once we're in range, do you think he will fire?"

"I have no doubt of it."

"We have no defense. We'll be ripped to pieces."

"If we're unable to lose him in the darkness, that's unfortunately true."

She looked up at him. "What about the meteorite?" she asked in a low voice.

"What about it?"

She lowered her voice, glancing at Lloyd. "If we drop it, we'll be able to increase our speed."

Glinn felt himself stiffen. He glanced over at Lloyd, who stood frowning at the bridge windows, trunklike legs planted wide apart. He hadn't heard. When Glinn answered, he spoke slowly, reasonably.

"To jettison it, we have to bring the ship to an absolute halt. It takes five miles to stop the ship. One half hour. That would give Vallenar all the time he needs to catch us. We'd be sunk before we came to rest."

"Then you've run out of answers?" she asked, her voice even lower.

He looked into her green eyes. They were clear, and steady, and quite beautiful. "There is no such thing as a problem without a solution," he said. "We just have to find it."

Britton paused. "Before we left the island, you asked me to trust you. I hope that I can. I would like to very much."

Glinn looked away, feeling an unexpected flush of emotion. For a moment, his eye fell on the GPS screen, and the dotted green line marked *Ice Limit* that ran across it. Then he looked back into her eyes. "You can trust me on this, Captain. I *will* have a solution for you. I promise."

She nodded slowly. "I don't believe you're a man who breaks his promises. I hope I'm right. Mr. Glinn—Eli—there's only one thing I want out of life right now. And that's to see my daughter again."

Glinn began to answer. But what came out instead was a hiss of surprise. He took an involuntary step back. In a blinding flash of insight brought on by Britton's final sentence, he understood what was driving Vallenar.

He turned and, without a word, abruptly left the bridge.

Rolvaag,
12:30 P.M.

Lloyd paced restlessly across the long expanse of the bridge. The storm battered furiously against the windows, but he had averted his eyes from the tearing seas. In all his life, he had never seen anything so frightening. It barely resembled water anymore, looking more like mountains, green and gray and black, rising, falling, sweeping, crumbling apart in gigantic creamy avalanches. He could hardly see how their ship—*any* ship—could survive five seconds in such a sea. Yet the *Rolvaag* plowed on. It was difficult to walk, but he needed the distraction of the physical activity. Reaching the starboard wing door, he pivoted brusquely and resumed pacing. He had been at it for sixty minutes, ever since Glinn had vanished without a word.

His head ached from the sudden reversals of fortune, the abrupt shifts in mood, the unbearable tension of the last twelve hours. Exasperation, humiliation, triumph, apprehension. He glanced up at the bulkhead clock, then at the faces of the bridge officers. Howell, his face set. Britton, expressionless, monitoring alternately the radar screen and the GPS chart. Banks, framed inside the door of the radio room. Lloyd felt like shaking some kind of answers out of them. But they had already told him everything there was to know. They had about two hours before the *Ramirez* would start edging into range.

Lloyd felt his limbs stiffen against a current of rage. It was Glinn's fault. It was overweening arrogance: he had studied the options so long the man believed himself incapable of failure. *Think long, think wrong,* someone had once said. If he'd been allowed to call in some favors, they wouldn't be helpless, like a mouse waiting for the cat to close in for the kill.

The door to the bridge opened and Glinn stepped in. "Good afternoon, Captain," he said nonchalantly.

More than anything, this air of nonchalance sent fury coursing through Lloyd. "God damn you, Glinn," he said, "where the hell have you been?"

Glinn's eyes drifted toward him. "I've been examining Vallenar's files. I know now what's driving him."

"Who the hell cares? He's the one who's driving us, right towards Antarctica."

"Timmer was Vallenar's son."

Lloyd stopped short. "Timmer?" he asked, confused.

"Vallenar's signal officer. The man who was killed by the meteorite."

"That's absurd. Didn't I hear Timmer had blond hair and blue eyes?"

"He was Vallenar's son by a German mistress."

"Is this another guess, or do you have evidence?"

"There's no record of a son, but it's the only explanation. That's why he was so anxious to get Timmer back when I visited. And that's why he initially refrained from attacking our ship: I told him Timmer was in the brig. But as soon as we left the island, he realized Timmer was dead. I believe he thinks we murdered him. That's why he pursued us into international waters. That's why he'll never give up until he dies. Or until we do."

The spasm of fury had left. Lloyd felt drained, exhausted. Anger at this point was useless. He controlled his voice. "And how, pray tell, is this psychological insight going to help us?"

Instead of answering, Glinn glanced back at Britton. "How far are we from the Ice Limit?"

"It's seventy-seven nautical miles south of our position."

"Can you see any ice on your radar?"

Britton turned. "Mr. Howell?"

"Some drift ice at ten miles. A few growlers. Just at the Limit, the long-range surface radar's picking up a massive ice island. Two ice islands, actually; it looks like one broke in half."

"Bearing?"

"One nine one."

Glinn spoke: "I would suggest heading that way. Make a very slow turn. If it takes Vallenar a while to notice the course change, we might gain a mile or two."

Howell looked questioningly at Britton.

"Mr. Glinn," said Britton, "it's suicide to take a huge ship like this past the Ice Limit. Especially in this weather."

"There are reasons," said Glinn.

"Care to share them with us?" Lloyd asked. "Or are you going to keep us in the dark again? Maybe we could've used some freelance decision making back there."

Glinn's gaze fell first on Lloyd, then Britton, then Howell.

"Fair enough," he said, after a moment. "We are reduced to two options: turn away and try to outrun the destroyer. Or keep to this course and try to lose the destroyer below the Ice Limit. The former has a close to one hundred percent probability of failure; the latter, somewhat less. This latter plan also has the advantage of forcing the destroyer through a beam sea."

"What is this Ice Limit?" Lloyd asked.

"It's where the freezing waters around Antarctica meet the warmer northern waters of the Atlantic and Pacific. Oceanographers call it the Antarctic Convergence. It's known for impenetrable fogs and, of course, extremely dangerous ice."

"You're proposing to take the *Rolvaag* into an area of ice and fog? It does sound like suicide."

"What we need now is concealment, time to lose the destroyer long enough to lay a course away from it. In the darkness, in the ice and fog, we might just escape."

"We might just sink, too."

"The probability of hitting an iceberg is lower than the probability of being sunk by the destroyer."

"What if there's no fog?" asked Howell.

"Then we have a problem."

There was a long silence. And then Britton spoke: "Mr. Howell. Set a new course for one nine zero. Bring her head around slowly."

There was the briefest of hesitations. Then Howell relayed the order to the helmsman in clipped tones. As he spoke, his eyes never left Glinn's.

Rolvaag, 2:00 P.M.

McFarlane slumped back in the uncomfortable plastic chair, sighing and rubbing his eyes. Rachel sat beside him, cracking peanut shells and letting the debris fall onto the metal deck of the observation unit. The only light came from a single monitor set high in the bulkhead above them.

"Don't you ever get tired of those damn peanuts?" McFarlane said.

Rachel seemed to consider this a moment. "Nope," she replied.

They lapsed into silence. Conscious of an incipient headache and low-grade nausea, McFarlane closed his eyes. The moment he did so, the roll of the ship seemed to increase dramatically. He heard the tick of metal, the occasional drip of water. Other than that, the holding tank that yawned beneath them was quiet.

McFarlane opened his eyes with an effort. "Run it again," he said.

"But we've already viewed it five times," Rachel said. When McFarlane did not reply, she gave a disgusted snort and leaned forward to punch the transport controls.

Of the three security viewcams in the holding tank, only one had survived the explosion. He watched as Rachel ran the tape forward at high speed, slowing to normal speed a minute before the detonation. They watched in silence as the seconds counted down. Nothing new. Garza was right: nobody had touched the rock. Nobody had even been close.

McFarlane leaned back again with a curse, glancing out of the observation unit and along the catwalk, as if searching for an answer on the walls of the tank. Then he let his eyes travel slowly down the forty-foot span to the top of the meteorite. The explosion had gone off sideways, killing most of the lights in the tank, damaging communications networks both fore and aft, but leaving the catwalk and observation unit at the top of the tank unharmed. The web looked largely intact, although it was clear that some struts had been knocked out. Molten steel had sprayed in foamy streaks across the walls of the tank, and some of the massive laminated oak timbers were charred. Flecks of blood and red matter could be seen here and there at points the scrub team had missed. The meteorite itself looked unchanged.

What's the secret here? he thought. *What is it we're missing?*

"Let's go over what we know," he said. "The explosion seems to have been just like the one that killed Timmer."

"Perhaps even stronger," Rachel said. "One hell of an electrical blast. If there hadn't been so much metal around to absorb the charge, it might have blown the ship's electronics."

"And afterwards, the meteorite threw off a lot of radio noise," he said. "Just like with Timmer."

Rachel picked up her radio, turned it on, made a face at the roar of static, turned it off again. "And it's still throwing it off," she said.

They lapsed into silence again.

"I wonder if *anything* triggered the blast," said Rachel, rewinding the tape. "Maybe it was random."

McFarlane didn't respond. It couldn't be random; something must have triggered it. And despite Garza's remark—and the increasing nervousness of the crew—he didn't believe the meteorite was some malignant thing, actively seeking to hurt them.

McFarlane wondered if perhaps Timmer and Masangkay had never touched the thing, after all. But no; he'd analyzed it too carefully. The key to the mystery had to be Palmer Lloyd. He had placed his cheek against the rock and lived to tell the story. The two others had been blown up.

What was different about their touches?

He sat up in the chair. "Let's watch it again."

Wordlessly, Rachel punched the controls, and the monitor flickered to life.

The surviving camera had been placed almost directly above the rock, just below the observation unit. There was Garza, standing to one side, the welding diagrams unrolled before him. The TIG welders were spaced evenly around the rock, working on various nodes. They were kneeling, their bright points of flame leaving red tracks on the screen. In the lower right corner, a time display ran rapidly through the seconds.

"Turn up the sound," McFarlane said. He closed his eyes; the headache and nausea were getting worse. Seasickness.

Garza's voice leapt into the small enclosure. "*How's it going?*" he shouted. There was an answering shout: "*Almost there.*" Scratchy silence; the trickle of water; the pop of a torch flaring out. Room tone, then a flurry of creaks and groans as the vessel began to heel. He heard Garza's voice: "*Hold tight!*"

And then it ended in a hiss of white noise.

McFarlane opened his eyes. "Back ten seconds."

They watched as it ran through again.

"It went off at the very top of the roll," Rachel said.

"But Garza's right. That thing was manhandled all the way down to the shore." McFarlane paused. "Could there be another workman, hidden by the rock? Somebody we're not seeing?"

"I thought of that. Six welders came in, plus Garza. Look, you can see them all there in the last frame, clearly visible. All well back from the meteorite."

McFarlane dropped his chin to his hands. Something about the video was nagging at him, but he couldn't put his finger on it. Maybe it was nothing. Maybe he was just too damn tired.

Rachel stretched, swept peanut shells from her knees. "Here we are, trying to second-guess Garza," she said. "But what if everybody's right?"

McFarlane glanced at her. "I don't understand."

"What if nobody touched the meteorite? What if it was something *else* that touched the meteorite?"

"Something else?" he replied. "But there was nothing else moving in that room—" He stopped abruptly, realizing what had been troubling him: the sound of water.

"Give me the last sixty seconds," he said. "Quickly."

He lifted his head toward the screen, searching for the source of the sound he'd heard. There it was, very faintly: a thin stream at one side, falling from above, disappearing into the depths of the tank. He stared at it. As the ship began the heavy roll, the stream of water pulled away from the bulkhead and began angling closer to the meteorite.

"Water," McFarlane said aloud.

Rachel looked at him curiously.

"There was a stream of water coming down the side of the tank. There must be a leak in the mechanical door. Look, you can still see it." He pointed up at a narrow stream trickling down the far longitudinal bulkhead. "The meteorite went off when that roll brought the water in contact with it."

"That's absurd. The meteorite's been sitting in waterlogged ground for millions of years. It got rained and snowed on. It's inert. How could water possibly affect it?"

"I don't know, but take a look." He replayed the video, demonstrating how, at the instant the water connected with the meteorite, the screen popped into snow.

"Coincidence?" she asked.

McFarlane shook his head. "No."

Rachel looked at him. "Sam, how could this water be different from all the other water that's touched the meteorite?"

And then, in a moment of revelation, it became clear. "Salt," he said. "It's *salt* water dripping into the hold."

After a shocked moment, Rachel suddenly gasped.

"That's *it*," she said. "And that's why Timmer and Masangkay set it off with their hands—their sweaty hands. There was *salt* in their touch. But Lloyd put his cheek to it on a bitterly cold day.

There was no sweat in his touch. It must be highly reactive to sodium chloride. But why, Sam? What's it reacting to?"

McFarlane looked at her, then beyond, to where the trickle of seawater still glistened in the gloom, swaying with the gradual motion of the ship.

The motion of the ship . . .

"We'll worry about that later," he said. He reached for his radio, snapped it on, heard the hiss of static.

"God *damn* it!" he said, shoving the radio back in his belt.

"Sam—" Rachel began.

"We've got to get out of here," he interrupted. "Otherwise, when the next big roll comes, we're toast."

He stood up just as she gripped his arm.

"We can't leave," she said. "Another explosion like that might break the web. If the meteorite gets loose, we'll all die."

"Then we have to keep the water from the rock."

For a moment, the two stared at each other. And then, as with a single thought, they sprinted down the catwalk toward the access tunnel.

Almirante Ramirez, 2:45 P.M.

Vallenar stood at the bridge, looking southward over the heaving seas, an old pair of binoculars cradled in his hands. The officers around him were struggling to remain on their feet in the wildly rolling ship, their faces frozen masks of neutrality. They were terrified. But now his regime of absolute discipline was paying off: the test had come, and those who remained were with him. They would follow him to hell, if necessary—and that, he thought as he glanced at the chart, was exactly where they were heading.

The snow and sleet had stopped, and the sky was clearing. Visibility was excellent. But the wind had, if anything, picked up, and the seas were mounting ever higher. When the ship sank into the bottom of the troughs, it became enshrouded in a midnight darkness, and the walls of black water rising on either side made him feel as if the ship were at the bottom of a vast canyon. At the bottom of these troughs, the wave crests were an astonishing twenty meters *above* the level of the bridge. He had never seen a sea like this in his life, and the increase in visibility, while useful to his plan, made it appear all the more dreadful. The normal procedure would be to head into the wind and ride it out. That was not an option. He had to keep a heading that put the wind and sea almost on his beam; otherwise, the heavier American ship would escape.

He watched as the bow of his destroyer plowed into the sea at the bottom of the long trough and came up slowly, the *castillo* thunderously shedding water; the ship leaned to starboard until the bridge was hanging over the open ocean, wracked with foam. Everyone grabbed a handhold. The bridge hung for frightening seconds, then slowly righted itself, the momentum dipping it to port. It was an especially ugly roll.

Vallenar knew the ship, knew what it could and could not do. He could feel when the wind and water took charge. They had not—at least, not yet. It would take vigilance, and adroit seamanship, to keep the ship from foundering. He would do it himself, not leave it to the conning officer.

He saw a foaming swell looming in the distance, towering over the rest, thrusting itself through the storm like a whale. He spoke calmly, almost nonchalantly. "Ease your rudder to left standard, starboard engine ahead one-third, port engine ahead two-thirds. Keep calling your head."

"Coming around easy, sir," said Aller. "Heading one seven five, heading one seven zero—"

"Steady on one six five."

The wave began to take the ship in its embrace; the *Ramirez* rose, strained, canted. Vallenar held on to the engine-room telegraph as they heeled sickeningly, the inclinometer reading close to thirty degrees, before the wave finally crested. For a moment, he had a long view across the southern ocean, all the way to the horizon. He quickly fitted the binoculars to his eyes and scanned the tumultuous sea until they subsided into the next trough. It was a terrifying sight: the monumental peaks and valleys of water, the absolute promiscuity of chaos. It temporarily unnerved him.

As the ship fell, he calmed himself. They rose again, and so did Vallenar's binoculars. He felt a sudden lurch in his chest: *there it was;* a dark silhouette against the sea, bordered in white. It was larger, and closer, than he thought it would be. He kept the binoculars trained, almost afraid to blink, as the ship subsided, then slowly began to rise on the next foam-webbed mountain of water. As they topped it, and the combing crest creamed over the port railing and slanted the ship over, Vallenar saw the tanker again.

"Port engine back one-third. Right standard rudder. Steady on one eight zero."

Once more the deck heaved up and fell to starboard.

"What is our fuel?"

"Thirty percent."

He turned to the *ingeniero de guardia*, the engineer of the watch. "Ballast the tanks." Filling the empty tanks with seawater would slow them down half a knot, but it would add a stability they would need for what was about to come.

"Ballasting the tanks," said the engineer, with evident relief.

Vallenar turned to the quartermaster. "Barometer?"

"Twenty-nine point two eight, falling."

He called his tactical action officer to the bridge. "We have visual contact with the American ship," he said, handing the man the binoculars.

The man raised them to his eyes. "I see it, sir," he said after a moment.

Vallenar turned toward the officer of the deck. "It bears one nine zero, or thereabouts. Have CIC give me a course to intercept."

The orders were relayed, the new course given. Everything now was crisp, correct.

Vallenar swiveled back to the tactical action officer. "Report when we are within gun range. Do not engage without my order."

"Yes, sir," said the tactical action officer, in a carefully neutral tone.

The destroyer began to yaw as it cleared another ugly wave, its prow dropping into the next trough with a rumble of water. The deck heaved, careening to starboard. The head began swinging to port, a heavy, uncontrolled motion.

"I can't hold her at one nine zero."

"Use full rudder to maintain your heading."

The ship steadied. Vallenar could see a *tigre* approaching from due west.

"Ease your rudder to standard. *Ease* it!"

The ship began a slow, dangling roll as it mounted the side of the enormous wave. When the wave broke, a sheet of water came racing across the deck: they were actually shipping water on the bridge.

"Right hard rudder! Right hard!"

The ship skidded sideways.

"Rudder's out of the water, sir!" the helmsman cried, the wheel loose in his hands.

"Port engine back two-thirds! Starboard ahead flank!"

The operator worked the engine telegraph. The ship continued sideways.

"She's not answering—"

Vallenar felt a twinge of fear—not for himself, but for his uncompleted mission—and then he felt the stern settle in the sea and the screws bite into the water.

He slowly released his breath, then leaned into the squawk box as if nothing had happened. "Report any air contacts." No ship would be coming to the aid of the Americans in this weather, he was sure of that; but he felt less sure about aircraft.

"No air contact out to two hundred miles," returned the CIC. "Ice to the south."

"What kind of ice?"

"Two large ice islands and assorted growlers and drift ice."

They're running to the ice, Vallenar thought with satisfaction. It was a desperate measure, taking a tanker below the Ice Limit, *deliberately* heading for the ice, in a storm like this. But it was their only move, and he had expected it. Perhaps they thought they could play hide-and-seek among the bergs, or escape under cover of darkness. Perhaps they were hoping for fog. It would not succeed. On the contrary, the ice would work to his advantage by dampening the heavy seas. And in ice, a destroyer was far more maneuverable than a tanker. He would kill them in the ice—if the ice didn't get them first.

"Drawing into gun range, sir," said the tactical action officer.

Vallenar looked out over the storm-tossed ocean. Now, even without the binoculars, he could occasionally glimpse the dark speck of the American ship. It was perhaps eight miles away, but even at that distance it made a big, fat target.

"Do you have visual contact acceptable for targeting?" he asked.

"Not yet, sir. Visual targeting will be difficult in this sea, at this range."

"Then we wait until we are closer."

The minutes dragged on as they gained, very slowly, on the American ship. The sky darkened as the wind held steady at eighty knots. The fear that had gripped the bridge remained, a healthy tonic. The sun was setting. Vallenar continued to issue a stream of carefully nuanced rudder and engine instructions, responding to the changing sea. The repairs to the propellers and rudder were holding well. The men had done a good job. Pity so many had died in the process.

Night would be falling soon, and the *Rolvaag* was running dark. He could wait no longer. "Mr. Casseo, bracket the target. Tracers only."

"Yes, sir," said the tactical action officer. "Loading tracers."

Vallenar looked down at the forward guns. After a minute he saw them turn, elevate to about forty-five degrees, and then fire in sequence: two bright shells. The barrels jerked backward in a gout of flame, and the bridge shook with the recoil. Vallenar clapped his binoculars to his eyes and watched the ranging shots arc into the storm. Both fell wild, well short of the tanker.

The ship subsided into another trough, then climbed again. Once more, the forward guns fired tracers in the pause at the top of their roll. These flew farther, but still fell short.

The tactical action officer timed additional shots for the wave crests, making slight adjustments. After a few minutes, he spoke again. "Comandante, I believe we have sufficient range data to lay a line of shells across the target."

"Very well. Fire for effect. I want to disable the ship enough to slow it down but not sink it. Then we will draw close for a clean kill."

There was the briefest of silences at this.

"Yes, sir," said the tactical action officer.

As the destroyer rose, the guns went into action once again, live rounds leaving the barrels now, screaming southward in deadly arcs of orange.

Rolvaag,
3:30 P.M.

McFarlane sank back against the bulkhead of the observation unit, ignoring the nearby chair and letting himself slide down to the metal deck. He felt utterly drained. Countless small muscles twitched spasmodically in his arms and legs. He could feel Rachel plop herself down beside him, but he felt too exhausted even to look over.

With the meteorite disrupting their radios, and no time to get help, they had been forced to find a solution themselves. Standing in the access corridor, behind the safely closed hatch, they had finally come up with a workable scheme. There were dozens of waterproof tarps in the storage compartments behind them, slung over the stacks of stores. They rigged a series of those tarps over the top of the web to shield the meteorite from seawater. It took a half hour of frantic activity, conducted under constant fear of another explosion.

McFarlane unclipped his radio, found it was still dead, and snapped it off again with a shrug. Glinn would learn all about it eventually. It seemed strange to McFarlane that Britton, and Glinn, and the rest could have been on that bridge all this time, preoccupied with their own work, completely unaware of the crisis that had played out half a dozen decks beneath them. He wondered what the hell was going on up there; the storm seemed to be getting worse.

He felt himself roll back with the ship. It was only a matter of time until the stream of seawater swerved toward the web once again.

They lapsed into silence. McFarlane looked over as Rachel reached into a breast pocket of her shirt, pulled out a jewel case containing a CD-ROM, and gave it an appraising glance. Then, exhaling in relief, she replaced the case.

"I'd forgotten all about that in the scramble," she said. "Thank God it wasn't damaged."

"What is it?" he asked.

"Before boarding, I dumped all the data from our meteorite tests onto this disk," she said. "I want to go over it again. If we get out of here alive, that is."

McFarlane said nothing.

"It must have an internal energy source," Rachel went on. "How else could it generate so much electricity? If it were just a capacitor, it would have discharged whatever electricity it had millions of years ago. It's *generating* the charge inside itself." She tapped the disk in her pocket. "The answer *has* to lie somewhere in the data."

"What I want to know is just what kind of environment it comes from. I mean, the thing reacts so violently to *salt water*, of all things." McFarlane sighed. "Ah, hell. Let's give the damn rock a rest."

"That's just the problem," Rachel said. "Maybe it *isn't* just a rock."

"Not your spaceship theory again."

"No. Maybe it's something a lot simpler than a spaceship."

McFarlane began to answer, then stopped. The rolls of the ship were growing ever steeper.

Rachel too had gone silent. It was clear she knew what he was thinking.

"Must be a hell of a sea up there," he said.

She nodded. "Anytime now."

They waited in silence as the rolls grew ever stronger. At last, at the very crest of a great roll, the stream of water once again parted from the bulkhead and angled through the air toward the tarps. McFarlane pulled himself to his feet and stared out the window of the observation unit, waiting. Over the rush of the ocean and the distant shriek of the wind, he heard the patter of water on plastic coming up from below. He watched it run harmlessly down the tarps to drip into the spaces between the bottom girders.

They paused, expectantly, for the space of a heartbeat. Then Rachel let out a long breath.

"Looks like it worked," she said. "Congratulations."

"Congratulations?" McFarlane replied. "It was your idea."

"Yeah, I know. But you figured out the salinity angle."

"Only through your prompting." McFarlane hesitated. "Listen to us," he went on. "We're a goddamn mutual appreciation society."

Despite his weariness, he found himself grinning. He could almost feel a huge weight lifting from his shoulders. They knew now what caused the explosions. They had taken the necessary steps to make sure it would not happen again. They were on their way home.

He looked down at Rachel, her dark hair shining in the dim light. Just a few weeks ago, the thought of sharing this easy, comfortable silence would have been unthinkable. And yet now it seemed hard to imagine a time when she had not been with him, working at his side—finishing his sentences for him, teasing him, providing speculation, wisecracks, and insight whether they were desired or not.

She was leaning back against the tank, gazing out at nothing as the ship went into an even steeper roll, unaware that he was looking at her. "Do you hear something?" she asked. "I could swear I heard a distant explosion."

But McFarlane was barely listening. To his surprise, he felt himself kneeling beside her and drawing her near with a very different feeling than the passion that had briefly filled him in her cabin.

She laid her head on his shoulder.

"You know something?" he said. "You're the nicest smart-assed, backstabbing assistant I've met in a long time."

"Mmm. I'll bet you say that to all the girls."

He stroked her cheek gently, then raised her lips to his as another large wave passed by. Water splattered loudly across the tarps.

"Does this mean I get to wear your MIT ring?" she murmured.

"No. But you can borrow my rock hammer."

They kissed again as the ship slowly righted, then went immediately into another heavy roll in the other direction.

Suddenly, McFarlane drew back. Over the general muttering and creaking of the hold, over the distant boom of the sea, he heard a new sound, a strange, high-pitched creaking, ending in a metallic crack, loud as a gunshot; and then another, and another.

He glanced quickly at Rachel. She looked back, her eyes wide and luminous. The loud reports ceased, but the echoes still sounded in his ears. They waited in shocked silence. With each fresh roll of the ship, there now arose a chorus of other sounds: the groaning of steel, the creak and crackle of splintering wood, the tearing of rivets and welds.

Rolvaag,
3:30 P.M.

Britton watched the first tracer shell rise lazily above the wracked surface of the sea and then fall away in a twinkle of light. Another one followed, still dropping well short of their position.

Lloyd was instantly at the window. "Christ, do you believe this? The son of a bitch is firing at us."

"Tracers," said Glinn. "They're getting our range."

She saw Lloyd's jaw set in a tight line.

"Mr. Howell, left hard rudder," she ordered as another pair of tracer shells arched over the sea, a little closer this time.

They watched in silence as more shells came on, creeping ever closer. And then one flashed directly overhead, a streak of light against the dark sky.

"We're bracketed," murmured Glinn. "Now they'll open up with live rounds, walking them through our position."

Lloyd turned on him. "What are you, a sports announcer? We need a plan, not running commentary. I can't believe this. Three hundred million and this is where you've brought us?"

Britton spoke, quickly but distinctly. "Silence on the bridge! Mr. Howell, right full rudder! Engines emergency astern!" In the crisis, she felt her thoughts begin to stream past with a crystalline clarity. It was almost as if someone else was doing her thinking for her. She glanced at Lloyd, standing there at the center of the bridge windows, his beefy fingers twined like a knot as he looked southward over the ruthless seas. How difficult it must be to realize that money couldn't buy everything—even one's own life. How different he was, in the last analysis, from the man who stood beside him.

Her eyes moved to Glinn. She found herself becoming dependent on his judgment now, in a way she would never have allowed before he had been proven wrong—*proven human*, she thought.

Beyond the two men lay the storm-tossed sea. As night had fallen, they had darkened the ship in an attempt to elude Vallenar's guns. But a huge southern moon, a day from full, had risen in a crystalline night sky to thwart their hopes. To Britton, it almost looked as if it was smiling mockingly at them. A *panteonero* was a strange form of weather: it usually ended in a clear night of maddening, murderous wind. In the moonlight, the moiling surface of the ocean had a ghastly luminescence. The surreal ocean continued to launch a procession of gigantic breakers past them, looming above the ship, periodically throwing it into darkness deeper than night, subsiding in huge roars as the ship broke out once again into the moonlight, the tumbling white water, and the banshee winds.

An abrupt report, faint but audible above the storm, shook the bridge windows. Others followed in measured cadence. Britton saw a row of geysers climbing down the face of a wave to the north, one after another, heading toward the *Rolvaag* along the line of its former course.

The great ship's head labored and wallowed in the seas. *Turn, you bitch*, she thought.

Suddenly, the ship bucked and shuddered. A great billow of ugly yellow smoke shot from the bow, hot metal whining upward, trailing streamers. A thunderous report immediately followed. One of the king posts jerked into the air, twisting as it fell back, the guy wires whiplashing across the deck. Then the geysers were erupting ahead of them and turning wide as the fire passed their position.

There was a deathly moment of stasis.

Britton was the first to recover. She raised her glasses and examined the bow area. It appeared that at least one shell had ripped through the forecastle. The great ship rose on the next wave; in the bright moonlight, she could see water running into the exposed chain locker and out a ragged hole, well above the waterline.

"General alarm," she said. "Mr. Howell, send a damage-control team forward. Assemble a fire team with AFFF foam and an Explosimeter. And I want a lifeline rigged up along the maindeck, bow to stern."

"Aye aye, ma'am."

Almost involuntarily, she glanced at Glinn.

"Cut the engines," he murmured. "Veer away from the wind. Cut ECM. Pretend we're crippled. That will stop his firing for now. Give it just five minutes, then we'll run again. That will force him to repeat his range-finding. We *must* make those ice islands."

She watched him step away to confer with his operative in low tones.

"Mr. Howell," she said. "All engines stop. Left thirty degree rudder." The ship continued forward under its immense inertia, slowly turning.

She looked at Lloyd. His face had gone gray, as if the firing had shocked him to the core. Perhaps he believed he was about to die. Perhaps he was thinking about what it would be like to be sinking in the cold, black, two-mile-deep water. She had seen that look before, on other ships in other storms. It was not a pretty sight.

She dropped her gaze to the radar. It was getting a lot of sea return, but it cleared every time the *Rolvaag* rose. They were now twenty-five miles from the Ice Limit and the pair of ice islands. The beam sea was slowing down the Chilean ship by as much as a knot, but it was still closing the gap steadily, relentlessly. As she looked out over the boiling seas, she wondered how the destroyer could possibly be surviving.

Suddenly the door to the bridge burst open. And there, framed in the doorway, was McFarlane. He took a step forward, Rachel following close behind.

"The meteoritc," McFarlane said as he struggled for air, his face wild.

"What about the meteorite?" Glinn asked sharply.

"It's breaking free."

Rolvaag,
3:55 P.M.

Glinn listened as McFarlane gasped out his story, feeling an unfamiliar—and unpleasant—sensation of surprise drift over him. But it was with his usual, unhurried economy of motion that he turned toward a telephone. "Sick bay? Get Garza on the horn."

In a moment, Garza's weakened voice came across the line. "Yes?"

"Glinn here. The meteorite's breaking its welds. Get Stonecipher and the backup team down there at once. You lead it."

"Yes, sir."

"There's something else," said McFarlane. He was still struggling for breath.

Glinn turned.

"The rock reacts to *salt*. Salt, not touch. That's what sets it off, what killed Garza's team. Rachel and I strapped tarps over the web. But whatever you do, for God's sake keep salt water off it. And it's still throwing off a lot of radio noise. Radio communication will be spotty, at least for an hour or so."

Glinn took this in, then raised the phone and spoke again to Garza. As he was finishing, he heard a fumbling sound on the other end, followed by the nasal, angry voice of Brambell. "What's this devilment? I forbid this man leaving sick bay. He has head trauma, concussion, a hyperextended wrist, and—"

"No more talk, Dr. Brambell. I must have Garza's expertise *at whatever cost*."

"Mr. Glinn—"

"The life of the ship depends on it." He lowered the phone and looked at Britton. "Is there any way to reduce the ship's list in these waves?"

Britton shook her head. "In seas this heavy, ballast shifting would only make the ship more unstable."

The *Rolvaag* continued driving southward, the raging sea alternately burying its maindeck in the water, then forcing it skyward, water thundering out the scuppers. Two of the containers had torn free and washed overboard, and several others were now shifting in their lashings.

"What the hell were those explosions?" McFarlane asked Glinn.

"We were fired on by the Chilean ship." He looked first at McFarlane, and then at Amira. "Do you have any idea *why* salt affects the meteorite?"

"It doesn't seem like a chemical reaction," McFarlane said. "None of the meteorite was consumed in the explosions, and there sure as hell wasn't enough salt to generate that kind of energy."

Glinn looked at Amira.

"It was too big an explosion to be either a chemical or catalytic reaction," she said.

"What other kind of reaction is there? Nuclear?"

"That's one unlikely possibility. But I think we're not looking at this problem from the right perspective."

Glinn had seen this before. Amira's mind had a tendency to jump out of everyone else's groove. What resulted was either genius or idiocy. It was one of the reasons he had hired her, and even at this extremity he knew better than to ignore it. "How so?" he asked.

"It's just a feeling. We keep trying to understand it from our point of view, thinking of it as a meteorite. What we need to do is look at it from *its* point of view. Salt is important to it, somehow—something either dangerous, or . . . necessary."

Howell's voice filled the resulting silence. "Captain, more ranging shots being fired from the *Ramirez*." The chief mate hunched over the Doppler radar. There was a long moment of silence, and he looked up, a grin on his face. "A snowsquall just cut us off from the *Ramirez*. The bastards can't see us, Captain. They're running blind."

"Come right, steady on one nine zero," said Britton.

Glinn moved to the GPS chart, staring at its arrangement of green dots. The chess game was drawing to a close; the board was cleared of all but a few pieces. Their fate had been reduced to a combination of four factors: two ships, the storm, the ice. He examined them intently for thirty minutes, the positions of the two ships changing ever so slightly, his mind intensely concentrated. He closed his eyes, retaining the image of the green dots in his mind. In that simplicity lay a deadly lack of options. Like a chess master, he had played out in his mind each possible sequence of moves. All but one led to one hundred percent probability of failure. And the probability of success on the last option remained exceedingly low. For this last play to succeed, everything would have to happen perfectly—and on top of that, they would need luck. Glinn hated luck. A strategy that required luck was often fatal. And now that which he hated, he needed most of all.

He opened his eyes, focusing immediately on the chart. The green dot representing the *Rolvaag* was now thirty minutes from the Ice Limit and a few minutes more from the two gigantic ice islands.

Glinn's radio chirped and he snapped it on.

"Garza here," came the weakened voice over a wash of static. "In the tank. There's a lot of radio interference, don't know how long we can talk."

"Go on."

"There are welds failing with each roll of the ship."

"Cause?"

"The meteorite's discharge snapped some critical points on the web and weakened others. Also, Rochefort designed the cradle for a maximum thirty-five-degree roll. We're still ten degrees below the limit—" For a moment, the radio cut out. "But of course the meteorite is two hundred and fifty percent heavier than Rochefort initially anticipated. We might be a bit short on the engineering."

"How short?"

"Hard to say without—" The radio cut out a second time. "Still a certain amount of overengineering was built into the design, even beyond double-overage. Stonecipher thinks we might be able to go a long way like this. On the other hand, if some key points go, the rest could fail quickly."

"I don't like these words 'might' and 'could.' "

"It's impossible to be more precise."

"So how quickly is 'quickly'?"

"We'd have five, ten minutes, maybe. Maybe more."

"And then?"

"The meteorite will shift. Even a few inches might be fatal, cause hull failure."

"Reinforce those critical point welds."

There was a crackling pause. Glinn knew what Garza was thinking about: what happened the last time they welded the cradle.

"Yes, sir," Garza said finally.

"And keep the salt water off it."

The only answer was another buzz of static.

The great ship *Rolvaag* drove southward, ever southward.

Rolvaag, 5:00 P.M.

At the rear of the bridge was an observation alcove, a small area sandwiched between the radio room and the chart room. Except for the tall expanse of windows, it was devoid of furniture or decoration. At the windows stood Glinn, binoculars to his eyes, looking sternward between the stacks. The snowsquall, a wavering gray line to the north, was passing. It had given them sixty minutes. They needed another twenty. But as the bright moonlight once again lay a carpet of illumination across the raging seas, it became clear that they were not going to get it.

As if on cue, the *Ramirez* came blowing out of the distant curtain of snow. It was shockingly close now, no more than four miles away, lights ablaze. Its bow rose and fell in the violent sea, and he thought he could even see the forward guns trained on them, etched against the night sky behind. The *Rolvaag* would be as clear to them as the *Ramirez* was to him. There was a sudden murmur on the bridge, followed by an unbearably tense silence. Vallenar was wasting no time: the forward guns quickly adjusted their elevation.

Even worse, with another gun the *Ramirez* began firing a string of white phosphorus "Willey Peters," which popped on and drifted slowly down, brilliantly lighting up the *Rolvaag* and the sea around it.

Vallenar was methodical, not rushed. He was being careful. He knew he had them. Glinn glanced at his gold pocket watch. At four miles, the *Ramirez* would just fire away, not bothering to get their range. The *Rolvaag* was twenty minutes from the ice islands. They would need twenty minutes of luck.

"Crossing the Ice Limit, ma'am," said Howell to Britton.

Glinn glanced down to the sea. Even in the moonlight, he could easily make out the abrupt color change in the water: from a deep green to a clear, almost bluish black. He came to the front of the bridge now, searching the southern horizon with his binoculars. He could see thin patches of brash ice lifting and falling, and as the ship rose he caught a striking glimpse of the ice islands—two low, flat lines of turquoise. He raised his binoculars and examined them more closely. The one to the east was huge, perhaps twenty miles long; the one to the west about five. They rode steady in the water, vast still mesas above the changeable sea—so large that even this violent sea could not raise and lower them. There was a gap between the islands of perhaps a thousand yards.

"No sign of fog," said Britton, coming up beside him with her own binoculars.

As Glinn continued gazing southward, a terrible feeling, perhaps the most terrible he had ever felt, constricted his solar plexus. The Ice Limit had not brought them cover. If anything, the sky to the south was clearer. The brilliant moonlight, silvering the enormous waves, was like a searchlight across the sea. The Willey Peters, slowly dropping about them, made the landscape as bright as day. There was no place to hide. They were completely vulnerable. It was intolerable, an exquisite pain unique in Glinn's experience.

With supreme self-mastery, he once again raised the binoculars and examined the islands. The *Ramirez* was not firing, taking her time, sure now of the kill. Minutes passed as his mind traveled back down all the dead avenues it had explored before. Again and again his mind probed farther, deeper down the branches of possibility, trying to reach another solution to their problem. But there were no others: just the one far-fetched plan. The silence stretched on.

A shell came screaming down past the superstructure, sending up a delicate plume of spray. And another, and another, closing on their position.

He quickly turned to Britton. "Captain," he murmured, "pass between the two islands, staying close to the larger island. Understand me now: as close as you possibly can. Then bring the ship into its lee and heave to."

Britton had not dropped her binoculars. "That's going to turn us into a sitting duck as soon as he comes around the island. This is not a viable plan, Eli."

"It's our only chance," he answered. "Trust me."

A geyser erupted off their port side, and another, the shells once again walking through their position. There was no time to turn, no point in evasive action. Glinn braced himself. Tall columns of water shot up around them, moving closer. There was a brief lull, pregnant and terrible. And then a terrific explosion jerked Glinn from his feet and threw him to the deck. Some of the bridge windows blew out, scattering jeweled shards across the deck and letting in the howling of the wind.

As Glinn lay on the deck, half stunned, he heard—or perhaps felt—a second explosion. And that was when the lights went out.

Rolvaag, 5:10 P.M.

The firing stopped. Britton, lying amid shards of Plexiglas, instinctively listened for the engines. They were still running, but the vibration was different. Different, and ominous. She rose shakily as the orange emergency lights snapped on. The ship rolled with the terrifying sea, and now the roar of the wind and waves, blasting through the broken windows, filled her ears, along with stinging sheets of salt spray and gusts of subzero air. The storm was now inside the bridge. She staggered over the main console, which was covered with blinking lights, shaking chips of plastic out of her hair.

She found her voice. "Status, Mr. Howell."

He was also on his feet, punching buttons on the console, speaking into the phone. "Losing power to the port turbine."

"Ten degrees left rudder."

"Ten degrees left rudder, aye, ma'am." Howell spoke briefly into the intercom. "Captain, it looks like we received two hits on C deck. One in starboard wing tank six, the other in the vicinity of the engine room."

"Get damage control on it. I need damage assessment and casualty count, and I need them now. Mr. Warner, start the bilge pumps."

"Start the bilge pumps, aye, ma'am."

Another gust of wind blasted through the bridge, bringing with it another sheet of spray. As the temperature on the bridge dropped, the spray was starting to freeze on the deck and consoles. But Britton hardly felt the cold.

Lloyd approached, shrugging glass from his clothes. A nasty cut across his forehead was bleeding profusely.

"Mr. Lloyd, report to sick bay—" Britton began automatically.

"Don't be ridiculous," he said impatiently, wiping the blood off his brow and flinging it to one side. "I'm here to help."

The blast seemed to have shocked him back to life. "Then you can get us all foul-weather gear," Britton said, gesturing toward a storage locker at the rear of the bridge.

A radio crackled and Howell answered. "Waiting on the casualty list, ma'am. Damage control reports fire in the engine room. It was a direct hit."

"Can it be contained with portable extinguishers?"

"Negative. It's spreading too fast."

"Use the fixed CO_2 system. And I want water fog on the exterior bulkheads."

She glanced over at Glinn. He had been speaking urgently to his operative at the EES console. The man stood and vanished from the bridge.

"Mr. Glinn, I need a report from the hold, please," she said.

He turned to Howell. "Patch Garza through."

A minute later, the overhead speaker crackled. "Jesus, what the hell's going on?" Garza asked.

"We've received two more hits. What's your status?"

"Those explosions came on a roll. They broke additional welds. We're working as fast as we can, but the meteorite—"

"Keep on it, Manuel. Smartly."

Lloyd returned from the locker and began distributing gear to the bridge crew. Britton accepted hers, pulled it on, and looked forward. The ice islands now loomed up, faintly blue in the moonlight, barely two miles distant, rearing two hundred feet or more out of the water, the surf tearing and ripping at their bases.

"Mr. Howell, what is the position of the enemy ship?"

"Just at three miles and closing. They're firing again."

There was another explosion off the port beam, a geyser of water that rose, only to immediately bend almost horizontal under the force of the *panteonero*. Now Britton could hear the distant reports of the guns themselves, strangely disconnected from the nearby explosions. There was another crash, a shudder, and she flinched as white-hot metal screamed up past the bridge windows.

"Glancing shot, maindeck," Howell said. He looked over at her. "The fire's being contained. But damage to both turbines was severe. The explosion knocked out the high- and low-pressure turbines. We're losing power, fast."

She dropped her eyes and watched as the digital readout blinked the ship's speed back at them. It dropped to fourteen knots, then thirteen. With the drop in speed, the motion of the ship became worse. Britton could feel the storm taking over, clutching her ship in its anarchistic grip. Ten knots. The bigger waves were shoving it hard, sideways, up, down, in a weird and sickening ballet. Never had she believed a ship this big could be so bullied by the sea. She focused on the console.

The engine warning lights were on. They didn't tell her anything she didn't already know: beneath her feet she felt the distant thrum of the wrecked engines, strained, stuttering, intermittent. And then the lights flickered again as the power failed and the backup systems engaged.

No one spoke as the great vessel plowed through the seas. Its great inertia continued to carry it forward, but every breaking wave robbed another knot or two from its forward motion. *Ramirez* gained on them ever more quickly.

Britton looked around at her officers on the bridge. Every one of them looked back with pale, steady faces. The chase was over.

Lloyd broke the silence. Blood from his wounded forehead trickled into his right eye, and he blinked it away absently. "I guess this is it," he said.

Britton nodded.

Lloyd turned to McFarlane. "You know, Sam, I wish I was down in the hold right now. I'd kind of like to say goodbye to it. I suppose that sounds crazy. Does that sound crazy to you?"

"No," he replied. "No, it doesn't."

Out of the corner of her eye, Britton saw Glinn turn toward them at these words. But the man remained silent as the dark shadows of the ice islands slipped ever closer.

Almirante Ramirez, 5:15 P.M.

"Cease firing," Vallenar said to the tactical action officer. He raised his binoculars and examined the wounded ship. Plumes of black smoke, thick and low, were pouring from the stern of the tanker and barreling across the moonlit seas. At least two confirmed hits, including what looked like a shell directly into the engine room and extensive damage to their communications masts. It was brilliant shooting in seas such as this: enough to leave the ship dead in the water, exactly as he had hoped. He could already see they were losing headway—*really* losing headway. This time, there was no feint.

The American ship was still aiming for the ice islands. They would prove a pathetic, temporary shelter from his guns. But the female captain had shown great courage. She would not surrender her ship until all courses of action had been tried. He could understand such a captain. Hiding behind the island was a noble, if futile, gesture. And, of course, for them there would be no surrender. Only death.

He glanced at his watch. In twenty minutes, he would pull through the gap and draw up to the *Rolvaag*. The slack water in the lee of the ice islands would give him a steady platform for precise firing.

He began to visualize the kill. There could be no error, no possibility of reversal. He would position the *Ramirez* at least a mile away, to prevent more underwater excursions. He would illuminate the entire area with phosphorus flares. There would be no haste: the operation would be executed with care. But he wouldn't tease it out, make things unduly slow; he was no sadist, and the female captain in particular deserved a respectful death.

It would be best to hull her aft, he decided; at the waterline, so she would go down by the stern. It was most important that none escaped to provide an eyewitness account of what happened here. He would turn the 40-millimeter guns on the first lifeboats; that would keep the rest on board until the end. As the ship went down, the survivors would crowd into the forecastle, where he could better see them. He wanted most particularly to make sure the smooth one, the lying *cabrón*, would die. This man was behind everything. If anyone had ordered his son executed, it was him.

The tanker, now slowed to five knots, was drawing between the ice islands, passing close to the larger one. Very close, in fact; perhaps the rudder was damaged. The islands were so tall, so sheer, that the tanker appeared to be slipping into some monstrous hangar of gleaming azure. As the *Rolvaag* disappeared from view between them, he saw the ship begin a turn to port. That would take it behind the larger of the two islands and into its lee, temporarily out of the reach of his guns. It was a sad, hopeless effort.

"Sonar?" he called out, dropping the binoculars at last.

"Clear, sir."

That was it—there was no unexpected underwater ice; it was a clean drop from the top to the root of the ice island. Time to finish the job.

"Steady through the gap. Follow their course."

He turned to the tactical action officer. "Await my orders to engage with the guns."

"Aye, sir."

Vallenar swiveled back to the windows, raising the binoculars once again.

Rolvaag, 5:20 P.M.

The *Rolvaag* passed between the ice islands, gliding into a tranquil, twilit world. The wind dropped, no longer gusting through the broken windows into the bridge. Suddenly the ship was released from the evil grip of the storm. Britton found the sudden silence in the midst of the storm unsettling. She stared up at the cliffs that rose up on either side, sheer as if cleaved with an ax. Below, at the waterline, the pounding surf on the windward side had formed an undercut of fantastic-looking caves. In the moonlight, the ice shone a pure, rich blue so deep she thought it one of the most beautiful things she had ever seen. Funny, she thought, how the nearness of death could heighten one's sense of beauty.

Glinn, who had disappeared onto the port bridge wing, now returned, closing the door carefully behind him. He approached her, wiping flecks of spray from his shoulders.

"Steady as she goes," he said quietly. "Keep the tanker's head at this angle."

She did not bother relaying the useless and cryptic direction to Howell.

The ship had lost even more headway making a ninety-degree turn behind the ice island. Now they were gliding parallel to the ice at about a knot, still slowing. Once they stopped, they'd never start again.

She glanced at his profile, at the unreadable face. She almost asked whether he really thought they were going to successfully hide their quarter-mile ship from the destroyer. But she kept silent. Glinn had made a supreme effort. There was nothing more he could do. In a few minutes, the *Ramirez* would round the ice island and that would be it. She tried not to think of her daughter. That was going to be hardest of all, letting go of her daughter.

In the lee of the island, everything seemed strangely quiet. There was a terrible silence on the bridge: there were no longer any orders to give or receive. The wind was gone, and the swell warping around the island was smooth and low. The wall of ice was only a quarter mile distant. Here and there, long fissures ran down from its top, deep runnels worn by icemelt and rain. She could see small waterfalls feathering into the moonlit sea, and hear the distant cracking and pinging of the ice. Beyond that came a distant keening sound of wind, raking the top of the ice island. It was an ethereal, otherworldly place. She watched an iceberg, recently calved off the island, drift away to the west. She wanted to be there when it slowly melted and disappeared into the sea. She wanted to be anywhere but here.

"It isn't over, Sally," Glinn said quietly, so that only she could hear. He was regarding her intently.

"Yes, it is. The destroyer killed all our power."

"You'll see your daughter again."

"Please don't say that." She brushed away a tear.

To her surprise, Glinn took her hand.

"If we get through this," he began, with a hesitation foreign to him, "I would like to see you again. May I do that? I would like to learn more about poetry. Perhaps you could teach me."

"Please, Eli. It's easier if we don't talk." She gave his hand a gentle pressure.

And then she saw the prow of the *Ramirez* nosing past the ice.

It was less than two miles away, slinking close to the blue wall of the ice island, following their own wake, approaching like a shark closing on its disabled prey. The gun turrets were tracking them with a cool deliberation.

As Britton stared out the rearward bridge windows at those guns, waiting for the final deadly fire to erupt from their barrels, time slowed. The space between her heartbeats seemed to grow longer. She took in the scene around her: Lloyd, McFarlane, Howell, the watch officers, silently waiting. Waiting for death in the dark cold water.

There was a popping sound from the destroyer, and an array of Willey Peters soared into the air, exploding into a crooked line of brilliance. Britton shielded her eyes as the surface of the water, the deck of the tanker, the wall of the ice island, shed their colors under the terrible illumination. As the worst of the brightness eased, she squinted out the windows once again. The guns on the *Ramirez* lowered their elevation, pointing at them until all that could be seen were the black holes of the muzzles. The ship was now halfway through the gap and slowing fast. The shooting would be almost point-blank.

An explosion cracked through the air, echoing and reverberating between the islands. Britton jerked back instinctively, and felt Glinn's hand bear down on hers. This was it, then. She murmured a silent prayer for her daughter, and for death to be merciful and quick.

But no burst of flame had come from the destroyer's guns. Britton's eyes scanned the scene in confusion. She saw movement far above.

At the top of the ice cliff above the *Ramirez*, splinters and chunks of ice were spinning lazily into the air, rising above four drifting puffs of smoke. The echoes died, and for a moment the stillness returned. And then the ice island seemed to shift. The face of the cliff above the *Ramirez* began to slip, and the blue fissure opened between it and the rest of the island, rapidly widening; now Britton could see that a gigantic piece of ice, nearly two hundred feet high, was peeling away. The great plate of ice separated from the cliff and began to descend, breaking into several pieces as it did so, in a kind of slow, majestic ballet. As it merged with the sea, a wall of water began to rise: black at first, then green and white. Higher and higher the water rose, propelled by the great plunging mass of the ice, and then the sound began to reach her, a mingled cacophony of noise that grew steadily in volume. And still the wave mounted, so precipitous it began breaking over itself even as it formed, climbing, breaking, climbing again. The vast block of ice disappeared, driven below the surface by its own momentum, and the steep-walled wave broke free and headed, broadside, for the *Ramirez*.

There was a roar from its diesel engines as the destroyer tried to maneuver. But in an instant the wave was upon it; the destroyer yawed, rose, and rose still farther, heeling, the rust red of its bow-plates exposed. For a sickening moment it seemed to pause, slanting far to starboard, its two masts almost horizontal to the sea, as the crest of the monstrous wave foamed over it. Seconds ticked by as the ship hovered there, clinging to the wave, poised between righting itself and foundering. Britton felt her heart pounding violently in her chest. Then the ship wavered and began to come upright, water shedding from its deck. *It didn't work*, she thought; *God, it didn't work.*

The righting movement slowed, the ship paused again, and then it sagged back into the water. There was a sigh of air from the superstructure, jets of spray shot in all directions, and the destroyer turned over, its slimy keel rolling heavily toward the sky. There was another, louder sigh; a moiling of water and foam and bubbling air around the hull; and then, with hardly a swirl, it disappeared into the icy deep. There was a second brief explosion of bubbles, and then those, too, disappeared, leaving behind black water.

It had taken less than ninety seconds.

Britton saw the freakish wave race toward them, spreading and attenuating as it did so.

"Hang on," murmured Glinn.

Positioned lengthwise to the wave, the tanker rose sharply, heeled, then came easily to rest.

Britton disengaged her hand from Glinn's and raised her binoculars, feeling the cold rubber against the sockets of her eyes. She could hardly comprehend that the destroyer was gone. Not a man, not a life raft—not even a cushion or bottle—appeared on the surface. The *Almirante Ramirez* had disappeared without a trace.

Glinn's eyes were on the island, and she followed his gaze. There, at the edge of the ice plateau, were four dark specks: men in dry suits, crossing their arms over their heads, fists together. One by one, the flares dropped into the sea, each with a faint hiss. Darkness returned.

Glinn raised his radio.

"Op accomplished," he said quietly. "Prepare to receive the launch."

Rolvaag, 5:40 P.M.

Palmer Lloyd found himself momentarily unable to speak. He had been so certain of impending death that to stand here on the bridge, drawing breath, seemed a miracle. When he finally found his voice, he turned to Glinn. "Why didn't you tell me?"

"The chance of success was too slim. I myself did not believe it would succeed." His lips twitched briefly in an ironic smile. "It required luck."

In a sudden physical display of emotion Lloyd leapt forward, wrapping Glinn in a bear hug. "Christ," he said, "I feel like a condemned man getting a reprieve. Eli, is there anything you can't do?" He found himself crying. He didn't care.

"It's not over yet."

Lloyd simply grinned at the man's false modesty.

Britton turned to Howell. "Are we taking in water?"

"Nothing that the bilge pumps can't handle, Captain. As long as we have auxiliary power."

"And how long is that?"

"By shutting down all but essential systems, with the emergency diesel, more than twenty-five hours."

"Splendid!" Lloyd said. "We're in fine shape. We'll repair the engines and be on our way." He beamed at Glinn and then Britton, and then faltered a little. He wondered why they looked so grim. "Is there a problem?"

"We're DIW, Mr. Lloyd," said Britton. "The current's moving us back into the storm."

"DIW?"

"Dead in the water."

"We've weathered it so far. It can't get any worse than this. Can it?"

No one answered his question.

Britton spoke to Howell. "Give me status on our communications."

"All long-range and satellite communications down."

"Issue an SOS. Raise South Georgia on the emergency channel sixteen."

Lloyd felt a sudden chill. "What's this about an SOS?"

Again no one answered. Britton said, "Mr. Howell, what is the status on engine damage?"

After a moment Howell reported back. "Both turbines beyond repair, ma'am."

"Prepare for possible evacuation of the ship."

Lloyd could hardly believe what he was hearing. "Just what the hell are you talking about? Is the ship sinking?"

Britton turned a pair of cool green eyes on him.

"That's my meteorite down there. I'm not leaving this ship."

"Nobody's leaving the ship, Mr. Lloyd. We'll only abandon ship as a last resort. Putting lifeboats out into this storm would probably be suicide anyway."

"For God's sake, then, let's not overreact. We can weather the storm and get a tow to the Falklands. Things aren't that bad."

"We have no steerage, no headway. Once we drift back into that storm, we'll have eighty-knot winds, a hundred-foot sea, and a six-knot current all pushing us in one direction, toward the Bransfield Strait. That's Antarctica, Mr. Lloyd. Things *are* that bad."

Lloyd felt stunned. Already, he could feel a swell rolling the ship. A gust of air came into the bridge.

"Listen to me," he said in a low voice. "I don't care what you have to do, or how you do it, *but don't you lose my meteorite*. Is that understood?"

Britton gave him a steady, hostile look. "Mr. Lloyd, right now I couldn't give a shit about your meteorite. My sole concern is my ship and crew. Is *that* understood?"

Lloyd turned to Glinn, looking for support. But Glinn had remained perfectly silent and still, his face its usual mask.

"When *can* we get a tow?"

"Most of our electronics are down, but we're trying to raise South Georgia. It all depends on the storm."

Lloyd broke away impatiently and turned to Glinn. "What's happening in the holding tank?"

"Garza is reinforcing the web with fresh welds."

"And how long will *that* take?"

Glinn did not answer. He did not need to; because now Lloyd could feel it, too. The motion of the ship was growing worse—ghastly, slow rolls that took forever to complete. And at the top of each roll, the *Rolvaag* cried in pain: a deep groaning that was half sound and half vibration. It was the dead hand of the meteorite.

Rolvaag,
5:45 P.M.

Howell emerged from the radio room and spoke to Britton. "We've got South Georgia, ma'am," he said.

"Very good. Put them on voice, please."

The bridge intercom came to life. "South Georgia to tanker *Rolvaag*, acknowledged." The voice was tinny and faint, and Britton could recognize a Home Counties accent barely recognizable through the static.

She picked up a transmitter and opened the channel. "South Georgia, this is an emergency. We are severely damaged, without propulsion, repeat, without propulsion. We're drifting south-southeastward at a rate of nine knots."

"Acknowledged, *Rolvaag*. State your position."

"Our position is 61°15'12" South, 60°5'33" West."

"Advise as to your cargo. In ballast or oil?"

Glinn glanced up at her, a sharp look. Britton closed the channel.

"From this point on," Glinn said, "we begin telling the truth. *Our* truth."

Britton turned back to the transmitter. "South Georgia, we're converted to an ore carrier. We're fully loaded with, ah, a meteorite, mined on the Cape Horn islands."

There was another silence.

"Did not copy, *Rolvaag*. Did you say meteorite?"

"Affirmative. Our cargo is a twenty-five-thousand-ton meteorite."

"A meteorite of twenty-five thousand tons," the voice repeated impassively. "*Rolvaag*, please advise as to your intended destination."

Britton knew this was a subtle way of asking, *What the hell are you doing down here?*

"We're headed for Port Elizabeth, New Jersey."

There was another silence. Britton waited, wincing inwardly. Any knowledgeable mariner would know there was something very wrong with this story. Here they were, two hundred miles off the Bransfield Straits, well into a major storm. And yet this was their first distress call.

"Er, *Rolvaag*, may I ask if you have the latest weather report?"

"Yes, we do." But she knew he would give it to her anyway.

"Winds increasing to a hundred knots by midnight, seas topping forty meters, all of Drake Passage under a Force 15 storm warning."

"It's almost Force 13 now," she replied.

"Understood. Please describe the nature of your damage."

Make it good, Glinn murmured.

"South Georgia, we were attacked without warning by a Chilean warship in international waters. Shells struck our engine room, forecastle, and maindeck. We have lost headway and steerage. We are DIW, repeat, Delta India Whiskey."

"Good Lord. Are you still under attack?"

"The destroyer struck an iceberg and sank thirty minutes ago."

"This is extraordinary. Why. . . ?"

This was not a proper question to ask during an emergency distress call. But again, this was a most unusual emergency. "We have no idea why. The Chilean captain seems to have been acting alone, without orders."

"Did you identify the warship?"

"The *Almirante Ramirez*, Emiliano Vallenar, CO."

"Are you taking in water?"

"Nothing our bilge pumps can't handle."

"Are you in imminent danger?"

"Yes. Our cargo could shift at any moment and the ship might founder."

"*Rolvaag*, please stand by."

There was a sixty-second silence.

"*Rolvaag*, we fully appreciate your situation. We have SAR assets standing by here and at the Falklands. But we cannot, I repeat, we cannot undertake a search and rescue until the storm abates to Force 10 or less. Do you have satellite communications?"

"No. Most of our electronics are down."

"We will advise your government of your status. Is there anything else we can do?"

"Just a tow, as soon as possible. Before we end up on the Bransfield reefs."

There was a whisper of static. Then the voice returned. "Good luck, *Rolvaag*. God bless."

"Thank you, South Georgia."

Britton replaced the transmitter, leaned on the console, and stared out into the night.

Rolvaag, 6:40 P.M.

As the *Rolvaag* drifted out of the lee of the ice island, the wind caught it and shoved it brutally back into the storm. The wind gathered force, and in moments they were soaked again with freezing spray. Sally Britton could feel that the ship, with no headway left, was completely at the mercy of the storm. It was a repulsive, helpless feeling.

The storm began to strengthen with a clockwork regularity. Britton watched it build, minute by minute, until it reached an intensity she barely believed possible. The moon had fallen behind thick clouds, and nothing could be seen beyond the bridge. The storm was there, inside the bridge, all around them: in the lashings of spray, in the bits of razor-sharp ice whipping through, in the smell of death at sea crowding in. But it was the sound that unnerved her most: a continuous dull roar that seemed to come from all directions at once. The temperature on the bridge was nineteen degrees Fahrenheit and she could feel ice building in her hair.

She continued to receive regular reports of their status, but found herself issuing few orders. Without power or steerage there was little she could do but wait. The feeling of helplessness was nigh unbearable. Based on the motion of the ship, she estimated significant wave heights at well over one hundred feet, and they were moving as powerfully as a freight train. These were the waves that circled the globe, pushed by the winds, never hitting shore, building, ever building. These were the waves of the Screaming Sixties, the biggest seas on earth. Only the sheer size of the *Rolvaag* was saving it now. As the ship rose on each wave, the winds climbed to a gibbering wail. At the peak of the wave the whole superstructure would vibrate and hum, as if the winds were attempting to decapitate the ship. Then there would be a shudder, and the ship would heel, slowly, achingly. The wave-by-wave battle was recorded by the inclinometer: ten, twenty, twenty-five degrees. As the angle became critical, all eyes stared at this normally insignificant instrument. Then the crest of the wave would pass and Britton would wait for the ship to recover: the most terrible moment of all. But each time the ship did recover, first imperceptibly, then more quickly, gradually righting into an equally unnerving overcorrection, as its great inertia caused it to lean momentarily against the wave. It would slide into the next trough, shielded by the surrounding mountains of water, into an eerie stillness almost more frightening than the storm above. The process would repeat again, and again, in an endless, cruel cadence. Throughout all this, there was nothing she—or any of them—could do.

Britton turned on the forward superstructure spotlights to check the *Rolvaag*'s maindeck. Most of the containers and several davits had been torn from their moorings and swept overboard, but the mechanical door and the tank hatches were solid. The vessel was still taking in water from the shell hole near the king posts, but the bilge pumps were compensating. The *Rolvaag* was a well-built, seaworthy vessel; it would be weathering the storm nicely—were it not for the monstrous weight in her belly.

By seven, the storm had reached Force 15, with gusts up to one hundred knots. When the ship topped a wave, the force of the wind coming through the bridge threatened to suck them out into the darkness. No storm could keep up this kind of violence for long. Soon, Britton hoped, it would begin to break. It *had* to.

She kept checking the surface scopes, irrationally, looking for a contact that might indicate a rescue. But they were streaked with grass, giving mostly sea return. At the crest of each wave, they cleared long enough to show a growler field—small bergs—about eight miles ahead. Between the ship and the growler field lay a single ice island, smaller than those they had passed but several miles long nevertheless. As the ship was pushed deeper into the ice, the waves would mitigate; but, of course, then there would be more ice to deal with.

The GPS, at least, was steady and clear. They were about one hundred and fifty miles northwest of the South Shetland Islands, an uninhabited row of fanglike mountains sticking up from the Antarctic seas, surrounded by reefs and ripping currents. Beyond lay the Bransfield Strait, and, beyond that, pack ice and the brutal coast of Antarctica. As they drew closer to the coast, the seas would drop but the currents would get worse. One hundred and fifty miles . . . if South Georgia could launch a rescue at 6 A.M. . . . It all depended on that *thing* down in the hold.

She thought of asking Glinn for a progress report. But then she realized she did not want a report. Glinn had been as silent as she, and she wondered just what was going through his mind. She, at least, could read the movement of the ship. For the others it must be simple, sheer terror.

The ship rolled; a frightening roll. But as the roll approached the apex, she felt an odd hitch, a catch, to it. At the same time, Glinn raised his radio to his ear, listening intently. He saw her look.

"It's Garza," he said. "I can't hear him over the storm."

She turned to Howell. "Patch him through. Maximum gain."

Suddenly Garza's voice boomed through the bridge. "Eli!" he was calling. The amplification gave the panic in his voice a ragged, desperate edge. In the background, Britton could hear the groan and screech of tortured metal.

"Here."

"We're losing the primary crosspieces!"

"Stick with it."

Britton wondered at Glinn's calm, steady voice.

The ship began to heel again.

"Eli, the whole thing's unraveling faster than we can keep up with—" The ship heeled farther, and another scream of metal drowned out Garza's voice.

"Manuel," said Glinn. "Rochefort knew what he was doing when he designed that web. It's much stronger than you think. Take it one step at a time."

Still the ship slanted.

"Eli, the rock—*It's moving!* I can't—" The radio went dead.

The ship paused, shuddered throughout its frame, then slowly began to right itself. Britton felt that little hitch again, like a pause, almost as if the ship had caught on something for a moment.

Glinn kept his eyes to the speaker. After a moment, it crackled once again. Garza's voice came back on. "Eli? Are you there?"

"Yes."

"I think the thing shifted slightly, but it came back into place."

Glinn almost smiled. "Manuel, do you see how you're overreacting? Don't panic. Focus on the critical points and let the others go. Triage the situation. There's a tremendous amount of redundancy built into that web. Double overage. Remember that."

"Yes, sir."

The ship began another roll; a slow, screeching, agonizing motion. Again she felt the pause, and then she felt something new, different in the motion . . . Something ugly.

Britton looked at Glinn, then at Lloyd. She could see that they hadn't noticed. When the meteorite had moved, she could feel how it affected the entire ship. The massive *Rolvaag* had almost pivoted on the crest of that last wave. She wondered if it was her imagination. She waited while the ship sank down into the unnatural peace of the trough, then began to rise again. She turned on the maindeck lights and sealights: she wanted to see the conformation of the ship on the water. It was rising, shuddering as if to shake off its burden, the heavy black water surging off its sides and out the scuppers. As they came up the thing in the hold began to groan again; slowly, the ship reared up the long face of the wave, shivering as it rose into the wind. The bow broke through the topmost comb of water, and the groaning became a shriek of protesting metal and timber, echoing through the bones of the ship. There it was: the *Rolvaag* made that same ugly motion at the top, a yaw that almost became a pivot, then a lying back down in the water. There was a hesitation before it recovered—and that was the worst of all.

Once, on a terrible storm off the Grand Banks, she had seen a ship break its back. The hull had come apart with a horrific noise; black water had boiled in, instantly flooding the ship's deepest compartments. Nobody had a chance to get off: all were sucked down into the deep. It was a sight that still disturbed her sleep to this day.

She glanced at Howell. He had noticed the slow recovery, too: he was staring at her, frame rigid, round eyes white in a deathly pale face. She had never seen him so frightened. "Captain . . ." he began, his voice breaking.

She gestured him silent. She knew what he was going to say. It was her duty to say it.

She glanced at Glinn. His face remained strangely confident and serene. She had to look away. For all his knowledge, the man did not know the feel of a ship.

The *Rolvaag* was on the verge of breaking up.

They began to subside into another trough, the wind abruptly dropping to zero. She took the opportunity to look around the bridge: Lloyd, McFarlane, Amira, Glinn, Howell, Banks, the other officers of the watch. All silent. All watching her. All waiting for her to do something, to keep them alive.

"Mr. Lloyd," she said.

"Yes?" He stepped over, eager to help.

This was going to be hard.

A hideous shudder rattled the consoles and windows as the ship took a major cross-swell. When the sound eased as the ship slipped back down, Britton could breathe again.

"Mr. Lloyd," she said again. "The meteorite *must* go."

Rolvaag,
7:00 P.M.

On these words, McFarlane felt a queer feeling in his gut. A galvanic charge seemed to spread through his body. *Never*. It was impossible. He tried to shake off the seasickness and fear of the last harrowing minutes.

"Absolutely not," he heard Lloyd say. The words were quiet, barely audible above the roar of the sea. Nevertheless, they carried a tremendous force of conviction. A hush fell on the bridge as the ship went deeper into the preternatural calm of the trough.

"I am the captain of this ship," Britton said quietly. "The lives of my crew depend on it. Mr. Glinn, I order you to trigger the dead man's switch. I *order* it."

After the briefest of hesitations, Glinn turned toward the EES console.

"*No!*" screamed Lloyd, seizing Glinn's arm in a powerful grip. "You touch that computer and I'll kill you with my bare hands."

With a short, sharp motion, Glinn twisted out of the grip, throwing Lloyd off balance. The big man stumbled, then drew himself up, panting. The ship slanted again and a metallic groan ran through the length of the hull. All movement stopped as everyone clung to the nearest handhold.

"You hear that, Mr. Lloyd?" Britton cried over the sound of

protesting metal. "That son of a bitch down there is killing my ship!"

"Glinn, stay away from that keyboard."

"The captain has given an order," Howell shouted, his voice high.

"*No!* Only Glinn has the key, and he won't do it! He can't, not without my permission! Eli, do you hear me? I order you *not* to initiate the dead man's switch." Lloyd moved suddenly to the EES computer, blocking it with his body.

Howell turned. "Security! Seize this man and remove him from the bridge."

But Britton held up a hand. "Mr. Lloyd, step away from the computer. Mr. Glinn, execute my command." The vessel had begun to heel still farther, and a terrifying crackle shot through the ship's steel, rising in pitch to a muffled howl of tearing metal, abruptly cut off as they began to right.

Lloyd gripped the computer, his eyes wild. "Sam!" he cried, his wild eyes seizing on McFarlane.

McFarlane had been watching, dumbstruck, almost paralyzed with conflicting emotions: terror for his life, desire for the rock and its boundless mysteries. He would rather go down with it than give it up now. Almost.

"Sam!" Lloyd was almost pleading now. "You're the scientist here. Tell them about all the research you did, the island of stability, the new element . . ." He was becoming incoherent. "Tell them why it's so important. Tell them why they can't dump the rock!"

McFarlane felt his throat constrict—and realized, for the first time, how utterly irresponsible it had been to take the rock to sea. If it sank now, it would drive itself deep into the abyssal mud of the ocean bottom, two miles down, never to be seen again. The loss to science would be catastrophic. It *was* unthinkable.

He found his voice. "Lloyd's right. It might be the most important scientific discovery ever made. You can't let it go."

Britton turned to him. "We no longer have a choice. The meteorite *is* going to the bottom—no matter what we do. So that leaves us with only one question. *Are we going to let it take us with it?*"

Rolvaag,
7:10 P.M.

McFarlane looked at the faces around him: Lloyd, tense and expectant; Glinn, veiled and unreadable; Rachel, clearly as conflicted as he was; Britton, an expression of utter conviction on her face. It was a haggard group, ice crystallizing in their hair, faces raw and bleeding with the cuts of the flying ice.

"We can abandon ship instead," Lloyd said, his voice panicky. "Hell, let the ship drift without us. It's drifting anyway. Maybe it'll survive on its own. We don't *have* to jettison the rock."

"It's close to suicide to launch lifeboats in this sea," Britton replied. "It's below zero out there, for God's sake."

"We *can't* just drop it," Lloyd continued, desperate now. "It would be a crime against science. This is all an overreaction. We've already been through so much. Glinn, for God's sake, tell her she's overreacting."

But Glinn said nothing.

"I know my ship," was all Britton said.

Lloyd veered wildly between threats and pleas. Now he turned back to McFarlane. "There must be something. Some *way*, Sam! Tell them again about the value to science, about the irreplaceable . . ."

McFarlane looked at Lloyd's face. It was ghastly in the orange emergency lights. He struggled against his own nausea, fear, and cold. They couldn't let it go. He seemed suspended: he thought of Nestor, and what it meant to die, and he thought of sinking in the cold dark bottomless water—and suddenly he was very, very afraid of death. The fear surged over him, temporarily usurping the intellectual functioning of his brain.

"Sam! Jesus Christ, tell them!"

McFarlane tried to speak, but the wind had risen and his words were lost in the howl.

"What?" Lloyd cried. "Everyone, listen to Sam! Sam—"

"Let it go," McFarlane said.

An incredulous look filled Lloyd's face, and he was temporarily speechless.

"You heard her," McFarlane said. "It's going to the bottom regardless. The fight's over." A feeling of hopelessness swept over him. He felt a warmth at the corners of his eyes and realized it was tears. Such a waste, such a waste . . .

Abruptly, Lloyd turned, abandoning McFarlane for Glinn. "Eli? *Eli!* You've never failed me before, there's always been something in that bag of tricks. Help me here, I beg you. Don't let them drop the rock."

His voice had taken on a pathetic, beseeching tone. The man was unraveling before their eyes.

Glinn said nothing as the ship began to roll again. McFarlane followed Britton's eyes to the inclinometer. All talk ceased as the wind shrieked through the broken bridge windows. Then the terrible sound began again. The *Rolvaag* hesitated, thirty degrees on its side, everyone clinging desperately, the vessel wallowing broadside to. McFarlane gripped a bulkhead rail. The terror he felt was now helping to clear his mind, sweeping away his regret. All he wanted to do was get rid of it.

"Recover," he heard Britton murmur. "*Recover.*"

The ship remained heeled stubbornly to port. The bridge hung so far out over the side of the ship that McFarlane could see nothing but black water below the windows. He was swept with a feeling of vertigo. And then, with an immense shudder, it gradually began to right.

As soon as the deck leveled, Lloyd let go of the computer, his face torn with a mixture of horror, rage, and frustration. McFarlane could see the same terror working in him, clearing his mind as well, illuminating the sole rational course left them.

"All right," Lloyd finally said. "Let it go." He buried his face in his hands.

Britton spoke to Glinn. "You heard him. Get rid of it, *now*." Relief sounded clearly through the tension in her voice.

Slowly, almost mechanically, Glinn sat down at the EES console. He placed his fingers on the keyboard. Then he glanced at McFarlane. "Tell me, Sam. If the meteorite reacts to salinity, what will happen when it hits the open ocean underneath the ship?"

McFarlane started. In all the mayhem, he had not stopped to consider this. He thought quickly.

"Seawater is a conductor," he replied. "The meteorite's discharge will be attenuated through it."

"Are you sure it won't blow up the ship?"

McFarlane hesitated. "No."

Glinn nodded. "I see."

They waited. There was no sound of typing. Glinn sat hunched over the keyboard, motionless.

Silence fell again as the ship subsided into another trough.

Glinn half turned his head, fingers still poised over the keys. "This is an unnecessary step," he said quietly. "And it is also too dangerous."

His long white hands fell away from the keys, and he stood up slowly to face them. "The ship will survive. Rochefort's work has never failed. There is no need to use the dead man's switch. In this instance, I am in agreement with Mr. Lloyd."

There was a moment of shocked silence.

"When the meteorite comes into contact with seawater, the explosion could sink the ship," Glinn went on.

"I told you, the charge will be dispersed through the seawater," said McFarlane.

Glinn pursed his lips. "So you *think*. We can't risk damaging the jettison doors. If they can't be closed, the tank will flood."

Britton spoke: "What's certain is that if the meteorite isn't jettisoned, the *Rolvaag will* go down. Eli, don't you understand? We aren't going to last *a dozen more rolls*."

The ship began to rise on the next wave.

"Sally, you're the last person I'd expect to panic." Glinn's voice was calm, confident. "We can ride this out."

Britton took an audible breath. "Eli, I *know* my ship. It's over, for God's sake. Can't you see that?"

"Not at all," said Glinn. "The worst has passed. Trust me."

The word *trust* hung in the air as the ship rolled farther and farther. The bridge seemed to have been shocked into paralysis, every eye on Glinn. And still the ship rolled.

Garza's voice came on the speaker, faint now, fading in and out. "Eli! The web is failing! Did you hear me? *Failing!*"

Glinn wheeled toward the microphone. "Stay with it, man. I'll be down there in a moment."

"Eli, the foundation of the cradle is being rocked to pieces. There's metal everywhere. I've got to get the men out of here."

"Mr. Garza!" Britton spoke into the ship's intercom. "This is the captain speaking. Are you familiar with the dead man's switch?"

"I built it."

"Then trigger it."

Glinn stood, impassive. McFarlane watched him, trying to understand this sudden change. Was Glinn right? *Could* the ship—the meteorite—survive? Then he glanced at the faces of the officers. The abject terror in their eyes told him a different story. The ship poised at the crest of the wave, twisted, groaned, sank back again.

"The dead man's switch must be initiated from the EES computer on the bridge," said Garza. "Eli has the codes . . ."

"Can you do it manually?" Britton asked.

"No. Eli! For God's sake, hurry. We don't have much time before this thing rolls right through the side of the ship."

"Mr. Garza," Britton said. "Order your men to their abandon stations."

Glinn spoke: "Garza, I contravene that order. We won't fail. Stay at your work."

"No way, sir. We're evacuating." The radio went dead.

Glinn looked pale. He glanced around the bridge. The ship subsided into a trough, and silence fell.

Britton stepped toward Glinn and put her hand lightly on his shoulder. "Eli," she said. "I know you have it in you to admit failure. I know you've got courage enough to do that. Right now you're the only one with the power to save us and this ship. Execute the dead man's switch, *please*."

McFarlane watched as she stretched out her other hand and clasped Glinn's. He seemed to waver.

Suddenly, silently, Puppup returned to the bridge. He was streaming wet, dressed once again in his old rags. There was a strange excitement in his face, an expectancy, that chilled McFarlane.

Glinn smiled and squeezed Britton's hand. "What nonsense. Sally, I really expected more of you. Don't you see we can't fail? We've planned far too carefully for that. There's no need to invoke the dead man's switch. In fact, under the circumstances, it would be dangerous to do so." He looked around. "I don't blame any of you. This is a complex situation, and fear is an understandable reaction. But you have to consider what I've just brought you through, virtually single-handedly. I can promise you, the web will hold, and the ship will weather the storm. We're certainly not going to end it here—not because of a regrettable failure of nerve."

McFarlane wavered, feeling a surge of hope. Maybe Glinn was right. The man was so persuasive, so confident. He had succeeded under the most unlikely circumstances. He saw that Lloyd, too, looked eager, wanting to be convinced.

The ship rose. It heeled. All talk ceased as everyone clung for their lives to whatever handholds they could find. The screeching chorus of warping, tearing metal began anew, rising in volume until it drowned out even the rage of the storm. At that moment, McFarlane realized, utterly and completely, just how wrong Glinn was. At the crest, the ship shook as if it were in an earthquake; the emergency lights flickered.

After an agonizing moment, the ship righted itself and fell over the crest of the wave. The wind howled once about the bridge and was cut off.

"You're wrong this time, Glinn, you son of a bitch," said Lloyd, terror back in full force. "Throw the switch."

Glinn smiled, almost to the point of sneering. "Sorry, Mr. Lloyd. I'm the only one who has the codes, and once again I will save your meteorite for you, despite yourself."

Suddenly Lloyd rushed at Glinn, a strangled cry rising in his throat. Glinn sidestepped him lightly, and with the briefest flick of the heel of one hand sent Lloyd crashing to the deck, gasping heavily.

McFarlane took a step toward Glinn. The man turned on him lightly, poised. His eyes remained as impenetrable, as opaque, as ever. McFarlane realized that Glinn wasn't going to change his mind. He was a man who couldn't fail, and he would die proving it.

Britton glanced toward the chief mate. One look at her face told McFarlane she had reached the same decision.

"Mr. Howell," she said. "All hands to abandon stations. We will abandon ship."

Glinn's eyes narrowed slightly in surprise, but he remained silent.

Howell turned to Glinn. "You're giving us a death sentence, forcing us out in that storm in lifeboats, you crazy bastard."

"I may be the only sane one left on the bridge."

Lloyd pulled himself painfully from the deck as the ship struggled once again to rise. He did not look at Glinn.

Glinn turned and, without another word, left the slanting bridge.

"Mr. Howell," Britton said. "Initiate a 406 MHz beacon, and get all hands to the boats. If I'm not back in five minutes, you will assume the duties of master."

Then she, too, turned and vanished.

Rolvaag,
7:35 P.M.

Eli Glinn stood on the iron catwalk above number three center tank. He heard a clanging noise as Puppup dogged the hatch of the access corridor shut. He felt a small twinge of gratitude for the Indian. He had been loyal to the last, when everyone else—even Sally—had failed him.

The hysteria he had witnessed on the bridge was very disturbing. He had succeeded at every turn, and they should have trusted him. A claxon horn was blowing in some faraway, echoing space: an eerie, unpleasant noise. In the coming hours, many would die in the rough seas. It was all so unnecessary. The great *Rolvaag* would survive; of that he was sure. It would survive, with its cargo, and those who remained with it. And at dawn, with the storm just a memory, they would be met by the towships from South Georgia. The *Rolvaag* would return to New York with the meteorite. It was a pity that so many others would not.

He thought of Britton again. A magnificent woman. He felt a great sadness when he reflected on her unwillingness to trust him at the end. He would never find another like her; that he knew. He would save her ship for her, but any question of a personal relationship was now dead.

He leaned against the longitudinal bulkhead, distantly surprised at how long it was taking to regain his breath. He clung as the ship heeled; an alarming angle, admittedly, but still beneath the critical limit of thirty-five degrees. He could hear the slippage of chains, the protests of metal, below his feet. At last, the ship began to right itself with a groan. A tragedy, that after all he had done—the quite extraordinary successes he had engineered—they were not willing to trust him this one last time. All but Puppup. He glanced toward the old man.

"Heading down there, guv?"

Glinn nodded. "I'll need your help."

" 'At's what I'm here for."

They stepped to the edge of the catwalk. There below sat the rock, the top of its surrounding web swathed in plastic tarps. The emergency lights bathed it in a dim light. The tank was still holding nicely, staying dry. It was a superb ship. The triple hulling made all the difference. Even covered with tarps the rock looked magnificent, the epicenter of their terrors and hopes. It was resting in its cradle, just as he knew it would be.

Then his eyes flickered down to the struts and braces. There was, it had to be admitted, a great deal of damage: bent spars, compression fractures, sheared metal. The transverse web brackets along the bottom of the tank were littered with broken rivets, snapped chains, and splintered wood. He could hear a residual creaking and groaning. But the web was still essentially intact.

The elevator was broken, however. He began climbing down.

The ship rose, heeling again.

Glinn steadied himself, then continued descending. It took longer than he thought it would, and by the time he had reached the bottom he felt more horizontal than vertical—splayed upon, rather than clinging to, the ladder. Hooking an elbow to it, he braced himself, waiting it out. Now he could see, under the tarps, the red flank of the rock. The sounds in the hold were growing, like some infernal symphony of metal, but they signified nothing. Toward the top of the roll he slipped out his pocket watch and held it at arm's length, dangling it from its chain, estimating the roll. Twenty-five degrees: well below critical value.

He heard a sudden muttering, groaning noise, and the massive crimson curve of the meteorite seemed to stir. The ship heeled farther, the meteorite moved with it, until Glinn was not sure whether the ship was shifting the meteorite or vice versa. The meteorite now seemed poised at the edge of its cradle, ready to tip out. There was a crackling, splintering sound. Twenty-seven degrees. Twenty-eight.

The ship shuddered, paused, then began to right itself. Glinn eased out a breath. Twenty-eight degrees. Well within tolerances. The meteorite shifted back into its cradle with a monstrous shudder. Abruptly, the screech of metal stopped. The screaming of the wind and water outside the hull abated as the ship sank down.

His eyes scanned the tank. What was necessary here was to tighten the chains closest to the meteorite. They had been designed so that one person could do it, using a motor-assisted "come-along" anchored to each tightening point. He was surprised Garza hadn't done this already.

Quickly, he scrambled to the main tightening point and switched on the key motor-assist. It lit up—in perfect working order, of course.

The ship continued to subside into the oncoming trough, giving him some peace and stability in which to work.

Glinn pulled the forward lever on the motor-assist, and was pleased to see the big rubber-coated chains that had come loose in the rocking of the meteorite tighten again. Why hadn't Garza done this? The reason was clear: he had panicked. Glinn felt a momentary disappointment at his trusted construction manager. This wasn't like Garza; not like him at all. So many had failed him; but at least he had failed no one.

The chains were tightening nicely, and he turned to Puppup. "Take this toolbox," he said, indicating a box left in Garza's retreat.

The ship rose; the roll began; the chains began to strain. And then, with a sharp ratcheting noise, the chains loosened. Glinn peered closely in the dim light. He saw that, in fact, Garza *had* already tried it. The gears on the motor-assist had been stripped, and the four-inch steel ratchet head had sheared off. The assist was useless.

The ship began to rise. And then he heard a voice from above. He ducked out from the web and glanced up.

Sally Britton was stepping through the hatchway onto the catwalk. She carried herself with the same natural dignity that had struck him so forcefully the first time he had seen her, coming down those sun-drenched steps, ages and ages ago. His heart gave an unexpected lurch. She had changed her mind: she would stay with the ship.

Britton had to pause during the long, screeching roll. They stared at each other while the meteorite rocked in its cradle and the ship screamed its pain. When it was over she called out again. "Eli! The ship's about to break up!"

Glinn felt sharp disappointment: there had been no change in her thinking after all. But all this was a distraction. He focused his attention on the cradle again. Now he saw it: the way to lock down the rock was to tighten the topchain bolt at the summit of the meteorite. It would mean cutting through the tarp. It was a simple matter, requiring no more than six inches of hand tightening. He began climbing up the nearest chain.

"Eli, *please!* There's an extra lifeboat in reserve for us. Leave this thing and come with me!"

Glinn pulled himself up, Puppup following with the toolbox. He needed to focus his mind on the objective, not suffer distractions.

Reaching the crown of the meteorite, he found to his surprise a small flap already cut in the tarp. Beneath, the topchain bolt was loose, as he expected. As the ship rose out of the trough and began to heel yet again, he fitted the wrench around the nut, anchored the bolt with a second wrench, and began to tighten.

Nothing moved. He had not comprehended—*could* not comprehend—what tremendous, what unimaginable pressure the bolt was under.

"Hold this wrench," he said. Puppup obliged, grabbing it with his sinewy arms.

The ship canted farther.

"Come back to the bridge with me, Eli," Britton said. "There may still be time to trigger the switch. Both of us might yet live."

Glinn glanced up for an instant from his struggle with the bolt. There was no pleading in her voice—that was not Sally Britton's way. He heard patience, reason, and utter conviction. It made him sad. "Sally," he said, "the only people who are going to die are the foolish ones in the lifeboats. If you stay here, you'll survive."

"I know my ship, Eli," was all she said.

Kneeling, hunched over the topchain bolt, he struggled with the nut. Someone else had tried this before him: there were fresh marks on the metal. As the ship heeled, he felt the meteorite shift, and he anchored himself more firmly, both feet braced against the links. He strained to the limits of extremity, but it did not move. Gasping, he refitted the wrench.

Still the ship heeled.

Britton spoke out of the darkness above, her voice rising above the sound. "Eli, I would like to have that dinner with you. I don't know much about poetry, but what I know I could share with you. I would *like* to share it with you."

The meteorite shuddered, and Glinn found himself gripping with both hands as the meteorite tipped with the ship. There were ropes up here, fastened to the frame plates of the tank, and he quickly lashed one around his waist to keep his position. He returned to the wrench. A quarter turn, that was all he needed. The yawing of the ship slowed and he once again grasped the handle of the wrench.

"And I could love you. Eli . . ."

Glinn stopped suddenly and stared up at Britton. She tried to speak again, but her voice was drowned out by the rising shriek of tortured metal, echoing madly in the vast space. All he could see was her small figure on the catwalk above. Her golden hair had become unpinned and lay wildly across her shoulders, glowing even in the dim light.

As he stared, he became dimly aware that the ship was not leveling out. He looked away from her, first at the bolt, then at Puppup. The man was grinning, his long thin mustaches dripping water. Glinn felt a surge of anger at himself for not focusing on the problem at hand.

"The wrench!" he called to Puppup over the screaming of metal.

The ship was very far over, the sounds of metal deafening. With a hand he wished was steadier, Glinn took out his pocket watch to once again calculate the inclination; he held it up but it swung back and forth. As he tried to steady it, the watch slipped through his fingers and shattered against the flank of the rock; he saw little glints of gold and glass skittering along the red surface and disappearing into the depths.

The yawing seemed to accelerate with a brutal suddenness. Or was it his imagination? Surely none of this could be real. Double overage had been brought to bear, the calculations run and rerun, every possible path to failure accounted for.

And then he felt the meteorite begin to move beneath him, and there was a tearing sound as the tarps rent and the web unraveled, the sudden red of the meteorite filling his field of vision like the opening of a great wound, the rock crisscrossed by tangled ropes and cables, rivets shooting and ricocheting past him. Still the ship yawed on its side, steeper and steeper. He scrambled desperately, trying to untie the rope from his waist, but the knot was so tight, so tight . . .

There was a sound beyond all description, as if the heavens and the gulfs below had opened up at once. The tank tore apart in a terrific shower of sparks, and the meteorite rolled into the darkness—a monstrous shambling like some deliberate beast—taking him with it. Instantly all was dark, and he felt a rush of chill air . . .

There was the faint tinkle of glasses, the murmur of voices. L'Ambroisie was busy on this balmy Thursday night, filled with art fanciers and wealthy Parisians. Beyond the restaurant's discreet front, the smoky autumn moon lent the Marais district a delicate shimmer. Glinn smiled at Sally Britton, who was seated across the fine white damask. "Try this," he said as the waiter uncorked a bottle of Veuve Cliquot and tipped a chilly stream into their glasses. He grasped his glass and raised it. She smiled and spoke:

> *. . . how everything turns away*
> *Quite leisurely from the disaster; the ploughman may*
> *Have heard the splash, the forsaken cry,*
> *But for him it was not an important failure*

An important failure . . .

As his mood turned to puzzlement, the recitation was drowned by a hideous laugh from Puppup. And then the scene vaporized in a pure flash of brilliant, beautiful light.

Drake Passage,
7:55 P.M.

McFarlane clutched desperately at the lifeboat's safety loops, riding it through the great peaks and valleys of a confused sea, Rachel clinging tightly to his arm. The last twenty minutes had passed in a terrifying confusion: Britton's sudden departure from the bridge; Howell's taking command and ordering them to abandon ship; the muster at the lifeboat stations and the harrowing launching of the boats into the raging seas. After the tense hours of the chase, the struggle against the storm and the meteorite, this ultimate calamity had happened so quickly that it seemed unreal. He looked around the inner walls of the lifeboat for the first time. With its single-piece hull, tiny entrance port, and tinier windows, it looked like an oversize torpedo. Howell was at the helm, guiding the inboard; Lloyd and some twenty in all were inside, including half a dozen whose own lifeboat had been torn from its davits during launch and who had to be plucked from the freezing waves.

He tightened his grip as the boat dropped in free fall, crashed, and was abruptly driven upward. Instead of plowing through like the *Rolvaag*, the sixty-foot craft bobbed like a woodchip. The staggering falls, the wrenching climbs up the cliffs of water, were exhausting and terrifying. They were drenched in ice water, and some who had been in the sea, McFarlane could see, were unconscious. Brambell was there, thank God, attending to them as best he could.

An officer in the bow of the boat was securing the provisions and security gear. Debris was wallowing and rolling in the water beneath their feet. They were all sick, and some were retching uncontrollably. None of the crew spoke, going silently through their duties. The tightly enclosed hull of the lifeboat sheltered them from the elements. But McFarlane could feel the terrible seas were battering the boat mercilessly.

Howell finally spoke, his voice hoarse over the sound of wind and water. He was holding a radio to his mouth, but he spoke so that everyone in the boat could hear.

"All boats, listen up! Our only chance is to head for an ice island to the southeast, and ride out the storm in its lee. Maintain a heading of one two zero at ten knots and keep in visual contact at all times. Keep channel three open. Activate emergency beacons."

It was hard to tell they were going anywhere, but the moon had come back out—and now and then, through the narrow oblong windows, McFarlane caught the faint lights of the other two lifeboats driving down the foam-webbed seas, struggling to keep in sight. At the heights of the terrible waves, he could still make out the *Rolvaag*, half a mile back, wallowing back and forth as if in slow motion, its emergency lights winking on and off. No more boats had been launched since their pack of three started out minutes before. He could not take his eyes from the sight of the gigantic vessel, held in the death grip of the storm.

A fresh roller tried to raise the tanker, but this time the *Rolvaag* hung back, almost as if it was tethered from below. It leaned farther and farther from the face of the wave, and as the crest boiled over the ship it slowly lay down on its side. McFarlane glanced over at Lloyd. The man's haggard face was turned away from McFarlane and the *Rolvaag* both.

Another bob; the seas completely submerged the lifeboat; then they struggled upward again. Although he too wanted nothing more than to avert his eyes, McFarlane found his gaze drawn once again to the great ship. It still hung sideways, motionless. Even after the crest of the wave had passed over, it sagged, dragged lower and lower by the ineluctable weight. Its stern began to peer through the retreating wave, dead screws exposed. A distant shriek, almost feminine, cut through the howl of the storm. And then, both bow and stern jerked apart and rose from the seas in a boil of white. There was a deep, intense blue light in the center of the cataclysm, so bright it seemed to light up the sea from underneath, sending an unearthly hue through the water. A huge gout of steam ripped through the surface and mushroomed upward, blanketing the doomed ship, while lightning flickered within it, breaking out its top in forks that stabbed into the night. At that moment the lifeboat sank back into a welter of water, obscuring the terrible sight. When it emerged, the seas were empty and dark. The ship was gone.

McFarlane sat back, shaking and nauseated. He did not dare look at Lloyd. Glinn, Britton, the three dozen crewmen, EES staffers, and Lloyd Industries workers who had gone down with the ship . . . the meteorite, plunging to the bottom, two miles below . . . He closed his eyes, tightening his grip on the shivering Rachel. He had never been so cold, so sick, so frightened in his life.

She murmured something unintelligible and he leaned close. "What's that?"

She was pressing something toward him. "Take it," she said. "Take it."

In her hands was her CD-ROM, containing the test data on the meteorite.

"Why?" he asked.

"I want you to keep it. Keep it always. The answers are there, Sam. Promise me you'll find them."

He slipped the disk into his pocket. It was all they had left: a few hundred megabytes of data. The meteorite was forever lost to the world; it had already buried itself deep in the abyssal silt of the ocean floor.

"Promise," Rachel said again. Her voice sounded slurred, drugged.

"I promise." And he hugged her closer to him, feeling the warm trickle of her tears upon his hands. The meteorite was gone. So many others were gone. But the two of them remained, would always remain.

"We'll find the answers together," he said.

A breaking crest slammed into the lifeboat, driving it sideways. They were thrown to the deck of the boat. McFarlane could hear Howell shouting commands as another breaking wave slammed the boat and pushed it sideways, almost flipping it over. It dropped back with a crash. "My arm!" a man cried. "I've broken my arm!"

McFarlane helped Rachel back onto the padded seat, helped her arms into the loops. The seas were roaring all around them, burying them in water, sometimes forcing the entire closed boat beneath the surface.

"How much farther?" someone shouted.

"Two miles," Howell replied, struggling to keep the boat on course. "Give or take."

Heavy water rinsed down the portholes, allowing only occasional glimpses of the black night beyond. McFarlane's elbows, knees, and shoulders grew sore from being battered against the sides and roof of the small vessel. He felt like a ping-pong ball tumbling inside a washing machine. It was so cold that he had lost all feeling in his feet. Reality began to recede. He remembered a summer spent on a lake in Michigan. He would sit on the beach for hours, bottom in the sand, feet in the shallows. But the water had never been this cold . . . He realized that frigid seawater was rising in the bottom of the boat. The punishing gale was pulling the lifeboat apart at the seams.

He stared out the little window. A few hundred yards away, he could see the lights of the other two boats, bucking and bouncing in the sea. A great wave would descend upon them, and they would struggle through it, corkscrewing wildly as the pilots worked to keep them from rolling over, the propellers whining madly as they rose out of the water. He stared, stupefied with exhaustion and fear, at the wildly gyrating antennas, the semicircles of ten-gallon water tanks knocking crazily around the sterns.

And then one of the boats vanished. One moment it was there, running lights winking, diving into yet another wave; and then it was gone, buried, its lights cut out as abruptly as if shut off with a switch.

"We've lost the beacon on number three boat, sir," said the man in the bow.

McFarlane let his head sink toward his chest. Who had been in that boat? Garza? Stonecipher? His mind did not work anymore. A part of him now hoped they too would go down as swiftly; he longed for a quick ending to this agony. The water in the bottom of the boat was getting deeper. He realized, vaguely, that they were sinking.

And then the seas began to quiet. The craft was still pitching and bobbing in ferocious chop, but the endless procession of watery mountains beneath them ceased, and the wind fell.

"We're in the lee," said Howell. His hair was matted and lank, the uniform beneath the foul-weather gear soaked. Blood mingled with water in pink rivulets that ran down his face. And yet when he spoke, his hoarse voice was steady. Again he had the radio.

"I need your attention! Both boats are taking on water, fast. They won't stay afloat much longer. We've got only one choice—to transfer ourselves and as many provisions as we can carry to the ice island. Understood?"

Very few in the boat looked up; they seemed beyond caring. The feeble beacon on their boat swept the flank of ice.

"There's a small ice ledge up ahead. We'll run the boats right up on it. Lewis in the bow will pass out supplies to each of you and take you out two at a time, fast. If you fall in the water, get the hell out—it'll kill you in five minutes. Now buddy up."

McFarlane drew Rachel protectively toward him, then turned to look at Lloyd. The man stared back this time, his eyes dark, hollow, haunted.

"What have I done?" he whispered hoarsely. "Oh my God, what have I done?"

Drake Passage, July 26, 11:00 A.M.

Dawn rose over the ice island.

McFarlane, who had passed in and out of a fitful doze, was slow in waking. At last he raised his head, the ice crackling off his coat as he did so. Around him, a small group of survivors had huddled together for warmth. Some lay on their backs, their faces coated with ice, their eyes open, frosted over. Others were half upright, on their knees, unmoving. *They must be dead*, McFarlane thought in a dreamy sort of way. A hundred had begun the voyage. And now he could see barely two dozen.

Rachel lay before him, her eyes closed. He struggled to a sitting position, snow sliding from his limbs. The wind was gone, and a deathly stillness surrounded them, underlined by the thunder of surf below them, worrying the margins of the ice island.

Before him stretched a tableland of turquoise ice, cut with rivulets that deepened into canyons as they snaked off to the edges of the island. A red line, like a streak of blood, tinted the eastern horizon, dribbling color across the heaving seas. In the distance, the horizon was dotted with blue and green icebergs: hundreds of them, like jewels, stationary in the swell, their tops glistening in the morning light. It was an unending landscape of water and ice.

He felt terribly sleepy. Odd that he was no longer cold. He struggled to bring himself awake. Now, slowly, it came back to him: the landing, climbing a crevasse to the top in the blackness, the wretched attempts to light a fire, the slow slide into lethargy. There was the time before, too—before all this—but he did not want to think of that right now. Right now, his world had shrunk to the edges of this strange island.

Here, on its top, there was no feeling of motion. It was as solid as land. The great procession of rollers continued eastward, smoother now. After the black of the night and the gray of the storm, everything seemed tinted in pastels; the blue ice, the pink sea, the red-and-peach sky. It was beautiful, strange, otherworldly.

He tried to stand, but his legs ignored the command and he only rose to one knee before falling back. He felt an exhaustion so profound it took a supreme effort of will not to sink back to the ground. A dim part of his mind realized it was more than exhaustion—it was hypothermia.

They had to get up, move. He had to rouse them.

He turned to Rachel and shook her roughly. Her lidded eyes swiveled around to him. Her lips were blue and ice clung to her black hair.

"Rachel," he croaked. "Rachel, get up, please."

Her lips moved and spoke, but it was a hiss of air, without sound.

"Rachel?" He bent down. He could hear her words now, sibilant, ghostly.

"The meteorite . . ." she murmured.

"It went to the bottom," McFarlane said. "Don't think about it now. It's over."

She shook her head faintly. "No . . . not what you think . . ."

She closed her eyes, and he shook her again. "So sleepy . . ."

"Rachel. Don't go to sleep. What were you saying?" She was rambling, delusional, but he realized it was important to keep her talking and awake. He shook her again. "The meteorite, Rachel. What about it?" Her eyes half opened, and she glanced downward. McFarlane followed her gaze; there was nothing. Her hand stirred slightly.

"There . . ." she said, looking down.

McFarlane took her hand. He pulled off the sodden, half-frozen gloves. Her hand was freezing; her fingertips white. Now he understood: her fingers were frostbitten. He tried to massage the fingers and the hand relaxed. She was holding a peanut.

"Are you hungry?" McFarlane asked as the nut rolled away into the snow. Rachel closed her eyes again. He tried to rouse her and could not. He pressed himself against her, and her body was heavy and cold. He turned for help and found Lloyd, lying on the ice beside them.

"Lloyd?" he whispered.

"Yes," came the faint, gravelly voice.

"We've got to move." McFarlane found himself growing short of breath.

"Not interested."

McFarlane turned back to shake Rachel again, but he could hardly move his own arm now, let alone apply force to her. She was inert. The loss seemed more than he could fathom. He looked out over the huddled, unmoving shapes, glistening under their thin coatings of ice. There was Brambell, the doctor, with a book crooked incongruously under his arm. There was Garza, the white of his bandaged head rimed in frost. There was Howell. Two, maybe three dozen others. No one was moving. Suddenly he found he cared; cared very much. He wanted to yell, to get up and start kicking and punching people to their feet, but he couldn't even find the energy to speak. There were too many of them; he couldn't warm them all. He couldn't even warm himself.

His head swam as a strange, inky sensation overcame him. Apathy came creeping. *We're all going to die here,* he thought, *but it's okay.* He looked over at Rachel, trying to shake the inkiness off. Her eyes were half open now, rolled up, just the whites showing. Her face was gray. He would go where she had gone. It was okay. A single snowflake drifted out of the sky and touched her lips. It took a long time to melt.

The inkiness returned, and this time it was good, like sleeping in his mother's arms once again, and he gave in to it. As he drifted off into delicious sleep, Rachel's voice kept going through his mind: *Not what you think. Not what you think.*

And then the voice changed: louder, more metallic. "South Georgia Bravo . . . In sight . . . Approaching for a high-line pickup . . ."

A light appeared overhead. There was a clattering, a rhythmic beating. Voices, a radio. He struggled against it all. *No, no, let me sleep! Leave me be!*

And then the pain began.

South Georgia Island, July 29, 12:20 P.M.

Palmer Lloyd lay in a plywood bunk bed in the infirmary hut of the British scientific station. He stared at the plywood ceiling: endless loops of dark and light wood, patterns his eyes had traced a thousand times over the recent days. He smelled the stale food that had been sitting by his bed since lunchtime. He heard the sound of wind outside the tiny window that peeked out over the blue snowfields, blue mountains, and blue glaciers of the island.

It had been three days since their rescue. So many had died, on the ship, in the lifeboats, on the ice island. *But one man of her crew alive, what put to sea with seventy-five . . .* The old sea-ditty from *Treasure Island* ran through his head, as it had run, over and over and over, since he had first regained consciousness here in this bed.

He had survived. Tomorrow, a helicopter would take him to the Falklands. From there he would return to New York. Distantly, he wondered how the media was going to report this one. He found that he didn't care. So little seemed important anymore. He was finished: finished with the museum, finished with business, finished with science. All his dreams—they seemed so ancient now—had gone to the bottom with the rock. All he wanted to do was go to his farm in upstate New York, mix a stiff martini, sit in the rocking chair on the porch, and watch the deer eat apples in his orchard.

An orderly came in, removed the tray, and began to put down another.

Lloyd shook his head.

"It's my job, mate," the orderly said.

"Very well."

At that moment there was a knock on the door.

McFarlane came in. His left hand and part of his face was bandaged, he was wearing dark glasses, and the man looked unsteady on his feet. In fact, he looked terrible. He sat down in the metal folding chair that occupied almost all the free space in the tiny room. The chair creaked.

Lloyd was surprised to see him. He hadn't seen McFarlane at all these past three days. He had just assumed McFarlane was through with him—as well he should be. Hardly anyone had spoken to him. His only visitor from the expedition, in fact, had been Howell, and that had been to sign some papers. They all hated him now.

Lloyd thought McFarlane was waiting to speak until the orderly left. But the door closed behind them, and still McFarlane remained silent. He did not say anything for a long time. And then at last he removed his dark glasses and leaned forward.

The change startled Lloyd. It was almost as if the man's eyes were on fire. They were red and raw, with dark circles beneath. He was dirty, unkempt. The loss of the meteorite, the death of Amira, had hit him hard.

"Listen," said McFarlane, his voice tight with tension. "I've got something to tell you."

Lloyd waited.

McFarlane bent even closer now, speaking directly into Lloyd's ear. "The *Rolvaag* went down at 61°32'14" South, 59°30'10" West."

"Please don't speak of this with me, Sam. Not now."

"Yes, *now*," said McFarlane with unexpected vehemence. He

reached into his pocket and withdrew a compact disc. He held it up, winking its rainbow colors in the light.

"On this disc—"

Lloyd turned away and faced the plywood wall. "Sam, it's over. The meteorite's gone. Give it up."

"On this disc is the last batch of data we gathered on the meteorite. I made a promise. I've been . . . *studying* it."

Lloyd felt tired—so very, very tired. His eyes strayed out the little window to the mountains wreathed in glaciers, their icy tops piercing the clouds. He hated the sight of ice. He never wanted to see ice again, ever.

"Yesterday," McFarlane continued relentlessly, "one of the scientists at the station here told me they'd been recording some very unusual, shallow seaquakes. Dozens of them, all below 3 on the Richter scale."

Lloyd waited for McFarlane to continue. It was all so irrelevant.

"The epicenter of those quakes is at 61°32'14" South, 59°30'10" West."

Lloyd's eyes flickered. He slowly turned his head back to meet the young scientist's eyes.

"I've been analyzing this data," McFarlane continued. "It mostly has to do with the shape and internal structure of the meteorite. It's very unusual."

Lloyd did not answer, but he did not turn away either.

"It's layered. It's almost symmetrical. It's not natural."

Lloyd sat up. "Not natural?" He was beginning to feel alarmed. McFarlane had suffered a psychological break. He needed help.

"I said, *layered*. It has an outer shell, a thick inner layer, and a tiny round inclusion right in the center. This is not an accident. Think about it. What else is like this? It's very common. It must be a universal structure."

"Sam, you're tired. Let me call a nurse for you. She'll—"

But McFarlane interrupted. "Amira figured it out. Right before she died. It was in her hand. Remember how she said we had to stop thinking from our perspective, start thinking from the meteorite's perspective? At the end, Amira knew. It reacted to salt water. It had been *waiting* for salt water. Waiting millions of years."

Lloyd looked for the emergency button near his bed. McFarlane was in much worse condition than he had initially thought.

McFarlane paused, his eyes glittering unnaturally. "You see, Lloyd, it wasn't a meteorite at all."

Lloyd felt a queer suspension, a stillness in the room. There was the button; if only he could press it casually, without exciting the man. McFarlane's face was flushed, sweaty, his breathing rapid and shallow. The loss of the rock, the sinking of the *Rolvaag*, the deaths in the water, on the ice—it must have broken him. Lloyd felt a fresh stab of guilt: even the survivors were damaged.

"Did you hear me, Lloyd? I said *it's not a meteorite*."

"What was it, then, Sam?" Lloyd finally managed to say, keeping his voice calm, his hand casually moving toward the button.

"All those shallow earthquakes, right where the ship went down . . ."

"What about them?" Lloyd said soothingly. He pressed the button; once, twice, three times. The nurse would be there momentarily. McFarlane would get help.

"That thing we just *planted* at the bottom of the sea. Guess what?"

"What?" Lloyd tried to sound normal. Thank God, he could hear the footsteps of the nurse in the corridor now.

"It's sprouting."

Authors' Note

The Ice Limit is, in part, inspired by a real scientific expedition. In 1906, Admiral Robert E. Peary discovered the world's largest meteorite, which he named the Ahnighito, in northern Greenland. He located it because Eskimos in the area were using cold-hammered iron spearpoints, which Peary analyzed and found to be meteoritic in origin. He ultimately recovered the Ahnighito, wrestling it to his ship only with tremendous difficulty. The mass of iron, when it was finally aboard, destroyed all the ship's compasses. He managed to bring it back to the American Museum of Natural History in New York, where it is still on display in the Hall of Meteorites. He recounted the story in his book *Northward over the Great Ice*. "Never," Peary wrote, "have I had the terrific majesty of the force of gravity so powerfully brought home to me as in handling this mountain of iron." The Ahnighito is so heavy that it rests on six massive steel pillars that penetrate the floor of the museum's meteorite hall, pass through the basement, and are bolted into the very bedrock under the building.

Needless to say, while many of the locales mentioned in *The Ice Limit* actually exist, Lloyd Industries, Effective Engineering Solutions, and all of the characters and ships described in the novel, both American and Chilean, are entirely fictitious. In addition, while an atlas will reveal a large island named Isla Desolación some three hundred fifty miles northwest of where much of *The Ice Limit* is set, our Desolation Island—its makeup, size, and location—is entirely our own invention.

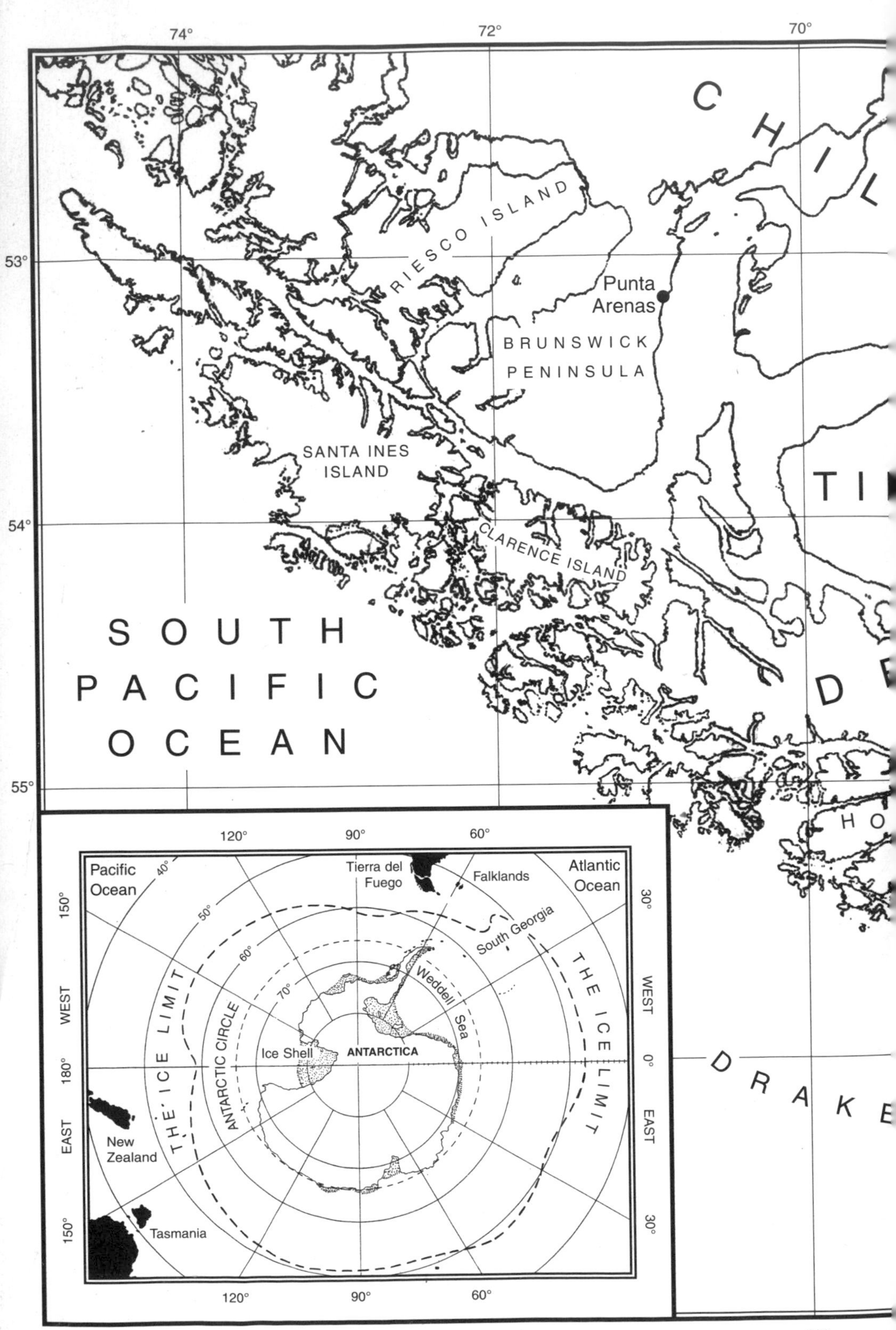

74°
72°
70°
53°
54°
55°
CHIL
RIESCO ISLAND
Punta Arenas
BRUNSWICK PENINSULA
SANTA INES ISLAND
CLARENCE ISLAND
TI
DE
HO
SOUTH PACIFIC OCEAN
DRAKE
120°
90°
60°
Pacific Ocean
Tierra del Fuego
Falklands
Atlantic Ocean
South Georgia
40°
50°
60°
70°
150°
30°
WEST
Weddell Sea
THE ICE LIMIT
ANTARCTIC CIRCLE
Ice Shell
ANTARCTICA
180°
0°
EAST
New Zealand
Tasmania